PRAISE FOR DiANN MILLS

BURDEN OF PROOF

"DiAnn Mills never disappoints. . . . Put on a fresh pot of coffee before you start this one because you're not going to want to sleep until the suspense ride is over. You might want to grab a safety harness while you're at it—you're going to need it!"

LYNETTE EASON, bestselling, award-winning author of the Elite Guardians and Blue Justice series

"Taking her readers on a veritable roller-coaster ride of unexpected plot twists and turns, *Burden of Proof* is an inherently riveting read from beginning to end."

MIDWEST BOOK REVIEW

"Mills has added yet another winner to her growing roster of romantic thrillers, perhaps the best one yet."

THE SUSPENSE ZONE

HIGH TREASON

"In this third book in Mills's action-packed FBI Task Force series, the stakes are higher than ever. . . . Readers can count on being glued to the pages late into the night—as 'just one more chapter' turns into 'can't stop now.'"

ROMANTIC TIMES

"This suspenseful novel will appeal to Christian readers looking for a tidy, uplifting tale."

PUBLISHERS WEEKLY

DEEP EXTRACTION

"A harrowing police procedural [that] . . . Mills's many fans will devour."

LIBRARY JOURNAL

"Few characters in Mills's latest novel are who they appear to be at first glance. . . . Combined with intense action and stunning twists, this search for the truth keeps readers on the edges of their favorite reading chairs. . . . The crime is tightly plotted, and the message of faith is authentic and sincere."

ROMANTIC TIMES, 4½-star review, Top Pick

DEADLY ENCOUNTER

"Crackling dialogue and heart-stopping plotlines are the hallmarks of Mills's thrillers, and this series launch won't disappoint her many fans. Dealing with issues of murder, domestic terrorism, and airport security, it eerily echoes current events."

LIBRARY JOURNAL

"From the first paragraph until the last, this story is a nail-biter, promising to delight readers who enjoy a well-written adventure."

CHRISTIAN MARKET MAGAZINE

DEADLOCK

"DiAnn Mills brings us another magnificent, inspirational thriller in her FBI: Houston series. *Deadlock* is a riveting, fast-paced adventure that will hold you captive from the opening pages to the closing epilogue."

FRESH FICTION

"Mills does a superb job building the relationship between the two polar opposite detectives. With some faith overtones, *Deadlock* is an excellent police drama that even mainstream readers would enjoy."

ROMANTIC TIMES

DOUBLE CROSS

"DiAnn Mills always gives us a good thriller, filled with inspirational thoughts, and *Double Cross* is another great one!"

FRESH FICTION

"For the romantic suspense fan, there is plenty of action and twists present. For the inspirational reader, the faith elements fit nicely into the context of the story. . . . The romance is tenderly beautiful, and the ending bittersweet."

ROMANTIC TIMES

FIREWALL

"Mills takes readers on an explosive ride. . . . A story as romantic as it is exciting, *Firewall* will appeal to fans of Dee Henderson's romantic suspense stories."

BOOKLIST

"With an intricate plot involving domestic terrorism that could have been ripped from the headlines, Mills's romantic thriller makes for compelling reading."

LIBRARY JOURNAL

AIRBORNE

AIRBORNE

DiANN MILLS

Tyndale House Publishers
Carol Stream, Illinois

Visit Tyndale online at tyndale.com.

Visit DiAnn Mills's website at diannmills.com.

TYNDALE and Tyndale's quill logo are registered trademarks of Tyndale House Publishers.

Airborne

Copyright © 2020 by DiAnn Mills. All rights reserved.

Cover photograph of airplane window copyright © franckreporter/Getty Images. All rights reserved.

Author photograph by Debi Wallace, copyright © 2018. All rights reserved.

Designed by Dean H. Renninger

Published in association with the literary agency of Books & Such Literary Management, 52 Mission Circle, Suite 122, PMB 170, Santa Rosa, CA 95409.

Airborne is a work of fiction. Where real people, events, establishments, organizations, or locales appear, they are used fictitiously. All other elements of the novel are drawn from the author's imagination.

For information about special discounts for bulk purchases, please contact Tyndale House Publishers at csresponse@tyndale.com or call 1-800-323-9400.

Library of Congress Cataloging-in-Publication Data

Names: Mills, DiAnn, author.
Title: Airborne / DiAnn Mills.
Description: Carol Stream, Illinois : Tyndale House Publishers, [2020]
Identifiers: LCCN 2020006486 (print) | LCCN 2020006487 (ebook) | ISBN 9781496427144 (hardcover) | ISBN 9781496427175 (trade paperback) | ISBN 9781496427182 (kindle edition) | ISBN 9781496427151 (epub) | ISBN 9781496427168 (epub)
Subjects: GSAFD: Suspense fiction. | Christian fiction.
Classification: LCC PS3613.I567 A75 2020 (print) | LCC PS3613.I567 (ebook) | DDC 813/.6—dc23
LC record available at https://lccn.loc.gov/2020006486
LC ebook record available at https://lccn.loc.gov/2020006487

Printed in the United States of America

26	25	24	23	22	21	20
7	6	5	4	3	2	1

Dedicated to Janet K. Grant, Books & Such Literary Agency.
Thank you for the years of friendship, wisdom, and guidance.

ACKNOWLEDGMENTS

Todd Allen—Your suggestions always make my books stronger. Where would I be without your knowledge of dialogue assassination?

Karissa Culbreath, PhD—My sincere gratitude for all your help. I couldn't have written this book without your immunology and microbiology expertise.

Lynette Eason—Love our brainstorming sessions!

James Hannibal—Your experience as a pilot and your knowledge of a quality story helped tremendously!

Mark Lanier—Your wisdom and insight into Scripture are an asset to grow me into a better person and writer.

Richard Mabry—Thanks for always explaining medical procedures.

Julee Schwarzburg—You are incredible! Your brainstorming, suggestions, and edits helped me create an amazing story.

Rachel Trusty—Thanks for helping me add a touch of reality to the story.

CHAPTER ONE

HOUSTON
EARLY JULY
MONDAY, 6 P.M.

Vacations offered a distraction for those who longed to relax and rejuvenate, but FBI Special Agent Heather Lawrence wrestled with the decision to take an overseas trip alone. Normally she arrived for a flight at IAH eager to embark upon a new adventure. Not this time. Her vacation expectations had bottomed out over four weeks ago after Chad had slammed the door on reconciliation. Was she working through her grief or avoiding the reality of a husband who no longer wanted her?

She waited to board the flight in a designated line at the gate. The hum of voices blended with airport beeps, and announcements swirled around her as though enticing her to join the enthusiasm. In the line beside her, passengers shifted their carry-ons and positioned their mobile devices or paper boarding passes. Ready. Alert. People eager to be on their way.

Heather offered a smile to those nearest her. An adorable little blond boy with an older woman found it hard to stand still. A middle-aged couple held hands. The bald head and pasty skin of the man indicated a medical condition. He stumbled, and the woman reached for him. A robust man held a violin case next to his heart. A twentysomething woman with pink hair and a man behind her with a scruffy beard exchanged a kiss.

Chad used to steal kisses.

If she pinpointed the exact moment when he chose to separate himself from her, she'd say when he returned from a third trip for Doctors Without Borders late last fall. He'd witnessed suffering and cruel deaths that had scarred him. She'd encouraged his desire to help others, not realizing their future would take a backseat. While he drove toward success, their marriage drifted across the lanes and stalled in a rut.

The boarding line moved toward the Jetway. Each step shook her to the core as though she should turn and try to reverse the past seven months. She'd ignored her and Chad's deteriorating relationship in an effort to make him happy. A huge mistake. But she didn't intend to add the labels *beaten* or *weak* to her dossier.

A cell phone sounded, and a man boarding in front of her stopped to answer it. His shoulders stiffened under a tan sports coat, and he talked in hushed tones. Heather dug her fingers into her palms and forced one foot in front of the other while the man pocketed his cell phone and proceeded into business class.

A flight attendant greeted her, a dark-haired young man wearing a wide smile, relaxed and genuine, an obvious sign he enjoyed his job. She returned the gesture. His black jacket with two rows of silver braid on the sleeves and black trousers were magazine perfect.

Heather walked to a rear aisle seat in business class and hoisted her tote bag into the overhead compartment. Although it held essentials for every emergency in case her luggage was delayed, the bulging piece weighed less than the burden on her heart.

Easing onto her seat, Heather pulled the brochure from her shoulder bag describing Salzburg's music festival, a celebration of musicians past and present. First a layover in Frankfurt and then on to her destination. She'd rented an apartment for ten days within walking distance of the historical center. The flexibility allowed her to choose her itinerary and cook or dine out. From the online photos, the centuries-old building had just enough updates to be comfortable without damaging its historic charm. She'd have hours to explore Mozart's roots, museums, the many churches, immerse herself in the culture, and think.

A female passenger, sporting red spiked hair and chin-length hooped earrings, stopped beside her. The woman carried a Venti Starbucks. "Excuse me." Her German accent a reminder of the destination. "Would you mind holding my coffee while I store my carry-on?"

"Of course." Heather held the cup while the woman shoved her small suitcase into the overhead bin.

"Sorry for the inconvenience. I wasn't thinking when I bought the coffee."

"It smells heavenly." Heather stood to let the woman pass and then handed her the cup.

"Thank you." The woman blew on the lid and took a sip. "I'm Mia."

"I'm Heather."

"Long flight ahead but soon I'll be home." She pointed to Heather's brochure. "Salzburg?"

"Yes. For a much-needed vacation."

"I'm from Frankfurt. Really missing my daughter and husband."

"You'll see them soon."

Mia broke into a wide smile. "We've done FaceTime and texted, but I want to touch their faces and hug them."

Heather continued to read the Salzburg brochure to avoid any personal comments from Mia, like whether she was taking a vacation solo. An elderly man wearing a straw fedora and a white mustache sat in the aisle seat across from Heather. He pulled his phone from his pant pocket and used his thumbs on the keyboard like a kid.

Mia placed her coffee on the tray and made a phone call. *"Wie geht es meinem kleinen Mädchen?"*

Heather translated the German. *How is my little girl?* The woman's excitement resonated through every word. Love. Laughter. Priceless commodities that Heather didn't possess. Yet this trip offered an opportunity to rekindle her faith in God and chart a course for the future.

While the attendants made their way through business class with drink orders, Heather longed to have confirmation she'd made the right decision to take this trip. No one knew of her vacation plans except her parents and Assistant Special Agent in Charge Wade Mitchell in Houston. No one needed to know the why of her trip until she made a few decisions.

Stuffing the Salzburg brochure into her bag, she snatched the aircraft's information and confirmed the layout for 267 passengers, restrooms, exit doors, in-seat power, on-demand entertainment, and three galleys. She always noted the details of her surroundings, another habit of working so many FBI cases. Always be prepared for the unexpected.

If the trip had been FBI sanctioned, her present circumstances might not hurt so much. How ironic she worked the critical incident response group as a behavior analyst, and she wrestled to understand her own life.

Right on time, the flight attendants took their assigned posts while miniature screens throughout the plane shared the aircraft's amenities and explained the passenger safety instructions. The captain welcomed them moments before the plane lifted into the clouds.

On her way. No turning back. She prayed for a safe journey and much-needed answers.

Food smells from business class caught her attention, a mix of roasted chicken and beef. Too often of late, she forgot to eat or nothing appealed to her. To shake off the growing negativity, she paid for Wi-Fi and grabbed her phone from her bag. Time to concentrate on something other than herself.

She glanced at the incoming notifications. No texts. Her emails were an anticipated list of senders when she longed for a change of heart from Chad. Sighing, she closed her eyes. Between her job, Chad, and stress, too often she fought for enough pillow time.

Two hours later, she woke from a deep sleep to the sound of a woman's scream.

CHAPTER TWO

HEATHER WHIRLED TOWARD the ear-piercing cry behind her. She released her seat belt and rushed back to the economy section. The overhead lights snapped on to reveal the middle-aged couple whom she'd seen at the gate. The panic-stricken woman beside him held a tissue to his nose. Blood dripped beneath her fingers and down her wrist.

Not a muscle moved on the man's face, and his eyes rolled back into their sockets. Heather approached him in the aisle seat. Before she could speak, the woman gasped, a mix of sobs and a struggle for composure. "Help me. I can't stop the bleeding."

Heather used tissues from the woman's lap to help block the blood flow. "Try to stay calm."

The woman nodded. "I shouldn't have let him talk me into this trip. He's been so weak."

From the front of the plane, the male flight attendant who'd greeted passengers earlier rushed their way. He carried two kits, one labeled first aid and the other biohazard. A female attendant trailed after him.

"Help is here," Heather said to the woman. She moved aside

for the attendant to administer aid. She prayed the ill man was undergoing a minor problem—an easily resolved issue—and for the woman's comfort. But his lifeless face showed a grim reality.

"Sir, how do you feel?" Not a sound or movement came from the man. Blood flowed from Heather's mass of tissues.

The male attendant twisted off the seal of the biohazard kit and searched inside. He drew out a pair of nitrile gloves and wiggled them on. The female attendant opened the first aid kit, ripped into a gauze package, and handed it to the male attendant, who applied it to the man's nose. She opened the biohazard waste bag to dispose of the soiled materials.

The male attendant captured the woman's attention. "Ma'am, I'm Nathan. Is this your husband?"

"Yes. He's very hot."

Nathan touched the man's forehead. "How long has he been feverish?"

"He was fine when we boarded. Perhaps over an hour into the flight?" Her sobs subsided to soft cries. "Do something. Blood's coming from his mouth."

Heather touched her shoulder with a clean hand. "Take a deep breath."

"How can I? Roy's not breathing."

"That's his name?" His gentle voice ushered in compassion.

"Yes. I'm Catherine."

He bent to speak to Roy. "I'm Nathan. Give me a few minutes to administer first aid." He replaced the gauze on Roy's nose for the second time and turned to the female flight attendant, who'd paled but didn't tremble. "Leave the kits. Call the flight deck and tell them what's happening."

She rushed to the front of the cabin.

"This is my fault." Catherine held Roy's hand. "He finished chemo and radiation for lung cancer, but his doctor hadn't cleared him for the trip."

"Catherine," Nathan said, "I know you're worried, but try to stay calm. Has he experienced these symptoms before?"

"No."

A voice spoke over the interphone. "If a licensed medical professional is on board, we have a medical issue. All other passengers, please remain in your seats."

Within moments, a lean man arrived from the right side of business class carrying a leather case. "I'm a doctor." Heather stepped back while he examined Roy and spoke to Nathan.

While the doctor stood over Roy with his back to Heather, Nathan turned to her. "We've got this handled. Please return—"

"No, please. Let her stay," Catherine said. "If she doesn't mind."

Nathan frowned. "Okay, for the moment. Our manual states we have to keep the aisle clear around the patient."

"I understand," Heather said. "I'd be happy to sit with her, and I'm Heather."

"Miss, if the pilots call our med service on the ground, I'll need you out of way so we can relay instructions."

The doctor and Nathan lowered Roy to the aisle and treated him. They blocked Heather's view of the procedure, but the doctor rummaged for something inside the leather case. For the next ten minutes, she waited for the doctor to reassure passengers of the man's recovery.

Catherine's hysteria spun in a cloud of uncertainty that left unchecked often spread panic. She unfastened her seat belt and rose on unstable legs. "Please, tell me my husband is all right." The female attendant gently urged her back onto the seat.

The doctor eased up from Roy and spoke reassuring words to Catherine. He peeled off his blood-covered gloves and tossed them into the bag. Had Roy succumbed to the lung cancer or a complication?

Nathan walked to a galley area. "Ladies and gentlemen, I am Nathan Howard, your lead flight attendant on board your flight today. We appreciate your concern for the man receiving medical attention. We will transport him to the rear of the cabin, where he'll be comfortable. A doctor is tending to him, and the medical concern is under control. Thank you."

Heather supported the airline's protocol designed to keep everyone from alarm and terror while the crew addressed issues. Yet a few people craned their necks to watch the scene as though it was a morbid form of entertainment more interesting than the recycled movies on the screens in front of them.

Nathan returned to Catherine. "I know you'd like for the young woman to sit with you, but it would be easier for the flight crew and safer for her if we placed an attendant here. Can we do that?"

"I guess." Catherine's lips quivered.

Heather bent to speak. "I'm not far." She understood how Catherine had latched on to her, a stranger, for moral support.

Nathan and the doctor picked Roy up and carried him to the rear. Roy was either unconscious or dead.

The female flight attendant sat in Roy's seat and held Catherine's hand. "I'll stay with you for as long as you like."

"Can I join my husband?"

"When the doctor is finished, I'll escort you back."

Heather returned to her seat—her mind weighed with concern.

"Gott hab Erbarmen," Mia said.

"Yes, God have mercy."

"You speak German?"

"A little. Spent a year in Frankfurt when I was in college."

"The sound of it makes me long for home." She hesitated. "What's wrong with the man?"

"His wife said he'd recently completed chemo treatments for lung cancer. I'm sure the doctor is doing all he can. The airline has doctors on the ground, and they'll consult with the doctor on board. Between them, they'll figure out what's best."

"Do you work for the airlines?"

"No." Heather smiled. "I'm with the Department of Justice."

Mia rubbed her palms together. She'd already stated her desire to see her family. "Will the flight be diverted?"

"It depends on lots of factors. The man may just require rest." Heather wasn't going to state the excessive blood from Roy's mouth and nose pointed to his death. By now the doctors at Medi-Pro-Aire, an advisory service for airlines, had been contacted and put in communication with the pilot.

"I read the airline's cost to emergency divert range from $10,000 to upwards of $200,000," Mia said.

"I don't doubt the cost, but with this airline, the safety and welfare of the passengers always come first. They don't blink at the cost of diversion. It's on management's mind post-action."

"Can the pilots be called to the carpet for making a safety decision?"

"I'm sure their procedure is in place to protect the passengers." Heather forced comfort into her voice. "We'll be okay."

Muffled voices around her prompted alarm.

A man shouted for help. "My wife has a terrible headache."

A man in business class vomited.

"My son has a fever," a woman said.

"Please, the man beside me has a nosebleed, and he can't stop it."

"What is going on?" Mia whispered. "All these people are suddenly sick. Frighteningly sick."

Heather wished she had answers while horror played out around her.

"I'm afraid." Mia's face turned ashen.

"We have to stay calm." Heather craved to heed her own advice.

Throughout the plane, people complained of flu-like symptoms. Another person vomited. Heather touched her stomach. A twinge of apprehension crept through her.

Nathan spoke over the interphone. "If you are experiencing physical distress, press your call button. Flight attendants will be in your area soon with damp paper towels. Use these to cover your mouth and the tops of beverages. As always, remain in your seats."

Heather messaged ASAC Mitchell in Houston with the medical emergency report, including the symptoms.

He responded. **The FBI, TSA, CDC, and Medi-Pro-Aire are on it. Are you okay?**

Yes. People's symptoms indicate a serious virus.

The doctor on board has given a similar conclusion.

She trembled as she typed. **Looks similar to what Chad described in Africa.**

The doctor said the same. Is the man dead?

I think so.

How many others are sick?

Heather surveyed the passengers within her sight and typed. **From my seat, I see around ten in business class, and I hear the sick in economy. Will the plane divert?**

No decision yet. Keep me posted. You are our eyes.

Beyond what the doctor on board relayed to those on the ground, ASAC Mitchell must believe she held the voice of reason and objectivity. The irony of their interpretation. The viruses were usually zoonotic or caused by insects, and the symptoms created intense suffering. She blinked to clear her head and not ponder the worst.

With panic gripping her in a stranglehold, she imagined what others were feeling. A man questioned why the plane hadn't landed. A woman bolted to the galley and held her mouth. The man who held the violin marched to the business class restroom but fell face-first and vomited.

The elderly man across the aisle from her coughed. His nose trickled blood.

Heather grabbed tissues from her bag and handed them to him. "Will this help?"

"Tell me this is a nightmare." He gripped her arm—fiery hot.

CHAPTER THREE

THE PASSENGER CALL BUTTONS dinged like stuck doorbells.

Heather faced Nathan. She'd waited in line with two other people who'd volunteered to help those infected by the virus. The Good Samaritan law applied to all of them who gave reasonable aid.

"I'm FBI, Houston." She displayed her creds. After he read her ID, she stuck it back into her jean pocket. "How can I help?"

"We need a miracle. I've never experienced a sickness outbreak of this magnitude. If it hadn't been for the extra freight freeing up thirty seats, we wouldn't have availability in the rear economy section for the sick."

"We're in a holding pattern?"

"Yes, over New York City and not headed over the Atlantic."

He didn't have to finish his thoughts. The aircraft might be seen as a danger to any country including the US. Who was she fooling? The entire crew and passengers jeopardized the safety of American citizens on the ground. "I'm sure we'll hear of plans to land soon," she said. "The every-fifteen-minute updates help ease the nervous jitters."

"In the flight deck, the captain is on SATCOM with flight ops determining a course of action. The goal is a combination of speed and locating proper facilities both for the aircraft and the passengers." He nodded at a beverage cart near him stacked with paper towels, cleaning fluid, plastic gloves, tissues, and plastic bags. "I'd take a double shot of anything to avoid the virus. But we can't serve food or drink as long as there's threat of contagion." He drew in a sharp breath. "It takes as long to spiral down into a city below us as it does to cut a straight path descent to a city a hundred miles away."

"Looks like we're a flying ambulance, racing the passengers toward the best and fastest medical care for a large volume of people."

"I'm counting on it. Sad thing is if we divert to another airport, more innocent people will be infected. What other flights have been targeted? Makes me question what ground control will determine."

Heather refused to discuss his statement. "I've reported our situation to the FBI and given them multiple updates. No news of any other outbreaks in Houston or other flights."

"Something contaminated this aircraft." He clenched his jaw. "I don't understand. Our air-filtration system is stellar."

"Does the same system handle the flight deck?"

"There's a pack that goes to the pilots and one to the rest of us. But both packs are combined and constantly filter recirculated air."

"Regardless, when the pilots use a lavatory in business class, they're exposed on a smaller scale."

What was the plan of action for infected pilots? Some aircrafts were equipped to fly, even land, through computer technology. She'd read nothing indicating this model had that technology.

If the plane didn't land soon, more people could die.

Nathan studied her. "What's the FBI calling the problem?"

"Not confirmed. They will notify the pilot once the ground

agencies finalize a plan." The virus reeked of weapons of mass destruction—WMD—and terrorism, but Nathan would find out soon enough how federal officials termed the virus outbreak.

"A shout-out to whatever deity you support might help."

"I've been praying to God since the first infection." She pointed to business class, where Mia had joined a small group. "People are gathered to pray in clusters near the front."

"In seat belts?"

"I assume so. A flight attendant is with them."

"An attendant has a massive headache and nosebleed." Nathan gulped, the sound of despair. "How did this happen since takeoff? I watched these people board. They looked healthy, happy."

Chad had relayed frightening stories about how rapidly viruses spread in third-world countries. He'd explained excruciating pain often accompanied the symptoms, but his description hadn't captured the vivid torment around her.

"Those versed in emergency medical care are strategizing how to help us," she said.

"Do they understand every minute that ticks by means another infected passenger?"

"I'm sure they do, but their path forward has to protect ground-based medical and law enforcement personnel from the virus while ensuring it stays contained."

Nathan tied up a plastic bag filled with paper products used to clean up the sick. The stench tore at her stomach, and she turned her head.

"Are you trained for emergencies?" Nathan said.

"A little. I want to help."

"What do you know that you're not telling me?"

She shook her head. "Nothing. Medical testing can put a name on this."

An attendant with bloodstains on the chest of her uniform sought Nathan's attention. "Any paper towels?"

"Three rolls left and two stacks from the lavatories. Take a roll." He gazed out at those in business class. "You've got to be kidding me." He marched to a man videoing the scene with a smartphone. "Sir, what's wrong with you?"

"The media need visuals to show the status of these people," the man said.

"Why don't you ask the victims if they want to be exploited?"

The man went nose-to-nose with Nathan. "Try and stop me."

"I'll contact the pilot. He has authority to order physical restraint."

"I've already sent pics and descriptions to the media."

"Stop now or face the consequences. Take your seat and fasten your seat belt."

"Who is in control here?"

Nathan reached inside his suit jacket and handed the guy a tri-folded pamphlet. The man read it, his face reddening. He slapped it against Nathan's chest and pocketed the phone. He whirled around to his seat, mumbling obscenities.

Whoa. Heather hadn't expected compliance. Nathan joined her, and curiosity gained ground. "What did you show him?"

Nathan gave a slight grin. "We have form letters that say, 'Order to Cease Objectionable Behavior.' It lists all the things a belligerent passenger can expect if he doesn't stop inappropriate behavior, like law enforcement on the ground waiting to arrest him." He stared at the man's back. "They're stored in the overhead, but some leads carry one with them for unique circumstances."

"Definitely adds weight to your instructions. I've seen how flight attendants struggle with lack of authority. For some passengers, they are simply waiters."

He faced Heather. "You asked to help, and I appreciate it. Whatever is on board appears to randomly attack people."

"Weak bodies are the most susceptible." She looked at those growing sicker before her eyes, a few elderly, and young children.

Whoever got in its path. Their immune systems couldn't handle the virus's attack. The flight crew had moved several passengers forward to make room for the ill in the back of the plane. Earlier, she'd witnessed two more faces covered with navy-blue blankets. "Where can I best be used?"

He handed her a pair of disposable gloves and demonstrated how to remove them to avoid contamination. "We have a few stacks of paper towels left to clean up blood and vomit on the floor and seats."

Heather wiggled into the gloves. Nathan handed her a stack of folded paper towels, a bottle of water, and a plastic bag. "I appreciate this. A good supply of water is on board, but don't use it on an unconscious person." He stiffened. "I don't mean to sound calloused. The flight has no one dead, and the doctor on board refuses to make a pronouncement. Can't blame him."

"I'm aware of the airline's policy."

"Thanks for your cooperation. Procedure. Rules. A passenger might claim an upset stomach and demand the plane land costing the airlines thousands of dollars." He glanced around them. "I wish a stomach virus swept through the plane. Not this tragedy." He shrugged. "Blankets from unoccupied seats are available to cover the unresponsive."

She returned to the elderly man who sat across the aisle from her. He wore a shirt soaked in blood and vomit, and she stopped beside him. "I'm here to help, sir. Do you have a change of shirt in your carry-on?"

"No. I'm sorry," he whispered through blood-coated lips. "Take care of the others first."

Heather wiped his face, neck, and shirt, then tossed the soiled paper into the plastic bag. Oh, for a breath of fresh air. She finished cleaning the man and prayed to a God she wanted to believe cared for these people.

She moved from business class to help others. A scruffy-bearded man seated in a middle row of the economy section blocked her way in the aisle. She recognized him from the gate in Houston. He wore jeans and a polo shirt. The pink-haired woman with him flipped through an airline magazine.

"I saw you talk to those flight attendants," he said. "When will the pilot continue on course?"

"We didn't discuss it, sir. I'm a volunteer to aid with the sick."

"I have business in Frankfurt, critical business."

"I'm not an airline employee, but these sick people take priority."

He swore. "Not my problem. If I'm late, the airlines will pay."

Was he blind to the surrounding people's condition? Heather peered at the woman who coaxed him into taking his seat.

Heather left the couple and moved on to the rear, where the blond-haired little boy sat beside the older woman—Heather had seen them at the gate. The woman had a blanket over her face. *No. No.* Maybe she was sleeping. Heather pulled the blanket back far enough to view vacant eyes staring back at her. She quickly replaced the blanket, the fear mounting until she wanted to scream. But breaking down served no purpose.

"Hey, sweetie." She bent to the little boy and noted his flushed cheeks. She adjusted his loose seat belt to his slender frame. Dampening a folded piece of a paper towel, she held it for him to see. "I'm going to clean the blood from your face."

He whispered, "Grandma," and touched the blanket of the covered woman. "She must have a headache."

So young to experience such an ordeal. "She's asleep, honey. Let her rest." She swallowed to keep the tears at bay. "What's your name?"

"Frankie."

"Where do you live?"

"Me and Grandma live in Kingwood, Texas."

"You're a big boy to take such a long trip." A piece of the paper towel stuck to his face, and she brushed it aside.

"I'll be in kindergarten again. I missed a lot of school 'cause I've been sick."

His explanation for repeating kindergarten ripped her heart raw. Fighting a virus required a strong and healthy body. "But you're better now?"

"Yes, ma'am. I haven't been in the hospital since April. Grandma says I'm growing out of it. Soon I can live with my dad. That's where we're going, to see my dad in Germany. He's a soldier. We're gonna have my birthday there."

"You are brave." His eyes dropped to half-mast, his pallor tugging at her fears for him. "Go ahead and sleep. Dream about your birthday and the time with your dad."

"Will we be there before Grandma wakes up?"

"Not sure." Poor Frankie would see his dad by himself. If he recovered.

Please, God, take care of Frankie and these helpless people. You know my concerns, my secret.

CHAPTER FOUR

HEATHER PEERED into Frankie's face and continued to pray for him and those on board. How often had she heard terror brought others to God? During the past eight years, her relationship with God had dwindled to a weak thread. Chad held fast to the god of science, and while he didn't ridicule her faith in the beginning, he often had plans for them on Sunday morning—for the benefit of their marriage.

In the early years, they debated their views of God, and Chad even attended church occasionally. Why hadn't she followed the Bible's instructions not to marry someone who saw no need for God? Heather had digested a lie. She thought she could influence Chad to change. But her pleas to invest time in exploring God collided against the soundproof wall of his heart.

"Agent Lawrence."

Heather gave Nathan her attention. "Do you need me?"

"Houston's FBI has requested you join a conference call in

progress regarding the sickness on board our aircraft. TSA, FAA, and CDC have already linked via audio. The pilot has arranged a special patch through our interphone. You can use the one near the flight deck."

Heather nodded and glanced at Frankie's closed eyes. She stared at the disposable gloves encasing her fingers, smeared with blood and vomit. If only attempts to make the victims comfortable helped. She peeled off the gloves, then tossed them into a full plastic bag and followed Nathan to the front galley.

A man grabbed her hand. Blood streamed down his arm, not from him but from his small daughter. "Please, help me."

Heather grabbed tissues from Nathan. The little girl's eyes stared vacant . . .

Nathan urged her toward business class, where he gave her the handset.

"Agent Lawrence here."

A drone of voices stopped.

"Heather, this is SAC Bischoff. Those of us managing the crisis on board flight 3879 need your input. Medi-Pro-Aire has requested CDC protocols, which we have put into effect. I've been told you're assisting with the sick. While your efforts are commendable, please take precaution. On the call is ASAC Mitchell and Dr. Jordan Radcom, the director of the CDC's Division of High-Consequence Pathogens and Pathology. I understand Dr. Radcom is a friend."

"Yes, sir. My husband, Chad, and Jordan attended medical school together, and we stay in close contact." She swiped beneath her eyes. "I can't be professional in this. What is being done for these people?"

"We're making progress. None of us have any idea what you are experiencing. Do your best to remain calm."

Impossible to numb her heart and mind to the suffering. "Yes, sir."

"I'll continue," SAC Bischoff said. "Dr. Radcom will direct the CDC operation."

Trained doctors could help these people.

"We'll now proceed," SAC Bischoff said. "Forty-five percent of the people on board flight 3879 have displayed symptoms of a virus, and an additional seventeen are unresponsive. None of the passengers or crew stated they were ill before boarding the plane. We've elected to divert the aircraft to JFK, where the CDC from the New York Quarantine Station will identify the health threat and conduct the investigative research. Those affected by the virus will be transported to Jamaica Hospital in Queens, which has an infectious disease service where trained medical persons can treat those who are ill.

"Those not exhibiting health issues will be taken to a quarantine facility. The FBI will oversee security in conjunction with Homeland Security, NYPD, the National Guard, and the New York State and City Health Departments."

"Sir, do you have any idea what's been unleashed here?" Heather said.

"We're hesitant to make a statement without confirmation."

"Has anyone claimed responsibility?"

"Negative," SAC Bischoff said. "We've not detected any online chatter. Until we gather evidence otherwise, the crime is classified as an act of terrorism with a WMD. Passenger and flight crew background checks are under way as well as those who came in contact with the aircraft in Chicago and Houston. Outbound aircraft in both cities are grounded until we can provide a safe solution. Airborne flights will continue to their destinations, and international flights are being diverted in compliance with FAA policy."

"We need everyone's medical records immediately." Jordan's voice heightened. "Where has the aircraft been the past five to ten days? What are the food and beverage sources? Was there recent maintenance on the air-filtration system? Are any of the passengers with a group?"

Heather's mind delved deeper into catastrophic mode. Had the culprit planned for other areas of the world to be exposed? Was this the first of many outbreaks?

"We'll gather the data and make sure everyone receives the information," SAC Bischoff said. "I'm disconnecting listen-only mode so Dr. Radcom and I can address further questions."

A woman introduced herself as an FBI agent from New York City. "Earlier we discussed the possibility of shooting down the aircraft. Why was the option abandoned when the virus is out of control?"

Acid clawed up from Heather's stomach to her throat, and she longed to shout a protest. The agencies on the ground had to find a better solution. But she understood the welfare of the American people was at stake. In truth, she didn't want to be on the call or hear the debate if the outcome meant sacrificing the lives of the people on board the plane.

And her baby.

"The consensus is we can treat the infected and confine the virus," SAC Bischoff said. "The president is concerned about the welfare of those on board the flight and the potential impact on the American people. He has advised against drastic measures."

The woman agent spoke again. "What safeguards protect Americans?"

"We have implemented protective measures to isolate the victims. White House staff are monitoring our call, and the president has pledged assistance to end the illness and stop the spread of contagion."

The director of the New York State Health Department introduced himself. "We are equipped to handle the treatment of those infected and exposed to the virus."

"Who are you trying to convince?" the woman agent said. "If

the health department were equipped, the dialogue to destroy the plane wouldn't have occurred. My recommendation is to eliminate the problem and keep US citizens safe."

"As stated prior to bringing Agent Lawrence onto the call, we are not willing to take extreme measures. The decision has been made. End of discussion. If there are no additional questions, we'll turn our attention to Dr. Jordan Radcom," Bischoff said. "Doctor, what are your thoughts?"

"The unknown virus sets the stage for nationwide panic," Jordan said. "In light of images and videos relayed from the aircraft, we can't delay a statement to the public. While our conversation is in the middle of the night, other parts of the world are aware of our crisis. They are looking to see what actions we take and if the virus is contained."

"The president has scheduled a press conference for 9 a.m. Eastern time. He'll address the media and provide information then," Bischoff said. "SAC Fielder from the New York City office will speak after the president."

"Heather," Jordan said, "I have a few specifics for you. Find out from those who are coherent if they recall conversations or actions to help us establish the virus's origin. Anything unusual. Smells. Tastes. Please message SAC Bischoff and me with the information."

"I'll get on it right away." Heather pushed logic into her words, but the emotions refused to dissipate. "Watching men, women, and children suffer is traumatic. They must have medical attention as soon as possible."

"We're expediting all personnel," Jordan said. "Have you experienced any symptoms?"

"No." In one breath she considered herself blessed. In the next, guilt rolled through her as though she were responsible.

"What are your observations?" Jordan said.

"The doctor has relayed to you medical information—"

"I value your perspective."

"Okay. It appears the virus begins with a severe headache accompanied by fever. The people who've verbalized their symptoms complain of muscle and joint pain followed by nosebleeds, vomiting with blood, abdominal cramps, and in the severe stage, respiratory distress. Something has to be done now."

"What are the reactions of the people who aren't showing symptoms?"

"Frightened. A few are busy making others comfortable. Others are glued to TV and electronic screens. I assume to avoid what's going on. The aircraft has Wi-Fi, so passengers will have access to live news reports and CDC press releases. If anyone here is responsible, I haven't seen any indications."

"Thank you," Jordan said. "The CDC will provide medical information to the public through our website. It will contain FAQ and methods of contacting the CDC."

SAC Bischoff picked up the conversation. "Dr. Radcom will be part of a task force with the FBI to coordinate communications with the media. I'll send a detailed report to everyone. Dr. Radcom has a plane to catch to New York."

Heather closed her eyes. Jordan was a man who loved God above all things. Surely his commitment meant he'd work to end the virus and help those who suffered.

Turbulence threatened her balance, and Nathan righted her, odd since they were circling in a holding pattern. Within moments the pilot requested everyone to take their seats with the familiar instructions to fasten their seat belts. Jordan and SAC Bischoff would have to wait for her passenger interviews until the plane stabilized.

CHAPTER FIVE

HEATHER REPEATEDLY TOLD HERSELF the queasiness came from turbulence or her pregnancy and not the initial signs of the virus. She didn't detect a fever. Neither did her nose bleed. *My baby must survive.*

Passengers remained in their seats while flight attendants tended to the sick. They wore face masks and disposable gloves, but what about the passengers? Holding wet paper towels to their mouths and noses was a nuisance, and few adhered to the safeguard. So little time had passed, but each moment brought pitiful cries that promised to haunt her the rest of her life. The bleeding and death were etched in eternity.

True to her word, she monitored everyone, but the pilot insisted passengers remain in their seats. She pulled her phone from her bag and read an email from ASAC Mitchell time-stamped five minutes ago. He wrote the welfare of the American people took priority, which meant critical medical attention for the ill on board the plane. With the various agencies' involvement, everyone faced a lengthy ordeal in New York. She anticipated the furious responses from those who hadn't been infected but would be transported to a quarantine facility, like the scruffy-beard man and the woman with him.

If only Heather had an idea what or who had initiated the dreadful disease. Instead helplessness sank into her flesh. All she could do was offer a sliver of hope to the sick and their companions.

Mia leaned back against the seat and appeared to sleep. Perspiration trickled down the side of her face while she held a tissue to her nose. Blood had seeped through and dried, showing her head position had stopped the blood flow. Others were too weak to keep their heads tilted.

Please, God, not this sweet lady. We've known each other for a few hours. She's prayed and cared for the sick and been a friend.

Heather spoke Mia's name, and the woman turned to her while maintaining an upward chin. "I learned the plane is being diverted to JFK. Once we land, you'll see a doctor. Lots of them."

"Feels like we're being stalked by an invisible demon."

"We are, and I'm scared, too."

"I'm ready to be pricked and a thermometer stuck anywhere they want to put it."

They laughed, a sweet reprieve from reality. How quickly relationships forged between people tossed into a crisis situation.

"I keep praying, but the arguments against God rush me," Mia said. "Look around us at the people who are too sick to move. It's unspeakable. Why does God allow it?"

Heather wished she had a theological answer. "Good overcomes evil, even when we don't think it's possible."

"Are you convinced?"

"I'm trying. Faith means I don't have to understand, just accept. But it's hard, and I'm angry." Heather's annoyance with God surfaced months ago. One critical problem after another surfaced between her and Chad after she'd worked so hard. Her thoughts halted . . . She longed for God's intervention in her life, and Chad's decision had drawn her closer to Him. The latest tragedy on the plane compounded her confusion about where God fit. Yet, hope in His desire and ability to make matters right was her only grip on faith.

"My husband witnessed hundreds of people in Africa fall victim to virus outbreaks—many men, women, and children died," Heather whispered. "He's worked with Doctors Without Borders, and he's talked about so much suffering. After his first trip, he returned home determined to complete his doctorate in microbiology and immunology. He denies a good God who allows senseless deaths and says science paves the way for the good of mankind."

Mia replaced her tissue with a clean one—the blood flow had slowed to an occasional drip. She dropped the soiled tissue into the disposable bag in the front seat pocket. "No one deserves a nightmare illness. We boarded a plane with no thought of the outcome. Passengers and crew looked forward to opportunities for work, play, or a return home to families." She offered a thin, shaky smile. "My husband says I overthink things. Perhaps I do. My point is, what good can God make of unspeakable agony? Will we live to thank Him?"

Heather wished she could promise more light in their miserable darkness. "Hold on, dear one."

"I must for my family's sake. Are you pregnant? I've seen you hold your stomach."

Heather hadn't been aware of the gesture. "Must be a subconscious reaction. And yes, I am."

"The protective action is instinctive. We mothers will do whatever it takes to keep our little ones from harm."

"With the many sick people surrounding us, I'm afraid the virus will hurt my baby." Heather swiped at a tear. "I don't sound positive."

"I pray your baby is healthy and perfect. Your husband has reason to worry."

His ocean-blue eyes and light-brown hair flashed across her mind. The sight of him still stole her breath despite their problems. "I haven't told him. We separated over a month ago."

Mia's features saddened. "I'm so sorry. You should tell him. Children change how husbands and wives view the problems between them. With a baby, commitment deepens, and couples are open to communicate and resolve their issues."

How many nights had she lain awake and silently begged for Chad to love her? Begged God for him to change? "The key word is commitment. My husband values his work above everything, but I thought love was enough to keep my spot secure. Even if he was aware of the pregnancy, he'd be upset with me. I followed the necessary precautions, but he'd accuse me of trying to trap him. Not my style." She shook her head. "I've said too much."

"You're terrified about circumstances beyond your control." Mia's empathy offered sincere comfort, insight that Heather appreciated.

"I am. I can raise my baby alone—except I hadn't expected exposure to a devastating virus."

"Do your parents live close? I'm sure they'd help."

"They live in Houston, and they'll be overjoyed with a grandchild."

"You haven't told them either?"

"I decided to wait until after my trip. My goals were to build confidence in my ability to function as a single mother." Mom had often said Heather couldn't function without organization, a schedule, and an idea of what would happen moment by moment. "My parents claim I mastered the art of order and levelheadedness. If I confessed my sketchy future, they'd be rattled."

"Do you always put others before yourself?"

"Whenever possible, but I'm not always successful."

"You love your husband very much."

"Does it show?"

"Yes. Your face softened when you said his name."

"Are you a counselor?"

"Just a wife, mom, and an engineer with life experiences. The three roles are a constant juggle. I'm a typical engineer but emotional at times." Mia shoved a slight smile into her words.

Heather attempted to keep a professional facade. "Chad's one fault is his career takes so much of his time. Unfortunately, he's certain I'm holding him back."

"Have you discussed counseling?"

"He refuses, doesn't see a reason to prolong the inevitable." She swung to Mia. "His words."

"I'm sorry."

"No, I'm sorry to burden you. How are you? Are you nauseous?"

"My head hurts, but my stomach is fine."

"Try to rest. Soon we'll be bombarded with a team of medical personnel, doctors, and CDC disease detectives. My guess, they will be dressed in full containment gear." Heather grimaced. "I keep talking on about trivial things. I'll be quiet and stop bothering you."

Mia dabbed at her nose, and red stained the tissue despite her tilted head. "I thought I'd run out of words to pray, but you, your baby's health, and your personal problems will reach heaven's gates."

"Thank you." Tears pooled in Heather's eyes. Drat hormones. "God put us together so we could stay strong." She held Mia's hand . . . minus a glove.

The flight deck garnered the passengers' attention. "Ladies and gentlemen, the ATC has ordered us to hold here for an additional thirty minutes. Once we have an update, we'll get back to you."

A sandy-haired man behind them in economy shouted obscenities about the delay. Nathan hurried from the galley to him. Heather refused to gawk. No point.

More time loss. More worries. The hours and days ahead loomed with a ghastly unknown—a nightmare.

CHAPTER SIX

THE TURBULENCE ENDED and Heather left her seat to assist with the sick again. What difference did it make if she was tossed onto the floor or inhaled the virus? At least she'd be tending to someone who needed care. Her head throbbed, but she blamed lack of sleep and stress. No other symptoms, and she'd rarely been plagued by morning sickness.

She hurried to Frankie in the rear. He held his grandmother's blue-veined hand, small fingers wrapped around life as he'd known it. The poor child didn't realize his grandmother had passed, and now wasn't the time to tell him. His grandmother had been the second victim to receive an unresponsive diagnosis. Fever ravaged Frankie's body, but no vomiting or nosebleed. His breathing appeared regular, and he responded to her tender whispers. She prayed he would celebrate his seventh birthday with his dad.

Heather longed to press Delete on life's computer and return them all to the boarding gate.

She walked to the galley in business class, where Nathan stored bottles of water. The faces of those she passed told of their intense fear. Some mingled with anger. None resembled the granitelike features of a killer.

Hours had passed since they'd left Houston. Authorities on the ground had made critical decisions, but they were slow in implementing them. She didn't want to fault the federal agencies involved, but still frustration mounted at the number of ill who suffered without medical attention. The doctor on board had his hands full.

A man who'd boarded the plane in front of her spoke to Nathan. He'd also volunteered with the sick from the beginning and needed supplies. Blood mixed with vomit stained the front of his tan silk sports coat. "Do you have any updates to share? We can't go on like this to Germany."

"Sir, the pilot will announce a decision soon," Nathan said. "Until then, we remain in a holding pattern."

The man glanced around them. "I understand, and it's not my desire to be part of the problem. I see the sick throwing up and crying out for help, and I must take action."

"You've helped tremendously by tending to the sick."

"Has to be more I can do." He drew in a deep breath and reached for a pair of plastic gloves and a roll of toilet paper. "I'm sure this will end soon."

"Arrangements are being made. You can best serve everyone by encouraging them to stay strong."

"It's difficult to watch an epidemic with no solution." The man moved to the nearest need.

Heather gathered more cleaning supplies. In her line of work, she longed to right the wrong, fix problems. She believed her emotional and professional skills could outmaneuver any of life's roadblocks. Violent crimes were met head-on. Storms required an umbrella. Grieving people needed comfort. Stomachaches called for an antacid. Face it. Cuff it. Right it. But the tragedy on board this flight threatened her ability to survive emotional and physical paralysis.

"Look around at those on their devices," Nathan said. "Trust me, the media know the misery here. If the person responsible is on board, he or she deserves to suffer more than the rest."

She refused to reply, but his version of retribution resonated. Not godly, but honest.

He bent closer to her. "Tell me, will the plane be destroyed?"

"No, sir. There are no plans to eliminate us. The process on the ground takes time."

Nathan had said nothing she hadn't already processed. But she didn't have authority to give him the information learned on the conference call. The woman FBI agent's persistent demand to shoot down the plane fired across her mind. The federal agencies running with this ball didn't care about the cost of landing the plane. They were concerned with the best way to treat the number of people who were critically ill.

Before Heather could assist another ill passenger, the pilot requested their attention. "Ladies and gentlemen, thanks so much for your patience. ATC has directed us to prepare for a landing at John F. Kennedy airport in New York. Please return to your seats and remain there with your seat belts fastened for the remainder of the flight. Once we reach the gate, please stay in your seats and keep the aisles clear so health care workers can evacuate the sick. The current situation is frightening for every person on board. Please stay calm. Houston and Chicago airports are closed to outbound flights as a precaution.

"While questions are flooding your mind about what to share with friends, family, and employers, a solution will be provided once the FBI, CDC, and New York health departments examine and question us. Thank you for your cooperation—and especially those who have risked their lives to volunteer with the sick. We're on our way to medical aid."

The cabin filled with sounds of those murmuring relief. Hope. Treatment. No matter what they faced on the ground, it held more promise than what they'd experienced.

"Listen up!" The sandy-haired man who'd shouted obscenities earlier stood sideways in the opposite aisle separating business class from economy. He held the throat of a dark-haired young woman in a viselike grip. No weapon, but he could snap her neck. The terrified look on her face reminded Heather of other critical incidents where she'd intervened. "This plane will not land in New York."

"Sir, what's the problem?" Heather inched toward the attacker.

Bolts of anger shot from his eyes. "Are you a PR rep from the airlines? Flight security? The spokeswoman for the doctor who's insisting we land?"

"Sir, I'm a passenger, too."

"Are you ignorant of passenger schedules?"

"Of course not. Like you, I have plans that don't include landing this plane prematurely." She had to persuade him to release the young woman.

He cursed, his voice resounding in the cabin. "I paid for a trip to Germany, and I intend to get there. If the plane lands at JFK, I'll kill her. Tell that to the pilot."

CHAPTER SEVEN

HEATHER WATCHED the sandy-haired man pull back the curtain that separated business and economy class. The young woman in a stranglehold tried to pull free, but he yanked her tighter.

He shouted at Nathan. "Are you deaf? Tell the pilot to fly the plane to Germany or the girl dies."

Heather understood how terror drove people to irrational behavior, beyond logic and often to accomplish a selfish goal. The enraged man's eyes darted around the cabin, and he jerked the hostage closer. The young woman trembled, and she didn't look much more than twenty years old. Was he the one who'd unleashed the virus? Or was he afraid and reacting in a panic state?

"Sir, the pilot has orders to follow." Nathan held up the communication device. "I'll talk to him now. With so many people sick, I'm not sure what's possible. His instructions are from those on the ground."

"Listen to me!"

Heather took another hesitant step toward the man. "We—"

"Get back to the galley or I'll kill her."

She complied. "I've done what you've asked. Can we talk from here?"

"Stay there." The man's attention swung in every direction. "You'd like to help? Get the attendant to contact the pilot."

"I'm speaking to him now," Nathan said.

"Landing on time in Frankfurt is important to me, too," Heather said. "What's urgent for you?"

"People expect me. I have a tight schedule. Stuck in quarantine until the government issues a stamp of approval? Not me."

"Like you, I have a life other than a flight in crisis," she said. "This huge interruption will cost us time and money. We'll figure it out together." She took another step.

"Stop where you are." His voice graveled low. "I've never met a woman who didn't have an agenda."

The male volunteer who'd just spoken to Nathan stood in the aisle ahead, midway between Heather and the abductor. "Hey, buddy, I agree. Women can be a pain. I've been lied to and manipulated by every one I've met. Finished with them."

"I'm right there with you."

"You think your reason to land in Frankfurt is important?" the volunteer said. "I have a huge deal to close, and if I miss the meeting, the deal's off. By the way, my name's Thomas."

The man's attention perked. "What are you gonna do, Thomas?"

"I hate to lose the money. I mean it's huge, and the financial impact will hurt those in my company who are anticipating a bonus." Thomas made slow strides toward the man while talking. "Bills won't get paid. College funds stagnated. Homes foreclosed. Planned vacations canceled. Get the picture?"

"Then help me get the aircraft to Frankfurt."

"I'm sure I can do something. Let's discuss options." Thomas slowed his steady pace. "Can we talk while you hold her?"

"My mouth moves just fine."

Thomas blew out a sigh and pointed at the man. "She looks sick, and if she bites you, you're infected."

The man lowered his arm to avoid her mouth. "She won't try."

Why had Thomas risked his life and the young woman's to intervene? Admirable move. But dangerous. Perhaps he was trained in hostage negotiation.

Heather retreated behind the galley. She caught Nathan's eye, crouched low to the opposite side, and crawled through the curtained area along the opposite end of the aisle. To reach the man and free the woman, she'd have to squeeze past another man seated in the same row. The other two seats had been occupied by the woman hostage and the man who held her.

"One problem is how do we handle the sick?" Thomas said.

"Doesn't matter. They'll get over it or they won't."

"True. So far I'm healthy."

"I'm good to go. Sure would help if the AC was lower." The man chuckled. "Add cooler temps to my demands."

"Good idea."

The man's gaze stayed glued to Thomas, as though he was captivated by someone who shared the same mind-set.

"I want to negotiate a deal with the pilot," Thomas said. "Let's give permission to land, unload the sick, and then fly on to Frankfurt."

"Your plan takes time."

Heather lunged at the abductor. She seized his left wrist and twisted it back, forcing him to release the young woman, who scurried away from his hold. Heather wrestled him to the aisle floor and pulled both arms behind his back.

"I'm FBI. You're under arrest." She glanced up. "I need something to tie his hands."

Thomas yanked off his tie. "Use this until we find a rope."

The tie cost more than six months of car insurance. She grabbed it without taking her eyes off the assailant and wrapped it several times around his wrists. After grabbing his wallet for ID, she pressed him into his seat and clicked the seat belt.

The man referred to Heather in curse words she'd heard before and didn't appreciate.

"Enough," Thomas said, his voice low. "No reason to use that language with women and children present."

"You FBI?" the man said.

"No. I'm just a passenger."

Heather turned to Thomas. Relief coated her words. "Quick thinking. Thanks."

"Glad to help. The hostage was upset. I would have been, too." He looked at the woman now near the business class galley, where a female flight attendant helped her sit.

Heather studied the scene. The attendant gave the young woman a bottle of water and urged her to sit. Assured the young woman was in good hands, Heather sat on the right side of the man in custody. Nathan appeared and suggested Thomas take his seat. She thanked him again.

"What do you need?" Nathan said.

"Actually, if you could keep our friend company, I'll retrieve my purse."

"Sure thing." He eased onto the right side of the man.

She walked to Mia, who opened her eyes the moment Heather reached for her shoulder bag resting below her seat.

"You are my hero," Mia said. "I saw the whole takedown, and I'm impressed with how you swung into action. I'm also relieved. Is the young woman all right? Wasn't hurt?"

"I believe she's fine. Clearly shaken, which can be expected."

"The man who helped you looks familiar, but I'm not sure why or from where."

"His name is Thomas. No clue of his last name." Heather shrugged. "He's been volunteering with the sick."

"Danger brings out the worst and the best in people."

"You're right, Mia. Heroes are built from adversity." Heather studied her new friend's features. Mia's shallow breath caused worry to creep through her mind. At what point would medical personnel administer drugs to end the vicious symptoms? "I should get back to my prisoner. Please rest."

"I'll try."

Heather touched Mia's forehead. Heat emanated from her skin. Heather grabbed a clean pair of gloves and walked back to relieve Nathan of her prisoner.

Seated on the aisle seat beside the detainee, Heather turned to him. "Okay, sir. We are in the middle of a high-stress emergency. What's going on with you?"

"My business, Ms. FBI."

"Without a statement, I can't speak on your behalf to the authorities."

"Who's asking you to? Leave me alone." He ended his comment with a few additional words not in her vocabulary.

"Why is getting to Germany so important? I'd like to understand."

He snorted. "As if I'd talk to a Fed."

"You might want to rein in your pride and cooperate."

"I haven't done a thing to deserve this but demand my rights."

"What about threatening to kill that young woman?"

The man curled his lip. "You Feds are all alike. Push people until they fight back, then make an arrest."

"Once we land, I have no choice but to turn you over to the FBI."

"Those were your plans anyway. What's new?"

She opened his wallet to his driver's license. "Braden Taversty. Houston address. The photo looks like you."

He sneered. "It's supposed to."

"Your attitude is commendable. Won't get you far in front of a judge." She pulled her phone from her bag and typed an email to

ASAC Mitchell with the incident and Braden Taversty's identification information. Now to see if the man had a record.

Until the last few hours, she'd counted on her training and stubbornness to get through adversity. But the disaster called for knowledge she didn't possess.

The pilot announced the plane's initial descent. Heather wanted to believe the ordeal would soon be over, but in truth, she suspected it was only beginning.

CHAPTER EIGHT

I AM SHIELD. The source of the virus and how I walked through security undetected is my secret—a stroke of clear genius. I put aside my mental research about how the virus posed symptoms sooner than calculated. The release is done, and I'll analyze my error in the near future. Meanwhile, I'll observe the virus do its best work. I need to contemplate what the next several hours mean to the success of my plan.

A more urgent matter drives a stake into my thoughts. The virus cannot spread if the victims are hospitalized or in quarantine. A problem for me to work through.

Once we land, the CDC will move its teams into action. *Dogged* best describes each person assigned to the flight. Every inch of the plane and its contents will be examined for traces of the virus. Feds will thrive on getting their job done.

A team will inspect the plane's air cycling system designed to maintain cabin pressure while keeping it fresh and at a comfortable temperature. I should know since I memorized the plane's components. One of the virus's characteristics is the ability to go undetected by advanced filtration systems, which comforts me in the midst of these sick and dying people. The virus spread as designed, and for that, I'm pleased.

Pushing aside the success of the virus, I concentrate on additional law enforcement teams who will assist the CDC. They'll have the responsibility to examine food, clothing, beverages, trash, the sewer system—nothing escapes scrutiny. They won't rest until the traces of the virus are found and they discover how it has been smuggled on board. I must believe my role is impossible to detect. They will have no choice but to concoct some tale to please the public.

Am I safe? The passengers and flight crew will have medical personnel discerning everything about our physical health, and I don't mind. The vaccine will never show up. I'm simply a strong human whose body is immune.

An idea strikes me, an excellent thought.

CHAPTER NINE

CHAD STARED AT THE SHADOWED CEILING FAN above his bed. Adjusting to his new furnished apartment came with a learning curve, as though the lease had embedded the warning in fine print. After four weeks, his body should be accustomed to the hum of the air-conditioning and the absence of Heather. Why did her light, citrusy body spray linger on the sheets and pillowcases when he'd bought them on move-in day? Or did his senses ignore her absence?

The wave in her shoulder-length auburn hair and the spark of mystery in her sea-green eyes held him captive. At their condo, the added touch of fresh flowers welcomed him home at night—something he never thought he'd miss. Chad sensed her presence the moment she stepped into a room. The lilt of her voice had an uncanny way of filling him with peace.

Adapting to the single life had drawbacks, and he'd find some way to unshackle her from his life and heart. He'd deleted her photo from his cell phone and every email and message she'd ever sent him.

But he'd never remove her memory.

Chad checked the time. Six hours until he unlocked the door to his office and delved into the lab results from the previous day. He could try sleeping at his office and lab, as if it mattered where he spent his nights. At least the familiarity of a sterile setting might help the insomnia, and his assistant never arrived before 7 a.m.

In three weeks, he'd welcome a permanent position in the National Center for Immunization and Respiratory Diseases, a part of the influenza division at the CDC in Atlanta. Heather had no clue—no one in Houston did. Here she'd be safe . . . protected.

Chad had his longtime friend, Jordan Radcom, director of the CDC's Division of High-Consequence Pathogens and Pathology, to thank for the coveted position. Over the past thirty-plus years, the CDC had investigated an average of one contagious disease per year, and soon he'd be a part of the federal agency's respected role in conquering disease.

He closed his eyes and willed sleep to draw him into the place where he didn't have to think about the past, present, and tomorrow. But roaming thoughts like trying to find a Wi-Fi signal in the middle of nowhere kept him awake.

His cell phone buzzed, but he ignored it. Probably Heather. She'd beg him to talk to her and want to do the prayer thing so they could restore their marriage. She seldom resorted to tears. . . . Tonight the loneliness might break his determination.

His phone stopped its incessant ringing. Finally peace. A beep alerted him of a message. Chad refused to fall for a plea to call her. Heather needed to accept the reality of their relationship.

His new bride now lived behind the locked doors of a lab among the vials, computers, and test tubes. She wore calculations and methodology while he wore a lab jacket. She demanded his valuable time. His commitment to her ensured relief from hideous diseases for thousands of people. His new wife didn't have emotions or complicate his life. His new bride didn't insist upon starting a family, getting involved with church, or make it known she'd never leave her Houston FBI team.

He respected Heather for standing up for her principles, but he didn't support them. She deserved more from a husband than a ring around her finger and his last name. He'd freed her to find a man who'd give her his total love and devotion, instead of less than part-time. Oh yeah, the Bible-reading type who professed serving God as a man's highest calling.

He flung back the sheet and rose from the bed. Rationale told him to forgo sleep and start the day. He showered and dressed. While packing up his laptop, his phone rang again.

"For heaven's sakes. Give it a rest," he whispered and silenced the device without looking at caller ID.

His doorbell buzzed. Heather applied persistence and confrontation to all her FBI cases. No stops there. Had she taken a new approach to get his attention? He waited while the doorbell repeated. He had no choice except to open the door, and he turned the knob, ready to lose his temper. In the hallway a square-built man and a petite woman stared back at him.

"Dr. Lawrence?" the man said.

"Yes. What can I do for you?"

"I'm FBI Special Agent Javier Rivera and this is Special Agent Laura Tobias." Both displayed their credentials proving their federal identity. "May we come in?"

"I suppose." Chad gestured the two inside. "Has Heather been hurt?"

Agent Rivera closed the door behind them.

"I asked if Agent Heather Lawrence is all right."

"Agent Tobias and I have tried to contact you since midnight," Agent Rivera said. "You haven't answered your phone or your doorbell."

"Neither have you answered my question." She must be fine

or the agents would have stated so from the beginning. "Why are you here?"

"A flight left George Bush Intercontinental Airport at 8:35 p.m. en route to Frankfurt, Germany. Two hours in the air, a man complained of flu-like symptoms. A doctor on board says it's a possible hemorrhagic fever virus. We are told some victims are unresponsive. Understand the airlines will not declare a person has died in flight. Several other passengers and crew members are experiencing the same danger signs."

Chad had watched death tolls rise with these symptoms in massive proportions. Did the CDC require his skills immediately and not in three weeks? He needed the diversion and the opportunity to prove himself. "Have any of the passengers or flight crew been in an area where there's a similar outbreak?"

Agent Rivera hesitated. "It's under investigation. We don't have a list yet of those who boarded from connecting flights."

"Does the virus have a name?"

"Not at this time. The doctor on the plane communicated with Medi-Pro-Aire, and the pilot has been in contact with the CDC."

"You're clueless about the illness." Chad stated the obvious.

"At the present."

Chad's head spun with the what-ifs of a viral outbreak. The impact of what Agent Rivera alluded to confirmed everyone on flight 3879 was at risk. "Is the aircraft headed back to Houston or diverted to Atlanta, where the CDC can handle it?"

"Neither."

"Then it's New York. The CDC has a station there."

"The plane's in a holding pattern. I believe you're correct about the New York CDC station."

"Is the flight scheduled to land there?"

"Under consideration."

Chad's thoughts focused on people without medical care, and

Agent Rivera offered scant answers or he didn't have any. "How many exhibit symptoms?"

"The last update quoted 45 percent of the 267 passengers and crew on board. Dr. Lawrence, while I've answered most of your questions, we're here to escort you to the FBI office for questioning. You have knowledge linked to the case. Please bring your laptop."

"As a consultant?"

"No. As a person of interest."

CHAPTER TEN

IN THE REAR SEAT of Agent Rivera's double-cab truck, Chad watched the darkened streets whiz by. He wrestled with his thoughts—the shock of the FBI's questioning his character climbed the tower of unbelievable. Handcuffs didn't restrain his hands, and the agents hadn't taken his cell phone, but they had his laptop in the front seat. He'd given it to them without argument. If he had something to hide, he'd have requested a search warrant.

"Why am I on your radar? Other than I live in Houston and have devoted my life to eliminating viruses?"

Agent Rivera cleared his throat. "We have sufficient evidence to bring you in for questioning. The agents who conduct the interview will provide details."

"You two are the gophers?" The silent agents reminded him of two marionettes. Chad attempted to manage his ire. "Look, I'm concerned the people on board the flight aren't receiving the proper medical care. Are you recording our conversation?"

"No, sir," Rivera said.

"Here's my permission. If you refuse, I'll press Record on my phone. Which is it?"

"Be our guest," he said.

Chad hit Record. "Let's discuss the crisis."

Agent Tobias, a pleasant enough woman with short salt-and-pepper hair turned from the front seat. "Dr. Lawrence, there's no reason to deny you information available to the public. You have your phone to search or—"

"I prefer your version."

"We prefer you use your phone."

Chad searched on one of Houston's media sites. After reading what he'd already been told by Agent Rivera, he reached new information from a live report at IAH.

"... The FBI, TSA, and CDC have formed a task force to better handle what those on-board flight 3879 may have contracted. The aircraft was inbound from Chicago O'Hare airport before scheduled to depart Houston and outbound to Frankfurt. At this time, there are no reported outbreaks in Houston or Chicago. However, the FBI has put Houston and Chicago hospitals on alert. The doctor on board suspects a severe and fast-acting virus. He has no means to confirm a diagnosis or determine what kind of virus has infected many innocent people."

Chad stared out at a midnight-blue sky. No ceiling of stars to light up the night or his thoughts. Fast-acting viruses had an incubation period of one to two days. Others were longer. The passengers could have been exposed to a contagion before they boarded, but how did they contract the virus and experience severe symptoms within a couple of hours?

The order of occurrence caught his attention. The virus began with a severe headache, high fever, body aches, nosebleeds, vomiting with blood, pain in lower stomach, and according to the doctor on board, respiratory distress occurred prior to an unresponsive state. He'd seen firsthand how dengue and Ebola attacked the body. None of the reports as yet indicated the victims convulsed.

So many strains of deadly viruses had a 90 percent fatality. The thought of a new strain and the implications had a probable epidemic attached to it. He contemplated the minuscule information, afraid to speculate what an unknown virus might do to those infected.

Until medical professionals and researchers had information and emergency procedures were implemented, no one could be sure what had stricken the passengers and crew. If he'd been permitted to make a recommendation, he'd suggest the pilot land ASAP so the sick could be treated. The truth swarmed his logic—who would listen to him?

"I'm not the guilty party here."

"Sir," Agent Tobias said, her voice even, "you are wanted for questioning. An interview doesn't imply guilt."

"When will the FBI take me off their list?"

Agent Rivera stepped in. "Depends on verification of your answers."

"The protocol is a waste of valuable time. Since it affected only those people on the Houston flight, business and economy, it seems the air-filtering system has been compromised. Agent Rivera, your thoughts?"

Silence, but what could Chad expect? The airlines had incorporated intricate systems, especially on newer aircraft like the Boeing 777. His idea implied a level of sophistication. But anything was possible.

By now, the TSA had been instructed to view all footage of those who'd passed through security, and even reached out for interviews. Finding the source of the virus, its characteristics, and developing an antiviral would take teams of researchers—a huge concern for those impacted. The CDC, where he should be, would be working round the clock.

The extended silence raised his anger level. Didn't these idiots comprehend he had the necessary skills? "Whether you want to hear this or not, I'm giving you a dose of the real world. If authorities are looking at a virus that's characterized by internal and external bleeding, there's no treatment or vaccine. Medical personnel can ensure the patient maintains proper oxygen levels, replace blood, deal with the clotting factors, treat any resulting infections, and closely monitor vitals. I've fought for victims to survive while my attempts were like putting a Band-Aid on a mortal wound. Now it appears we have a deadly virus on US soil?" He shivered.

In many cases, medical workers were handicapped except to support the patients and evaluate their test results while consulting with international researchers how to effectively and efficiently treat them. Until epidemiological studies were conducted, confirmation was impossible.

They were not just patients, but victims. Until a vaccine was found or developed, a medical team's goal, his goal, was to find ways to prevent the spread of hazardous disease agents while pinpointing the causes.

Chad's thoughts focused on his limited knowledge and mentally listed the stats.

Typical to flu symptoms.

Typical of a viral hemorrhagic fever.

Highly contagious.

Unidentified.

Deadly.

After driving through a secured gate, Agent Rivera parked the truck in a well-lit area behind Houston's FBI. Chad glanced at his phone for the time. The passengers had spent nearly seven hours with an unidentified virus. Their mental and physical conditions nudged at him.

What kind of mindless Neanderthals accused a crusader who battled disease of biological terror?

CHAPTER ELEVEN

CHAD NEVER EXPECTED to pass through security and the rear employee entrance of the FBI building as an accused criminal. He had questions, plenty of them, and every one served to billow his anger. *Tamp it.* Creating a scene served no purpose but to make him look like a fool. He pondered the virus dilemma and hoped plans were under way to land the plane and begin health measures.

Chad rubbed the chills on his arms. He'd treated a friend stricken with Ebola. The man's initial struggle with high fever and body aches advanced to diarrhea and vomiting with blood. Chad still fought the nightmares that stalked him . . . how he'd fought day and night to ease the man's suffering. Misery beyond words. Helplessness. The alarm of approaching death.

In the reception area, a woman behind a glass enclosure kept his phone. Rivera and Tobias disappeared with his laptop. A separate agent escorted him to a room where he sat at a table and waited for the next step. Chad refused to succumb to the depression swirling through his senses.

Agents Rivera and Tobias entered the room from another door. He carried a file folder. "Dr. Lawrence, Agent Tobias and I will conduct your interview."

Were they aware of their role on the drive here? Was that why they let him talk? Share information that could incriminate him? "You have some answers recorded on my phone."

"Yes, sir. Do we have permission to image your cell phone and laptop?"

"Whatever makes you feel better." He should control his sarcasm. Should.

The agents seated themselves across from Chad. After the requisite identification questions, Rivera scooted the folder toward him. "Dr. Lawrence, in this file is the manifest of the passengers and crew on board flight 3879. Please open it and scan the names in business class."

He'd appease the man. Midway, Heather's name shone like a neon light. He shot fire into his gaze. "Why didn't you tell me Heather was on the flight?"

"Were you aware your wife had plans to fly to Frankfurt, Germany, and on to Salzburg, Austria?"

"Why didn't you give me her whereabouts sooner? I asked if she was all right at my apartment. Has she contracted the virus?"

"I'm sure you'll be notified if she's among the stricken."

He squeezed his fists under the table. "Are you questioning every family member of those on board the aircraft?"

"The investigation involves many agents and assignments."

"Who?"

"That's not information we can relay. For public information, I suggest you follow what the FBI and CDC report to the public. Dr. Lawrence," Rivera said, "I'm waiting for an answer to my previous question. Were you aware your wife was on the manifest?"

"No." Chad's emotions spun to the edge of out of control. Why was he here and not assisting the CDC?

"Why?"

"Heather doesn't tell me everything. Is she on a case for the FBI?"

"I suggest you pose that question to your wife."

"Can't you tell me if she's all right? I am her husband." Chad punched the last few words. The interview had turned into an interrogation.

"If you're so concerned about your wife, why did we find you living at a separate address?"

"My personal life is my business." Chad bolted from his chair. "I must talk to Heather now."

"Sit down, Dr. Lawrence." Rivera lifted his chin.

"Not until I talk to Heather."

"Sir, the best way to help your wife is to cooperate with us."

Fury rose from the soles of his feet. But what could he do? Demands put a dent in his innocence. He slowly lowered to the chair. "We discussed a trip months ago, but I told her to cancel it."

"What was your reason?"

"I saw a separation in our future."

"Do you have access to her online calendar?"

"I do, but I haven't checked it lately. Obviously."

"Isn't it true you filed for divorce, and she refused to sign the papers?"

"Agent Rivera, I don't see what my private life has to do with the current crisis."

"How did you react to her refusal?"

How did he answer when he owned his decision? "I wanted to know why she insisted we stay married."

"What was her reasoning?"

"You mean after her profession of love and how we shouldn't give up?"

"Yes."

"It's complicated."

"How?"

"Are you married?"

"I am, and so is Agent Tobias. But we're asking the questions here."

"Then you know marriage has its rough spots," Chad said. "Mine has more than most, and it's time to call it quits."

"What happened?"

"We changed."

"How so?"

"Change is a part of the human cycle. We grow with it or stagnate and die. In our case, our marriage didn't survive. Look, if either of you have been married more than a year, then you understand people are complex. It's impossible to provide a single answer to why I no longer want to live with Heather." He sighed. "I simply want out."

"Your reasons are important to our interview."

"I have no idea what is going on here, but I'll play. I got tired of the nagging."

"About what?"

"She has this God-thing going. Wants me to go with her to church, and her parents have identical ideals."

"Do they go to the same church?"

"Yep. Every other word is religion and questions about the status of my soul. One of them sent a pastor to persuade me about God. His final words were a reminder of where I'd spend eternity." He stretched his neck. "The man meant well. Just religion is not for me."

"Anything else?"

"She wants to start a family, and I don't have time for parenting."

"Did she know this prior to your marriage?"

He stared at Rivera. "The choice not to have children was one I made after we were married."

"I see. What else?"

"Don't you have enough for your records?" Chad blinked. "All right. She insists Houston is the only location where she can work with her FBI team. There, you have it all."

Rivera leaned back in his chair. "You're a person of interest in a serious crime. Your lab is a level 3 capable of developing a virus similar to what has infected flight 3879. Dr. Lawrence, are you responsible for the virus that has infected numerous people, motivated by revenge against your wife?"

Chad slammed his fist onto the tabletop. "I wouldn't hurt her. Check my background. You'll find I've placed my life in danger multiple times to treat people who've been infected by deadly viruses. In three weeks, I'm scheduled to begin work at the CDC in Atlanta."

Agent Tobias raised her palm to speak. "We're on a fact-finding mission. The same knowledge required to manufacture a disease is used to develop a vaccine. The two go hand in hand."

The implication rang loud and clear. "This is outrageous. Nothing I've said backs up your accusations. Your actions show the FBI's desperation. Are you looking to save your rear before the media attacks you?" Chad rubbed his face as though he could wipe away their unreasonable line of questioning. The core of his thoughts centered on how to clear his name. "What's next?"

Agent Tobias folded her hands on the table as if attempting to relax him. "Progress depends on many factors."

"My name has to be erased from this insane atrocity." He held up a palm. "Who accused me? Heather?"

"The information isn't available to you."

"I understand confidentiality, but this is a pack of lies." Many agencies would be involved with the problem. If only he were among them.

Rivera lifted his chin. "Dr. Lawrence, our interview has concluded. You are under investigation until the FBI makes a determination. For now, don't leave town. We imaged your mobile phone and laptop, and those devices will be returned upon leaving the building. I'll escort you to the visitor area, where the receptionist will call a taxi at our expense."

The truth hit hard. Chad's decision to leave Heather had made him a murder suspect.

CHAPTER TWELVE

THE THUD OF THE PLANE'S TIRES touching down on the runway offered Heather a moment to thank God for a safe landing and a prayer for healing and strength. The sick desperately needed relief and a vaccine to prevent further contagion. She longed for testing to show her unborn child hadn't experienced trauma. . . . Were her ideals selfish?

She captured her last thought and tossed it aside. Anxiety for others and her unborn child was far from self-centered. She'd experienced a mother's innate reaction like Mia had stated.

She'd weathered crises and navigated storms before, and she would again.

She glanced at a sleeping Braden Taversty seated beside her. The man wasn't concerned his hostage plans had been foiled. He'd swung his head away from her, and she peered closer. A bead of sweat trickled down the side of his face followed by another.

An internal alarm sounded. Had the virus seized another victim? He'd complained about the lack of AC before Heather had taken him into custody. Taversty's nose trickled blood. With his hands tied, he had no ability to clean his face.

"Mr. Taversty." When he didn't answer, she repeated his name.

He turned her way, his features pale. "What?"

"I'm going to wipe the blood from your face. Do you mind?"

"Knock yourself out."

She retrieved the last tissue from her purse and swiped his nose, mouth, and chin, then deposited the tissue into a plastic bag. "How long have you had virus symptoms?"

He shook his head.

"Did you infect these people and yourself?"

Taversty moaned. "No. Wish I'd thought of it."

"Please, if you have any information about what is happening, I need to know."

He closed his eyes. "Wouldn't say if I did."

What kind of monster planted death? Whoever at fault was someone with an agenda, a madman who should be behind bars.

The plane crept ahead on the tarmac to where a team of medical personnel and researchers held the passengers' and crew's futures in their hands. Admittedly, her energy level pointed at zero. But she'd do whatever it took to find how the virus had been unleashed.

Nathan joined her in the aisle. "Are you okay?"

"Yes." She hadn't expected the flight attendants to be up and about. "Mr. Taversty is sick." She peeled the blood-coated gloves off and tossed them into a plastic bag.

"Are you afraid of contracting the disease?"

She struggled to control the trembling. "Of course. I'd be a liar if I didn't admit it. But fear's not only for me but for all those on this plane. Everyone's at risk." Her stomach churned. She might be nauseous or . . . maybe she'd contracted the virus. Heather touched her stomach, a habit over the past few hours.

"Are you ill?"

"I'm not sure. The conditions on board our flight are enough to give the strongest person a nervous stomach."

"I understand. Will you be all right with Mr. Taversty until medical workers transport the sick?"

"I'm fine."

"Thank you again for helping out. You and others made our job easier."

"I promise to do all I can to find answers. Have the pilots escaped symptoms?"

"Fortunately yes." Sweat beaded across Nathan's forehead.

"Do you have symptoms?"

"I think so. Hope I haven't contaminated too many people."

As much as Heather despised a long quarantine, she'd not complain as long as others were protected.

Her phone alerted her to a message from ASAC Mitchell. "Excuse me while I check this."

"I have many things to do." Nathan offered a half smile before walking away.

Heather read the text. **Braden Taversty has Middle Eastern terrorist connections. Lived with two other guys with same MO. One is in jail awaiting trial for bombing a senator's car, and the other fled the country.**

She typed. **He claims innocence. Are you investigating a possible suicide mission?**

Yes.

The pilot's voice drew her attention. "Ladies and gentlemen, we won't be exiting the aircraft but taxiing near a hangar where the CDC can board, analyze the sick, and give instructions to those who aren't displaying symptoms. Their priority is the ill, who will be examined and transported to Jamaica Hospital. The team is trained and equipped for our emergency. They request patients to travel to the hospital individually as instructed, absent any family members, except in the case of children under twelve years of age who are not vomiting or bleeding. Have patience as we work to make the transition as smooth as possible. Every inch of the plane and its contents will be examined. We all want answers, help for the ill, and guidance."

How could chaos be smooth?

CHAPTER THIRTEEN

HEATHER STUDIED A CDC TEAM, dressed in white personal protection equipment—PPE—weave through the aircraft's cabin. The first time Chad wore the complete gear, he hadn't expected the confining uniform to bring on a panic attack. He didn't give up, and if he were in New York, he'd be here helping.

The ill received care while other workers handed out surgical masks. A little late now. Heather doubted the wet paper towels distributed hours ago to cover passengers' and crew's mouths prevented any contamination.

She responded to two FBI agents, also clothed in PPE, and asked for facial tissues. They were prepared to take Braden Taversty into custody. Blood flowed more freely from his nose and mouth, and Heather dabbed at his face with clean tissues. No matter what he'd done, he deserved humane treatment.

Heather extended Taversty's wallet to an agent. "Looks like he has the virus."

"Sir," the agent said. "We're getting you help. If you're involved with the virus, we need to know."

Taversty shook his head. Did he speak the truth, or could he be responsible? The agent summoned a CDC worker who supplied a stretcher.

From the looks of him, Taversty wouldn't live to face a judge. The stretcher moved him toward the exit.

The agent turned to Heather. "He'll remain at Jamaica Hospital in federal custody for suspected terrorism. Has he given you a statement?"

"Only his denial of having anything to do with the virus. He also said if he had info, he'd not offer it."

"A definite person of interest."

Heather nodded. No need to speak of Taversty's Middle East connections and frighten anyone within hearing distance.

The agent sighed at the procession of those leaving the plane on narrow stretchers, the ill and otherwise. Frankie's grandmother, then Roy were wheeled past, recognizable by visible articles of clothing. Heather held her breath. She was afraid to breathe in the stench of death and yet afraid not to hold on to life. After the unresponsive were pronounced dead, they'd undergo autopsies to determine the cause. The findings provided data for the forensic medical research team.

Grim. Incredibly grim.

The process of checking and recording vitals as well as questioning each person's health history took much longer than she anticipated. Medical personnel entered data on tablets, eliminating the loss of any critical information.

Heather moved to a window and observed the frenzy of activity surrounding the aircraft. Bright lights flashed on multiple emergency vehicles. Peculiar to be looking at first responders from a victim's perspective. Not a position she'd ever want to be in again.

After a separate team recorded vitals and inserted an IV, the patients were each placed in an isolation pod, a mobile transportation unit designed to keep the patient from exposing others to contagion, and driven to Jamaica Hospital.

Flight attendants and those traveling with the ill tagged personal items for each one who displayed virus symptoms and made sure the items accompanied them. Not a single item left the aircraft without being labeled and placed in a contamination bag. Workers instructed a couple accompanying a sick child to add a face shield to their surgical mask and wear two pairs of gloves.

NYPD vehicles and officers, ambulances, fire trucks, and a National Guard unit stood ready as first responders to protect those on the plane and outsiders from being exposed. Media parked beyond the police barricade, and cameras rolled while reporters held mics. Weren't they afraid?

Thomas, the man who'd helped her with Braden Taversty, gazed out a window nearby. He reeked of vomit, but then again, so did she. "I'm hoping we're released in the next twenty-four hours," he said.

"You'd be wise to add days to your estimation," Heather said. "None of us want to infect others."

"You're right. Wishful thinking on my part." He gestured around the cabin. "Just hate what has happened to the passengers and flight crew. Except it beats lying on a stretcher with our faces covered."

She watched the medical team. Rather frightening, and she'd witnessed atrocious crimes involving shoot-outs that left bullet-ridden bodies.

Thomas cleared his throat. "I've studied the healthy and the sick. None but the man you apprehended gave an indication of guilt."

"Would the guilty person volunteer their name and motive?"

He chuckled, but the sound bore no mirth. "Guess not."

A man called for help, and Thomas rushed to his aid. Him and others like him were unsung heroes. Unlikely any of them had boarded with the idea of making sacrifices to help keep people alive. She observed Thomas to see if he needed assistance. Odd, he didn't appear as the nurse-type, but then who did?

Her thoughts trailed to Chad. In the beginning, they had adored each other. They fell in love and married within two years. She had a crazy work schedule, while he spent hours with his doctorate studies. Yet every spare minute found them talking, laughing, sharing. They stole moments for long walks in the park. They cooked together . . . planned for their future while they journeyed through their dreams.

She should have seen his commitment to healing would always take first place. Still she said yes.

Heather walked back to her seat. Dried blood covered Braden Taversty's seat. What were the odds that she'd be on an aircraft attacked by a mysterious killer, and the virus's description fits Chad's specialty?

"You're in my way, a liability. I can't move ahead in my life saddled with a wife. Trust me on this one, Heather. I'll do anything to make it happen."

Her heart ached with the accusations bannering across her mind. . . . She hadn't explored the similarities to that level. Her emotions further unraveled. If she ignored her doubts, she was withholding information to the bureau. Concealing potential evidence put her in line for a prison sentence without her baby. If she relinquished her thoughts, and Chad discovered she'd pointed a finger at him, she lost any illusions of reconciliation.

Did anyone else suspect Chad's involvement? Choices . . . the substance that framed a person's character. Where was her loyalty? Her husband? Her commitment to enforcing the law? God? A poison of shame assaulted her.

If she suspected Chad might have committed a vile crime, others were in the same camp.

Weariness settled into her body, and for the next hour medical personnel and investigators swarmed like bees in a hive. Although each assigned worker had a role and the passengers were treated with dignity, another forty minutes passed before the uninfected were addressed.

"I'm pregnant," she told a CDC worker. "No signs of the virus at this point."

The worker made notes.

The pilot asked for their attention over the interphone. "For those who remain on the aircraft and are free of symptoms, flight attendants will be issuing containment bags for your carry-on items. You'll be escorted to a CDC medical treatment unit inside a hangar. There a team will draw blood, collect urine samples, and record your vitals. In addition, the FBI and CDC will be conducting interviews. Again, thank you for your cooperation during these distressing circumstances."

Heather slipped her bag over her shoulder and secured her tote from where she'd sat with Mia, who'd been taken to Jamaica Hospital. Maybe she'd be allowed to visit her new friend if the quarantine unit's location was close by. She secured a containment bag and joined the line to disembark.

Another worker escorted her to the portable medical unit, where she sat on a folding chair at the end of a row. Messages from Chad rolled into her phone except answering them had no appeal. The hum of voices lulled her closer to sleep. She'd always been on the other end of an investigation, caring for those emotionally, physically, and mentally damaged by tragedy, but nothing compared to the compassion and empathy that had taken residence in her heart.

Beside her sat a pilot. Blood dripped from his nose. "Oh no," he whispered.

A medical worker escorted him to an ambulance.

Over two hours later, the health assessments, drawn blood, swabs, and questions were completed. In the predawn hours of morning, the group moved toward rows of luggage. Passengers identified their belongings and waited while their items were loaded into three awaiting buses. Heather ached from her toes to the hairs on her head.

"Where is the quarantine unit located?" Heather said to a CDC worker standing near her.

"You're FBI, right?"

Heather confirmed, and the man continued. "You'll be taken to an island in Jamaica Bay. It's ample to handle those from flight 3879. It's best the public isn't aware of the destination until you are safely transported. We need to avoid mass hysteria and a possible attack."

"Is the island inhabited?"

"Not at this time. It's occasionally used in the summer as a camp for troubled teens and for military training."

Isolation of another type. Sounded like a prison to her. The person responsible for the virus likely inoculated themselves. The survivors might be living with a killer.

On the bus, she sat next to Catherine, who dabbed tears beneath her eyes. Heather placed her arm around the grieving woman's shoulders. "I'm sorry Roy was unable to fight the virus."

"Thank you." She swiped at more tears. "He stopped breathing before they moved him to the back of the plane. He's with God now. No pain from cancer or the effects of the treatments."

"It's impossible for me to understand what you're going through, but I'm here."

Catherine patted the hand on her shoulder. "You're a sweet girl to risk getting sick to help others."

Heather didn't feel sweet or giving, only scared. What awaited them? A male CDC worker stood at the front near the driver.

"We're ready for a short bus ride. A ferry will transport you to a facility where a full staff will make you as comfortable as possible throughout the quarantine. I can't tell you how long you'll be guests. The duration is up to those analyzing what we've learned and will learn. Once we identify the cause of the illness or confirm you're not contagious, you'll be free to return to your homes. Testing and time are the contributing factors here. A counselor has been assigned to help you contact family and employers."

"Do we have a choice?" a woman said.

"No. I'm sorry. Under 42 Code of Federal Regulations parts 70 and 71, 'the CDC is authorized to detain, medically examine, and release people traveling between states who are suspected of carrying communicable diseases.'" He lifted a phone from his coat pocket and turned to the driver. The bus moved ahead.

"Who pays for time lost on the job?" a well-dressed woman said.

"The counselor at the quarantine unit will handle your questions."

Discontent swept around the bus. Heather understood the tapestry of angst—concern for loved ones stricken by the virus, the anxiety of contracting the virus, and panic at the possibility of facing financial devastation.

Killers were motivated by scores of reasons to inflict harm, and they were a dangerous lot. Out of control fear had the ability to do much worse. If the person responsible for the virus confessed, he or she might not survive.

CHAPTER FOURTEEN

CHAD WAITED OUTSIDE SECURITY of Houston's FBI for a taxi, his body no longer tense with the worry of being charged for a crime he hadn't committed. Soon the FBI and anyone else who suspected his involvement with the virus would discover the lies against him.

His concern for Heather mounted, and he sent her an audio message. "Heather, I learned you're on flight 3879." He paused so his words would sink in. "I was told the virus hasn't infected you. Good news." Was she aware of his FBI interrogation?

The early July morning hadn't met the intense heat of the day, but humidity hung thick, and his shirt stuck to his body. How he longed to be on a plane to JFK, making history and changing lives for the better. Agent Rivera had told him not to leave town, but once the FBI cleared him, he'd catch the next flight out.

While he waited for Heather to return his message, he checked in with Andy, his assistant. Got the young doctor out of bed. Chad asked him to be at the office by 6 a.m. He ended the call, and Heather still hadn't responded. This time he text messaged her.

Check your audio message. Are you okay? Please contact me.

Twenty minutes ticked by without hearing from her or the taxi. Why the delays? If the taxi ever arrived, he'd head straight to his lab. No place else to go. Certainly not his apartment. Other projects awaited his attention, despite the responsible investment in Heather's circumstances. He chose control instead of allowing uncertainty to rule his actions. His mild blowup during the interview showed a lack of discipline.

A creeping thought rooted. He'd signed the CDC employment contract and worked with HR to secure an apartment. They'd note he'd done his best to cooperate with the FBI during the questioning.

Who was he kidding? The FBI's questioning and his newly acquired status could destroy his chances to be a leading authority of a possible new contagion.

The trip to Salzburg had been Heather's dream for the two of them, to experience the music festival and explore everything the city had to offer.

If he hadn't moved out, he'd have been with her.

If he hadn't applied at the CDC, he'd have been with her.

If he'd been with her, he'd not be a suspect in a despicable crime.

But a promise made to shield Heather drove him to stop the worst viruses known to medicine.

Once the plane landed, authorities would inspect the plane microscopically for evidence. But what if the answers didn't lie within the metal encasing the aircraft? What then?

Chad swallowed hard. Heather had faced the full effect of a tragic illness, and so far, she'd escaped the deadly sickness. While she prided herself in strength, she also had a tender heart. Knowing her, she'd volunteered to help with the sick and increased her exposure to the contagion. Planes didn't carry a supply of masks.

Haunting memories of his friend's sickness floated across his mind, all too vivid. Paul's condition had deteriorated, and his internal organs hemorrhaged . . .

Heather deserved happiness and a good life. Neither he'd supplied. He placed his trust in medical science, the only reliable deity.

Chad checked his phone and logged into a secure medical site that provided information for those working around the world in various areas of disease control. Before he could read the latest reports, a man called his name.

Agent Rivera pulled his truck into the visitor area and powered down his window. "Your taxi hasn't arrived? Need a ride?"

"It'll be here soon."

"Have you talked to your wife?"

"No. Has she implicated anyone else or just me?"

"The answer is above my pay grade."

"I'll find out."

"The people who requested your questioning aren't important."

"As in more than one? I don't understand. The who is critical to me."

"I'd feel the same way if others suspected my involvement in this."

"What's with the sudden empathy?"

Rivera frowned. "The idea of all the people sick from an unnamed virus hits home. My sister died of flu three years ago. Fever, vomiting. Seizures. Until her body gave up. I can relate to the passengers and crew."

Chad sympathized with what Rivera had witnessed, but he didn't trust the agent, especially if his congeniality stemmed from digging for evidence against him. "How old was she?"

"Thirty-two. She left three children under the age of six. My wife and I are doing what we can to help their dad give them a normal life." He narrowed his gaze. "Dr. Lawrence, you're either a proficient liar or blameless. But if you had any hand in spreading the virus, I'll personally make sure you're prosecuted."

Lights from an incoming car ended the conversation. The taxi came to a stop near Chad and Agent Rivera. Once inside and after Chad had given the driver his lab's address, he again navigated to the secure medical site on his phone. According to the doctor on board the aircraft, the order in which the symptoms appeared for each victim was systematic. No deviation for Chad to pinpoint an exact origin.

The aircraft had been cleared to land where people could be treated. Medi-Pro-Aire agreed with the pilot for CDC guidelines to take precedence.

Chad huffed. Good to read the organization had initiated a health focus instead of profit and loss. Those who were sick might live to thank Medi-Pro-Aire. The aircraft should have landed when the first victim succumbed.

He slipped his phone into his pant pocket. What virus strain had attacked these people? Anything was possible with today's technology. A deadly mutant strain? Panic rippled through him. Was the virus contained to the aircraft or were other areas facing the contagion?

CHAPTER FIFTEEN

QUIET PERVADED THE FERRY RIDE, similar to the lack of conversations on the bus. Heather knew she wasn't the only person who choked in a thick fog of uncertainty. Nathan had been taken to Jamaica Hospital. Sad. Sad for all those sick.

Catherine might go into shock, and Heather stayed close by. The woman needed a friend, a silent presence to hold her hand. The two found bench seats on the lower deck with many of the others. Chains of doubt hung like the artificial light swinging above them. The FBI had trained Heather to face the unpredictable—yet she feared for her own sanity.

Normally she'd be on the deck searching the sky for constellations, but she didn't care if any stars or planets filled earth's ceiling. In the ferry's belly, nothing expelled the shroud of uncertainty.

She texted Mom and Dad a simple message about her quarantine status. Phone alerts wakened them, but they needed to know she had so far escaped the virus. The media would gain access to the manifest, and it would devastate her parents to see her name.

Within five minutes, Dad returned the text. **Glad you're okay. Be safe. Praying for you and the others. Call us soon. Chad must be worried sick.**

I'm sure he's fine.

I'll contact him.

Heather typed. **Don't please. I'll explain when I talk to you.** How would she ever tell them their marriage lay in the trenches?

She studied Catherine. "Are you managing? Do you need medical attention?"

"Just time, dear." Catherine laid her hand in Heather's lap.

"How long were you married?"

"Fifty-three years. I pray you never lose someone the way I lost my Roy."

Catherine's comment settled on Heather's own dilemma. "Thank you. I don't think we have a choice." She'd read walking through a divorce was worse than death—in death, the deceased had no choice. Chad claimed she clung to him because of her archaic beliefs. At this point, his reasoning didn't matter. She touched her stomach. She lived for what nestled deep inside her, and she'd do anything to keep her baby alive.

"I need to talk if you don't mind," Catherine said.

"I'm right here."

"What we've experienced tonight will reshape our lives. We'll never be the same. I intend to think more about others than myself." Catherine breathed in deeply.

"How so?"

"Relationships that I've taken for granted. Roy's cancer seemed inconceivable, and at times he comforted me more than I cared for him." She shook her head. "High time I gave back, beginning with my sister, who isn't getting any younger. And what will you do differently?"

"I want to find joy in small things. Never ignore a sunrise or sunset."

"Roy used to say a silver lining is always behind a cloud. Maybe I'll do hospital visits for my church."

Twenty minutes later, the ferry pulled to a stop. Slivers of dawn crept from the eastern horizon. Toward New York, lights flickered signaling a new day. Heather stepped into a line of people with Catherine. With the weariness attacking her body, she craved a bed. Floodlights paved a gravel walkway to a compound. Two armed National Guard soldiers flanked each side of the line. Other soldiers held various positions. Procedure and guidelines were in place to protect the quarantined group and others onshore from contagion. Simply not the welcome she'd anticipated for her vacation.

They hurried to a concrete and steel building. Before entering, a man dressed in scrubs gave each person a new mask and gloves with the instructions to wear the protective gear. He pointed to a metal barrel to dispose of soiled items. Inside, they walked on gray concrete floors. The pale greenish-yellow walls reminded her of bile. The musty smell woven with the hint of unwashed bodies permeated the housing. But they could be in a plane hangar under a germ-free tent and exempt of privacy.

Or at Jamaica Hospital.

In a huge concrete cafeteria containing long functional metal tables and benches, an Asian woman wearing a mask and light-blue scrubs greeted them from a small podium.

"Welcome to Adam's Island. My name is Lacy Skaggs, and I'm the director. Please, have a seat. First, I'm sorry these tragic circumstances have brought you here. While your luggage is unloaded from the ferry and carried inside, I'm here to give you a few instructions.

"Are any of you experiencing symptoms?" No one spoke up. Lucy smiled. "Good. You will hear this question repeatedly. If during your stay, you feel ill, contact one of the staff here immediately. Wear a mask and gloves at all times. Even in bed. We provide extras in your assigned rooms. We are isolated here, but we are not alone. In addition to a complete medical staff, a psychologist is available to help you through the loneliness, depression, and mental fatigue. Quarantine can alter the mood of the strongest of people. If you need spiritual assistance, we have a chaplain. I repeat, you are not alone."

"How will we hear about our friends and family at Jamaica Hospital?" a man said.

"Once the patients are evaluated and initially treated, I'll receive the updates and contact you personally. You can access their information and condition anytime through me."

"My husband died on the plane." Catherine's voice shook, and Heather held her hand. "What happens to his body?"

"If a person passes or has passed, I'll notify you as soon as the ME makes the ruling."

"How do we handle funeral or memorial services?" Catherine said. "Can you explain the procedure?"

Compassion filled Lacy's features. "The bodies must be burned to avoid the spread of contagion. If a deceased's family or loved one is in quarantine, appropriate services can be held once we are released." Her gaze panned the crowd. "I regret the condition of many of your loved ones. Please accept my condolences."

Catherine mumbled a thank-you. Sobs rose across the room.

"We are here to help. Don't suffer alone. You'll see many of us roaming around. We're doctors, nurses, and CDC staff dedicated to making your stay as comfortable as possible. The New York National Guard is in place to keep us safe. From the looks of you, you're exhausted. So let's get you to your rooms, and we'll sort out your concerns in the hours ahead. However, if you have critical questions, stay and I'll do my best to provide answers." She gestured to the rear of the room. "In the back are your escorts and your luggage. Families and married couples can exit now."

Shortly thereafter, female escorts divided the women traveling alone into groups of six. The young woman Braden Taversty had accosted joined Heather's group. For the first time, Heather noted multiple tattoos and ear piercings. The two women hadn't spoken. Silence had a way of masking hurt.

Catherine also stood in Heather's line. She hadn't stayed behind to request grief counseling, but perhaps she'd schedule it after a few hours of sleep. They walked down a hallway with a white-haired woman dressed in blue scrubs. She stopped to open a door and flipped on a bright overhead light. Cold and uninviting.

The escort beckoned them inside. "Come in, ladies. My name is Doris. Find a bed and we'll chat a little."

Heather entered a dorm room—six beds with crisp white linens and blankets lined three to a wall. One side of the room had draperies pulled over windows. When the sun rose, they'd have a view of Adam's Island and their surroundings. Heather was grateful for lighting over each bed and an outlet to charge devices. She chose the bed at the farthest end facing the window wall and set her suitcase and tote beside it.

"The staff share the same goal, to ensure your stay is in the best environment," Doris said. "We even have earplugs if the gal next to you snores." No one smiled at her attempt at humor. "The CDC medical team will be drawing blood later on today. While I encourage you to rest, be aware med techs will be in and out.

"Place your belongings inside the metal chest beside your bed. Note there are masks and nitrile gloves in the top drawer. As Lacy instructed, wear both at all times. Make sure you have a can of disinfectant spray. Take this to the bathroom and spray before and after each use. The smell isn't as bad as others. Also use the spray after making your bed. If you run out, we have plenty. If you are hungry, thirsty, or require personal hygiene items, I will secure them for you. I won't leave this room until I have your requests and answered your questions."

She pointed to a phone attached to the wall beside the overhead light switch. "The phone is for you to request help or speak to a CDC person. It can't call outside the facility, but there is decent Wi-Fi connectivity here. Find me if you don't have a mobile phone, and I'll help you place a call. On your beds are plastic bags containing a towel and washcloth. Use the towel and washcloth once and seal them back into the plastic bag. These will be picked up, laundered, and clean ones provided each day. Inside a second plastic bag are shampoo, conditioner, liquid soap, toothbrush, toothpaste, notepad, pen, and a marker for you to write your name on the outside of the bag. Just as your mama use to say, let no one use the items assigned to you. One of you may be infected, and we don't want the virus to spread. If you're ill or suspect someone else is, contact us immediately."

"How long will we be here?" The lines fanning from Catherine's eyes had deepened. Every former passenger looked terrible from the ordeal and lack of sleep.

"I have no idea."

Catherine continued. "Are you saying we might be quarantined for days?"

"The period depends on CDC jurisdiction," Doris said. "Truthfully, ma'am, they haven't given us a time, and we are all sympathetic to your plight. I promise, as new information is released, we'll pass it on. Right now, concentrate on settling in. Having one bathroom and shower for six women may be inconvenient." Doris snorted. "What am I saying? Sharing a bathroom is a pain. We workers are in dorms, too, and the arrangement lacks privacy. But this is our hotel for the time being. Write your questions on the notepad provided. Include dietary and medical needs. Media will learn what is going on here, but they aren't permitted on the island."

"Has the virus broken out on any other planes?" the young woman said who'd been held hostage by Braden Taversty.

"Not to our knowledge."

A chorus of relief spread through the women.

"Make friends with those who are here." Doris pointed to the young woman, who'd taken residence opposite Heather's bed. "Let's begin with names and something brief about yourself. Mine is Doris in case you missed it the first time. And yours?"

"Tatum." She turned to Heather. "I never thanked you for helping to save my life."

Heather smiled. "Glad you're okay."

The next woman spoke. "Maria. My sister is at Jamaica Hospital."

"Ada. I'm scared for all of us."

"We understand." Doris pointed to Heather.

"Heather. I was on my way to vacation in Salzburg."

"Catherine. My husband is gone."

"Jackie. I just retired and planned to tour Germany."

"We will get through this together," Doris said. "Please, ladies, try to sleep. If you need to speak to me or anyone privately, the phone's right here or walk back to the cafeteria. The staff are stationed 24-7. We don't lock your room door or the outside doors. You are not a prisoner or being punished. A member of the National Guard will be stationed in the cafeteria during every meal. At times tempers flare, and none of us need additional problems. Our goal is to keep you healthy and safe while monitoring and testing your bodies for any signs of infection or discovering a reason you are currently immune to the illness.

"Inside each metal chest is a brochure that explains what quarantine means. Meals will be in the cafeteria at designated times. Snacks and beverages are available 24-7. Later today, you'll be given more information about Adam's Island and what's available for your use. Recreational equipment inside and out is designed to alleviate stress. Any questions before I speak to each one of you privately?" They shook their heads. Like Heather, sleep evaded them. Doris gestured to Heather. "I'd like to see you privately."

Heather followed her into the hallway. "Is this about my pregnancy?"

"Yes. The CDC worker who talked to you on board the plane alerted us."

"I gave her my doctor's name. But what precautions do I take for my baby?"

The woman held up a finger and spoke into a radio. A few moments later, she clipped the radio onto her belt. "Dr. Natalie Francisca is on her way by ferry from the city to speak to you. She's a gynecologist who works with the CDC. I'll notify you when she arrives."

"Thanks."

"I'd like for the other women staying with you to know your condition. In the event of an emergency—"

"All right."

Back inside the room, Heather sank onto her assigned bed and buried her face in her hands. She managed one breath after another to gain control—for her baby, those who'd died, for the sick hospitalized, and Chad. She grappled for strength.

Doris called for the women's attention. "Heather and I agree you should be aware of her pregnancy. Needless to say, she has more than one concern as do many of you. I encourage you to support each other."

Arms enveloped Heather, and she looked up to Catherine and Tatum.

"I'm sorry," Tatum said. "What can I do?"

Heather should tend to them, not the other way around. She was the behavior analyst for the FBI, trained to provide logic and comfort. "I'm just hormonal."

"Right." Tatum clasped Heather's arm. "You're FBI, pregnant, wrestled down a jerk on the plane, and in need of sleep."

Heather fought for composure. "We all fit on the exhausted list. Everybody's hurting."

Catherine wrapped her arm around Heather's shoulders, the woman who'd lost her husband only hours ago. "Dear, I watched you in action with sick people. You deserve a good cry."

Heather wiped her eyes. "Thanks." But she craved confirmation God had not abandoned them.

CHAPTER SIXTEEN

A SHOWER AND CLEAN CLOTHES failed to rid Heather of death's cloud. A lingering bitterness on her tongue added to the mix. No point slipping into pajamas. She didn't want to keep the doctor waiting. A snuggle beneath a sheet and blanket provided the best creature comforts on the face of the earth. The mask and gloves proved cumbersome, but those were the instructions.

She read Chad's attempts to contact her. *Was she okay?* As though he cared about her health or safety. She listened to the voice message and deleted it. How had he seen the manifest? She should text him, but her attitude stank. He'd find out the plight of flight 3879 when the rest of the country learned what happened.

Strange how his words were unlike recent conversations. In the last seven months, he'd avoided her as though she'd grown a wart on her nose. He failed to look at her even in the same room, preferring grunts to handle their communication.

Unless his recent caring covered up something else . . . someone else?

She shook her head in the darkness. The doubts were simply a part of hormones and sleep deprivation while witnessing the night's terror.

He'd be furious about the baby. At some point, she'd have to tell him. He'd accuse her of not taking her pill and purposely getting pregnant to wreck his career. As if he was ever home anyway. He'd made it clear fatherhood wasn't in his future. Why would she bring a child into that environment? When she'd learned about the baby, she chose not to tell him in light of their noncommunicative marital status. Mixed emotions had assaulted her—hope and fear of potentially facing single parenthood.

At least Chad wouldn't accuse her of having an affair. He knew her better than that. She'd accepted the responsibility of single parenthood, and her parents would help teach her child about life and God.

She hadn't decided if requesting child support made sense. Stubbornness mostly. Chad claimed he no longer loved her, so what made her think he'd be willing to contribute financially for his child? Legally, he'd be forced to pay, and she could save the money for the baby's future. He might offer a generous amount as a bargaining tool for her signature on the papers. Broken promises, words hurled like bullets, regrets, and the many tears had left her weary and drained.

A sickening apprehension persisted. What if the virus damaged her baby? She forced down the perpetual lump in her throat. Abortion for any reason was not an option. She'd face the future with her baby regardless if it was born with defects. Her mind drifted to images of infants whose mothers contracted the Zika virus. She cherished the life inside her.

Don't worry, little one. You are my gift, and I will take care of you.

CHAPTER SEVENTEEN

CHAD SAT AT HIS LAB DESK and pressed in Heather's cell phone number in another effort to contact her. If she'd escaped the virus thus far, surely the prognosis was good. Media reported the CDC had been inside the plane and conducted preliminary treatment of the ill. They questioned every passenger and flight crew member according to protocol. Another report claimed the FBI had arrested a man from the aircraft who'd been hospitalized. They hadn't released the man's name or the charges. Neither had they spit Chad's name to the media. Not yet anyway.

What to believe . . . He read a report from the press secretary for New York City's mayor. The aircraft had been moved into an isolated hangar at JFK for further analysis after the CDC and FBI examined and interviewed those on board. Every person, no matter their health status, experienced a battery of tests. A press conference was scheduled for later on. Chad longed to see the test results and evaluations, an impossibility until the FBI signed off on his potential guilt.

The phone call to Heather rang a fifth time. Panic whipped through him. . . . The virus spread rapidly through a victim's system. *Heather, answer.*

"Chad."

He closed his eyes and exhaled. "Are you okay?"

"Yes. I'm trying to sleep. Why?"

"I'm worried about your health."

"How noble."

"Five minutes from now, you'll apologize."

"Don't count on it. Some people impacted by tragic circumstances choose to move on. Grow stronger. Take what life tosses them and throw it back. Learn a few things along the way."

A nagging thought persisted. "Are you aware the FBI questioned me as a person of interest?" Silence met him. "Did you accuse me of developing the virus?"

"Who conducted the interview?"

"Agents Rivera and Tobias."

"I know them both. They're good agents. The FBI didn't consult me on their decision to bring you in. The protocol indicates you're a suspect."

"Right. I specialize in viruses, and you're on the aircraft." Chad bit back his real concern . . . her exposure to a deadly virus. "The ordeal was extremely humiliating. I save lives. I don't take them."

"You're also clawing your way to the top."

He ignored her scorn. "You've seen firsthand how a virus affects victims. Maybe you finally understand why I'm committed to finding cures."

"I forgot the world revolves around you. I'm sure you can envision the high fevers, bleeding from the nose and mouth, vomiting, and agony with some drifting into unconsciousness and death. The latter is more appealing than watching them suffer. In death, they have peace." She'd never spoken to him with such rancor.

"I'm sorry to take my FBI ordeal out on you, so I won't offer my thoughts on your taking a trip during a critical time of our relationship."

"I'd be disappointed if you didn't. But you've been very clear my future isn't your problem."

"That's reality."

"This is a pointless conversation. You called me."

"I'm glad you're not among the afflicted. Wish I was there to help."

"Your résumé would raise a notch. Never mind. What else?"

He pictured lightning flashing from her sea-green eyes . . . and how the sprinkling of freckles across her nose darkened when she was angry. "You're in a stubborn mode, which means you won't ask for help. I'll explain the CDC's procedure."

"Go for it." Her weak voice indicated exhaustion. But as she said, life moved on, and with a little adjustment, she'd be fine.

"According to the preliminary reporting, this is a type of hemorrhagic fever virus, HFV for short. Not confirmed, but it's a strong contender. Here are a few influenza facts—its nucleic acid is not DNA but RNA, and it exists in eight different segments. These eight segments can have mutations, and it can have mutations within the segments."

"Will a blood test identify the flu virus?"

"Possibly."

"Would it also show an antivirus?"

"Doubtful."

"Are the symptoms described by the doctor on board the flight a disease you've seen?"

He should deceive her, calm her mind, but why hide the truth? "The way it affects the body, to some degree, yes. Honestly, not even in third-world countries have I heard of a virus with such a rapid incubation period. It's unlike anything on record. The CDC is pulling together top researchers in the field. They will determine the type and begin the process to develop a vaccine."

"Researchers have been working for years on a vaccine for Ebola, dengue fever, and other viral diseases," she said. "So far the diseases still attack and kill thousands of people. A cure for this could take weeks, months, years, or never."

He delayed his answer. "Heather, I won't fill you with feel-good nonsense. It's unlikely a cure or antiviral is available."

"For once I'd rather be lied to."

"So far you've escaped contracting the virus. An amazing accomplishment with the high number of infected people." Chad fought for words devoid of how his heart ached for her. She'd witnessed the very suffering that pushed him to help others. "Feel relieved. Follow instructions. Law enforcement will search until they find where the virus originated, which is critical. The source is always a strong indicator of determining the best treatment. Then there's the r-naught factor to consider."

"A percentage of those who will walk away without ever being infected?"

"Correct," Chad said. "An hour from now, the CDC could announce answers, and the whole scenario would take a different turn. How many new cases since you've been quarantined?"

"I'm not sure."

"Why not? Aren't you monitoring the situation?" Some of the infected would be slower to display symptoms as if the virus had been momentarily abated.

"I'm not working the case."

Right. She was a victim. "Do you recall if the majority of the cases are among the young or old?"

"A range of people. How long will the quarantine be in force?"

"Depends on the incubation period. The first man showed signs under two hours after takeoff. Others at four and upwards of five hours—a positive indicator for a short quarantine. The other factor is Ebola and some other HFV viruses require up to a twenty-one-day incubation. With the limited information on this strain, I can't give you an accurate time frame."

"Do you suspect Ebola?"

"I have no access to the testing and won't as long as the FBI continues with its ridiculous investigation of my integrity."

"Poor Chad."

"Guess I had that coming."

"So far I'm one of the lucky ones. I'm alive, a positive."

"I'll not push for divorce until the virus scare is over."

Silence came from her end.

"Heather?"

"Really big of you to postpone your plans. If I contract the virus, my signature won't stand in your way."

"Why won't you sign the papers?"

"I'll consult with my attorney. The more I think about it, I'm not surprised you're under the FBI's microscope."

He swore.

She ended the call.

He held his cell phone and waited for her to call back or message an apology. She had hardened with what she'd been through. No point in holding a grudge against her when she might never fully recover from the worst imaginable death he'd ever witnessed.

Nothing erased the powerless urgency of sitting beside Paul while his body fought Ebola. He hadn't wanted to take this trip, but Chad persuaded him. On the plane, Paul claimed to have a bad feeling about it.

Blood had filled Paul's tear ducts, then moved to his ears, mouth, and nose. Plasma filled his lungs, and he coughed up blood. Seizures attacked him before he slipped into a coma and died. Chad's stomach rolled . . . just like it did after every nightmare reminder.

Chad texted Jordan and requested Heather's test results.

If she contracted the virus, would the FBI cancel their investigation or raise the level of suspicion?

CHAPTER EIGHTEEN

CHAD MULLED OVER the morning press conference from New York City. Not sure he approved of the measures to inform the public. In his opinion, contagion information encouraged panic to spread worse than the virus. But no one had asked him.

He wrestled with the reality of a deadly virus, Heather in danger, and his future with the CDC. His eyes stung from the constant glare of the computer screen and sleep deprivation. The CDC's inconclusive report stated the unknown virus had claimed three more lives, and they'd transported two new cases from those quarantined to the isolation unit at Jamaica Hospital.

How could he investigate the virus so far away from the source? Long hours awaited those who worked directly with the infected people and medical personnel who researched a cause and a cure. Chad craved to work alongside the researchers for reasons he might never be able to vocalize.

Andy, his geek assistant, gulped coffee, the second pot this morning. The guy drank his weight in caffeine, claiming it fired his brain cells. Once he started talking, he rarely stopped—an annoying personality trait. Chad had called him into the lab early with the hope his name would be cleared, and he'd be involved in identifying the strain of flu.

An updated post on the CDC site flew into his in-box. At least he was still receiving notifications. "Andy, listen to the latest. As we suspected, the molecular/PCR test is negative indicating the HFV is a new virus. So we wait while they attempt to grow the pathogen in culture. They've expedited autopsies, but the reports may take days or weeks."

Andy stretched his neck muscles. "Doc C., what can we accomplish here? I can't sit and read reports. Depressing."

Chad's assistant had hit the target. Previous research on other viruses gave them variables, but without direct involvement, all they had was a theory and speculation.

They couldn't grow different cell line types without access to blood samples. Even if they had cultures, New York had a biosafety level 4 lab, and the closest level 4 to Lawrence Labs was in Galveston. He buried his face in his hands. They could get lots of work done as a class 3, but they didn't have what was necessary to make a decent hypothesis.

"You're right," Chad said. "We're spinning our wheels, wasting time. Having Heather exposed to the virus and stuck in quarantine has—"

Andy startled. "You didn't tell me she was on the plane. Is she all right?"

"Yes. I found out early this morning."

"Another reason you're off."

Chad glared. "What do you mean? Since when haven't I been in the game?"

"You're off." He shrugged.

"Preoccupied. Hey, before you hear the latest from another source, I filed for divorce."

Andy tapped his thumb on the desktop. "I'm not surprised. You two are from different planets. Sorry to hear it."

"Been coming for quite a while. We don't share the same ideas and vision for the future." Chad stopped himself before he unloaded too much personal info.

"Doesn't she hassle you about church?"

"Among other things. Has the FBI contacted you?"

"I'm to be at their office at 11:30 today."

"They have me in their sights."

"An agent told me the same thing. Are they crazy?"

"Someone provided enough evidence to put me on their list." Chad swung back to his computer.

"Heather's all over this."

"Maybe." Chad stared into his computer screen.

"Did you schedule an appointment with an attorney?"

"This afternoon at two." Chad didn't say he'd picked a name at random. Heather had retained the couple's usual go-to attorney first.

His phone alerted him to a call, and he didn't recognize the number. With a deep breath, he answered. Had the FBI exonerated him?

"Dr. Lawrence, this is KHWX TV. Your wife, FBI Special Agent Heather Lawrence, was on board flight 3879 bound for Frankfurt, Germany. What can you tell us regarding the virus and the medical emergency?"

"I have the same information available to you."

"Is it true you and your wife are separated?"

Chad's anger meter rose, one more time. Two realizations had occurred to him in the early hours of the morning—one, he'd not give up until those stricken by the virus found relief, and two, he needed to get his life settled. He'd do everything within his power to keep Heather and others healthy.

"I have nothing to say. I suggest you contact the FBI or CDC for updates." He ended the call and gripped his shaking hands. Alarm or anger? Both sensations were like a predator nipping at his heels.

"The FBI has a man in custody." Andy scrolled through his phone. "He's listed in serious condition. Unconscious. Someone on board the plane said he was on a suicide mission."

"Unless a cure is available, the suspect will die before anyone can question him."

"Doc C., I know you want access to the man's stats. It will happen. First we need to clear your name so you can help with the research."

The frustration of bitter truth. "Has the FBI added WMD to the federal assault charges?"

Andy peered into his phone. "Not yet."

"If the FBI asks, don't hold back on anything I've said or done. I must get my name out of the mud."

"Sure. Can't figure out their ridiculous reasoning unless they're fishing." Andy set his phone beside his computer. "This is so stupid. Why aren't they running down real leads?"

"They're doing their job, like us dealing with dangerous substances." Chad forced a smile. "Appreciate you. I don't say it enough. Something else. I accepted a position at the CDC in Atlanta. Supposed to start in three weeks, but now I question if the job offer will be withdrawn. Previously I arranged for a doctor to handle the day-to-day operations here. Should have told you sooner."

"I'll miss working with you. You're innocent until proven guilty. Remember?"

"Depends on who's asking. Makes me wish, along with a truckload of other things, I had a background in law enforcement. Then I'd have an idea of the next step."

"With any luck, the FBI will find a lead and make progress today. That would toss out your worries. In any event, I'm on your side."

"Thanks. We could use good news." Tension hung over the lab, ready to strangle him. He needed the truth broadcast from every media outlet in the country.

CHAPTER NINETEEN

IN THE CAFETERIA, Heather studied Dr. Francisca, a slight woman with dark hair and expressive eyes. The east windows behind the woman showcased a fiery midmorning sun that did little to mask Heather's turmoil.

"I'm sorry for disturbing your sleep." Dr. Francisca spoke sensitivity into her words. "I understand how you need rest after hours on the plane and what has transpired. You've experienced the terror of a contagion."

"Add concern for my baby and the inability to fix the virus problem to the list."

"Makes sense since you're a part of the FBI. How are you feeling?"

"Tired. Nausea assaulted me on the plane, but lack of sleep has always affected my stomach. I haven't vomited, just a rolling sensation. So far I've had little morning sickness, and the first trimester is over." Heather blinked the stinging sand from her eyes.

"Do you want something for the upset stomach?"

"I'd rather not take anything."

"Understandable. Let me know if you change your mind. I've obtained the online records from your ob-gyn, and you have a healthy baby growing inside you. I want to run tests and compare them with your previous prenatal work. My testing will be separate from the CDC's evaluations."

Heather breathed a prayer for courage. "What are the dangers for my baby since I've been exposed to a hemorrhagic virus? Is—?"

"While medical researchers have identified the type of virus, more information and testing are necessary before a treatment plan can be implemented."

Throat and nasal swabs completed at the airport could show a different result, but Heather wouldn't press the issue. "Perhaps today medical authorities will have data to share."

"We all could breathe easier."

"Is there a threat of miscarriage or birth defects?"

"Studies show normal flu doesn't increase your chances of miscarriage. But any contagion has the potential for birth defects, which is why I plan to monitor all of your activities."

"What other hemorrhagic viruses have stats? The pregnant women often miscarry or their babies are premature and don't survive."

"Heather, worry and stress are enemies to you and your baby. Let's figure out what has made people sick and how to treat it. All you can do is take good care of yourself. Report to a medical person any bleeding, weakness, fatigue, dizziness, fever, diarrhea, or intense muscle aches. The point to remember is many virus symptoms mirror pregnancy. What have you experienced with the baby?"

"Fatigue, backaches, a little dizzy at times."

Dr. Francisca made notes. "I've ordered an ultrasound and additional blood work once you and I are finished talking."

"What are you looking for?"

"An increase in a protein or a hormone in your placenta. I'll compare the results with what your doctor originally noted."

"For chromosome abnormality?"

"Correct. And the ultrasound will allow me to take a look at your baby. Does your husband have permission to view your medical records?"

"Yes. I'd prefer waiting to find out the sex unless you advise otherwise."

"Of course. Dr. Radcom will receive copies of the results. They should be available later today."

"Are you ordering an amniocentesis?" Heather said.

"Only if test results give us a reason."

Heather had spent enough fretful moments craving answers. She'd manage a few more. "You're asking an always-in-control person to relax. Okay, I'll do my best."

"Good. I'll walk you back to the lab area. We have everything we need here."

After the blood draw and the ultrasound, Heather ate breakfast, not for herself but for her baby. A healthy mommy meant a healthy newborn. At least it made sense. The smells of bacon, eggs, and mile-high biscuits were tantalizing, and she complimented the cook, who thanked her with an accent straight out of Texas. No wonder the food tasted homemade. Strange how something she often took for granted became a precious gift.

A few people and families were up and in the cafeteria. Some talked in hushed tones. Perhaps they found it difficult to sleep in the new surroundings. She should force herself to speak to them, invite an environment of friendship. All she managed was a smile beneath her mask and a muffled "Good morning."

TV news flashed on the screen with the president's earlier announcement of flight 3879's medical emergency. By his side were SAC Fielder from New York City, SAC Bischoff from Houston, and a representative of the CDC. The two men spoke briefly as figureheads. She listened to what she'd already heard before plodding down the hall back to her room.

Two techs raced past her pushing a gurney. Heather saw Maria's face, the quiet woman from her room whose sister was at Jamaica Hospital. She held tissues to her nose, and blood stained her white blouse. Heather wanted to stop the gurney and reassure Maria that she'd be fine.

"Is she going to the hospital?" Heather said.

"Yes."

What about the other women rooming with her? Would this ever end?

CHAPTER TWENTY

FROM THE DEPTH OF SLEEP that paralleled drug-induced unconsciousness, Heather stirred at the sound of her name. She opened
her eyes to Doris's kindly face. "I'm sorry to bother you again. Dr.
Jordan Radcom wants to see you."

Was Maria okay? Did he have her test results? Was Dr. Francisca
with him? *Shake it off, Heather. Be an agent, not a neurotic pregnant
woman.*

She glanced at the clock: 2:15 p.m. She'd slept hard for a few
hours, but she craved more—so much more.

Doris walked with her to a room beyond the kitchen. She
knocked and announced Heather's arrival. Jordan invited Heather
inside. His eyes were his most prominent feature, intense and
penetrating. Chad referred to him as the Eagle, a nickname from
medical school.

Jordan grasped her gloved hand lightly. The gloves and the
masks were a uniform—rightfully so. They were an army of soldiers

battling a virus. "I'm sorry for the circumstances that have brought you here." Deep lines fanned from his eyes. "Have you been able to sleep?"

"Yes. And you?"

"I'll rest when the virus is under control." He pointed to a folding chair in front of a metal desk. "Why don't we sit?"

She obliged, and he did the same. "I wasn't expecting you on the island."

"And miss not spending time with you? Directing the quarantine is my job, which means I'm here for the duration."

"I'm selfishly glad, if that makes sense. How's Erika? The girls?"

"They're good. My daughters are growing much too fast for my liking."

"Erika sent pics a few weeks ago. They've changed so much and very pretty."

"They take after their Swedish-born mother." He glanced out the dirt-streaked window behind him, where light attempted to stream in. He turned back to her. "Is our hotel treating you okay?"

She summoned lightness into her words. "The vampires are doing a splendid job."

"I'll give them your commendation. I spoke to Dr. Francisca, and I have your test results. She put a rush on them."

"Before I hear the details, how is Maria?"

"I checked before you walked in." He breathed in deeply. "Experiencing respiratory problems."

The fear factor threatened to take control. She'd fight it, and she'd claim victory. "I'll continue to pray. . . . Is my baby okay?"

"Yes. No issues or indications of potential problems. But if the baby is affected, it may show up later."

Heather shoved aside what could happen. "I have to believe my baby will survive this."

"Lots of prayer. Dr. Francisca included the baby's sex in her report."

In the time since she'd met with the doctor, she'd changed her mind about knowing the gender. "What is it?"

"A boy."

She smiled despite the circumstances. "Thank you. I wanted a son." Oh, for him to have Chad's blue eyes. She shut down the notion. No point going there and upsetting herself.

"Do you have any health issues not mentioned to Dr. Francisca or a member of the CDC?"

"None other than the pregnancy. I have a nasty headache, but I'm attributing it to the current situation. Stomach's queasy, but I'm not surprised with the emotional stress. The last several hours haven't been normal. . . . The possibility of the virus hurting the baby has me scared."

"Dr. Francisca is an outstanding ob-gyn. She'll take good care of you."

"I like her." She folded her hands in her lap as though she had to find something to do with them. "On the plane, I scrutinized and talked to many people, but none looked suspicious other than Braden Taversty."

"He's in critical condition." Jordan paused. "Not expected to recover."

Which meant he might never be questioned. "Any intel pointing to a suicide mission?"

"You'll have to ask your friends at the FBI. I'm the medical guy."

"Right." As the man in charge of the CDC's investigation and research of the virus, he'd be aware of a suspect. The information might be off-limits to her. She'd talk to SAC Mitchell. She could be of assistance if they had their attention on someone in quarantine. "Have you identified the virus?"

"Not yet. Additional testing will show us what strain."

"You know this, but whoever developed the virus has more. The source has to be found before others are infected."

"That fact is on everyone's minds."

"And I just reminded you. My apologies. What's being done for those in the hospital?"

"They're receiving broad-spectrum antibiotics, and we're treating the symptoms. That's all we can do without conclusive test results."

Jordan's words sounded bleak. She craved a taste of good news. "A German woman by the name of Mia was taken to the hospital. Can you tell me how she's doing?"

Jordan turned to the computer on his desk. "Last name?"

"I have no idea. She sat beside me on the plane."

He studied the screen. "Okay, we have one woman named Mia from Germany. She's in stable condition and holding her own."

Had it been only hours ago since she'd held Mia's coffee while the woman placed her carry-on in the overhead bin? How had Heather escaped the virus? Except it wasn't over yet. "What about a little boy named Frankie? I don't have a last name for him. He's six, almost seven years old. He was seated with his grandmother, and she left the plane on a stretcher."

Jordan again peered into the computer screen. He typed, studied the screen, and frowned. "Frankie is unconscious. Not responding to the antibiotics."

A well of despair rose from the pit of her soul. She sobbed and tried desperately to stop. *Stay strong. Others need me.* The breakdown was a repeat of when Tatum and Catherine comforted her. Jordan stood from his desk, but she held up her palm. "No, Jordan. I can handle my own problems. I'll be okay."

Heather fought the grief not only for Frankie, who might not see his seventh birthday, but for those who might never see tomorrow. *Where are You, God? How can good come from young and old suffering and dying?* She managed a gulp of air. "I apologize."

He handed her a tissue. "Considering the pregnancy and everything surrounding your flight, I'm surprised you're not hysterical.

Grown men here have cried over the sick and the plight of these people. I'd be worried if you weren't affected. In my mind, the animals who planted the virus deserve whatever punishment the court gives them."

"Doing nothing frustrates me. My job is to analyze bad guys and help determine the why of their behavior and a method to reach them in a way they'll understand. I want to be on the street turning over rocks and interviewing anyone who might have information. Has anything been uncovered by the CDC, health departments, or FBI?"

His gaze bored into hers. "Between us, I assume the FBI will filter all information before it's brought to my attention. For the CDC, the process requires hours of testing and evaluation. Acquiring medical records takes time, and for those who traveled alone and died or are unconscious, we need hours, days to locate answers."

She recalled the hopelessness in Chad's recollections of an Ebola outbreak. The dire conditions took root in her very bones. "You're overwhelmed and I get it, but can you keep me posted? Mia and Frankie are new friends."

"Sure." He peered at her. "In view of his upcoming CDC position, I regret Chad won't be joining us here on the island. Probably not even when his name is cleared."

"He accused me of contacting the FBI to bring him in for questioning. I haven't talked to the FBI for a copy of the interview. No excuse except I'm preoccupied." Confusion clouded her mind. "What CDC position?"

Jordan startled. "He didn't tell you?"

"What's going on?"

"Chad should discuss his decisions with you."

"We aren't communicating well at the moment. Please explain how Chad has a position at the CDC."

"Guess it doesn't matter. He has a new role in Atlanta where he'll be working directly with the National Center for Immunization and Respiratory Diseases—the influenza division."

Far too similar to what flight 3879 was experiencing. She despised her suspicions of Chad's recent behavior and preoccupation with . . . something.

His new apartment was a furnished month-by-month lease. She thought he'd chosen the apartment's rental flexibility because of the possibility of working out their problems. "He hasn't told me anything, much less about a move to Atlanta." She shoved strength into her words instead of another meltdown. "When was he hired?"

"The interview process began after the first of the year."

The same time Chad chose to distance himself. His actions made calculated sense. The coward didn't have the guts to tell her his plans.

"When is he scheduled to start his new responsibilities?"

"Three weeks." He glanced at his desk and back to her. "Not sure why he kept the job change from you."

"I do, and it's okay. We're separated." She drew in a breath. "I question why he hasn't passed on his marital status."

Jordan frowned. "I asked him if you planned a transfer to the Atlanta FBI office, and he didn't respond. I hate to hear you're not together, but I suspected problems when the FBI found him at a different address from yours."

"I'm not thrilled about it either." Heather refused to offer her sentiments. She'd either thrown a wrench into Chad's plans for a career in the CDC or he gambled on her not surviving the virus. "He has motive to plan my death."

"You're kidding, right?"

"He said I was in his way. He couldn't move ahead in his career with a wife." She pressed her lips together hard enough to bruise them.

"Why does he believe you're in his way?" Jordan said.

"I have no idea."

"You can unload, Heather. Whatever you tell me stays right here."

She stiffened to regain her composure. "So . . . the relationship headed downhill, and I tried to fix it. It made matters worse."

Her previous doubts hung over her, dark and menacing. What were the odds that she'd be on an aircraft attacked by a mysterious killer and the virus's description fit his specialty?

CHAPTER TWENTY-ONE

LATE AFTERNOON, Heather viewed the news from the cafeteria TV. Angry crowds protested the restrictions on the outbound flights from Houston and Chicago airports. Per the president, the FBI, Homeland Security, local law enforcement, and the CDC were working together to end the virus panic and bring answers to the American people. Quarantined passengers and crew had arrived safely on an island off the coast of New York until further threat of contagion had passed.

The media placed the country's reaction in diverse camps—terror, outrage, and blaming the current administration for causing business and travel delays. Watchdog journalism shared interviews from those inside the quarantine, often using photos and videos taken on the plane to raise their ratings.

Heather blew out her irritation. She couldn't fault those who demanded explanations. She had the same concerns and questions. But the ones who protested the inability to book travel hadn't experienced people in misery and dying a horrible death, or they'd run for the safety of their homes and lock the doors.

She logged into the FBI security site for the latest on the investigation. Agents worked the case with no solution to stop the virus or find the culprit who'd spread it. Task forces of trained personnel labored around the clock. If she were there, she'd be in the thick of it, too.

CDC workers had stripped Maria's bed and disinfected the room, the empty bed a reminder of the death stalker. Tatum scrolled on her phone, and Catherine read her Bible. Jackie and Ada were watching a movie in the recreation area. Both women had bonded in the ordeal.

Heather needed to get out of the room for a while. The cafeteria had a coffee bar, and she needed a jolt of caffeine. She grabbed her shoulder bag and slipped her phone inside. In the cafeteria, the aroma of coffee brought back memories of sharing coffee with Chad. . . . Once upon a time, things were good between them.

A few others sat on metal benches that lined the cafeteria. She saw a mix of grief, panic, and frustration. A preteen girl screamed for her mama, who was at Jamaica Hospital. A man held her and she sobbed. No doubt bad news. A CDC worker escorted them toward the wing of offices.

God, when will this end?

Thomas shoved his hands into jean pockets and walked her way. "Nothing is more unfair than a child attacked by tragedy."

"I agree."

"Children are the seeds of a beautiful future. They should be nourished and loved."

"That's beautiful. I'll remember it," she said.

"Are you busy?"

"I needed to get out of my room."

"I understand. Do you mind if I get a cup of coffee, a couple of cookies, and join you? If you prefer being alone, I get it."

Talking would pass the time. "Sure. I smell chocolate chip, and I could use a chocolate anything."

He returned with a stack of her favorite cookies piled onto a paper plate and wrapped his legs over the bench opposite her. "They look like they're still warm. Good of them to offer creature comforts."

Heather gave him a thumbs-up. "The coffee's not bad." Thomas wasn't a handsome man but pleasing, as her grandmother would say. Worry lines fanned from his eyes, like the rest of them. "How are you doing?"

"Much better than many others. I've experienced blood drawn. Urine samples. Tongue depressors. Q-tips pushed up my nose. A few hours of sleep. Daytime TV. A shower improved my attitude. Breakfast and lunch reminded me of my high school cafeteria, carbs and mushy vegetables. Pushing the mask up to eat has a trick to it." He managed a faint smile. "How about you?"

"We've had a similar day."

"After dinner, I want to take a walk outside. It may help to process our situation."

She held up her phone. "At least the CDC provides access to the world beyond our quarantine."

"Have the authorities determined a vaccine to protect us against the virus?"

"Not yet." If only she had promising news. "No arrests for who is responsible either. Braden Taversty is in critical condition."

"Some reporters are labeling his stunt a suicide mission. The world is filled with fanatics, and he could be one of them. Our faces are plastered across the screen of the free world. We are being called a lot of things—fortunate, guinea pigs, victims of bureaucratic decisions. Shall I go on?"

Heather sensed his downward spiral, and hers trailed right behind his. "I'm sure a long list of groups and psychopaths are taking credit." She sipped her coffee. "Enough gloom. We can't allow our current circumstances to destroy us." She pushed the plate of cookies his way. "I'll do what I can while we're here."

"I found a game room and offered to spend time with the kids. Most of them have hospitalized parents or siblings."

"They may need a sounding board. Let me know if I can help."

"I will. Lacy Skaggs said they lacked men, so I jumped in." He rubbed his hand over his face. "I bet the kitchen has the ingredients for me to whip up a batch of these."

"You bake?"

"Paid for grad school by working at a bakery in Austin. Learned a sweet trick or two. Real butter. Real chocolate chips. Refrigerate the dough before baking. Correct temp." He shook his head. "Odd how things pop into your mind when you're away from a normal routine." He tilted his head. Sadness settled dark on him. "The bakery's name was Flour Power. What I wouldn't give to be back there instead of here with the grim reaper around us."

She nodded. "If we're here very long, you can volunteer for a baking spree."

"Might help me keep my sanity."

"Do you have family in Houston?"

"No. Guess that's a good thing. What about you?"

"My husband and parents are there."

"I imagine they're worried sick."

"Thomas, hold on to a glimpse of tomorrow, no matter how thin or fragile. We're the lucky people who are blessed to be healthy. Every minute we escape the virus ups our chances of survival."

He captured her gaze. "You're right. Optimism for the future is our best asset. I appreciate the reminder." He rose from the bench with his empty cup. "Think I'll take that walk before dinner. The fresh air may help my outlook. Thanks for taking a few minutes with me."

The moment Thomas walked away, Chad's words echoed through her mind.

You're in my way, Heather. I can't move forward in my career with a wife.

106

CHAPTER TWENTY-TWO

CHAD SURVEYED LIFE below his apartment through a half-inch gap in his living room blinds. The sights and sounds reflected a world untouched by chaos while he evaluated a worthless day. He hadn't moved ahead on research projects and neither had he heard from the FBI investigation, leaving him in a sour mood. The appointment with his lawyer added no value to the legal conundrum other than the establishment of a retainer fee and for Chad not to talk to the FBI without the lawyer's presence.

A video call from Jordan sounded on his phone. Chad hadn't expected his old friend to make contact so soon after the FBI questioning. Unless he bore bad news about the position in Atlanta . . . or Heather had contracted the virus.

Chad tapped the video messaging app. "Hey, Jordan. Good to hear from you. I assumed you'd be knee-deep handling the virus situation."

Exhaustion spread over Jordan's face. "Up to my eyeballs in this mess. I have an important matter to discuss with you."

"Has Heather contracted the virus?"

"No. You must be frantic with the rapid spread of the virus. If Erika or my girls had been subjected to this, I'd be insane with worry. Our families take priority, and it's hard to have objectivity."

Chad fumed that Jordan doubted he could separate career and personal life. "I'd be happy to assist in New York. I'm able to dissimulate emotion."

"Not with your FBI person of interest status."

His words ripped off the scab. "The memo travels fast."

"Why does the FBI suspect you?"

"Fishing."

"What aren't you telling me?"

Jordan could learn the reason on his own.

"Okay, you aren't ready to talk about it. When you're cleared, the CDC may approve you in an advisory capacity. We're calling the virus H9N15, and it appears to be the most rapidly spreading flu virus in contemporary medical history. Authorities all over the world are on alert for another breakout. I'm sure you've viewed the constant updates to the CDC file."

"Yes, I have. What can I do?"

"Have you formulated a hypothesis from your past studies?"

"For a thorough analysis, I must be on-site. Examining conclusions of other researchers is valuable, but I can't give the problem my full attention in Houston."

"Understandable but impossible. The only way we're going to end the threat is to examine data." Jordan squinted. "There's another reason for contacting you. It's about Heather."

Maybe she'd confided in him about their personal problems, and Jordan planned to give him the God and family lecture. "You indicated she's okay." Chad softened his voice. He couldn't stop where his heart led.

"She's not displaying any symptoms. You requested results from her blood work, and I prefer giving them to you myself. Why didn't you tell me your marriage was in trouble?"

"A face-to-face conversation made more sense."

"Heather and I briefly discussed your relationship. She was unaware of your position in Atlanta."

"Past tense says you told her."

"Yes."

"I hadn't found the right time to have that conversation. Her blood work didn't raise a red flag?"

"No signs of the virus. She's one of the lucky passengers and crew."

His whole body relaxed. Another problem kicked out the door.

"More good news," Jordan said. "The baby is fine."

Blood pumped hot through Chad's body. "The baby? She's pregnant?"

"From the look on your face, you aren't the only person keeping a secret. What's going on between you two?"

"In order to continue my work, I must eliminate all other obligations."

"I gave you a new one, a baby. Technically two considering Heather is the mother of your child. For the record, I'd be an empty man without Erika and my daughters. Their support and encouragement empower me to be not just a CDC director, but a man who loves his family. My desire is to make them proud."

Chad's heart hadn't slowed since the beginning of the conversation. What he craved was freedom from the accusations and a single life. Not another interruption, which was what a pregnancy entailed. He'd told her several months ago—no kids. "Your requirements for success and mine aren't the same."

"At the end of your life, what will you have to show for it? How will you answer to God?"

Jordan's faith had always been an irritation. "My life will have been dedicated to medical research. My hope is to leave the world a better place, a healthier environment. Science is the one verifiable discipline in the universe."

"Science is God's tool to learn and use for good purposes. I'm working to bring good from evil in the field of medicine."

"And I can't answer to a fallacy."

"See how far your view goes when you breathe your last breath."

Chad ignored the remark. "How many weeks is Heather?"

"Sixteen."

She had confirmation of the pregnancy before he'd moved out. She hadn't said a word. The baby was his child, although he wasn't ready for fatherhood, and she'd hidden the information from him. The prospect drew a longing, real and vital. He paced his apartment. A baby scared him witless . . .

"Chad, say something."

He turned from the phone's camera and breathed in and out. "I'm shocked. What's the baby's sex?"

"Ask Heather."

"I'd rather hear it from you. Our communication is edgy."

Jordan frowned "Okay. A boy. I learned about her pregnancy from a CDC worker and requested a reputable ob-gyn, Dr. Natalie Francisca. No matter who the passenger, I'd ensure any pregnant woman on the aircraft received expert care."

A son? Was his promise worth abandoning his wife and unborn child? Confusion assaulted him. Heather took precaution, and she wasn't the devious type to trap him. Besides, unless she tossed the pills in the trash, sixteen weeks ago he still lived at the condo then. Or had she tricked him?

What mattered? His love for her pushed him to make a sacrifice, and he'd given his word, and what was a man's word but his integrity?

"Are you going to talk to her?" Jordan said. "If you're deaf, I can restate the importance of family."

Chad pondered how to respond. Logic told him confronting her gave an illusion of them staying together. Not happening. "A baby doesn't change my original outlook on the future."

Jordan's eyes narrowed. "Are you an idiot? Heather loves you. She worked while you completed your first and second doctorate. Supported you before and after you were married. I remember she paid the rent on her apartment *and* yours. A divorce is how you thank her? You've never complained about her. Now you're successful, she's pregnant with your baby, surviving exposure to a killer virus, and you aren't sure if a family is in your future?"

"It's complicated."

"Makes me wonder if you have a negative IQ."

"It's taken me eight years to realize I'm not what she or a baby needs. They deserve a man who will love and be there for them. That's not me. Neither will it ever be."

Jordan huffed. "Got to go. Work's waiting for me."

"I'll check back later. I'll figure out a plan for Heather and the baby. Don't tell her you talked to me."

"I'm not playing your fool's game. If she brings it up, I'll tell her." Jordan leaned back in his chair. "For the record, Heather is a remarkable and intelligent woman, quite capable of taking care of herself. Your actions make me want to strangle you. You're a brilliant doctor, and the CDC is lucky to have you. But the world doesn't revolve around the next scientific discovery by a man who doesn't accept his humanity. Relationships matter."

CHAPTER TWENTY-THREE

HEATHER WALKED ALONG the rocks of the island's shoreline and deliberated Chad's position with the FBI. Whatever lay ahead was in God's hands, but she wished He'd send a text.

"Heather Lawrence."

She turned to the scruffy-beard man and the pink-haired woman walking toward her. According to the manifest, she'd learned their names. "Hi. You're Parker and Sonya Karey?"

"We are." Parker peered at her down a long nose that nearly touched his mouth. "I'd like to talk to you."

"Sure. How can I help?"

"We understand you're FBI."

Although Parker must have disagreeable as his middle name, he and his wife were victims of the contagion. They all shouldered the stress of sickness and death. "Right. What's going on?"

"Earlier I searched online for information about you. Your husband is Dr. Chad Lawrence, owner of Lawrence Laboratory."

"Correct."

Parker crossed his arms over his chest. "He's an expert in his field. Worldwide recognition. He claims the health of the world is his priority." He tugged on his scruffy beard.

"Do you have questions? Have you read something confusing?"

He eyed her, his hostility as transparent as glass. "I don't mince words. Looks to me like your husband might have developed the virus."

"Where did you hear that?"

"Latest news." He held up his phone. "Got it right here. He's a person of interest."

"The FBI is interested in him. Chad hasn't been arrested or accused of a crime."

He waved away her statement. "Doesn't matter. Something about him has their attention. Why isn't he in New York or here with you in this godforsaken quarantine?"

She wasn't going to add to the conversation. He needed someone to vent his frustrations to.

Parker sneered. "A peculiar situation."

"What do you mean?"

"Your husband is a specialist in the same field of what has attacked the plane. You're on an overseas flight alone, and we're exposed to a killer virus. Fill in the blanks."

Heather hid a wave of dizzying fury and tried to eliminate anger from her voice. "I assure you, Chad has dedicated his life to the betterment of others. His FBI status is a misunderstanding, and I'm confident the status will soon be removed."

"How can you say he's uninvolved? Our situation isn't an accident or circumstantial." Disgust coated every word. "My statements about your husband wouldn't bother you so much if you didn't think they held a grain of truth."

Survivor's guilt and Parker's implications slashed her heart.

Sonya moved closer to her husband. "You should know motive for murder comes in different shapes and sizes. And reasons."

The two walked away as though on cue. The Kareys' statements held a measure of truth. Yet the implications dug a ridge into her heart. The idea of Chad at the root of an evil crime bordered on ridiculous. Right?

Tuesday night, each time Heather drifted off to sleep, Chad's insistence upon the divorce melded with motive for murder . . . like Sonya had insinuated.

She grabbed her phone and navigated to her secured access on the FBI site to read Chad's interview from Agents Rivera and Tobias. Used to be she termed his sarcasm as witty, but then his comments grew caustic. His interview showed a man disturbed by the accusations against him and willing to aid in the investigation. She requested the video. Viewing it would be hard, but she had to study his face, read his actions, and analyze his responses.

If he'd developed the virus, she'd never be able to forgive herself for trying to hold on to him.

She stretched her neck to shake the doubt—and the overwhelming emotions that whirled through her. Sorting them out required time, but not while lack of sleep robbed her of good judgment. Tomorrow had to be a better day.

Backgrounds on many of those on the plane had been added to the FBI secure site. The Kareys were an average young couple traveling to Frankfurt for a job interview. Mia headed home to her family. Frankie's story about him and his grandmother flying to meet his dad had been confirmed. Curiosity zeroed in on Thomas Powell, the man who'd helped her with Braden Taversty. She scanned his information—CEO of Software Developers International, or SDI, a software company worth millions. She studied every name and background and a few raised suspicions. But none like Braden Taversty.

Her phone alerted her to a text from Jordan. He requested they meet at his office.

The hour neared midnight. It had to be urgent. If he'd stumbled onto a viable threat and the FBI were accurate in their assessment of Chad, how did she proceed? What if she learned her tenacity to secure their relationship had killed so many people?

She typed to Jordan.

15 minutes okay?

Perfect

She dressed, splashed water on her face, and tied her hair into a ponytail. Freshening up failed to soothe the anxiety about the future.

At Jordan's office, he greeted her minus a smile. "Please sit." He studied her face. "How are you feeling?"

She eased onto a metal chair. "I'm okay. Take a look in the mirror. Jordan, you can't give your best without rest." She shrugged. "I sound like Dr. Seuss."

"He probably could make more sense out of this than I am. We've had four more cases transported from here to Jamaica Hospital. Three additional deaths."

"One hundred twenty-five ill and twenty dead." The madness swung back and forth like a pendulum. "I need to be doing something, but what?"

"Pray for guidance, God's grace, and mercy. And a quick determination of how we can help the victims." She promised, and he went on. "The CDC is calling the virus H9N15, a new strain. Once researchers identify the virus's genetic sequence, we can create the diagnostic test to pinpoint patients who have been infected with the virus."

"Thank you for filling me in."

"Friends do what they can for each other." Jordan paused. "I also received an update on the virus investigation. This has been cleared for your ears only through all channels, but the information must remain private." His graveled voice and slumped shoulders pointed to the hours already invested in the panic. "I preferred you hear the news from me first. The CDC and FBI have uncovered a critical piece in the investigation. A team searching the plane discovered how the virus infected the passengers and crew."

Heat rose in her face—Parker's words stomped across her mind. "How and where?"

"We found a crushed breath freshener in one of the plane's sewage tanks. When the pieces were tested and compared to blood samples from victims, we confirmed a high concentration of the new virus strain."

She blinked with the realization. "Someone sprayed it throughout the cabin and disposed of it down a toilet?"

"It appears so."

"If spreading the virus was a deliberate act, is the murderer among the dead, the sick, or here in quarantine?" she said.

"Good question."

"Which restroom was the container found?"

"One in business class," he said.

"Were fragments found anywhere else?"

"Not yet."

Which meant investigators were scouring the area. "A piece could have been kicked or carried elsewhere by attaching itself to someone's shoes, which means finding who's responsible is slim."

"Currently it's our singular piece of evidence."

"It's a high probability the one who unleashed the virus sat in business class or was a member of the crew." Heather pictured her original assigned seat. She'd tended to the sick all over the aircraft and later sat in economy when she took Taversty into custody. She didn't recall a passenger or attendant using a breath freshener. But she'd also been asleep.

"Where are your thoughts?" Jordan said.

"A suicide mission implicates Braden Taversty, except he wasn't seated in first class. A flight attendant policed the restroom in business class, and no one got past her." She paused to review the facts. "Nothing in his background indicates he had the skills to develop the virus. But he does have contacts who are capable. If he had the whole suicide thing going on, why isn't everyone dead including himself?"

"Or was this a trial run to spread contagion to other flights or areas of the world?"

"I wish we had answers because this is complex. You've seen the results of what viruses can do. Not anything to mess with. If how the virus passed through security is leaked to the public, we'll have copycats. Another nightmare."

"Heather." Jordan caught her gaze. "Don't you think the findings clear Chad?"

"Do they?"

He startled. "You still have doubts about his innocence?"

CHAPTER TWENTY-FOUR

HEATHER HATED THE PERPETUAL LUMP in her throat. "At first I denied Chad's involvement—an incredulous idea. But I applied my investigative skills, and uncertainty consumed me. Had I been blind to deceit? What kind of agent misses the signs of a potential criminal, a man who has the ability to plan her death and display no conscience?" She breathed in to gain control. "If he'd threatened me that he'd develop a killer virus if I didn't agree to his demands, I'd have arrested him. And signed his papers."

She shook with the words. "I've chosen to deal with this through an agent's eyes. He's intelligent, ambitious, and the FBI uncovered enough data to bring him in for questioning."

"Chad is like a brother. I can't go along with it."

"Really? Who told you about the separation and request for a divorce?" Jordan didn't answer, and she spilled more into the conversation. "His feelings for me are gone. If I were dead, he'd be a free man." She lifted a finger. "I'm being cynical, but it's true."

"I'm convinced he's wrestling with a tough jolt of reality."

"Imagine his response if he knew I was pregnant."

Jordan stared back.

"You told him. Why?"

"You didn't ask me to keep the information private, and you'd given him permission to view your health records. Anyway, I talked to him before dinner."

"His name is still there because I never thought he'd check. This is my fault. He's had a few hours to contact me, which says he doesn't care."

"Maybe he's trying to figure out how to approach the subject."

"When our son's born?"

"You're under emotional stress for a multitude of reasons. Get through the quarantine and then deal with Chad's stupidity."

She raised a brow.

"He's an idiot," Jordan said. "I told him so."

"I'm sure he handled your comments well. Jordan, I don't have time for Chad to find himself or decide his life's purpose or how he can reach his status of success in the medical world. I have a son to raise who matters more than a selfish grown man. It's not fair to subject a child to a father who's a revolving door."

"Don't give up. I'm praying for God to work on his heart." He shook his head. "Chad couldn't have developed the virus. Impossible."

"False hopes are what I banked on in our marriage. His god is what he can see and touch. I meant a lot to him when I worked to help him finish his doctorates. Look where my blind love got me—my husband's a suspect in an FBI investigation where people are sick and dying."

She stopped herself before saying something she'd regret later. "Our relationship has ended. He's not going to change, and neither do I trust him. In all sincerity, I'd like evidence to prove his innocence, but where is it?"

"Let's put aside the Chad discussion. Neither one of us can clear or convict him while in quarantine."

"You're right." She shifted her attention. "It's conceivable the virus was planted for a distinct purpose, to target an individual or people group. But like most viruses, it attacks all ages with an emphasis on children and the elderly. So far a link hasn't been established. With those parameters, does the culprit term the mission a success? My question goes back to why create a deadly virus and not ensure everyone is eliminated?"

"You mean if a bomb was assembled and detonated on board the plane? A terrorist's approach, possibly Braden Taversty."

"Terrorists seldom work alone. Think about this. If not Taversty, the culprit could be right here on the island with us, watching how the virus plays out." She wrapped her arms around her chest to avoid the chill from the drafty building, so odd for July. "How many people were involved in the scheme to place the virus inside a breath freshener? A level of sophistication that escaped TSA. Security cameras at Houston's and Chicago's airports haven't uncovered anything, not even a follow-up. This had to take weeks or months to plan. Who or what are we dealing with?"

Jordan pressed his lips together. "Time's our deadliest enemy. We require stats and analysis, and those for H9N15 aren't available yet. Look at the snail-paced progress made on some of the most feared viruses in the world—Marburg, hantavirus, Lassa, Junin, Machupo, smallpox, strains of Ebola, bird flu, dengue, and the list goes on. Meanwhile people are infected and die."

"Seems a new virus pops up every week. I should have asked Chad pointed questions so I'd better understand what we're dealing with. They're tiny germs made of genetic material inside a protein coating?"

He nodded. "Viruses invade a body's cells and then use them to reproduce cells just like them. What makes them so dangerous is they can kill the cell, damage it, or change its composition and make the person sick. The life-threatening viruses attack the cell systems that must retain their normal function for the body to survive."

"Chad refers to them as hijackers."

"Right. They seize control and take over."

"I've studied behavior for the past nine years. I've assessed the minds of people who've committed horrendous crimes. What I experienced with this virus ranks as one of the most perverse of my career." She recalled moments with Roy, Frankie, Mia, the elderly man who'd sat beside her, and a sea of suffering and vacant faces. She clenched her fist. "I long for release from quarantine so I could help end the scare."

"Heather, would you want to risk infecting otherwise healthy people?" His gentle tone was meant to ease her worries, but she teetered on being overwhelmed. They all were reacting out of helpless misery. "Our goals—all of us—are for an arrest and a vaccine," he said. "At this moment, I'd settle for effective treatment."

"Circumstances could change in the blink of an eye."

His shoulders relaxed. "Makes me think of that Scripture. I needed a reminder of who's in control."

"Remind me, too, because every person on this case is consumed with worry, which produces zero results." She let her words sink into her heart before moving on. "Interviews will continue until arrests are made. Earlier today, I checked a secure site for online chatter. All I saw was admiration for whoever is responsible."

"The FBI press conference in the morning will give the public information," Jordan said. "That gives us several hours to pull together research from the various agencies. If they choose, the authorities have two factors to report—the discovery of how H9N15 traveled through security and how a person on board the aircraft released it, then attempted to destroy the evidence."

"Thankfully, the report is progress. I despise the public claiming the FBI as inept."

"I don't blame you."

She navigated to a secure site on her phone. "Give me a moment to check for new developments." She finished and glanced into Jordan's wide-set eyes. "I'm sorry. There's nothing new to report confidential or secured. All the passengers, flight crews, and families or significant others in Chicago and Houston remain under scrutiny. Those near the aircraft five days prior to the virus's release are being questioned and thorough background checks conducted."

"I assume the FBI has scrutinized cameras positioned during the boarding process to connect passengers and employees for a possible link."

"Yes, and I'm sure the FBI continues to replay the footage for missing details," she said. "An associate of our person could have boarded a different plane with a separate virus container."

His jaw tightened. "Our worst scenario is an outbreak in another area. With death occurring in a matter of hours for so many, the idea shakes me to the core."

Heather believed in a future built on good, not evil. "I'll do everything I can from here. My attempt to mingle and observe behavior today got me nowhere. Most people are afraid, a mental paralysis." She stared out the window behind Jordan's desk to the dark unknown. "The devastation of Chad leaving me took a backseat to the virus outbreak." She shoved aside the surge to assume control. "I pray God will guide me to the right people."

"We've all been on our knees."

One of Chad's criticisms of Jordan was his bold faith. She'd not ask Jordan why God allowed the virus to attack those on the flight—he wouldn't have an answer either. God was God, and the why was His. Senseless to protest and rant when God didn't ask humans to help Him make decisions.

An idea soared into her mind. "Is it possible for me to talk with those in the hospital who are stable? We have a connection, have gone through the same ordeal. They might confide in me."

He appeared to contemplate her request. "We could establish an audio or video link." He offered his first smile of the evening. "I agree your bond is stronger than anyone within the CDC or FBI."

"It's a small thing and has potential to bring huge results."

"I'll check to ensure we have no roadblocks. The patients must be willing to talk to you, and some aren't physically able. Best time to arrange the calls is early afternoon tomorrow."

CHAPTER TWENTY-FIVE

CHAD BELIEVED THE FORCES OF LIFE held on to secrets, mysteries that unlocked cures for catastrophic diseases. Viruses were evil incarnate that added to the world's suffering and created useless deaths. Relentless resolve intensified Chad's struggle to overpower the evil, a vicious tug-of-war between science and whatever spearheaded the contagion. In his thirty-five years, whatever had approached him as evil never turned to good. That proved Jordan and Heather's answer to life wasn't a deity.

Heather despised his rants against Christianity. She said God is love, righteous, and just. So very wrong, but he no longer had to hear her uninformed inadequacies. His parents had the religious mantra going. Mom died in a nursing home with Alzheimer's, and Dad died of a broken heart. Where had faith gotten them?

The exterior door of the lab buzzed with someone requesting entry. Chad glanced at his computer screen for a visual. They seldom had visitors and never unannounced ones, especially this time of evening. He groaned. Agent Rivera and other agents wearing FBI jackets and weapons were there.

Andy peered over his shoulder. "The FBI, huh? Want me to welcome them? Shake a test tube full of green goo at them?"

Chad wished for a semblance of humor. "My dilemma. I'll handle the Feds."

"Make sure they're told a lab tour isn't for Boy Scouts."

Chad made his way through one set of locked doors where he removed his protective gear before he opened the door to the front office. He pressed the intercom. "Lawrence Laboratories."

"Special Agent Javier Rivera with a search warrant. The FBI has probable cause to suspect criminal activity may be found here that relates to the H9N15 virus. Five agents are with me to search your lab."

He'd been betrayed by the legal system. Reality shook him with a fusion of bitterness and unfairness that knotted his stomach. The reasoning behind his implication in the FBI's investigation, and the irony, fueled his anxiety. He squeezed the doorknob and faced Rivera. Agent Laura Tobias and four other agents joined him. All were ready to pursue invisible evidence. Javier handed him a document.

Chad looked for a federal judge's signature on the warrant, and it appeared large, legible, and recognizable.

Not a muscle twitched on Rivera's face. "Sources within and outside the FBI point to probable cause."

"Who besides the FBI lied and placed me in a vulnerable position?"

"Dr. Lawrence, as I told you previously, the information is unavailable."

Chad glanced away to slow his heart, pounding loud enough to summon the dead. The accusations about his ability to develop a virus provided motivation for murder. "Excuse me while I check with my lawyer." Chad made the call and had to leave a voice message. Resistance crawled inside his resolve to cooperate. Everything he knew about himself defied their intrusion into his life.

Drawing in a breath destined to rid his rattled nerves, he gestured the investigators inside his front office. "Search every inch of my office and lab. When you're finished, take apart my car. Then I'll direct you to my apartment. Trust me, you won't find a thing."

"We will proceed as stated in the search warrant." Rivera's tone reflected a professional investigator. "We're equipped to conduct the sweep."

"Did your sister die of flu or did you fabricate the story to gain my sympathies?"

"I told you the truth." Devoid of emotion, Rivera stared into his face.

"My assistant is inside the lab. Shall I ask him to leave?" A show of temper served no purpose with the serious allegations against him.

As if timing his arrival, Andy appeared from the inner door after shedding his protective gear. He stuck out his hand to Rivera. "Dr. Andy Sheehan. How can I help?"

"Dr. Sheehan, there's no reason for you to stay while we conduct our search."

"I'll stick around."

Supportive Andy. The man deserved a raise. "I'm good. I'll call or text you when the agents are finished."

"Okay." Andy clasped Chad on the shoulder. "Sure?"

"Yes. We're good."

Andy grabbed his backpack before leaving.

Chad forced a cooperative attitude into his facade, but he'd rather reach for a bottle of Jack Daniel's. "With all due respect, Agent Rivera, you must take precautions before entering the lab, during your search, and afterward."

"We've been briefed on the safety requirements for a class 3 lab," Rivera said. "We all have experience in handling hazardous materials."

"But I didn't train you, and you didn't bring protective gear. No one approaches my lab without my instructions. I'm cooperating with the FBI to prove you accused the wrong man, so placate me." Chad led the group to a dressing area inside the first set of doors to his lab. He pulled a tan gown, nitrile gloves, a mask, and booties from a drawer for each agent and himself. A sense of control dulled the tension in his body. "Put these on over your clothes and shoes."

"Dr. Lawrence, our work will take a while," Rivera said. "You're not permitted to interfere. I'd prefer you wait in your office."

"I'll observe to make sure no one is contaminated. Are you up to date on your vaccines?"

The agents confirmed and dressed in the gowns—each garment designed to open in the back.

"Although you claim previous experience, I intend to give you a tutorial," Chad said. "My lab handles life-threatening microbes. Are you sure you want to continue?"

Rivera slipped into his booties. "We are prepared to conduct our job."

Chad bit his tongue to keep from unloading a truckload of sarcasm. Instead he slipped into his own protective gear. "Put on everything I've given you. We have two sets of self-closing doors here for safety reasons. When we're finished in the lab, everything comes off within the door behind me and tossed into a container marked *Hazardous*. There are no transmittable viral hemorrhagic-fever type viruses that could cause fatal diseases here. Pathogens are clearly marked. Without precaution, someone could get sick."

Rivera tugged on the nitrile gloves and captured the attention of the agents. "We're ready."

Chad released the second door and sealed it behind them. Anger at the agents who'd invaded his domain tingled his fingers.

The audacity of their suspicions. He unlocked the third door and allowed them to enter the lab.

Rivera did a 180. "Spotless. Computers. Equipment. Work-stations. Biosafety cabinet to work with contaminants. According to the lab's plans, you've upgraded the airflow system. Are you positioning your lab to better adhere to standards before diving into your new job for the CDC?"

"Not at all. There's a level 4 lab in Galveston. My reason for adding extra safety measures was to ensure everyone inside was protected. Another safety element is the absence of sharp edges that tear the gloves."

"Shows your dedication."

Rivera's somber tone caused Chad to study him. "Are you surprised?"

"No, look, Dr. Lawrence, we have a job to do. We're not here to judge, only gather facts. We conduct our work and a separate team analyzes the results."

Hours later, the agents removed their protective garments and tossed them into the hazardous waste receptacle. The longer Chad had viewed their test tube search and scrutiny of his refrigeration system, the more his blood pressure soared.

"I insist you examine my car." They'd gone through his desk, briefcase, and mirrored his electronic devices. "I'll sign whatever the protocol."

"Vehicles in question are towed to headquarters," Rivera said.

"Permission granted." He kept his temper in check. "I'll take a taxi. Why not escort me, then sweep my apartment?"

"I'll drive you home."

Questions rolled through Chad's mind gathering storm clouds. Despite the late hour, he'd call Heather at his apartment and ask if she supported this unfair accusation. During the day he'd talk to Jordan, find out his reaction. Could Jordan have insisted the FBI conduct the search? Could this be a good thing and force the FBI to clear him?

A vital factor weighed on his senses. A virus test gave positive or negative results in fifteen minutes. "What's the operational status of my lab?"

"Closed until test results."

"How long?"

"When those making the decision have affirmed there's no evidence of H9N15 in your possession, we'll inform you. We project three days before you can reopen. But the lockdown may be up to twenty-one."

What was he supposed to do in the meantime? "Am I under arrest?"

Rivera shook his head. "As stated during your interview, do not leave Houston."

"What if I tell you where I'm going?"

"Not advisable."

"Will the media be told of my investigative status and the lab's closed doors? Or is my question above your pay grade?"

"I suggest you call ASAC Mitchell." He reached into his pocket and handed Chad a card.

"Mitchell is Heather's ASAC." Chad held the card while suspicions mounted against his wife. He stared into the faces of each agent before settling his attention on Rivera. "I expect a formal apology when you've proven I'm blameless in the accusations."

"I'll deliver it myself."

CHAPTER TWENTY-SIX

HEATHER'S CELL PHONE SOUNDED—Chad's ring, the music from "Wild Thing." She silenced the device before the call woke the other women. Besides, she had no desire to talk to him. He had no doubt spent a rough night with the FBI executing their search warrant, and now sleep evaded him. She'd be on his to-blame list.

Her phone alerted her again with an annoying vibration. She checked the time: 3:13 a.m., 2:13 for him. Avoiding him put off the inevitable. What happened to those moments when she clung to his every word, when she trusted their love would survive any crisis?

Heather carried her phone and disinfectant spray into the bathroom and closed the door. "Yes, Chad." She poured boredom into her words. "What's going on?"

"Are you convinced I developed H9N15?"

In the darkness, she closed her eyes. From the tone of his voice, he was beyond furious. She expected it.

"Yes or no, Heather?"

"Does it matter?" She despised the way they spoke to each other.

"The person who should know me best believes I'm capable of infecting passengers and crew with a killer virus?"

"For the record, I find the thought abhorrent, at times inconceivable. But you've surprised me over the past several months, and evidence shows you could have targeted all those people. You're not the man I married. You're quick-tempered and have more patience with a broken test tube than you do with people. You're eaten up with some kind of poison."

"So you supported the humiliating intrusion into my life. Out of revenge?"

"Seriously, Chad? Haven't you listened to a word I've said?"

Silence hovered over the conversation like dying sparks on a smoldering flame.

Like their ashen vows.

"If you're finished, I'm tired," she said.

"I'm overwhelmed with what's happened to me. I forget you're the one stuck in quarantine, alone, and pregnant. I'm way out of line."

"Yes, you are."

"Maybe I am when I look at it from your point of view. Peculiar, don't you think?" he said. "The one thing I'm committed to smacks me in the face—my career, life purpose, research. Were you told the FBI closed my lab until they receive results from their sweep? I can't work. My projects are at a standstill. I'm sure you have the ability to speed things along."

"You're asking me to help you?" Surely she'd heard wrong. "Under no circumstances will I attempt to influence an FBI investigation. If you're innocent, why stop an opportunity for positive proof?"

"Spoken as a true Fed."

"I'm dedicated to truth, whatever the cost."

"Now who's eaten up with self-importance? I want someone to confront and find out why. Who has accused me other than you and the FBI?"

"No clue, and I didn't initiate the interview. If I had a name, it would be confidential." Crackling tension swirled around her. "What else is on your agenda?"

"Why did you keep the pregnancy a secret?"

"Would the news of fatherhood have made any difference since you'd already stated your aversion to fatherhood, accepted the job in Atlanta, and moved out?"

"Don't forget your nagging about church and how you could never leave your FBI buddies in Houston. A baby alters the terms, which means I'll have my attorney include it."

"My apologies for the inconvenience," she said.

"Are you feeling okay?"

"I'm perfect."

"The baby's all right?"

"You contacted me because you're angry, not about my health or your child's."

"I suppose it sounds like a mixed message."

Heather swiped the tears, despising her emotions. At least he couldn't see her response. Whoever said love was the most powerful force in the universe had not met Chad Lawrence. But a surge of another kind rose in her . . . anger for being used. She'd helped to fund his education, supported him when his studies consumed his time, catered to his every whim—her own fault—and now he was finished with her. "I bet you need another doctorate."

"I had that coming, but you're not being fair."

"This has nothing to do with fairness. I've been a fool to put up with your sorry attitude. Follow through with your original ambitions, but I won't be on the other end of the phone to ease your frazzled nerves."

"I respect your wishes. I made a choice, and I'll stick by it."

Had he climbed the pole of selfishness? "Any regrets?"

"I wish I'd acted sooner."

His words stabbed at her heart. "The divorce or the virus?"

"You're way out of line."

"I'm finished with us, Chad."

"And I'll financially support our child. We can be friends, just not married."

"No thanks. Sign off on parental rights, and you'll be free of both of us." How she longed for the man who'd said, "I do," the man who'd bubbled with excitement whenever they discussed their future.

"I have a right to be apprised of the baby."

"Apprised? A child isn't something you check off a list or fit into your life when you have nothing better to do. You want your freedom? Leave me and my son alone."

"That's your stipulation?"

"Instruct your attorney to prepare a new set of papers with my conditions, and I'll sign them. I'm finished being used. Don't contact me again."

She pressed End, filled with loathing for the man who'd discarded her and his child like trash.

CHAPTER TWENTY-SEVEN

HEATHER REGRETTED THE WAY she'd allowed Chad to upset her. She'd attempted to sleep after his call, but fitful dreams, ghosts, voices, and even billboards blamed her for the virus.

The 9 a.m. press conference this morning could encourage viewers to offer evidence and free her from the torment. She massaged her arms as though the filth of whoever was responsible had rubbed against her.

And maybe he had.

Last night before going to sleep, she'd read her Bible. She prayed for those caught up in the virus, even those responsible. Thanked Him for the new life growing inside her and prayed the baby's test results continued to point toward good health. Her prayer concluded with a plea for the culprit to be stopped and face a jury. That pious action happened before Chad called, when she was convicted to kick-start a new prayer for forgiveness. Now she'd have to start all over again.

Today she'd concentrate on spending time with quarantined people. They needed to see her as a friend, to establish trust before

she could help calm their fears and find out if they knew anything to assist the investigation—whether they were aware or not.
Late morning, she'd remind Jordan about talking to patients in
isolation.

A jiggle in her stomach, then a second caused her to giggle.
So unexpected. She touched her womb. Her sweet baby boy had
kicked her, not once but twice. *Little one, I love you. Kick me 24-7.
Let me know you're alive and healthy.*

"I heard you laugh," Catherine whispered. "It was a sweet
sound."

"My baby moved for the first time."

"Boy or girl?"

"Boy."

"Congrats," Tatum whispered. She tossed back her blanket and
sat on Heather's bed between her and Catherine. "I've been praying for you and your baby."

"Oh, thank you." Heather's eyes moistened. "The initial testing
shows he's fine. The ob-gyn will monitor me until we're released."

Tatum took her gloved hand. "Any names rising to the surface?"

What a blessed diversion. "Since I was a teenager, I'd planned
to one day use my dad's name for a boy, Levi, and my mom's
maiden name, McCoy, for Levi McCoy."

"Love it." Tatum covered her mouth, but a laugh escaped
anyway.

"A strong name." Catherine scooted up in her bed and leaned
back against her pillow. "A baby is a gift, and your baby is hope
for all of us."

"What's all the whispering?" one of the women said.

"Heather's baby kicked for the first time."

"Aw, I'm sure you're excited. This is Jackie."

"Thanks," Heather whispered.

Ada chimed in with her congrats.

"So sorry to wake you," Heather said.

"Good news is never an interruption," Jackie said. "Be sure to write down the date and time your baby moved."

"Great idea." Heather grabbed her phone and calendared his little kick so she'd never forget how God blessed her in the midst of chaos. A news pop-up stole her breath.

> Dr. Chad Lawrence of Houston, Texas, is a person of interest in a deadly virus case on board quarantined flight 3879.

The embedded link to Read More urged her to continue, as though she hadn't already guessed the contents. As predicted, the report offered Heather's refusal to give Chad a divorce as motive.

"What's wrong?" Tatum said.

"Nothing I haven't heard before. I'd love to talk for hours and forget about why we're here, but I need to get ready for the press conference before everyone heads for the shower."

"Catherine and I are your friends."

"Me, too," Jackie said, and Ada echoed her.

"Your support means everything to me. Thanks y'all. We are in this together, the survivors." Heather used her phone's flashlight and grabbed her plastic bags of bathroom needs to begin the day. A slight smile spread over her face . . . little Levi had kicked twice, and she'd experienced a breakthrough with the other women in the dorm.

Heather reviewed the list of those quarantined and concentrated on the thirty-six people who'd sat in business class. Not all passengers originated in Houston. Three had red flags in their past activities—a woman had been in prison for grand theft, and she'd been transported from the plane to the hospital in critical condition. Two men were in quarantine. One man recently traveled to

China, where he disappeared for five days. He claimed mission-ary status while not showing a church affiliation in the States or Canada. A second man had a cousin living in Sudan. Agents were digging deeper, but so far nothing linked any of them to the crime.

Parker and Sonya Karey appeared to be an angry couple who'd sold everything to make a life change in Frankfurt. Heather watched them in every situation, always analyzing their behavior for signs of deceit.

Braden Taversty's contact in Frankfurt was Decker Anslow, a man from Houston who'd fled the country. German authorities held Anslow for questioning. Both men were booked to fly to India the day after the flight was supposed to land in Frankfurt. Houston agents swept Taversty's apartment and imaged his laptop. Agents in New York confiscated his mobile phone and learned both had been wiped clean before he boarded the plane. Taversty's par-ents owned a granite and tile company in Houston. They claimed not to have a relationship with him, Braden's choice. Although the older couple checked out squeaky-clean, a surveillance team kept an eye on them.

Heather entered the cafeteria for the press conference and sur-veyed the number of people scattered around the room. Some of the passengers and flight crew who hadn't exhibited signs when they entered quarantine were now hospitalized. Many around her appeared impassive. A few mingled in line for breakfast, and others sat at the tables. A haunting quiet pervaded as though they antici-pated their own death notices.

A female reporter spoke from a large TV monitor mounted to the right of a podium where Lacy Skaggs had spoken to them in the early hours of yesterday morning. Eight thirty-five a.m., and reporters were on the scene in the media room of New York's FBI building.

Heather grabbed coffee and scrambled eggs with sausage and toast. She attempted pleasantries with those nearby while keeping an eye toward the scrolling newsfeed. A few snubbed her, and many preferred an incommunicative state. Heather accepted their reluctance when her husband was on the FBI's radar. For most of them, a welcomed entrance into their lives required trust. They were frightened and angry. So was she.

She lowered her tray near Parker and Sonya. He glared, and the two picked up their trays and moved to a separate table. Catherine invited her to join the women from their dorm. Perhaps after the press conference, others would be open to friendship.

Her gaze settled on the TV monitor. SAC Bischoff from Houston and SAC Fielder from New York stood in front of a podium.

"Bet they don't board a ferry for here," Parker said.

Catherine turned and glared at him. "They can't figure out how to arrest who's responsible if they're infected."

"Did you notice there are fewer of us?" He snorted. "The sick and dying aren't receiving any notice from the suits. We're stuck here while they're collecting big bucks from taxpayers."

Catherine shook her finger at him. "You'd look a lot smarter if you'd hold your tongue until we hear what they have to say."

Heather hid a smirk.

Jordan walked to the front near the side of the TV monitor. "In a few minutes we'll hear from the FBI. At the conclusion, I'll take questions that pertain to the CDC. We're calling the virus H9N15. As information becomes available, the public can read on the CDC and FBI websites the latest developments. On the CDC site, viewers can ask questions, and those inquiries will be posted with responses."

Bischoff pointed to a reporter who had a question. "Why isn't a representative of the CDC with you?"

"Dr. Jordan Radcom, the director of the operation, is with those at the quarantine facility. We are in constant communication with Dr. Radcom. This press conference is to address the safety and well-being of American citizens. No reports exist of an outbreak outside of flight 3879. We are asking family and friends of those who were on the aircraft to reach out for medical attention if symptoms occur. We're also asking for any who have information leading to how this tragedy happened to contact the FBI using the number shown on the screen."

Another reporter asked to speak to SAC Fielder, and SAC Bischoff moved aside. "What is the current scenario for the passengers from the flight?"

"Our stats are accurate as of 8 a.m. Eastern. Of the 267 passengers plus crew, 152 have been infected. Of that number, twenty-nine have died. Those in quarantine will remain up to twenty-one days. The length may shorten if we're able to develop an antiviral."

Many in the cafeteria moaned and grumbled about the number of days they'd remain on the island. Heather shuddered at the increase in deaths. She dug her fingers into her palms. She was stuck in quarantine, yet she could be useful.

The press conference crowd buzzed.

"Is there a treatment?" a female reporter said.

"We are looking at a virus, which means medical personnel are treating the symptoms. Researchers are working around the clock to gather data before making recommendations."

"The virus you call H9N15 is termed an act of terrorism. Are there suspects other than persons of interest Braden Taversty and Dr. Chad Lawrence?"

Heather cringed at the sound of her husband's name.

"We are interviewing anyone linked to the case. I'm not at liberty to say more. The FBI and Homeland Security are working with various federal agencies for confirmation and interviews."

The persistent female reporter spoke again. "Do you believe Dr. Chad Lawrence could have developed the deadly virus?"

"The press will be updated as we have information. We—"

"Braden Taversty was arrested for an attempt to take over

the flight," the woman continued. "He's in serious condition at Jamaica Hospital. What's his statement?"

SAC Bischoff resumed the dialogue. "Ma'am, Mr. Taversty claimed he was innocent of any dealings with the virus. He is unconscious. We have an update to report from an investigative team. We believe early into the flight, the virus was released, its container destroyed, and remains flushed into the aircraft's sewage tanks. The new evidence has narrowed the guilty person's identity."

"Which one of the plane's restrooms held the evidence?" a male reporter said.

"We aren't at liberty to say," Bischoff said.

The male reporter spoke above the onslaught of shouts. "How was the virus transported through security? Isn't TSA responsible?"

"We are confident TSA did their job, and we are partnering with them in the investigation," Bischoff said.

"And you've confirmed no other international aircrafts have experienced the virus?" the same reporter said.

"Yes, sir."

"Any individuals or terrorist groups claim responsibility?"

"There are always those who want to take credit, but we haven't confirmed anyone. We encourage you to pose your questions regarding the investigation and medical situation on the websites and read all available information in the site's FAQ." He paused. "We will keep the media apprised of new developments. This concludes the press conference. Thank you for joining us."

The camera followed SAC Fielder and Bischoff exiting the platform. Heather listened to media comments and those quarantined around her. Her original assessment of grim stayed intact.

Jordan walked to the podium. "We are distressed and frightened, so let's get our questions out into the open. I'll be as honest and straightforward as possible."

CHAPTER TWENTY-EIGHT

HEATHER RESPECTED JORDAN'S ABILITY to show compassion in his verbal and nonverbal communication. He cared for these people, an honorable trait, and a man of prayer.

Again her heart ached for Chad and how the evidence stacked up against him. His integrity forbade him to devise such a plan, but "the end justifies the means" catchphrase shot through her mind like the crack of a rifle. The probe into Chad's motive had agents in the FBI's and other law enforcement's attention. Many could say he worked in conjunction with an accomplice, someone on board the plane.

She stiffened. Chills raced up her arms.

She could be implicated.

Married to a suspect in a criminal case.

Unaffected by the virus.

Jordan's voice jarred her alarm. "The staff must be informed of all illnesses," he said. "It's the best way we can stay on top of new outbreaks. Although the CDC is being pressured to release all those in quarantine, we can't comply or we stand to face uncontrollable contagion."

Catherine leaned toward Heather. "So many are sick while I've escaped the signs. Makes me feel guilty, ashamed."

"You're not alone." She rubbed her cold arms. "Many in this room are experiencing the same thing. Yet we're afraid we'll be next."

"Sobering. What disturbs me about this tragedy is the emphasis on whoever may have committed a detestable crime. Forever people will remember the guilty person. Why isn't the media focusing on the names and plights of the victims? How families are coping? Why aren't they reaching out for human-interest stories?"

"I agree," Heather said. "Possibly authorities are still contacting next of kin."

"The moment we are released, I will make sure the world knows about the victims. This can't be forgotten."

Heather wished she had words to convey the eruption of feelings pulsating through her.

"Not sure how I can ever board a plane again," Catherine said.

"Prayer. Courage beyond ourselves." Heather should heed her own advice.

A man stood from an adjacent table. "On a scale of 1 to 10, how does the H9N15 virus rate with Ebola?"

Not a muscle twitched on Jordan's face. "We don't have the stats yet for me to give you an answer. Ebola is not the only deadly virus out there, and there are various strains of it. Every virus has the potential to take lives. The CDC will not rest until we have answers. Federal, state, and local agencies are committed to investigating and researching who unleashed the virus, why, and developing an antiviral."

Tatum raised her hand. "What's next for the CDC?"

"To confirm what we grow in culture is what has caused the disease. The microorganism or other pathogen must be present in all the cases. Then the pathogen can be isolated from the diseased host, grown in pure culture, and be used to cause disease in another host."

"Dr. Radcom," Tatum said. "I need an explanation in language I can understand."

"I'm sorry. Let me break this into four steps. Number one, we'll test for all of the common viruses. So far nothing has been confirmed. Number two, because viruses are too small to see in a microscope, we'll look at infected cells through a microscope. Cells infected by a virus look different than normal cells or those infected by bacteria. Number three, to find what virus is causing the infection, we'll take a sample from an infected patient and use it to infect cells in the lab to grow and isolate the virus in a flask. After that, we'll perform a test to figure out the virus's genetic fingerprint. We'll map the sequence to similar viruses, although it will also have parts that are different."

"Won't the process take months? Because if what you described can't be done quickly, then a cure could take years."

"We are expediting every area, but we must be thorough. Again, if any of you are experiencing illness, please tell us. The sooner we can treat you, the higher the probability of recovery. Cooperation is key. We all must look out for each other and work together. Your concerns and questions will be confidential. My office is located down the hall behind me on your left." He pointed to Heather. "An FBI special agent is among us. Heather, would you join me up here?"

She walked to Jordan's side. Not a time for smiles.

"This is the woman who's responsible," the scruffy-bearded Parker said.

Heather wasn't surprised at his outburst. Neither would she address it.

Catherine snorted. "Deal with it and grow up. You're blaming a woman who puts her life on the line to protect you. You should be ashamed. She wiped up blood and vomit on the plane while you sat there with your eyes closed. I observed her heroism and your ignorance. You're a sniveling coward."

"If she'd given her husband a divorce, none of us would be imprisoned on this island. She's to blame for every sick person at Jamaica Hospital and those at the morgue."

"I will not tolerate any accusations," Jordan said.

"What if you were inconvenienced and losing money?"

"What if your wife was at Jamaica Hospital?" Jordan's even tone hushed the crowd. "What if you were dying?"

Parker grumbled but kept his mouth shut. A lot of bark.

Jordan caught Heather's attention. "From your perspective, how can we make the quarantine easier?"

"Patience is difficult under tragic circumstances, but we must follow CDC guidelines and stick together to survive the mental, emotional, and physical stress. Make friends."

Parker waved his hand. "I'm not receiving pay while I'm stuck here. As a federal salaried employee, you still get your money. Sit back and wait out the quarantine, Ms. Fed. What's the government doing for us?"

"I'm sure compensation is being discussed," she said.

He swore.

Thomas strode to the front dressed in jeans and a cream-colored knit shirt. His demeanor was pure professional mode. "If Dr. Radcom and Agent Lawrence would permit me to speak, I'd like to address one of the gentleman's concerns."

"Go ahead," Jordan said.

"My name is Thomas Powell. I'm the CEO for Software Developers International. For every person here who would otherwise be employed, I'll deposit an equivalent amount for lost wages into your bank account at the end of our quarantine. In turn, I ask for teamwork with the CDC, FBI, and law enforcement who have their lives on hold until the problem is resolved. For those hospitalized, I will offer monetary compensation to their families."

The room thundered with applause. Heather respected his position, a way to help ease some of the rising fears.

Jordan grasped Thomas's hand. "Mr. Powell, we appreciate your generous offer. When you proposed this to me earlier, I knew then I wanted you to speak directly to these good people."

"I'm honored to relieve some of the pressure. In addition, I'm prepared to contribute $4 million to the virus research." He returned to the back of the room.

His humble approach coupled with benevolence increased his likability meter among the crowd. Thomas Powell was known for his charitable contributions and his company's excellent reputation in the business world.

The room thinned, and Thomas approached her. "Morning, Heather."

She nodded a greeting. "These people and the CDC are fortunate to be the recipients of your kind gesture. Many people face financial worries, but you've alleviated their burden."

"It's something I'm equipped to do." He shoved his hands into jean pockets. "Are you helping the CDC and FBI keep peace here?"

"Something along those lines."

"What's important is treating the sick and arresting those responsible. Impossible for me. My comfort zone is to make things happen, not to watch life in a rearview mirror. If there's anything I can do to help Dr. Radcom, the CDC, or the FBI, please let me know."

"I'll pass on your offer. Understand medical and investigative authorities are trained to handle the matter."

"Can't be more dangerous than surviving the flight."

Parker stepped between her and Thomas while Sonya hung

back. Thomas excused himself, leaving her alone with the man she disliked.

He glanced around the room as though someone might hear him. "I'm positive many of the people here have their own version of justice. Just warning you I overheard two men state what they'd do to the killer."

"Did you offer to help them?" she said.

"I just listened."

"Perhaps they need a reminder that taking a vigilante attitude is followed up with jail time. You can help by providing any names of suspects."

He jutted his jaw. "Other than you, my list is just what I heard."

"Law enforcement can sift through the information. Providing a name will give you peace of mind, a sense of heroic satisfaction."

Parker swung back to Sonya, and she encouraged him to go ahead. "Okay, I'll cooperate with the local FBI." He grinned as though he held a game piece. "The blonde woman in her late thirties who sat adjacent from me in economy class. Wore a white sundress. First name of Irene or Renee. She was transported to the hospital's isolation unit late yesterday afternoon. She walked the plane and spent quite a bit of time in the bathroom."

Heather hid her recognition and typed the information to ASAC Mitchell. The FBI monitored the same woman who'd been in prison. "Thank you."

"Just doing my civil duty."

CHAPTER TWENTY-NINE

HEATHER MET JORDAN at his office to talk to the patients at Jamaica Hospital.

"I'll be with you the entire time," he said. "Due to the sensitivity of the patients' conditions, I'll monitor their responses for signs of distress. We have seven patients on the list."

"Only seven who are stable enough to carry on a conversation?" All those who'd been taken from the aircraft to Jamaica Hospital isolation made her nauseous.

"A few saw no point in talking to anyone from the flight. Several are too ill to speak."

"They're aware of why I'm calling?"

"Only of your desire to see how they're doing. Some recognized your FBI status, and others remembered your help on board the aircraft."

"Is it possible for me to have a copy of the recordings? I want to replay them later. Analyze the words and how they're spoken, then send my analysis and the recording to the FBI."

"Great idea." He set his phone on the desktop. "I'll request permission to record the conversation. Understand if a patient becomes agitated, the discussion is over."

"Is Mia on the list? She's the one I asked you about yesterday."

"She's our last person. The hospital tells me she's sleeping after a rough night."

"Has she gotten worse?" Heather's pulse sped.

"She's stable. Any of the patients can deteriorate at a moment's notice."

"Not my goal to upset anyone. I want to be a friend and listen."

"The little boy you mentioned? Frankie? He's termed in serious condition, but stable, a miracle since he has a history of medical issues. He's not able to talk today but soon. He was told you've been checking on him."

Sweet relief warmed her. "Thanks."

"Are you ready?" He handed her the piece of paper. "The first man sat in the economy section. He's recovering better than most patients. Excellent physical shape prior to the virus." He pressed in numbers. "Is Mr. Engels able to speak to Agent Lawrence?" He nodded at Heather and requested permission to record the conversation. With the man's consent, Jordan pressed the Record and Speakerphone buttons.

Heather introduced herself and thanked the man for agreeing to talk to her. "Sir, I'm glad you're feeling better."

"I'm one of the lucky ones." Mr. Engels's weak voice alarmed her. Hadn't Jordan claimed the man was recovering? "You apprehended the man who had a hostage." His labored breathing forced him to pause. "As ex-military, I regret my dormant reaction when you needed me. My symptoms hit with fever, vomiting, and a nosebleed at the same time the hostage problem occurred."

"You had yourself to manage," Heather said. "As a passenger and an FBI agent, I have a stake in finding the responsible person."

"You're free of symptoms?"

"So far I'm fortunate. Doesn't mean the memory of watching the virus unleash on the plane will ever go away."

"The killer deserves the chair."

She didn't care how a federal court sentenced the person, only for justice to rule. "The FBI discovered someone had brought the virus on board in a container. Looks like the container was smashed and flushed down a toilet, but that's all the info we can share at this time."

Mr. Engels used an expression she never used. "And we inhaled the poison."

"Possibly so. Do you remember anyone or anything suspicious?"

"Not at the moment." He coughed. "I have a foggy recollection of what went on, but I'll give it thought."

"If you can help, would you let a medical person contact me?"

"Sure thing."

"What can I do for you?" Heather said. "Is there family or friends I can contact?"

"My wife and kids would appreciate hearing from someone besides medical people or law enforcement. I mean you're FBI, but you were on the flight."

Jordan mouthed he had Engels's phone numbers.

"I was told your wife's number is available. I'll call her this afternoon."

"Thanks. She's germophobic, and the virus thing is freaking her out."

Heather finished the call and turned to Jordan. "Can his wife talk to him?"

"She'd have to make a request."

"I'll ask her. This could relieve some of the family's stress, and perhaps he could talk to his kids."

"We've encouraged communication to family and friends on Adam's Island, and it helps morale."

Over the next thirty minutes, Heather spoke to five more

patients—two men and three women. One man was Kirk Durgin, whom she'd seen boarding and again in business class. He expressed concern over his violin, and she promised to talk to the hospital about his possessions. He thanked her for offering to contact his wife. In the midst of their conversation, he developed respiratory problems and ended the call. A woman used the opportunity to rail against Heather for not having answers about Taversty's or Chad's suspected guilt. The others claimed appreciation for her call but had no information.

"Is it possible to talk to Frankie's dad?" she said. "He has to be an emotional wreck while grieving the loss of his mother."

"He calls the nurses' station several times a day." Jordan gave her Master Sergeant Franklin Dyer's contact information. "Not sure he's available now. In any event, you can leave a message."

She pressed in the numbers, and Franklin Dyer answered with full rank. "This is Special Agent Heather Lawrence. I'm at Adam's Island in New York with those quarantined from flight 3879. I spent a little time with Frankie on board the plane. He's a brave little boy, and we became friends. After your mother showed signs of the virus, I looked after Frankie."

"Thank you. Crazy worried about my son. You must have been one of the last people to talk to Mom."

"We didn't chat, sir, but we exchanged smiles while waiting to board."

"I took all she did for me for granted. Guilt's a nasty poison. Seems to eat me alive. Thanks for calling. My leave has been approved and I will be at Jamaica Hospital late tonight. I'm told I can't visit my son, but I can be persuasive. He'll know I'm there."

"Are you aware you can speak to him providing he's up to it?"

"No. I'm told he's conscious. I'll call the hospital now."

She gritted her teeth to control her emotions. "He's a special little boy, and I pray he continues to recover. Thank you for your service to our country."

"Thank you for checking on Frankie."

Heather ended the call. So many people victimized by one evil person's act.

"You okay?" Jordan said.

"Yes, I think."

"Heather, what you said eased the man's mind."

"He's carrying a huge load."

"As are so many dealing with the crisis. If you're ready, I'll see if Mia is awake."

"I am. She and I connected on the flight."

Jordan greeted a medical person and activated the speakerphone.

"Mia, this is Heather."

"How wonderful to hear your voice." Mia's labored words struck a distressful chord.

"Are you strong enough to talk? We can do this another day."

"I . . . want to. Arrests made?"

"Not yet."

"You okay?"

"I'm fine. Mia, you need your rest, so I'll talk fast." Heather explained how the FBI had uncovered evidence.

"Jerk."

Heather laughed despite the situation. "Wish I had a lead."

"Me . . . too. I'd kill them."

Heather had no reason to doubt her. "If you recall anything unusual, would you contact a medical person? They'll call me."

"K."

"I wish we had hours together. We can do those things when you're feeling better."

"Look forward to it."

"Oh, I learned my baby is a boy."

"Congrats." Mia's voice faded.

"Can I contact your husband and daughter for you? Dr. Radcom has the number."

"Please. I'd love that."

"Consider it done, and I'll make sure your husband has the number. He can talk to you directly. Get better so we can carve out some girl time." Heather ended the call and seized a moment to gain control.

If the responsible person was on Adam's Island, she'd find out.

CHAPTER THIRTY

CHAD BREWED THE LAST of his organic blend coffee from Whole Foods—a reminder of his life's work trickling away. He clamped both hands on the counter and fought the depression climbing into his whole body.

Since the FBI closed his lab, he'd found plenty of time to run trivial errands, the ones Heather used to do. He wanted to contact Jordan and vent, except the action gave *stupid* a new definition in the dictionary. Jordan wasn't pleased with his decision about divorcing Heather, and Chad feared losing his temper discredited his reputation. That would end his career. As of this morning, he'd been barred from the CDC secure site. He'd now learn new data as though he were an average person. But he wasn't the only person in history who'd been successful after an attack on his good character.

Keep telling yourself that.

Tomorrow the FBI should grant permission to reopen the lab, and he'd resume his projects. He longed to begin at the CDC with a spotless and vindicated record—even more, find a cure for H9N15 and deliver Heather and their son out of danger.

Useless to labor over his problems. Nothing within his power sped up the process. The one thing going for him was his laptop perched on the kitchen counter. His desktop sat behind the locked doors of his lab, but he could access his files here. This allowed him to catch up on paperwork until the FBI exonerated him from all charges.

Chad paused in his deliberation. The class 4 lab in Galveston had the equipment to test the contents of his lab, and he had credentials to log into many of their reports. They might have answers. He opened the lid to his laptop and typed in his password.

Assurance of one item gave him momentary peace—he hadn't been denied entrance. The downside was the FBI hadn't used Galveston's lab in growing cultures. How long before Houston authorities deleted his credentials to their lab?

After he poured a mug of coffee and added cream, Chad checked the various media for what gained the most attention. The top reporting networks offered a mix of New York's CDC research, the FBI investigation, and the latest fake news on his criminal status. Not the desired national acclaim Chad craved.

A report from NCN indicated Heather could have a role in the virus scare. Media requested a full investigation of her and a credible link to Chad's crime. Where did people come up with these outlandish ideas? What benefit could he or Heather have in spreading an uncontrollable virus?

He massaged his temples—a tension headache surfaced. Weariness settled on him, and his taste buds rejected the coffee. Without sleep, his productivity fell flat. He made his way to the bedroom and crawled under the sheets. He tossed and turned, played and replayed his conversation with Heather during the wee hours of the morning.

She'd never spoken to him with such . . . finality. The determination in her tone rattled across the miles separating them. Good for his future. But why didn't he want to celebrate? He'd soon be free to carry out his life's purpose unfettered. Aside from the dev-astation of being accused of a horrendous crime, he should break open a bottle of wine and make reservations at the finest steak house in town.

His mind spiraled to the depths of misery. He thought they'd be friends. She'd fly to Atlanta a few times a year, and they'd go out to dinner, but she wasn't interested. Motherhood had changed her. She refused friendship and demanded he sign off on parental rights. Not sure he wanted to accept both stipulations.

In the long run, a complete break made sense.

Chad's cell phone rang, and in his sleep-laden stupor, he snatched it from his nightstand without looking at the caller ID.

"Dr. Chad Lawrence, I'm a reporter for National Critical News. Lawrence Laboratories has been closed due to the incriminating evidence against you. What's your statement about the FBI's probe of your lab, and are you a developer of the H9N15 virus?"

"What?"

"Are you concerned of what the sweep will reveal?"

"I'm innocent, so why would I care?"

"Don't sound naive. Is it true you developed the killer virus to eliminate your wife?"

Chad ended the conversation. His blood pressure soared while anxiety battled his emotions.

His phone sounded again—the same number. *Forget it, buddy.*

Less than thirty seconds later, his phone alerted him to a call from a different number. No thanks. He wasn't an idiot to subject himself to repeated abuse.

Solitude usually calmed him when faced with problems, but unfair circumstances rumbled through his gut.

A third call unnerved him. Trembling, he silenced the device and navigated to a news network. One report claimed he was in

FBI custody. Another blamed the FBI for not arresting him. Still another network exploited his CDC position. NCN gave the most damaging report. One of their social media commentators labeled him a mass murderer, a killer who should be put out of his misery.

Chad's career in Atlanta was now flushed down the toilet like the remains of the container holding H9N15.

Who'd leaked the FBI's sweep of his lab? Had Heather changed her mind after their verbal exchange?

His phone vibrated with calls from unknown numbers. People left questions, threats, and accusations via messages. And Chad couldn't blame them. Whoever had infected so many people deserved a cruel death. Couldn't the media figure out it wasn't him? He tossed off the sheet and walked into the kitchen. The last of his coffee tasted lukewarm.

Chad's gaze panned his furnished contemporary apartment resembling his current state of mind—cold, sterile, and yet functional. It seemed to mock his alienation from the rest of the world. Why had this happened at a crucial time in his life when his dreams looked close enough to grasp? He'd sacrificed so much to keep his promise while he projected his goal focused on grasping a holy grail in medical research.

The doorbell alerted him. No point putting himself out there for a photographer or reporter. The person on the other side of the door could be an irate family member from one of the victims with a loaded gun. The doorbell repeated. Out of curiosity, Chad checked the security peephole.

An unidentifiable young man dressed in khaki pants and a loose knit shirt waited outside the door. He wouldn't get an interview or snap a pic.

An unbidden whisper swept across Chad's mind and squeezed his heart. Had his choices led to his miserable predicament?

CHAPTER THIRTY-ONE

THE FOLLOWING MORNING after Heather instructed Chad to leave her and their son alone, two more people died at Jamaica Hospital—Braden Taversty, who'd never regained consciousness, and the woman Thomas and the FBI suspected of distributing H9N15. The deceased woman's record showed she'd been clean since her prison stay. Still the FBI probed her background.

Taversty and his Middle Eastern connections had the FBI's attention. His death meant additional questions for Decker Anslow in Germany.

In the cafeteria, where the Wi-Fi signal was the strongest, Heather searched online for worldwide outbreaks of the virus. Satisfied the H9N15 appeared isolated to those on board the flight, she read through the plane's manifest again. She'd reviewed the people so many times her eyes blurred. Were any of them a part of the conspiracy? Doubtful a single person planned and carried out the crime.

Always Chad's involvement haunted her, like she'd exchanged her logic for stupidity. Suspicions continued to challenge what she remembered in the early days of their marriage. Had it all been an act? A buildup to the present?

She searched for links throughout all 267 passengers and crew. Did any share the same occupation or work for the same company, past or present? Had any attended the same elementary, middle, high school, or college? Ever share the same zip codes? Some searches would take time, and some links investigators might never discover. She typed requests to check for those who frequented the same restaurants, coffee shops, medical complexes, stores, gyms, faith houses and churches, and organizations. What were the passengers' destinations? She continued her search for those who could have been incarcerated in the same facility, belonged to sports affiliations, and even used the same travel agency. The FIG had the ability to obtain the information at their fingertips, much quicker than it took her to type out the request, but the process kept her involved.

She glanced at her in-box with work-related items that required her attention. A new email arrived from Mom, and Heather should answer it. Her parents knew the virus hadn't affected her, but the issue remained of not telling them the truth about her personal life. Hesitation showed disrespect for the two people who loved her most.

She pressed in Mom's cell number. Heather longed to hear their voices as though a glimpse of normal waved in the future. Her news would be bittersweet, and she'd much rather their conversation center on the baby than depressing topics. She clung to a grandchild boosting their spirits.

"Hi, Heather. We were just watching a virus update on TV. The reports are devastating. Are you still okay?"

"I'm good, Mom. Is Dad available? I'd like to tell you both a few things."

"He's right here. I'll put the phone on speaker." A moment later, Dad greeted her.

"Is it true, Heather?" Mom said. "Is Chad a suspect in the virus? What a loathsome accusation. We had no idea you two were having problems."

She closed her eyes. "Unfortunately, yes. Chad is under investigation. So far there's no evidence of his involvement. I'd like to believe him, except his guilt is possible. His lab's been swept and closed until he's cleared. I planned the trip to Salzburg to rethink my life as a single woman. But the media is now questioning if I'm involved."

"Oh, honey, I'm so sorry."

"Sweet girl," Dad began, "be honest with me. Is the media on target?"

"I'm not sure how to answer in view of what's been uncovered. One thing I'll say about the media. They present news in a way that initiates responses, emotionally charged ones. The truth will be exposed, but in the meantime, we'll hear facts and opinions. I apologize for not telling you our relationships had taken a nosedive. I wanted Chad and I to work it out, find what we'd lost."

She fought for strength. "But I have an announcement to cheer you up. You claimed at Easter you'd given up on the grandparent scene . . . but I'm pregnant. In January, you'll be the proud boasters of a grandson."

Mom gasped. "I'm happy and yet the circumstances make me sad."

"I feel the same," Dad said. "I'm super pumped a grandson is on his way, but I'm also worried. Is the baby all right with the exposure to the virus?"

"He's healthy. I'm under the care of an ob-gyn who works for the CDC. She's run tests, and I've received the initial results, which are good."

"Praise God." Dad's voice rose a notch. "Is Chad having an affair?"

"I have my doubts. It's all about his career, and he's supposed to take a position with the CDC in Atlanta in three weeks."

"Fat chance of him strutting his stuff there now."

"I imagine you're right. He moved into an apartment over a month ago." Silence met her, and she continued. "He learned about the pregnancy yesterday, but fatherhood hasn't changed his mind. Like a fool I thought he'd eventually agree to counseling. But earlier today I told him if he'd sign off on parental rights, I'd consent to a divorce."

"After all you've done for him, and now he doesn't want to be married?" Dad's voice escalated toward tilt. "Makes me want to take him hunting and use him as the target. You're better off without him and so is our grandson. Your mom and I will do whatever it takes to help."

"I appreciate it, Dad." Emotion threatened to overpower her. "I love both of you so very much."

"I detected something was wrong since Easter when you went with us to church and lunch without him," Mom said. "I'm sorry for not digging deeper. A successful marriage takes two committed people."

"He's become a selfish man I no longer recognize. Life centers on him and his work." Heather hesitated. "Truth is, I've changed, too."

"God will see you through this," Mom said. "Do you want your dad to pray?"

"Yes," Heather whispered.

Her phone buzzed with an incoming message. Right now the world could take a number.

Dad finished the prayer. He even asked for supernatural power to forgive Chad. "We'll be praying for you, the baby, those responsible, and investigators. Although I'm furious with him right now,

I can't see him resorting to murder unless his ambitions have left him deranged."

"Thank you," she said.

"Do you still love him?" Dad said.

How did she respond? "I'm back and forth on it. Rejection is a hard pill to swallow."

The call ended, and Heather brushed away tears beneath her eyes, filled with thankfulness for parents who gave her unconditional love. Weariness settled on her, a common occurrence over the past several weeks. She'd digest updates on her phone and take a nap. Her gaze settled on the words on her phone screen.

The media posted interviews and videos of families who'd been stricken with H9N15 and released grotesque images of the dead and suffering. An anonymous person sent several media outlets a photo of Chad and Braden Taversty together at a restaurant located near Lawrence Laboratories. She'd inspected plenty of altered images from editing software, and this one looked fake. Still it carried a buzz and that raised ratings.

Dread rolled through her veins. All the nights she'd sat home alone while Chad claimed his work kept him at the lab. Too tired when he got home to do anything but sleep. Sometimes she'd find him the next morning on the sofa still dressed. Had he lied or told the truth? She attempted to find any past behavior that plunged him into criminal status.

She believed his claims to be working all those empty nights.

She read nonverbal communication as habit, and nothing came to mind.

She hadn't overheard phone conversations to rouse suspicion.

He did have unexplainable hours away from home.

He had the skills to develop a killer virus.

He had motive to eliminate her from his life.

If the FBI proved Chad's participation in the virus, she'd lose confidence in her job as a special agent and behavior analyst.

Confusion over her myriad mixed conclusions washed over her. Had she crossed the line from love to contempt?

Answers . . . she craved answers.

Heather pressed in ASAC Mitchell's number. He responded on the first ring. "Who leaked the investigation? The media has charged Chad with murder."

"We did our best to keep his name quiet."

"The reports and the image of Chad and Braden Taversty are fake."

"We've determined the same. How will you handle the verdict if Chad is charged and arrested?"

"I despise the implication. If he is—"

"Love's blind, Heather. I have a meeting in five minutes."

"Please, how did the media get the info?"

"We have no idea of the origination."

CHAPTER THIRTY-TWO

HEATHER WALKED A FAMILIAR rocky path to the eastern shore of Adam's Island, past green maple, pitch pine trees, variegated brush, and yellow and purple wildflowers. Bleached white boulders lined the island's perimeter like a fortress. Add to the rock formations the presence of the National Guard, and those who intended harm kept their distance. She waved at a soldier who held a solitary post.

Heather stopped to admire the quiet beauty, wishing the fraudulent cloak of peace permanently masked the turmoil. A wisp of a cloud spread across the sky, reminding her of a child who fought for autonomy . . . or a husband's flight from a woman he no longer loved. With sadness engulfing her, she walked closer to the water.

The afternoon sun moved over Brooklyn and northeast to Queens, leaving shadows of the day behind. People busy with their lives breathed in the activity of their worlds.

Heather believed in the media's commitment to inform the public of breaking news as long as their reports raised the banner of truth. She sided with their constitutional right to free speech, but today a broadcaster supported the murmur of eliminating every person on Adam's Island. Another interview from a grieving woman, who'd lost a sister to H9N15, blamed Chad, the FBI, and the CDC. The woman went on to say she despised Heather's reckless and irresponsible behavior. "As a member of the FBI, Agent Heather Lawrence knew her husband's ability to inflict harm and chose to ignore him. Why isn't she speaking out?"

Far-fetched, and yet people clamored for more.

Heather leaned against a huge rock and listened to the waves slap and claw against the shore's edge. Rhythmic. Hypnotic. Each wave represented a lapse of time, moments when she longed to be back in Houston working alongside her team.

Would her son one day blame her for the shattered lives and premature deaths, a red stain in history as a result of her neglect?

Her intent to explore Salzburg had vanished for a crisis she'd never anticipated, but her desire to rekindle her relationship with God deepened. If anything, she needed Him more than before. How sad it took the reality of raising a child by herself to inch back to Him.

Oh, God, I'm so sorry to have replaced You with Chad. Please forgive me and guide me through today and tomorrow. I'm scared for my baby and the many people stricken with the virus.

She stared at the soldier who guarded the island. He held his rifle ready to swing into action. Did he fear contracting the disease? Did he have loved ones who needed him? Like those in quarantine, did he fear he'd be the next victim?

Heather walked toward the soldier to thank him for his service. He raised his rifle and bolted to his right, away from her. "Stop! Now!"

Her gaze swept his direction. A woman scrambled to the water's edge. She waded in. The water splashed at her waist . . . shoulders . . . A second soldier raced into the water. The woman swam with the agility of an athlete, but so did the soldier. He grabbed her and pulled her back to shore.

She screamed. "Let me go, you idiot. I don't have to stay here."

The woman could have drowned.

Or been shot.

Maybe stealing an opportunity for freedom looked better to her than staring down a killer virus.

Heather sat across from Tatum and Catherine in the cafeteria and listened to Tatum talk about her life in Houston. The young woman loved the vibrant city.

"You're a senior in college and plan to graduate early," Heather said. "Where are you attending? What's your major?"

"Rice University, and my major is communications, with minors in Spanish and Russian. I'll work for my dad while in grad school."

"What does he do?"

Tatum grinned. "He's the senior pastor at Mercy Community Church. Dad also has a radio and Internet ministry."

Catherine glanced up from a crossword puzzle, one of Mom's favorite pastimes. "My sister goes to Mercy and has tried to get me to change my current membership. The church is huge, a little intimidating."

"I understand. Our life groups provide a community environment and family feel."

"Once home, I'll attend to appease my sister and because I like the senior pastor's daughter."

"God's where His people worship," Tatum said. "I've grown up in the church. Can't picture not spending my life anywhere but in God's service. Dad's goal is to expand online ministries worldwide and in various languages. And God is calling me to jump on board the train, too."

Heather had envisioned Tatum's life anything but a Christian, confirmation first impressions were often wrong. Could the same judgment error in her psyche affect discovering the real culprit? Who hid their identity on Adam's Island?

"You have a noble calling," Heather said. "If we must be in quarantine, I'm glad it's with believers."

"Amen." Catherine closed her crossword puzzle book and turned a tender glance at Heather. "Are you praying?"

"Always. Afraid to stop in case the enemy gains a stronger foothold."

"You should be home enjoying your pregnancy, designing a nursery," Catherine said.

"I will when this is over."

"How far along are you?"

"Sixteen weeks."

Catherine shook her head. "You're not showing yet."

Heather patted her stomach. "Sad, and I keep checking for a bigger bump. My shape resembles a fence post. I'm sure to put on a few pounds soon—I'm looking forward to wearing maternity clothes."

"You'll get tired of them." Catherine laughed. "In my pregnancies, I resembled a barn with legs. Any morning sickness?"

"Queasy a few times. Mostly tired."

Catherine scanned the cafeteria, where others chatted and watched TV. She lowered her voice. "Bad enough you're stuck here pregnant, but now your husband's suspected of causing the problem. All the gossip gives people something to talk about."

Heather peered into the older woman's kind face. "After knowing him ten years, I thought I had him figured out." Chad's betrayal assaulted her. Love for him hadn't ended or changed her desire for his innocence. But if he had developed the virus, he deserved to spend the rest of his life in prison.

"I read where his lab in Houston is closed until the FBI is

certain there are no traces of the virus," Tatum whispered. "I can't imagine how you feel."

"The earliest testing results won't be released until tomorrow."

Tatum sighed. "I'm right here for you no matter what happens."

God had given her friends to walk through the maze of confusion. "Friendship works both ways. You two okay? No symptoms?"

"I'm too rotten to get sick." Tatum wriggled her shoulders like a kid. "The virus looks at me and runs."

"Dear Roy should have given it to me," Catherine said. "I miss him so much, and if I were with him, we'd be together in heaven." She lifted her chin. "Except it's a relief he's there and not in pain, and I won't be gloomy. He and I promised each other we'd be happy for whoever met Jesus first."

An image materialized of the many people who'd left the plane on stretchers . . . faces covered with a sheet or blanket.

The TV volume increased. A male newscaster appeared on the screen. "Live to you from the CDC building in New York City."

A hush rose over the cafeteria.

"At 3:15 p.m. today, an angry mob stormed the New York CDC building with violent demands for answers in the H9N15 crisis. The protestors, many armed with hammers and clubs, destroyed the lobby area and assaulted security personnel. Three workers were attacked. An NYPD officer intervened and was struck by a ball bat. Backup arrived on the scene and rescued him. He is listed in critical condition.

"NYPD used pepper spray to disperse the aggressive mob. Shots were fired, and a CDC worker received a leg wound from one of the protestors. At least ten people have been charged. Security in and around the CDC building has been tightened. The CDC facility will maintain an increased level of security until the threat of the H9N15 virus no longer exists.

"One of those arrested claimed the CDC has failed in their investigation. The man went on to say other breakouts in the city and in Houston have not been reported to the public. Houston has increased security at their CDC building."

"Can the situation get any worse?" a woman said. "My husband is in isolation. My daughter's dead. Now we hear the CDC may be covering up other cases."

"We'll never leave this island alive." A man raised his fist, his voice a roar of anger. "The National Guard will see to that."

The woman continued. "Even if we got away, where would we go? Our own country is keeping us prisoners."

"High time we took care of our own situation," another man said.

A male medical worker rushed to the platform. "Calm down. No new cases have been reported in other cities."

"Prove it!" The first man lunged at the medical worker and tackled him to the floor.

A woman shouted for help.

A child cried out for her daddy.

A man and woman knocked down a female nurse pushing a tray of blood samples.

Heather bolted from the bench as soldiers reached the chaos and rescued the workers. The assailants disappeared with soldiers while others silently challenged the crowd.

The medical worker stumbled to his feet and raised his hands to garner everyone's attention. Blood poured from his nose. "Please, we can't be caught up in fear. The CDC and law enforcement are on our side. It does no good to turn on each other."

Like the woman at the beach pulled from the water, people wanted a quick solution.

For now, the chaos had ended . . . but not the pounding in Heather's heart.

CHAPTER THIRTY-THREE

JORDAN WELCOMED HEATHER into his office. He'd texted her, said it was important. Most likely to hear what she'd witnessed in the cafeteria. She'd rather hear the case moved forward on all fronts.

The lines that once fanned from his eyes now reminded her of Midwest plowed fields, and the loss of sleep aged him each time they met. Her last look into the mirror showed she didn't look much better.

"What happened in the cafeteria?" he said.

She filled him in.

"I've asked for increased security." He motioned for her to sit, and he took a seat behind his desk. "The FBI requested your participation in a conference call."

She inhaled professionalism. No excuses for the bereaved wife and hormonal mother-to-be. "Has the FBI completed the initial testing of Chad's lab?"

"I'll let them explain the—"

"Have they found additional evidence against him?"

"No. But the CDC has Chad's job on hold. I contacted him earlier, so he's aware."

She imagined him fuming and pounding his fist into his palm. "The conference call isn't about the lab?"

"They will explain the investigation on their end." He pointed to his phone. "Three people are on the line—FBI SAC Fielder from here in New York, SAC Bischoff, and ASAC Mitchell."

"Can you brief me first?"

He sighed. "I'd rather not." He pressed a button. "Heather Lawrence is with me."

Fielder led the discussion. "Agent Lawrence, our conversation is to be held in strict confidence. Once I've finished, SAC Bischoff and ASAC Mitchell may have additional insight regarding sensitive intel."

"Yes, sir." Her pulse shifted into overdrive.

"Decker Anslow, the man being held by German authorities, confessed to his relationship with Braden Taversty," Fielder said.

"Tell me they were behind the virus." She held her breath.

"Pending. Taversty and Anslow were on a mission to fly to New Delhi, then drive to a remote area of Pakistan where they'd been recruited by the Taliban. Anslow claims they were interested in weaponry and training to bring down the US. Their specialty wasn't biowarfare."

"Sounds fuzzy to me. Evasive," she said. "Did he admit to meeting with Chad?"

"Said he'd never met or heard of Dr. Chad Lawrence, but Taversty had been advancing their cause and hadn't relayed his actions. Has Chad ever mentioned Braden Taversty or Decker Anslow?"

"No, sir."

"Had you ever come in contact with Taversty before the flight?" Fielder said.

"No, sir."

"Decker Anslow?"

"Not until his pic on the FBI secure website."

"When we make our statement this evening regarding Lawrence Laboratory's status, we'll confirm that the image of Taversty and Chad was Photoshopped."

"Is there evidence they were working together?"

"Just this link. We're questioning Chad again."

"Has Anslow made any other statements?"

"Nothing we can use for the current case. Agent Lawrence," Fielder said, "on July 3, Chad wrote you a check for $50K from his Lawrence Laboratories account, and you purchased a car. The balance is in your personal checking account."

How could the FBI conceive she'd betray her commitment to justice? But they needed to have answers, and she'd ask the same questions if she worked the case. "I'm glad you're thorough. I purchased a Ford Escape, and I can provide a receipt once in Houston."

"The dealership confirmed the cash purchase. Why did Chad fund you a new vehicle?"

"He came to see me on July 3. He had divorce papers with him. I'd refused to sign previously. He handed me the check to buy a new car and said mine needed replaced."

"But you didn't sign?"

"No, sir. If the check was a bribe, he lost." How much should she reveal? Why hide anything? "Since the quarantine, he's learned I'm pregnant. I'm sure you have access to my medical records here and are aware. Today I agreed to whatever he wanted if he relinquished parental rights."

"Appreciate your candid answers, Agent Lawrence. Nothing in your activities implicates you in the case. Are you and your husband communicating?"

"No longer. Our discussion today terminated reconciliation. He accused me of the media leak, and I didn't handle it well."

"Do you suspect Chad?"

"I'd be a fool if I didn't have reservations. I'm in the process of recalling past conversations and behaviors for a clue. Nothing's surfaced yet." She'd state the obvious. "Except I haven't contracted the virus, and my husband is a suspect. Do Chad's financials show a discrepancy?"

"We've found no irregularities. Taversty's finances are supported from an unknown source out of Europe."

But for many, the denial of Chad linked to Taversty at least in this context meant zip. "Did Anslow provide names regarding what he and Taversty were doing as part of the Taliban?"

"Authorities in Germany are working with their terrorist informants. The surveillance team on Taversty's parents hasn't reported anything unusual. Anslow's wife is in Pakistan. She'd been in the US illegally. His parents are deceased," Fielder said. "Two men have been cleared. The man who traveled to China and went dark for five days works underground for a Christian mission organization. And the man who has a cousin in Sudan was there due to a cousin's illness. A new development prompted this call. I'd like for you and Dr. Radcom to know our findings."

She glanced at Jordan, who gave a thumbs-up. "We're ready."

"The investigation has uncovered evidence from the aircraft that leads to another suspect. A fragment of the breath freshener containing the virus was found beneath the seat of a passenger in economy class, Parker Karey, who was flying with his wife, Sonya, one-way to Frankfurt. For the record, we received an anonymous call soon after the plane landed at JFK with sufficient info to back up our concerns leading to Chad's interview."

"A name?"

"Untraceable. The Kareys have our attention. Have you had any dealings with either of them?"

"Parker has been quick to accuse Chad and me of being responsible for the virus. Very verbal. Even a subtle threat. Reminds me of a barking dog." She ventured on. "Were fragments found throughout the cabin?"

"Only in the business class restroom where the remains were flushed and in the vicinity of Karey's seat. We understand it could have been transported by someone's shoes or anyone in the area."

Heather needed time to analyze the new info. "Dr. Radcom relayed to me about the shattered breath freshener found in the business class sewage tank. I told him the flight attendant wouldn't have permitted anyone from economy to use the restroom. However, someone could have slipped by."

"Exactly what we're thinking," Fielder said. "Or a coincidence."

"Have any traces of the virus been found in Chad's lab?" Heather said.

"So far the sweep of the lab, office, apartment, and vehicle are free of H9N15, and a surveillance team remains in place. He won't be exonerated until investigators are assured his lab is clean. We're waiting the minimum of seventy-two hours, but authorities may recommend the lab's closure for a longer period. Are Parker Karey and your husband friends or associates?"

"Chad's never mentioned him. Why?"

SAC Mitchell interjected. "Heather, look beyond the man you're married to. Karey and Chad live in the same city, and both may be involved in a heinous crime that has killed several people and placed many in the hospital. H9N15 has the potential to spread across the globe. Online buyers are digging for means to purchase it. Your husband has the ability to develop the virus and present a vaccine to the masses and gain worldwide acclaim. Can you imagine the monetary returns? What are the chances the two men are connected?"

"Higher than I'd like to think."

SAC Fielder stepped back into the conversation. "Neither Parker nor Sonya Karey has been infected. Are they lucky or vaccinated?"

Heather stated the obvious. "I haven't either. That fact decreases my credibility."

"Agent Lawrence, if we believed you participated in the crime, we wouldn't be having this conversation. We appreciate your answers to our questions. We're interviewing business and personal acquaintances and the organizational affiliations who have any dealings with Chad, Parker, or Sonya. Two terrorist groups are taking credit with no proof, and we're making inquiries."

"Have you questioned the Kareys?"

"Everyone has been interviewed. Nothing hit our radar about the couple until now. If they are behind the virus, they've covered their tracks. Can you get closer to Sonya?"

"I'll try. She doesn't say much. Her body language tells me she's bullied, does whatever Parker tells her, and they're always together. But it wouldn't be the first time a man took orders from a woman."

"Do any others in quarantine have your attention?"

"Just frightened people whose lives are upside down." She glanced at Jordan, who gave her a thin-lipped smile. "I'm concerned my efforts to befriend the people have been met with opposition. But I'll continue. Those in isolation at Jamaica Hospital seemed pleased when I offered to call their families, which I've done. May I remain in contact with the patients?"

Jordan spoke up. "I can give you the direct number to each person's room. If any of them refuse communication, for the sake of their well-being, I expect you to honor their wishes."

"I understand." Now she comprehended why Jordan listened to the conversations—welfare of the patient and a report to the FBI of her loyalty. She wasn't upset. Every precaution needed to be taken.

"Dr. Radcom, keep us updated. Heather, do whatever it takes to get close to the Kareys," Bischoff said. "You're the best, Heather. We're counting on you."

Heather left Jordan's office with her mind in investigative

mode. She'd done her homework on the Kareys. Updates gave her more information. Ten years ago while in college, Parker was arrested for possession of an illegal substance. Nothing since then. He'd recently been dismissed during a downsizing of an oil company. Sonya taught second grade for Houston Independent School District. They'd filed bankruptcy. They liked to collect things. Problem was, they couldn't pay for their expensive tastes—two Harleys, two new cars, a boat, high mortgage payments, and credit card debt. The one-way tickets to Frankfurt necessitated an explanation—unless one of them had a job to cure their financial woes. Or they'd arranged for a payoff.

What the people on board flight 3879 experienced must never happen again.

Heather dropped her phone into her shoulder bag and walked back toward her room. There she'd weigh all she'd compiled about the flight, manifest, Taversty, Chad, and the Kareys. She zeroed in on the women in her dorm, but they'd been cleared and Maria's condition at Jamaica Hospital declined. She'd scrutinized every person in quarantine, examined their records, and studied them again. Had her ability to read people slipped?

Terror coiled around her heart. Other agents claimed she saw personality issues before others. Agent Heather Lawrence had the punctual, organized, manicured, and compassionate set of standards going for her. She'd lived up to it by filing away at the rough places in her life. Then her life crumbled. She still had professionalism in her walk and talk. Right?

Heather turned a corner into the hallway. The Kareys and Thomas talked together.

"There's our destroyer of dreams," Parker said. "Hope you're careful. The rocks near the water are treacherous."

Heather stopped and marched toward the threesome. "Mr. Karey, twice you've threatened me."

"Can't prove it." He sneered.

Thomas lifted his gray eyes that were neither warm nor hostile. "Agent Lawrence, as a federal agent you have a right to arrest Parker, and I wouldn't blame you. He might consider an apology instead of facing a different type of isolation."

"Please," Sonya whispered, "apologize."

Heather waited, allowing her irritation to simmer.

"You misunderstood me," Parker said without eye contact. "I was suggesting everyone should be careful walking the shoreline. The rocks are treacherous."

CHAPTER THIRTY-FOUR

FRIDAY LATE MORNING, Chad paced his apartment, a man locked in a dungeon not of his own making. If all went well, he envisioned opening his lab later tonight. The FBI said they'd have their test results for H9N15 in three days, and that was hours away.

Who'd flashed the phony image of him and Braden Taversty across the Internet? Somebody fed the media just enough candy for the vultures to crave more. He silenced his devices until he had the intestinal fortitude to read the reports.

Who was he kidding? His career had exploded, and not in a good way. Jordan had used "on hold" to describe his CDC position. He poured a third cup of coffee, though his stomach burned from drinking the stuff on an empty stomach.

Solitude had never bothered him, actually his preferred method of concentration. He longed for the comforts of his lab, familiar sights and the hum of equipment. The satisfaction of contributing to the welfare of the world soothed him. The trick would be how to leave his apartment without an onslaught of reporters.

His doorbell rang, and he stared at it while anger burned hot for the unfairness. Next came the incessant knocking.

The doorbell repeated, and the person knocked. Chad walked to the door to see who was on the other side of the peephole. A text sounded.

This is Agent Javier Rivera outside your door. We need to talk. Are agents with you?

I'm alone.

Good news or devastation? What if Heather had been stricken with the virus? He typed. **Okay. Not in the mood for a trick.**

He opened the door, and true to his word, Rivera was solo. The agent took a step inside and Chad locked the door behind them. Rivera scrutinized the apartment as though weapons were stashed in the woodwork.

"Do you have an official apology?" Chad said.

"Depends." Rivera studied him. "I smell coffee. Mind if I get myself a cup?"

The agent used audacity as a platform. "Sure, why not? You're not worried I'd add a deadly virus to it?"

"Nope. That would be stupid on your part." Rivera walked into the kitchen and grabbed a mug from the cabinet.

"Cream's in the fridge. Sugar beside the coffeemaker. Spoons are in a drawer on the left."

"Thanks." Rivera opened the fridge door.

"The FBI has exonerated me?"

"Not yet. Let's talk, figure out the who and why of the virus."

Chad blew out his frustration. "Excuse me for my lack of trust."

Rivera turned to him and gulped a drink. "Great coffee."

"You've finished the last of my beans. Learned last night that I can't venture outside with reporters perched."

"The disruption won't end until someone stamps the case

Solved." Rivera pointed to the kitchen counter. "As you'd expect, questions lie beneath the surface."

The agent thought he had the situation under control. Chad grabbed his own mug and pulled out a stool. "I'll give you five minutes."

Rivera led the market in impassive stares. "The official word won't be until after 6 p.m. tonight, but so far you're cleared of H9N15 in your lab, office, home, and vehicle. I don't have the jurisdiction to approve reopening the lab. Medical authorities may impose the closing for the total twenty-one-day period."

"I told you my lab held no traces of H9N15. Eighteen to nineteen additional days is extreme."

"Not my call and the virus is as fatal as Ebola or Marburg."

Rivera had done his homework. "What else? Why didn't you send me a text with the update?"

"I have questions. How are you connected to Braden Taversty and Decker Anslow?"

Chad rose from the stool and sent it crashing to the floor. "I keep up on the news, and I've never seen or talked to either of them. The photo of me with Taversty is a fake."

Rivera glanced at the floor. "Lose your temper much?"

"When I've been falsely accused of murder."

"Then help me."

Chad's labored breathing slowed, and he righted the stool while Rivera observed him. "Taversty and Anslow are strangers to you?"

"Yes."

"Do you know Parker or Sonya Karey?"

"Names don't sound familiar. Do you have a photo?"

Rivera handed him his phone with a pic of the couple.

"No clue. How are they connected to the virus?"

"They were on the plane and now on Adam's Island." He stared into Chad's eyes. "Are you certain they aren't familiar?"

"Positive. You've given me the names of two people who haven't been infected by the virus. Have they accused me? Stated I know them?"

Rivera finished his coffee, as calm as if they were discussing the summer heat. "My questions are part of the investigation."

Chad concentrated on what Rivera didn't say. "They have implicated me, but so has half the world. The FBI works in pairs. Where's Agent Tobias?"

"At the office."

Chad knew protocol. "Were you sent to secure my trust in hopes I'd unload evidence?"

"I'm not convinced you're at fault. If you're connected in any way, tell me now."

"Are you reading my body language for signs of deceit? Did you expect me to crack under the pressure of losing my career and facing prosecution?"

"I have other reasons to work this case than my job. I told you at the FBI office my sister died of flu. While my instincts point to your innocence, the investigation's not over."

Discouragement weighed on Chad's shoulders as though he wore a five-hundred-pound yoke. He prided himself in his achievements—performance meant everything to him, and the FBI had snatched it away. He wanted to throw another stool. How could he convince the idiots at the FBI he was on their side? Heather interpreted how much a person knew by what they displayed in their body language. Was Rivera blind?

"Agent Rivera, I have no knowledge of the virus. I've read and heard the accusations. All lies. I swear I'm not your man."

Rivera's scrutiny offered no indication of his conclusions. "I'll contact you later with the determination of your lab."

Once Rivera left and Chad bolted the door, reality strutted across his thoughts as though someone had bannered it across the sky. The Kareys and Heather were in quarantine together. Had she gained their sympathies? Did she believe Chad tried to kill her?

He'd walked away from her, and she hadn't taken it well. Some rejected women turned to a new man. Some chose vengeance, a way to get even in the worst way. And she was pregnant . . .

Neither sounded like the woman he'd known for ten years.

If the virus hadn't taken over his life, he'd be packing for Atlanta.

CHAPTER THIRTY-FIVE

CHAD PURSUED EXONERATION from all charges, suspicions, and gossip of H9N15. If the FBI couldn't find the responsible person, he'd proceed with his own investigation.

He pulled a hardbound journal and smart pen from inside his computer case and sat at the kitchen counter. Some termed his method of note taking as old-school, but his preference fit into his brain's method of operation. Later he'd download his thoughts to his laptop and review them.

He wrote every detail since the first of the year. With the same mind-set he examined medical data, he read and reread his copiously written recollections.

He'd never threatened Heather.

He'd never looked at another woman.

He loved his wife more than his work, but no one understood his actions.

He'd made it known that fatherhood was not for him.

He'd asked Heather to stop the God nonsense.

He'd told no one about his CDC application and acceptance.

Had someone else applied for the position at the CDC and regretted Chad's appointment? Out to get him? He crossed that off his list. The organization recruited those who were committed to helping others, not stabbing competition in the back.

Chad jotted down meetings, phone conversations, and text messages from every contact since February, when Jordan told him his application had been accepted. He backed up minutes of the day and who was with him. His life didn't prompt a diabolical plot to kill his wife or the many people affected by the virus. How could he smuggle the virus on the aircraft without an accomplice?

Braden Taversty provided the means, and the man's terrorist affiliations made it all feasible. Were investigators working on the theory that Chad developed the virus and ensured Taversty would die when it was released?

Why question Chad about Parker and Sonya Karey?

If Chad wanted Heather dead, he'd have cut her brake lines, arranged for an accident at the condo, or poisoned her. Those methods negated placing him center stage. Yet someone disposed of evidence in a sewage tank, but the FBI hadn't announced where on the plane or the type of container. Why? Did they conclude they should deny the public details while they worked a different angle? A person or people on flight 3879 had an agenda for murder?

At 12:15, he navigated to the CDC website and read the manifest. He checked the list of deceased and infected people, confirming a suspicion. How many investigators arrived at the same stats? Surely media had made the deduction. Some reports added Heather to the list of accomplices, using her business class presence and noncontraction of the virus with her tie to him.

Chad paced across the small room. Opening the blinds tempted him, but a reporter in at least one building waited to tap into the next story with a fresh pic of Dr. Chad Lawrence. Where did he go from here? His experiences with crime limited itself to evaluating cells under a microscope.

A conversation with Heather was impossible with her ultimatum, but Rivera might drop a few bread crumbs. The clock read after three on a Friday afternoon.

He texted the agent.

Are you available to talk?

Tonight's fine. 6:30 okay? I'll bring dinner.

Good news?

FBI will announce fake photo of you and Braden Taversty.

I'll take it. When?

10 p.m. news.

Do you have the final word on my lab?

Not until 6. I'll bring the determination with me.

Agent Tobias?

Not sure.

CHAPTER THIRTY-SIX

HEATHER CHECKED THE TIME on her phone and the clock on the dorm wall. Nearing 5 p.m. in Houston, she waited for ASAC Mitchell's call to give her the FBI's stand on Chad's lab.

She craved answers, but where were they? If traces of the deadly virus were found, her husband faced imprisonment . . . her son's father.

She rubbed her arms. How could she ever return to her job with any confidence? She might not have a job. Then what? Cowards refused to face the truth about themselves, and the label crushed her. How could she ever explain to their son what his father had done and how she'd been too blind to recognize the signs?

She was overreacting. Hormonal.

She'd do whatever was asked of her to end the turmoil.

An antiviral found.

An arrest made.

An end to the helplessness of quarantine.

A twinge of white-hot pain seared her abdomen. She jerked

and grabbed her stomach. What had happened? What did it mean? The knife-piercing intensity lessened and disappeared. Could be something she ate.

"Are you all right?" Catherine eased onto the side of Heather's bed.

"I'm okay. Must have been a muscle spasm."

"Shall I call for a nurse?"

Heather shook her head. "It's gone."

Tatum walked across the room and sat on a small rug on the floor. Jackie and Ada were gone from their room. Since the latest media blast with the image of Chad and Taversty together, Jackie and Ada kept their distance as though she carried the virus.

Her phone buzzed. ASAC Mitchell's name spelled across her screen. "Yes, sir."

"Chad's cleared of H9N15," Mitchell said. "Included is his lab, office area, apartment, vehicle, and the imaging of his devices. His online calendar details every minute of his time, and although we'll continue to observe his activities, his background checks out. Neither do phone records link Chad to controversial numbers. The investigation isn't conclusive. Recommendations are to keep Lawrence Labs closed for the full twenty-one-day period."

The extension of the lab's shutdown had merit. "I'm glad. We'll all have assurance no traces of the virus exist. Like you, I want solid proof."

"Has blackmail crossed your mind?"

"Makes sense on some level. But it's hard for me to think Chad would agree to pursue a deadly virus no matter what the stakes."

"What if you were the target?"

Her deliberations hadn't taken her there.

"Quiet on your end," Mitchell said. "What haven't you told me?"

She touched her mouth as though forbidding reality. "Chad's a realist. He'd sacrifice my life to save others."

"Is that what he attempted and failed?"

"You nailed the big question," Heather said.

"How many victims does it take for a killer to prove his point, whether it be Chad, Taversty, the Kareys, or someone else? We're not discarding any possibilities or links in the investigation."

She relayed Parker's latest remark and the result.

"You're in a prime position to find evidence. I'm reiterating what SAC Bischoff said earlier, but you're our ace." He ended the call.

Heather studied Catherine's hand wrapped around hers. The woman had heard way too much of a one-sided conversation.

"My hearing's bad," Catherine whispered. "Memory's bad. Must be age."

"And I didn't understand any of it," Tatum added.

Dear friends. She explained the status of Chad's lab.

"Semi-good news." Catherine hugged Heather. "Now you can breathe easier while those on the outside search for the killer. If nothing's surfaced in your husband's lab at this point, aren't the remaining days a formality?"

"Depends on who's talking, and I'm fine for an arrest to happen today."

Catherine smiled at Tatum. "The three musketeers can celebrate a step forward at dinner."

Heather nodded. "I'm ready for dessert. Cookies, cake, pie—bring it on."

Truth. Betrayal. Fault. No solid answers. But she'd not spoil the mood for Catherine and Tatum. They deserved a reprieve.

"Oh, my goodness." Tatum held a tissue to her nose. Blood soaked through.

Heather rushed to retrieve a fistful of tissues from her own box and slid to her knees to hold them on her friend's nose. Heat radiated from Tatum's face. "I've got this." *Keep calm. This could have a legitimate explanation.* "Are you nauseous?"

"A little." She coughed, and blood stained her mask.

Catherine headed for the door. "I'm going after help."

Heather didn't glance up. "Have you vomited?"

"About an hour ago." Perspiration dotted her forehead. "Please, stay back. I don't want you to be sick."

"If I haven't contracted it yet, then I'm good."

"That's what I thought." Tatum coughed. "Be careful."

Watching Tatum disappear inside a medical helicopter to Jamaica Hospital moved Heather to shed one tear after another. What if she never saw her new friend again?

The young woman who'd embraced God's call on her life.

The young woman who'd been held hostage on board the virus-ridden plane.

The young woman who'd befriended her.

Heather wrapped her arm around Catherine's waist, and the two walked inside the building. The older woman sobbed, most likely reliving Roy's suffering and death.

CHAPTER THIRTY-SEVEN

AT 6:30 P.M., CHAD RESPONDED to his doorbell after Rivera had texted of his arrival. The agent held a bag from Whole Foods, a dinner option they'd decided upon in the afternoon—healthy eating. Chad invited the agent to come inside.

Rivera walked to the small kitchen counter and pulled out organic coffee beans from the Whole Foods bag. "First things first. Good coffee makes for good friends. I drank the last of yours earlier today."

Difficult to befriend a man who investigated him. "Thanks." Chad ground beans while his mind whirled along with the grinder's hum. He sympathized with Rivera losing his sister. The agent's quest to find the guilty person stemmed from personal and professional experience.

Life always tossed in complicated obstacles, and one man's drive was another man's incentive to push ahead and solve problems. For Chad, he'd go to his grave blaming himself for Paul's death.

He poured filtered water into the coffeemaker while tamping

his desire to dive into the obvious. Ridiculous to wait. "What's the status on my lab?"

"The FBI chose to wait the full twenty-one days."

"Not exactly what I wanted to hear." He refused to show the intensity of his fiery emotions. "Yet, I'm not surprised."

"Which is why I wanted to tell you myself." Rivera unloaded the food on the table according to the individual orders. "I have hot rolls and butter. Not on the wife's diet for me, but they are a weakness."

"They smell good."

"We got off to a rough start. What do I call you?"

"Chad. Your first name is Javier?"

"Yes. Gets us on a first-name basis."

"I don't have a confession or evidence. So wipe a promotion off your radar." Chad poured coffee and handed a mug to him. "You know where the cream's kept."

Javier grabbed half-and-half from the fridge, dumped in a healthy amount, and handed it to Chad. Something they had in common. Reaching into the cabinet, Chad pulled out his two plates and silverware. He preferred a real plate and utensils to Styrofoam and plastic. He looked at the kale salad and grilled chicken breast. Javier had meat loaf and tomato soup.

"I'm starved. No time to eat today," Javier said.

"Me either."

Javier crossed himself before grabbing his fork. Another one of those religious fanatics.

After a few minutes of silence, Javier downed his coffee and refilled it. Chad sensed he was ready to discuss something. "Sorry about your lab. Sorry your marriage is ending. Sorry Heather doesn't support you."

Chad gripped his cup. "We aren't discussing my personal life."

Javier frowned. "All right. What happens to the lab when you leave for Atlanta?"

"You mean if the CDC doesn't yank the position?" Chad pushed his salad around the plate. "A doctor is interested in managing the day-to-day operations. My assistant's incredible, but he doesn't have enough experience. I can oversee operations from Atlanta. The FBI's investigation may have me flipping burgers." He remembered a critical detail. He hadn't arranged for Heather to split his retirement in the settlement. None of Javier's business.

"What topics aren't off-limits for you?"

"I'm sure you have an agenda. Two visits without your partner in one day signals desperation to make an arrest. I do have a topic to toss out." Chad hoped Javier didn't laugh at the bizarre idea. "Would you help me clear my name? Unreachable for me to tackle by myself. You claim you're driven to take vengeance for your sister's death. Says to me you're a perfect candidate. We could work on the case after your scheduled FBI hours."

Javier laid his loaded fork on his plate. "You want me to assist you in finding who developed and spread H9N15 while I'm also investigating you?"

"Exactly. Put yourself in my shoes. Could you live with yourself if people believed you'd developed a killer virus? I figure SAC Bischoff will claim the idea is ingenious. He'll commend you on your ingenuity to spend extra hours in my company and the many opportunities for you to scrutinize my words and actions."

"Even if I received permission for your insane idea, you cannot be privy to FBI reports or activity on the case. If the public doesn't receive the info, you won't either."

"I don't expect preferential treatment. My proposal unites our private goals."

"Unites? Strange choice of words." Javier excused himself and stepped into the hall of Chad's apartment building.

He expected him to call SAC Bischoff with the request. The two men would strategize how to make the arrangement work for the FBI, which was what Chad wanted. He reached for his journal and pen on the counter. Ten minutes passed before Javier entered the apartment.

"What's the decision?" Chad said.

"Off the books. I'll go along for a while."

"And you'll make SAC Bischoff aware of what we do?" Javier confirmed, and Chad moved forward. "Take a pic of my notes so you can follow my thoughts. Been at this most of the day."

Javier snapped his phone camera over the journal while Chad turned pages. He hadn't taken time to note how much he'd written.

"Where do we start?" Javier said.

"Honesty. I've looked at every name on the manifest, specifically those seated in business class."

"The FBI has conducted interviews since the case started."

Irritation threatened to spoil his facade, but Chad recognized Javier's limitations. "It's clear more people are sick from the business class section."

"I've read the data."

"A no-brainer that the virus was released there, and the remains were placed in one of the toilets. That narrows the suspect list. No need to respond, Javier. I'm right."

"You are entitled to an opinion."

"While you were outside my apartment door, the media concluded the same thing. Ironic, don't you think? Still the same report didn't negate me as the developer because Heather was in business class. I've been accused by the best of well-meaning citizens. But you've only questioned me about Taversty, Anslow, and the Kareys. Why?"

"You have no idea who's been interviewed."

"How do you intend to work the trust issues between us?" Chad said.

"Like any other case. Has to be earned."

"Deal."

CHAPTER THIRTY-EIGHT

HEATHER WOKE with the same pain in her navel area as earlier in the evening, a sharp, knifelike twist. She'd been asleep since after dinner. Nausea added to the mix. She tossed back the thin blanket and rushed from the bed to the bathroom and vomited. The virus had invaded her body. What about her baby son? The dread of facing a miscarriage covered her like a death shroud. She should have gone to Jordan's office when the pain first appeared.

Please, God.

Death chased her baby, and she had no bullets to protect him. She should trust God, but an assault against her precious gift was unfounded. Anger rolled and rumbled against God for the injustice. The unfairness.

She'd taken care of the sick on the plane. The fingers of guilt pointed back at her. If she were infected with the virus, her baby's life was in danger. And it was her fault.

She vomited again—her body doubled over with pain. After

washing out her mouth, she stared into the mirror. A ghastly pale woman looked back at her. Hollowed eyes and sunken cheeks.

A knock on the bathroom door and Catherine's voice met her. "Heather, what's going on?"

"I'm cramping, throwing up, and I hurt in the upper right part of my back."

"Spotting?"

"Thank goodness no. I need a nurse or a doctor."

"Hold tight. I'll get help." The second time Catherine had raced for medical assistance.

Heather sat on the floor with her head between her knees. Her baby boy had to be okay. If she lost him, she had nothing left.

Fight, little one. Fight.

Jordan arranged a helicopter to transport Heather to Jamaica Hospital. Masked paramedics lifted her onto a stretcher. She was on her way to isolation with the passengers and crew from flight 3879. Although the whirling, deafening sound shared no resemblance to a plane, the flight held raw reminders of how the nightmare had started. Jordan held her hand and whispered a prayer. Later she'd thank him for filling the shoes of a man who'd once loved her, except Chad would never pray.

Dr. Francisca met her on the hospital's roof helipad. At the sight of the ob-gyn, Heather attempted to stop her fear, but the tears refused to stop. The putrid smell of sickness filled her nose, and the pain in her abdomen grew worse. The horror of losing her baby pounded against her head and heart.

Dr. Francisca held Heather's other hand and walked beside the stretcher from the roof to the elevator. "We're going to run tests and see what is going on."

"Whatever it takes to save my baby. Please, no tests that threaten his life."

"I won't order any procedure without your permission. Try to stay calm."

Heather turned to Jordan and peered into his kind face. "You are the best of friends. Thank you."

"I'm staying here until Dr. Francisca makes a diagnosis and establishes a treatment."

"Those on the island need you."

"It's a short helicopter ride."

Two hours later, blood work, a urine test, an ultrasound, and MRI—in which Heather was assured the test had no radiation to harm the baby—provided the results Dr. Francisca needed to make a diagnosis. A ruptured appendix. Heather required immediate surgery.

"Whom do I contact?" Dr. Francisca said.

Heather gave her parents' information. She turned to Jordan. "Would you let Catherine know what's going on? She's a great prayer warrior."

He nodded and Dr. Francisca continued. "The baby's father?"

Heather reached deep for control. "He isn't in the picture."

CHAPTER THIRTY-NINE

INSOMNIA HAUNTED CHAD and taunted his murky life. His cell phone sounded, and although awake, he startled. He read the ID and snatched it before the second ring. His fingers fumbled over the green Answer key while a hundred scenarios fired at his mind.

"Jordan, what's wrong?"

"I have bad news. Heather is scheduled for emergency surgery. Appendicitis."

He bolted from the bed. "Where is she?"

"Helicopter transported her to Jamaica Hospital. I'm here with her. She's under the care of a reputable ob-gyn who recommended a surgeon. They're prepping her now."

"How is she? How's the baby?"

"Both are stable."

"Does exposure to the virus risk their lives?"

"That's an unknown."

"Has she shown any signs of the virus?"

"No."

"Hold on. Is she on the same floor as those who are infected?"

"Yes. Chad, calm down. She's receiving excellent care."

He rubbed his face. "She's pregnant, has appendicitis, and with people who are dying. How would you react?"

"Probably the same."

Fear continued to ripple through him. "Can you have her transferred to another floor?"

"She's in isolation. Safe."

"Why don't I feel confident? I'm sorry. That wasn't necessary. I'll take the next flight to New York."

"I'd hoped you say that. I'll keep you posted."

"Did she ask you to call me?"

"No."

He didn't expect Heather to contact him, but he had Jordan as a friend to keep him informed. Hadn't she gone through enough? "Okay. I'm on my way." Chad drew in a breath filled with anxiety. He snapped on the light and booked a flight online. Once he secured a seat for 6 a.m., Javier's words repeated.

Do not leave town.

He fumbled through his wallet for Javier's card and pressed in the number. The agent answered as quickly as Chad had responded to Jordan.

"Chad Lawrence here. I just heard from Dr. Jordan Radcom in New York City." He slowed his words. "I'm sorry to wake you. Heather has appendicitis and is headed into surgery. I have a 6 a.m. flight."

Silence met him.

"I intend to go with or without your permission. Unless you plan to arrest me. I can forward you my itinerary and send flight status, the hotel, and she's at Jamaica Hospital."

"What's the point? Your attorney can handle the communication."

"Personal reasons. Doubt you'd understand."

"Because of the surgery and pregnancy? Guilty conscience?"

"All of those." Chad sighed. "An assault against my conscience for her situation, nothing else."

"Makes sense to sit tight. Why rush to New York? Stay here and find out the surgery results. Will she even see you?"

"I'll deal with it." Surely the medical team would permit Chad in her room.

"Although the FBI's initial statement cleared your lab, you're not out of deep water yet. There are people who are convinced you're a murderer. Without protection, a step outside your door is dangerous."

"I don't hear the FBI offering a means to keep me alive. Look, I'll take my chances. I need to confirm she receives the best medical care."

"I'm not the one authorized to give you permission to leave the city. Send me your travel plans, and I'll make the necessary calls."

"Better check in with your buddies at the FBI office in New York. They can put my presence on their surveillance list."

"This isn't funny. The news will leak. Reporters will be all over it. Someone will recognize you, and you could end up dead."

"At least I'd have ensured my wife and child are healthy."

"Since when did they mean so much to you?"

He wished he had an answer. "Nothing's changed there. My goal is to know how she feels about my involvement in the virus. One look into her eyes will tell me the truth."

Javier yawned. "You didn't answer my question, or maybe you did."

Chad ended the conversation. He opened his closet door and yanked out clothes. No point in going back to bed for a couple of hours. He was wide-awake.

Javier wasn't the only person who'd want to know why he had to check on Heather. He loved her, which meant he had to keep up the facade of separating himself from her. What morsel of truth made the most sense? Their child? Responsibility? Loneliness? Clear his name and resume his career goals?

His phone rang and he grabbed it. Number unrecognizable.

"Chad Lawrence?" a distorted voice said.

"This is he."

"Cancel your flight to New York."

"Who is this?"

"Get on the plane and you'll regret it."

"You have the nerve to threaten me." Chad pressed End.

Chad clicked his seat belt for the flight to JFK in New York. His patience level registered at nonexistence. The flight arrangements had been confirmed after 3 a.m. when the FBI finally gave their consent. He'd fought hard—and persistence won. He had pulled an Astros baseball cap over his eyes and wore jeans and a long-sleeved green camouflage T-shirt. His own mother wouldn't recognize him. He arranged for a taxi to transport him to the airport.

Javier's warning of what an irate person could do whispered danger, but a force stronger than himself pressed him on. He needed to support Heather, make sure she and the baby survived the emergency surgery. Her welfare took precedence over his own life, even if no one ever learned the truth about his promise to Paul's widow.

The caller's threat echoed—someone who knew he planned to board this flight. Technology boasted of ways to spy on people, and software made it happen. To toss out his phone for a new one broke his trust with Javier. As if he owed the man a concession. Once in New York, he'd borrow Jordan's phone, contact Javier, then dispose of his current device.

Could the caller have been the one responsible for the virus? Someone out for revenge? In any event, the person had the means to monitor Chad's actions. He looked behind him, forward, and on both sides. What did a criminal look like?

While on the tarmac, he phoned Jamaica Hospital and requested an update. He stated he was Heather's husband, but that got him nowhere. Jordan's latest text said the surgery had taken longer than expected, and she rested in recovery. The procedure should have been completed long before now.

"Mr. Lawrence," a nurse from OR said, "your wife is in ICU."

He drew in a ragged breath. "What's her condition?"

Before the nurse could respond, a flight attendant requested Chad turn off his phone. But he ignored her for the second time. "Why is Heather in ICU?"

"Sir," the nurse said, "I suggest you contact her doctor."

He hadn't asked Jordan for the doctor's number.

The attendant bent over him. "This is the last time I'll ask you to place your phone on airplane mode. Please do it now."

Chad obliged before the flight attendant kicked him off the plane for not adhering to the rules. A qualified medical team surrounded Heather, and Jordan was with her.

He closed his eyes. He regretted the physical dangers of Heather's job, the emotional stress of their relationship, the pregnancy, the horror of H9N15, and now emergency surgery. The same persistent questions beat against him. Had he been mistaken to leave her when he didn't want to go on without her in his life? Would the truth help her understand his behavior?

He clenched his eyes shut to stop the incessant questions. Why deliberate this now? His plans were in motion.

He'd orchestrated the past seven months to reflect apathy. He often claimed Andy's and other medical colleagues' company were more stimulating than hers. He followed up with many late work nights followed by drinks and dinner in which he chose not to call her. He tossed his discontent of her at every opportunity.

He wished she'd left him.

With the CDC job, he longed for a renewal of energy to improve the health for thousands of people. It was a worthy diversion. But what did "on hold" mean? While he stated research ignited his soul, a utopia where his future held more excitement than Heather, he died a little every day. What happened when the newness of the position wore off? And what would he do if the CDC canceled the contract?

Muddled thoughts fogged his mind. Glimpses of the past . . . her incredible impish smile. The ways she showed love—tender notes in his computer case, texts, heart-shaped cookies, soft music, and an emphasis on his needs. He missed her and what they once had together. Why did confusion shake his decision? The undercurrent of swimming in a sacrificial promise might have carried him away from all that mattered.

At the moment Chad had neither his marriage nor little hope for a promising career.

The plane lifted into the air.

The attendant announced the ability to use his phone. Fumbling for his device, he arranged for Wi-Fi and messaged Jordan.

The hospital said Heather's in ICU.

Minutes dragged until Jordan responded. **Hypovolemia. She lost too much blood during the surgery. Monitoring the baby.**

Is he okay?

Stable.

You're at the hospital?

Yes. Will see you later.

Heather and the baby had to pull through the surgery.

CHAPTER FORTY

HEATHER SLOWLY EMERGED from a deep sleep. Twice before she'd attempted to surface but drifted back. From the low, rhythmic beeping around her, she must be hooked up to machines that recorded her vitals. Sleep urged her into a peaceful world. She forced her eyes to open, but dizziness spun, and she closed them again.

"Is my baby okay?" she whispered to anyone nearby.

"This is Jordan, and your baby's fine. Strong heartbeat. It's Mama who needs to regain her strength."

Thank You. "My appendix is gone?"

"Forever. Because of potential infection, the surgeon chose not to remove it laparoscopically."

"Life has hit me with a few challenges," she said. "Am I in recovery?"

"ICU in the isolation section."

She opened her eyes. "Why do I feel so weak?"

"Low blood pressure."

She lifted her head to read her vitals, but the machine was turned, and the movement increased her queasiness. For the next few minutes, she pushed strength into her body until she felt strong enough to carry on a conversation. "How am I now?"

"You've made a little progress."

"When can I leave?" she said.

"Are you missing the five-star amenities of Adam's Island?"

"And to find who's responsible for the virus."

"Right now your mission is to get better. Qualified people are on the case."

"Not on the island. Any updates?"

"Not since I last checked. Catherine sent her love, and so do Jackie and Ada."

"Tatum? Maria?"

His eyes pooled. "Maria passed."

She wanted to yank out the IV and run down the halls screaming unfair. Instead she wept and cradled her stomach. "Tatum?"

"Her condition hasn't changed. Thomas Powell contacted me while you were in surgery. He hoped you were resting comfortably."

"Tell him and the others thanks. Jordan, I'm so thirsty."

"Would you like a few ice chips?"

"Please."

He spooned some into her mouth. They tickled her tongue and throat . . . a rare delicacy.

"Are you in pain?"

"A little. But I'm okay."

"Ever the strong FBI agent."

"I wish, and I'm tired. Will you fly back to quarantine?"

"Later. A few things are on my list first." He expelled a sigh. "Chad will be here soon."

She groaned. "He probably brought papers for me to sign."

"Don't think so. He's upset. I won't leave you alone with him."

"I'm a big girl."

"I might need to protect him."

She smiled.

"Go back to sleep."

And she did.

CHAPTER FORTY-ONE

CHAD PAID THE UBER DRIVER a generous tip to drop him off at Jamaica Hospital in New York City. He hoisted a backpack onto his shoulder and adjusted the bill of his cap lower on his forehead. At least it wasn't a hundred degrees with 100 percent humidity but a mild seventy-four degrees with a wonderful breeze. Did every circumstance revolve around him and his comfort level or was it his imagination? Grasping his carry-on, he stared at the impressive glass hospital and studied those in the immediate area for signs of trouble.

Heather's welfare consumed him. Even when he treated the sick in a remote area of the world, he longed to hear her voice . . . see her face. Could he ever eradicate those once-precious moments from his heart? He thought so, told himself so, but now doubts swung like a pendulum.

Was Heather aware of his visit? Would she refuse him into her room? He couldn't blame her since he'd rejected her countless times.

Outside, he texted Javier and told him he'd made it to the hospital. Reporters didn't swarm the outside entrance, a relief. He walked inside the hospital and searched for a familiar face. The time confirmed Jordan's tardiness. Earlier Chad promised to wait on his old friend for an escort. He refused to creep into a dark spot in his mind where Jordan had changed his mind, and Chad would face Heather alone. He wasn't a coward, just needed moral support. Jordan's last text concluded they'd enter Heather's room together.

Perhaps he'd been stupid to fly here. He'd told Javier part of his reason was to uncover the truth about Heather's feelings. But he had reasons difficult to admit, and twisted soul-searching pushed his confusion into off-limits. Heather referred to an off-limit topic as the issue beneath the issue.

"Hey, doc."

Chad turned to Jordan, who pulled him into a hug. Years of solid memories and recent emotional tension caused a lump in Chad's throat.

"Good to have you here despite the circumstances. I'm sorry."

"How is Heather?"

"Better. She's asleep but we can go on up." Jordan handed him a mask and gloves. "Hardly recognized you."

"My intentions."

They rode the elevator to a floor where everyone wore protective masks and gloves. The two men walked down a hallway to ICU. Jordan flashed his badge, and they gained entrance to the area and room where Heather rested.

He hadn't expected Heather's pallor to be more gray than white. She'd always been the poster child for health—thin, muscular, exercised every day, and ate a healthy diet. Seldom a sniffle. Except right now with her sea-green eyes closed, and the splatter of freckles faded against her cheeks, a peculiar blend of sadness and protectiveness overwhelmed him. He viewed her vitals. Blood pressure—80 over 46. Heartbeat and pulse were normal.

"Have you eaten?" Jordan said.

"Not hungry."

"You never change. Nerves take over and your appetite disappears."

"No medical exams to take today." His voice cracked. "That would be easier."

Jordan motioned for him to sit. "We can talk until she wakens. Anything you need to do?"

He wanted Heather to open her eyes, but her body required rest. "I should make a call to Houston FBI. Can I use your phone while I recharge my battery?"

Jordan handed him his device, and Chad stepped into the hall.

"Got your text," Javier said. "How's Heather and the baby?"

"She's asleep and the baby is okay." He glanced around and saw no one but a woman in dark-blue scrubs who emptied trash. "I received a call after we talked earlier this morning. A distorted voice told me to cancel my flight, said you couldn't protect me in New York."

"Who knew about our conversation and your New York plans?"

"You, Jordan Radcom, and I suppose SAC Bischoff."

"How did you make the flight arrangements?"

"Online."

"Then you received an email confirmation?"

"Yes."

"I suspect someone's bugged your phone or hacked your email account."

"What do you suggest?" Chad said.

"Pick up a burner phone at your first opportunity. Call me with the new number. Do you have your laptop?"

"Yes."

"I'd like to borrow it and your phone for a few hours. The New York techs can look at access logs and determine if, when, and how someone gained knowledge through your devices or online activity. In the meantime, if you receive any more threats, call me immediately."

Chad joined Jordan. Heather's eyes remained closed, and her BP had risen to 84 over 48. Improvement.

Jordan crossed, then uncrossed his legs. "Where are you? The Chad Lawrence I remember loved his wife, and his dedication to medicine came in second. He told her every detail of his plans."

He could remind Jordan she'd kept the pregnancy from him, but bitter words solved nothing but put him on the defense. The hours on the plane where he attempted to put Heather into a niche rolled back into his mind. He massaged his arms.

Chad needed transparency. "I'm trying to muster up the guts to discuss what I don't understand." He stared at Jordan. "I apologize. You have enough on your plate already, far more important than my problems."

"I always have time when friends are involved."

He hesitated. "I'm a realist, which makes the situation with Heather, the baby, and the charges against me difficult to shove into a neat compartment."

"Try me."

Chad looked for a loophole in the conversation as though whatever he said could be used against him. "I've attempted to put a scientific spin on my unexplainable emotions. It's useless."

"Are you denying your internal reactions? Because you're human, not a machine. We are created for relationships."

Chad almost laughed. "I'm well familiar with Maslow's hierarchy of needs. I want to find where I fit."

"A journey or a search?"

"For an answer to why my life is difficult and how to compartmentalize each happening."

"I know you well," Jordan said. "You spend far too much time shoving life experiences into mental files. You try to force them to fit instead of examining them for what they are."

"One problem after another stands in the way of a promise I made."

"Your commitment to medicine?"

Chad rubbed the back of his neck. "That's part of it."

"What is God saying?"

"You and Heather have a faith element in perspective while I look at how I can leave the world a better place. Prove to me there is a God in this rat's nest, let me see a deity in action who cares. So where is your God, the one who supposedly loves us? 'Cause He hasn't shown me His face."

"You blame God or He's not in the equation?"

"God isn't a factor and that makes it difficult for you to comprehend my method of reasoning. I want a solid future for Heather and the baby."

"Explain the issue to me."

"I will sometime soon."

"I believe God is in control of all things."

Chad ignored the faith debate sure to come if he cleared the road. *Move on. No use.* "How many people vied for the CDC job?"

"Four applicants." Jordan held up his hand. "The FBI went down the same path. They've been cleared."

"Are you talking to one of them in the event I'm barred?"

"I'm not doing a thing until the virus is under control."

"That's fair. How long will the CDC wait for my complete exoneration?"

"Chad, why are you here?" Heather's weak voice captured his attention.

He walked to her bedside. "To make sure you and the baby are okay. A ruptured appendix is dangerous."

"So is boarding a plane. Did you bring legal documents for my signature?" The hand with the IV protected her womb.

"No." He studied her vitals. "You're making progress."

"We'll be fine. Both of us are fighters."

"Jordan tells me your doctors are excellent."

"Relax, Chad. Your future doesn't include a funeral, at least not at this point. Do me and my son a favor and go back to Houston."

Chad sensed a catch in his chest. He grabbed his personal items and left the room. His body burned hot with her pronouncement. Wouldn't her signature free him of responsibility? No wife? No son? Why did he feel lost?

"Chad," Jordan said from behind him, "where's your hotel?"

He kept his attention on the hallway ahead. "I'll catch the next flight back to Houston."

"No need to walk through this alone."

"I already am."

On the main floor, he exited the elevator. He'd wait in the lobby for the New York agent to pick up and return his devices. Later he'd grab a ride to the airport and work until his flight left. A crowd of people with cameras and mics rushed toward him.

"Dr. Lawrence, why are you in New York?"

"Why are you at Jamaica Hospital?"

"Is your conscience bothering you?"

The whoosh of cameras.

"Did you infect your wife with the killer virus?"

"Are you here to observe your dirty work?"

A large bearded man bolted his way. "Murderer." His fist landed in Chad's face and shoved him backward. His head cracked against the tile floor.

CHAPTER FORTY-TWO

CHAD STRUGGLED TO MAKE SENSE of his world. An ax cut into the back of his head and chopped into his skull. The excruciating pain limited his ability to think straight. Words formed but they were rooted in his mind.

"Dr. Lawrence, move your fingers if you hear me."

The urgency in the woman's voice told him this was important, but her voice sounded distant, muffled. He tried to wiggle the fingers on his right hand.

"Good. I'm Dr. Weslyn. You're in the emergency room."

"Head . . ."

"You had a nasty fall." She lifted his eyelid and shone a blinding light. Then the other. "Your pupils are dilated." She took his hand. "Squeeze once if you are nauseous."

He followed instructions with a slight touch.

"Is your hearing impaired?"

He concentrated hard despite the pain. He squeezed her hand again.

"What you're experiencing is normal for your type of head trauma. I've requested a CT scan to give us a better idea of potential injuries. We're ready to roll you to imaging. You also require stitches."

"Wait a moment," a man said. "Let me talk to him."

"Make your conversation brief," Dr. Weslyn said.

"Dr. Lawrence, I'm Special Agent McNally from the New York FBI office. Agent Rivera requested we pick up your phone and laptop. I walked into the hospital shortly after you were assaulted. Do you remember anything about the situation?"

Chad recalled the reporters . . . the questions . . . He fought the relentless pain and willed his eyes to open. Through blurred vision, he glimpsed a suit, but the agony in his head forced his eyes shut again. "A man attacked me."

"A reporter?"

"No idea. Media was there."

"Did you recognize him?"

"No."

"Did he say anything?"

"Sir," Dr. Weslyn said, "Dr. Lawrence requires medical attention. He has a concussion, but we need to know the extent of his injuries. Your conversation can wait."

"Thirty seconds won't make a difference," McNally said.

Chad moistened his lips. "Called me a murderer."

"We're interviewing the reporters for ID of the assailant," McNally said. "Where are your devices?"

Chad fought to stay conscious. "Phone. Laptop . . . in backpack."

"Thanks," Agent McNally said. "I'll swing back and return these in two to three hours. In the meantime, security cameras should help us ID the assailant. I assume you'll be here at the hospital."

"I'm flying home tonight." The results of the CT scan wouldn't change his plans.

"I'll be in contact." Agent McNally grabbed Chad's backpack, and his cell sounded a text.

"Please . . . read."

McNally obliged. "From Agent Rivera. 'Can you talk?'" He looked at Chad. "What do I say, or do you want me to handle it?"

"Go ahead."

McNally texted on Chad's phone. Immediately it sounded again. "I explained your condition. He asked for you to call later."

Did Heather face the same backlash because of their relationship? Odd, in the moments before the head pain registered again, his mind explored a fresh start with her. Her smile welcoming him, things they could do together, and how to raise a son. Chad drifted into blackness.

Heather stared at the steady trickle of fluids dripping into her veins. How long would she be in the hospital? Most procedures were day surgery, but those patients hadn't squared off with appendicitis, pregnant, or been subjected to a killer virus. Depressing but true.

As a girl when life threw her into a tailspin, Mom and Dad always proposed the thankful game. She despised it at the time, but today she'd play.

Her appendix was in some depository of mangled medical waste, never to cause problems again.

Her baby son rested safely in her womb.

So far the virus had passed over her.

Her heart pumped blood to the rest of her body.

Thank You, God.

Stubbornness stopped her from concentrating on Chad's visit. The Heather from last week would have viewed his presence with the enthusiasm of a vulnerable woman. No longer did she believe

Chad deep down cared and would one day return to the man she married. Whoever said lonely people ate lies when they were hungry needed to spit out the garbage.

A hint of his visit crept across her mind . . . The cavernous pits etched beneath his eyes. He'd lost weight.

She picked up the TV remote and flipped through the channels. *An earlier scene from Jamaica Hospital* scrolled across the screen in bold letters.

A female reporter spoke a voice-over about an incident in the lobby of the hospital. "Dr. Chad Lawrence of Houston, suspected of masterminding the life-threatening H9N15 virus and collaborating with terrorist Braden Taversty, arrived at Jamaica Hospital earlier today. His wife is reportedly hospitalized there as well as the victims of the virus. When Lawrence exited the elevators, an unknown person shouted, 'Murderer' and assaulted him. Lawrence is listed in stable condition at the hospital. No arrests or suspects. H9N15 has taken the lives of thirty-one people and infected 152 . . ."

She muted the TV and texted Jordan. **Is Chad okay? Just saw the news.**

Will be. Concussion. Had a CT scan. A doctor is stitching the back of his head.

Any witnesses?

No.

Being admitted?

He refused.

If you can't persuade him to stay, ask if he'll see me before he leaves.

Will do my best.

The pain meds made her sleepy, but before she gave in to rest, she wanted to process what Chad had experienced since the virus unleashed. The events bombarding his life grew worse, and the persistent topic of why refused to leave her alone.

The FBI had scores of agents across the country on the case. Dead ends sent agents scrambling in many directions. Until the FBI found the person, another area of the country or world could experience an outbreak. The person had gained access to the aircraft, unleashed the virus, and done what? Rode the wave with feigned concern? Attempted a suicide mission? Survived with an antiviral?

CHAPTER FORTY-THREE

HEATHER WOKE TO THE SOUND of the door's click. Jordan walked inside the hospital room, and Chad staggered behind. She stopped audible alarm. The right side of Chad's face was swollen in blue and purple, sure to darken. A white bandage wrapped around the back of his head. Jordan assisted him onto a small sofa near her.

"Chad, you should be in a hospital bed."

"I'll schedule a neurologist appointment in Houston."

"There are plenty here." She bit her tongue to avoid an argument. "I'm sorry you were attacked."

"My own fault. Agent Rivera warned me the wrong people could track me down." He relayed the conversation with Agent McNally from New York's FBI.

"Can we talk if you feel up to it?"

"Why? Haven't we said it all? This—"

"Chad, Heather," Jordan said, "I'll be in the hallway to give you two a few minutes alone. Good thing neither of you is in good enough shape to kill the other. If I hear screams, I'll come running." He left the room and closed the door.

His humor should have eased the tension, but instead the walls closed in. She vowed to think before she spoke. She'd shed enough tears, both grief and anger. No crossing her arms over her chest or touching her face. "I regret the way I spoke to you earlier. No reason for my rudeness. I was cruel, and I'm sorry."

"I deserved it. Both barrels."

Twice he'd admitted fault, a rarity for him. "You flew a long way to turn around and head back."

He wrung his hands, and she sensed the wheels turning inside his super-IQ brain while he managed pain.

"You need evidence to confirm I had no part of the virus," he said.

"Guilt seems inconceivable. The man I married wouldn't have considered a horrible crime, but you changed with your . . . ambitions."

"So there's doubt."

"I wish there wasn't."

He leaned forward as though he planned to stand, then shook his head. Pain emitted from his eyes. He needed hospital care. "I thought a face-to-face would strengthen my resolve to follow through with my original plans, but I'm not so sure. I'm confused."

Whatever he said had to be his words. She'd made life easier for him since they'd met. They shared the same name, but they were strangers.

He massaged his temples. "Should have told you this before. On my last trip to Africa when Paul contracted Ebola and I couldn't save him . . . grief and failure leveled me." He stared at her with moist-ridden eyes. "Treating the symptoms for those who are nameless is difficult, but Paul and I had worked alongside each other for three years. Before he slipped into coma, he cried for me to end his misery. His tears were mixed with blood."

The memory clearly ripped raw. "Bleeding from every orifice of his body. I'd seen it many times yet not on a close friend. I'll never forget it. *Never.* Paul died leaving a widow and two small kids. I returned home and visited Tami. She begged me to find a cure for Ebola . . . to never give up. To protect you from the torment she was going through. What if the tables were turned? What if I died trying to help others, and you were left to raise our child or children alone?

"From the moment I left her house, I planned how to slowly dissolve our marriage, how to push you away. When you said you wanted to start a family, I couldn't wait any longer." Chad shook his head, the anguish pouring from his eyes.

"Why didn't you tell me? I pleaded for you to talk about Paul's death."

"Couldn't. Words refused to come. Paul didn't want to accompany me on that trip because his daughter was having her first dance recital. I persuaded him to have Tami video the performance. If it hadn't been for me, he'd be alive today, and I wouldn't feel obligated to keep the promise."

"I'm not Tami," she whispered.

"I know that now. Once the decision was made, I applied at the CDC and landed the job. Then the virus with the threat on your life, a baby on the way, and my possible role in the virus. Rather ironic. The woman I wanted to protect got caught up in a deadly virus."

She walked through the past several months, stumbling over the rocks of confusion. His unpredictable behavior held new meaning.

"Not sure what tomorrow holds," he said. "Did a reporter need a notch on his résumé, and I drew the short stick? With answers, I could move forward." He gripped his head.

"Did the doctor give you a prescription for pain?"

"Yes, but I don't know how my body will react. I might take the meds once I'm home."

"You could lean back on the sofa. Close your eyes."

"I will. But first, I need to finish what I started." He raised his head. "The one thing I have is knowledge and experience about viruses to add quality of life, not take it. But my efforts are futile. The CDC isn't sure my association with them is appropriate, and I understand. I can't be trusted when I'm viewed as a killer. The uncertainty makes me crazy. Always has. On the flight here, the truth hit me hard. I weighed my future or lack of and the vicious accusations, and my wife and unborn son are all that matter."

Her pulse sped. Had Chad experienced an epiphany? She should divert her gaze, but the task was deemed impossible. "I went to see her, too. She said for me not to contact her again, wanted nothing to do with you or me. I assumed her grief had prompted the anger, and I'd give her time."

"I'll tell Tami my family is more important. I made a promise without thinking, and it caused me to break one I'd already made."

"What are you saying?"

"I want to rebuild the trust you once had in me. When the virus predicament is over, can we find what we lost?" He bit into his lower lip. Was his hesitancy to manage the pain or form his words? "I own our problem. You've always put me first and sacrificed yourself."

Heather searched for a response, but she needed prayer and time to work through her hurt and betrayal. She despised the vicious words he'd said, the ugly actions conceived and acted upon.

She studied Chad's face, a vivid display of lined agony. Was it mental or physical? Or both?

His blue eyes clouded. "I love you, Heather. In my effort to cover my guilt, I chose to sacrifice what we'd started together. I'm sorry I hurt you and made demands that I didn't even want. Truth is, I don't deserve you."

Why hadn't she seen what Paul's death had done to him?

"You're not planning to give me any slack, are you?" he said.

"I share in our brokenness."

"Not really. You encouraged my dream of medical research when friends said one doctorate was enough. You saw my passion for people who suffered with disease." He touched his temples. "On the plane here, I remembered the night we used our budget on a movie and came back to the apartment starved. We had two pieces of bread for toast and four eggs." Chad peered into her face. "You put the last slice of cheese on my eggs and left the heel of bread for yourself. Your unselfishness showed me the power of love, and I was afraid you'd always love me more than I could ever love you."

Heather recalled the night of eggs and cheese. They'd been married less than two years. "We put strawberry jelly on graham crackers for dessert. Finished the jar."

"We laughed and agreed the movie had no plot."

Jordan opened the door. "Could we have a little while longer?" Chad said.

The door closed. The moment between them faded.

After several seconds, Chad spoke. "Is it too late for us? I'm determined to change. The future's shaky, but I don't want to spend it without you."

She longed to say the words he wanted to hear, but something held her back. Was it heartbreak that he'd walk out of her life forever, and she'd never again see the man she'd promised to love? But without God as the center of their relationship, reconciliation was doomed.

"Heather, say what's on your mind."

She inhaled to put off a flow of tears. "First, I can't focus on us until you're cleared, and the FBI has made an arrest."

"I understand. Whatever it takes."

"Over the last several weeks, I resigned myself to raise my baby alone. Mom and Dad will help, but the responsibility falls on me." She prayed for courage. "My son deserves a father who's active in his life and whose priority is God."

AIRBORNE

Hurt crested his eyes. "I can learn how to be a father. But my stand on religion hasn't changed. If a God exists, why doesn't He right this screwed-up world?"

"Ask Him."

"God hasn't ever talked to me. Will you accept a compromise?"

Her past decision to give in to Chad and relinquish her faith had tainted her relationship with God. "I can't. When I substituted you for God, we spiraled downhill."

"Does your stipulation involve a time frame?"

"No. I'm not going anywhere."

He lay back on the sofa. "My life is fine without God."

"I see your great life, hear your positive attitude."

He moaned. "You're not being fair under the circumstances."

"Your circumstances?"

"Right." He blew out his words. "Some changes will take time and counseling. Jordan will expect a report."

"Tell him whatever you think is best."

"You've asked me to give up my identity for something that doesn't exist."

"I gave you my terms. It's your task to search for God. No one else can do it for you." She fought the old habits to rush to his aid, quote Scripture.

"I'll tell Jordan we don't have plans to kill each other today, and the divorce is on hold while we work through our issues."

"We've got to be careful, and today reinforced the caution. Tell only Jordan."

"Makes sense. The news could jeopardize the investigation."

"Once you walk out of this room, don't contact me until we have burner phones. Give Jordan your number, and I'll get it from him."

"I'll pick up a phone at the airport. Please, be careful. If the person who spread the virus is on Adam's Island, he has every step of your life memorized."

"I can take care of myself."

CHAPTER FORTY-FOUR

CHAD SLEPT IN HEATHER'S HOSPITAL ROOM while he waited for his Houston flight. Jordan shook him awake every thirty minutes and asked a few questions before allowing him to close his eyes again. The small sofa didn't fit his over six-foot frame, but he didn't care.

He told Jordan with Heather present the divorce might not follow through, but no one dare find out.

"About time," Jordan had said. "Always wondered what Heather saw in you. Maybe it was your potential. Wise decision to keep this private."

Chad suspected Jordan had inside info about the Adam's Island investigation. But he kept his hunches to himself. The secrecy and who had access to secure information was privileged, and Chad didn't qualify.

Forty minutes before he planned to leave for the airport, Agent McNally arrived with Chad's laptop and cell phone. The agent closed the door, and Chad introduced Heather and Jordan.

"Dr. Lawrence, do you object to Dr. Radcom and your wife being privy to our conversation?" McNally said.

"Should I?" Chad reached for the Tylenol and a bottle of water. He swallowed three gel-coated capsules. An hour before he'd taken three Aleve. He preferred his head to buzz than pound.

Jordan pulled a chair closer to the bed for McNally. "Agent Lawrence and Dr. Radcom have clearance regarding the virus investigation," McNally said. "Shall I continue?"

"Go for it. Is my phone bugged?"

"No. But someone has compromised your email. Confirmation of travel plans and a forward to Agent Rivera are there, the source of where they learned about your flight plans and made the threat."

"Why? Makes no sense." Chad shifted, and the movement sent bolts of agony through his head. "Isn't there enough junk stacked against me?"

"We have examined possible motives. None of our speculations are conclusive."

Chad inwardly groaned at the textbook-formal-Quantico answer. "You traced the source? Who's responsible?"

"Only as far as an IP address in Spain. We aren't excluding additional exposure based on hacks to your online activity. They've covered their tracks with the use of a virtual private network."

Chad craved a clear head, but his brain needed to mend first. "Whoever is responsible doesn't know you're tracking them?"

"Theoretically. We can lead the hacker to exposure as long as the person isn't aware of what we've discovered. If someone is smart enough to develop the virus and invest in these tactics, they have an expert watching any online activity."

"Which means the FBI has no way to identify them?"

"Our tech team is on it. We're monitoring things, and I'll notify you when an answer is available."

"Agent McNally," Heather said, "this is the first I've heard threats were made. It's irrelevant at this point. My concern is since the H9N15 case is termed terrorism, doesn't that put a priority on nailing the hacker?"

"Yes." He turned to Chad. "I suggest you tell me everything you haven't already told the FBI in Houston."

"If I had evidence, I'd give it to you." Chad closed his eyes in an effort to sound coherent. He wanted to say the good guys and the bad guys were after him. But he'd resolved to sound less self-centered.

"Is the name Braden Taversty familiar?"

Chad sighed, a mix of the hammer to his head and frustration. "Agent Rivera and I discussed him. He was in the news as a suspect for the virus. He died here at the hospital. Never met him or corresponded with him."

"Decker Anslow?"

"Agent Rivera asked me about him, too. Taversty and Anslow are strangers to me. Who is this Anslow guy? How is he connected?"

"Isn't important."

"Then why have you and Rivera brought up his name?"

"Just part of the investigation," McNally said. "Are you planning to return to Houston tonight in your condition?"

"Yes. I'll request an Uber as soon as we're done here. Agent Rivera has my flight itinerary."

"I'll drive you to the airport."

Might keep him from another beating. "All right."

McNally handed him his devices, and Chad stuffed them into his backpack.

"Change nothing about your email patterns or behavior. We don't want to clue the hacker in on what we've discovered."

Chad's head beat harder. Focusing was a challenge. "Why not set up a separate email address for a trap?"

"We have eyes on your email. It's being monitored by our techs. We will find out who's behind this." McNally walked to the door. "I'll get my car and text you when I'm ready."

"Whoa," Chad said. "You told me in the ER those who were in the lobby faced interviews. Who attacked me?"

McNally huffed. "No one saw a thing."

"You mean no one saw the man suspected of developing a life-threatening virus knocked unconscious? A crowd of reporters shoved mics in my face and snapped pics. Doesn't the hospital have security cameras?" Chad gripped his fists to manage the pain. "I'm done," he whispered. "I'll sort this out at home."

"Dr. Lawrence, we have agents on every angle. The man who did this to you avoided security cameras. Media still swarm the lobby, so I'll arrange another exit point. Hospital security will escort you to my car."

CHAPTER FORTY-FIVE

AT THE AIRPORT, Chad purchased a burner phone, activated it, and texted the number to Jordan and Javier. He also bought a Bible and challenged himself to read it because God meant so much to Heather. While the last seat in business class offered slight comfort, the flight home weakened his ability to fight the steady throb of his injuries, and a stay in New York centered on illogical. Why put himself in the line for another attack or worse—endanger Heather or Jordan?

In Houston, the taxi ride to his apartment jarred his bruised brains and sore muscles. He closed his door and double-bolted it behind him. Pain meds with a concussion made little sense when he lived alone. Instead, he set his phone alarm to go off every two hours, took three Tylenol, then walked around his apartment before giving in to another two hours of sleep.

Midmorning, Chad staggered from his bed, fighting dizziness and the sledgehammer pressuring his skull. How strange the future held more promise than ever before while his mind and body clattered in agony. Perhaps after the FBI arrested the mystery killer, he'd regain his CDC and career focus. Yet where did the future lead? Heather wrapped around his heart, and he wanted her back. She insisted his exoneration must come first. Yet one of her terms leaped toward an inconceivable zone.

"My son deserves a father whose priority is God."

What did the God thing mean for a man torn between his dedication to medical research and a woman he loved? Jordan made faith fit, but they weren't the same men.

Javier arrived before noon. "Sure you're up to a visitor?" He handed Chad a bag from McDonald's. "Brought you a breakfast sandwich."

Chad forced a grin. He smelled coffee and an intoxicating mix of eggs, cheese, and bacon. "Do you take food wherever you go? Or is interrogation on the menu?"

"My mom raised me to treat friends right." He squinted at Chad. "You look awful, and the whole right side of your face is black and purple. Can you see out of that eye?" He frowned. "I should have flat out refused you to leave Houston."

"I'm okay." Pain, like a vise, enveloped his head. "Probably should sit." Before he fell on his face. He eased onto the sofa, and Javier took a chair. "Want to split the coffee?"

Javier waved away his response. "Had enough today."

"Where's your partner?"

"Agent Tobias? This is Sunday. She's with her family."

"I'm surprised you're not in church."

"Went to the first service. Wanted to give you the latest on your email hacker."

Chad flipped the seal on the to-go cup and inhaled the greatest creature comfort ever made. "Glad to hear we're still in this together."

"If you survive."

Chad forced a smile. "Tell me what you've learned."

"We noted the first hack occurred approximately seven hours after flight 3879 left Houston. This would have been while the CDC evaluated the passengers and crew at JFK."

"And during the same time, you and Agent Tobias brought me in for questioning." Chad peered through his distorted vision at Javier. "So did the FBI bug my devices?"

"No reason. We use legal means."

Chad rubbed his temples. "Explain what I'm up against." He noted a thin layer of dust on the table, reminding him Heather kept their condo spotless. He didn't need a maid or a cook—he missed his best friend.

"Are you sure you're okay?"

Javier's words pushed him to pay attention. "Sure. What are you permitted to tell me?"

"You just heard it. Unless you want my opinion." Chad nodded, and Javier continued. "If you're guilty, you've been set up by a partner to take the fall. If you're innocent, a guilty party has set you up. The third option is you have no clue what's going on but have information that threatens the bad guys. You're in danger no matter the option."

Chad bit into the sandwich. He'd spent cycles on the first two possibilities on the flight back to Houston. Didn't change his resolve. The third left a few holes. "How could I be a threat?"

"You tell me."

"Any ideas?"

"I've tossed this around several times. Possibly repercussion from one of Heather's cases. If you're arrested of a crime, she looks like a lousy agent. The other stronger thought is you have upset someone who is linked to your medical research."

Chad shrugged and drank the coffee. "I don't have an answer to either possibility. Tell me, how is Decker Anslow involved?"

"Why?"

"Both you and Agent McNally asked me if I knew Braden Taversty and Decker Anslow. The BBC reported Anslow is in German custody with alleged terrorist activities. The report's from Frankfurt. Not a coincidence Taversty headed to the same city, and media says he had terrorism interests. So what's the deal?"

"As updates are made public, I'll share."

Chad frowned. "Then I'm right. I suspect the two men collaborated treason, and one of them is dead. Of course you can't confirm it."

"That's the way of the FBI. Did Heather give you clarity?"

"You mean does she think I'm blameless?" He laid the sandwich on the napkin and stretched out on the sofa. "Let's just say we're not on the best of terms."

"Sorry to hear it."

"It's the way of a shattered marriage."

"I can tell how much you don't care in your voice." Javier eyed him. "How is she?"

Chad must do better to hide his feelings. He gave the agent a quick overview. "The surgeon came in while I was there. He wants to keep her under observation a few days before releasing her to quarantine."

"Any new virus cases?"

"One of the women who shared a room with Heather. Two more deaths." Chad recalled the names on this morning's news . . . a mother and a child. "Better news would be an antiviral and an arrest. The people exposed on the flight are entitled to resume normal lives."

"Time is a huge adversary."

Chad dug his fingers into his palm to channel the throb. "I will clear my name. Help stop the insanity directed at innocent people and me. Tell me what to do while people stomp my name through the mud."

"Leave the investigation to the professionals and pray for answers."

Chad hadn't forgotten Javier's religious views.

Except Chad had a plan, one neither the FBI nor Heather would approve, and he didn't intend to pray about it.

Javier's cell phone rang. He lifted a finger. "Hold on. I've got to take this." He listened and raked his hand through coal-black hair. "I'm with him now." He glimpsed at Chad. "He's in no shape to be anywhere but a hospital. Send me the pic. Thanks." Javier held on to his phone.

"What's the problem?" Life couldn't get much worse.

"A reporter came forward and ID'd the man who attacked you. Said she'd experienced a temporary memory lapse. If you're awake enough, here's a pic for you to identify."

Chad struggled to sit. The phrase *Physician, heal thyself* crossed his mind. He reached out to take Javier's phone. The bearded man who'd punched him sneered back. "He's the one. What's his name?"

"Simon Peale. In and out of jail. Robbery, drugs, breaking and entering."

"My guess is he cared less about anyone on the plane."

Javier snorted. "Spot on. He says a man offered him $8,000 to walk into the hospital, join the reporters, and punch you."

"Who?"

"Peale never met the man. Arrangements were made by phone."

"How convenient." Chad's anger matched the incessant pain. "He's in custody?"

"Yes."

"I want to talk to him face-to-face."

Javier held up a hand. "No rush—he'll stay behind bars."

"His benefactor could bail him out."

"Chad, give yourself a few days to heal, then take a trip to New York."

"Tomorrow."

"Tuesday at the earliest. How do you plan to avoid the email confirmation?"

Chad's thoughts had ventured there. "It's the perfect time to catch whoever's behind this."

"When we met, you didn't come across as a risk taker."

"Depends on the stakes. A lot's happened since you and Agent Tobias picked me up."

CHAPTER FORTY-SIX

HEATHER'S DOCTORS INSISTED she stay two additional nights in the hospital, but she received permission to drag her IV pole down the hall to visit Mia. The criterion was to wear a mask and gloves. Nothing new since she'd stepped off the ferry and entered Adam's Island.

Jordan had kept her up to date on how the patients responded to care. Some lingered over death, holding on to life with a faint glimpse of recovery. Tatum was on that list. Death chased them and often succeeded. A few patients continued to recover—Mia, Frankie, Mr. Engels, and a few others who fought the virus with supernatural strength. The violinist had passed, and she hoped his wife had been able to talk to him. The staggering toll of people infected with H9N15 renewed her commitment to find whoever was responsible.

Heather stopped at the entrance to Mia's room. If the visit didn't exhaust Heather, she'd check on Frankie later. Mr. Engels would need to wait until tomorrow. She walked into the room and viewed Mia, whose thumbs danced across her phone's keyboard.

"Hey," Heather said. "Ready for girl time?"

Mia's brown eyes widened. "Oh, my goodness. How wonderful to hear your voice over the phone, but here you are." She lifted her chin. "Why are you in a hospital gown?"

"Actually, two of them." Heather laughed. "One for each side of me."

"Not a fashion statement I'd recommend, but you didn't answer my question. Are you infected with the virus?"

"Nope. Ruptured appendix, and it's gone."

Mia touched her heart. "Good. And the baby?"

"He's fine."

Mia tilted her head. "A blessing in the middle of tragedy. I'd hug you, but we probably shouldn't."

"Right." Heather pulled a chair to the bedside. "I wish we were having a mani and pedi. This works, though. Tell me what you've been doing."

"Twice a day I talk to my daughter and husband. They'll fly here when the quarantine is over to escort me home. I told them how you've checked on me since I've been here."

"You'd do the same for me. Have you spent any time with others from the flight?"

"No. My closest companions are books, magazines, TV, and my phone. I'm too much of a coward to risk getting sicker." Mia tilted her head. "I stopped watching the news because it repeated the same dreary junk. I assumed if the CDC discovered an antiviral, I'd hear about it from the hospital staff. Has the FBI arrested a suspect?"

"Not yet." Heather gave her a high-level summary of what the news had shared, including Chad's visit and his attack. "The doctor wanted him admitted, but he refused. No surprise there. He flew back to Houston last evening. In short, our differences are irreconcilable. My baby and I are better off without him. I'll be released the day after tomorrow, and a helicopter will take me back to Adam's Island."

"Is the jerk who spread the virus in quarantine?"

"I wish I knew. I'm watching, listening, and analyzing behavior."

"And you can't tell me much else, right?"

"True. But you can update me on your family. Do you have pics?"

Mia reached for her phone and displayed an array of recent photos and videos. Heather complimented and aahed.

"I've reflected on those hours on board the plane countless times and if anyone looked or acted strangely," Mia said. "It's human nature to handle crisis according to our personalities, and we were overwhelmed with what was happening around us."

Heather took Mia's hand and remembered the last time she attempted to comfort her. Heather's gloves had been covered with blood and vomit. At least now they were pristine clean. "If something is wrong, tell me so I can help."

"The man you apprehended?"

"Yes, Braden Taversty. He died."

Mia glanced away. "This may be useless. Before boarding, he sat behind me at the gate, and I heard him on his phone talking in Hindi. Since I speak the language, I listened. He said, 'I'll be there in time to make it happen. Don't worry.' He didn't mention a name or anything else."

The conversation lined up with what the FBI had uncovered. "Thank you, my friend. I'll pass it on."

She chatted with Mia a few more minutes, then excused herself with a promise to keep in touch and to stop by in the morning. Back in her room, Heather closed the door and texted ASAC Mitchell with what Mia had observed.

Now to visit Frankie. The sweet boy sat in a chair and held an iPad. His color looked much better than she expected. Even with his past health issues, he'd beaten the odds. His eyes sparkled as though she were an old friend.

"Are you sick?" Frankie said.

"No. I'm in the hospital for something else. I'm fine. How about you?"

"In two days is my birthday. I hope Grandma can visit me."

Heather cringed. "Early happy birthday. Glad you're better."

"Thanks. Dad's here. I mean he stays at a hotel. He's normally with me, but he had to make some kind of 'rangements. Whatever it is, he was real sad. He wears a mask and gloves like everyone else. He says it keeps him healthy."

"And he wouldn't want to bring in any germs to make you sick."

"Yep. Will you see Grandma?"

A huge knot in her throat threatened to choke her. "Just you." She smiled into his angelic face.

"Grandma must be bad sick 'cause Dad won't talk about her. Says he'll tell me when I'm out of the hospital."

Wise man.

"If you can visit me," Frankie said, "why can't she?"

"I'm sure there's a good reason."

Heather played a card game of animal rummy and made sure he won. Frankie deserved wins in his life, even if many parental guides claimed children should learn how to lose. He'd lost enough.

CHAPTER FORTY-SEVEN

DR. FRANCISCA RELEASED HEATHER to return to quarantine in the morning. She could sleep as well in the dorm as in the hospital. The baby kicked as though he were excited.

Chad needed to share in his son's preparation for the world. They had each other's burner numbers, but he should make the initial call. Eagerness on her part wouldn't bring restoration. Heather had no desire to fix him. Not ever. Took her eight years to accept God changed people according to His plan.

She looked at a microscope and saw a creator God.

Chad looked at a microscope and saw man's scientific advances.

Her phone buzzed, and she answered.

"Feeling better?" ASAC Mitchell said. "You gave us a scare."

"On the mend, thanks."

"Chad's visit at the hospital wasn't a smart move. Was your conversation civil?"

"It resembled a pulled grenade."

"If you're feeling well enough, SAC Bischoff has information to relay."

Heather sat up in the bed to discourage her need for immediate sleep. "I'm ready, and my door is closed."

SAC Bischoff greeted her with his concern about her health. "We continue to probe into Parker and Sonya Karey, and they are still a vital part of the investigation. We contacted a company in Frankfurt where he'd been scheduled for an interview. The position is on hold due to the current virus situation. In addition, we're looking into the background of a vague suspect, one who is on Adam's Island. A few items in his background have the FBI's attention and our discretion. He's a high-profile figure, Thomas Powell, the CEO of Software Developers International."

She startled. "The all-American hero?"

"We understand he was instrumental in bringing down Braden Taversty and later he offered financial aid for the virus victims as well as donated $4 million to the virus research."

"That garners suspicion?" Thomas's attorneys would tear the FBI's suspicions to shreds. "He plays with the kids and rocks babies. The people in quarantine have him clothed in red, white, and blue."

"Are you vouching for him, Agent Lawrence?" Bischoff said.

"Only sharing how he's viewed."

"How would you characterize him?"

"Just what I've already said. What would be his motivation? I've read his background and didn't see a thing that demonstrates a criminal mind-set. Quite the contrary. What's the payoff? With proper evidence I could see Chad's involvement but zilch for Thomas Powell." She paused. "Have you found a connection between him and Chad? Other than an occasional charity event, they don't run in similar circles."

"We're investigating all possibilities."

"If Chad developed the virus, why would he need Powell? Doesn't make sense. His lab is fully funded."

"We have a series of discrepancies that may mean nothing. His family originated in Dallas, and he has a twin brother," Bischoff said. "They were separated when the boys were eleven years old. The father took the brother, abandoned Thomas and his mother, and left the country. Current residence for both men is in London."

Her interest spurred. "Does he have a relationship with them?"

"We're digging to find out. The father's name is Oliver Powell, and the twin is Jackson. Both are musicians and scheduled to perform this week at the Salzburg music festival. At one time, Oliver Powell played for the Dallas Symphony. An agent in Germany contacted them for interviews. Both refused to discuss Thomas, and neither used the festival's activities as a reason."

"Have you discovered why the family split, each taking a son?"

"No. We learned from Thomas's elementary and middle school records that he experienced bullying. In middle school he was suspended for threatening another student with a knife. Could have been to protect himself. We're looking for people from his school or a teacher, someone who witnessed the behavior. While in college, his mother died of complications with pneumonia. Neither Oliver nor Jackson returned for the funeral."

"A history of being bullied doesn't make a man a killer," she said. "It has the potential to damage the victim's self-esteem and lay the groundwork for inappropriate behavior."

"Three of his former girlfriends were interviewed," Bischoff said in his typical no-nonsense fashion. "Two women had nothing to say. The woman who had a yearlong relationship claimed he was a perfect gentleman. After their breakup, she received two hundred grand deposited into her bank account."

"From Powell?"

"Overseas account. Our agents questioned her about the transaction, and she claimed the funds were a gift from an anonymous sender."

"Did she expect the FBI to believe her story?"

"She's sticking to it, and she has no criminal affiliations."

"Sir, if he gave her the money, why deny it? Rhetorical, I know, unless Powell wasn't the sender."

"We were unable to find a current woman in his life. His range of acquaintances encompasses many people, but he has no close friends whom we can locate. Granted, none of what we've learned makes him a suspect."

"We have a history of bullying, family dysfunction, an ex-girlfriend who doesn't know where she received two hundred grand, and a probe into a possible link to Chad."

"Correct. You could give us solid insight into his personality."

Heather called Powell's hint of involvement weak—at best. But with so many lives at stake, who was she to judge? Many times the motivation to a crime surfaced after the criminal was arrested.

"Another matter may mean nothing. Jordan reported Powell stopped by his office and complained of severe headaches since exposure to the virus. From the symptoms, Jordan concluded they were migraines with aura type. He suggested Powell take over-the-counter meds and asked if he'd agree to tests. Powell preferred to postpone the testing unless the pain grew worse."

"What do his medical reports show?" she said.

"No issues with headaches. Jordan is concerned the H9N15 stats are in the beginning stages, and severe headaches could be part of it. But to date, no one has reported them. I wanted you to have all our information. Jordan said he'd encourage immediate testing in the event the virus has affected Powell differently."

"I'll approach him back at the island. We've had a few verbal exchanges but little else."

"Don't jeopardize your health in the process."

"Sir, my baby comes first. I know my limits."

"Thanks."

Heather spent the next several minutes on her phone reading through all secure and available information on Thomas Amadeus Powell. His brother also shared an unusual middle name—Wolfgang. Maybe hopeful expectations for a parent's love of music.

Difficult to believe a man of Thomas's caliber possessed the motive to kill. His charitable contributions and business practices were emulated by countless entrepreneurs. Online and print articles cheered him on. Colleges and universities applauded his philanthropy. Why would Powell risk all he had to spread a virus? With millions of dollars, power, and international contacts, what did he lack that lined him up as a killer? What, if anything, was hidden beneath his facade?

Heather concentrated on the traits of power and control, the ability to dominate and build self-importance. Chad fit those traits—so did Thomas. She'd studied the profiles of those who'd committed unimaginable atrocities. Positioning herself to befriend Thomas was a challenge . . . and a probable waste of time.

A text from Jordan seized her attention.

A flight attendant just passed.

Who?

Nathan Howard

Flashes of his caring, kindness, and fear on board the flight swept through her mind. She closed her eyes and let the tears flow.

CHAPTER FORTY-EIGHT

CHAD RETURNED HOME from a neurologist appointment and texted Andy using the burner phone.

This is Doc C. New phone. Are you available for a call?

Sure thing.

If anyone could assist in discreet, amateur detective work, Andy fit the bill. While the FBI hadn't found a bug in his phone, he wasn't taking any chances. Chad pressed in Andy's number. He hadn't spoken to his assistant since the day the FBI had swept his lab.

"Hey, Andy. I apologize for not checking in. I went through the whole feel-sorry-for-me game. Trying to recover. How are you?"

"Bored out of my mind. Heard what happened in New York. What's the deal?"

He gave a thirty-second overview of why the trip to Jamaica Hospital, Heather's negative reaction, and the attack. "The neurologist did an eval this morning. Told me I had a concussion." Chad chuckled to lighten the mood.

"Not funny, Doc C. Need some company while your head heals? We can talk shop or whatever you want."

"Sounds like a plan. Would you bring me a large bottle of extra-strength Tylenol?"

☆ ☆ ☆

In thirty minutes, Andy arrived with his laptop and the Tylenol. Chad had freshly brewed coffee ready. The essentials. They set up in the living area, where Chad took advantage of the sofa.

"I'm sorry about your rotten luck," Andy said. "You tried to do the right thing by supporting Heather, and you're punched. How did anyone know you were in New York?"

Chad relayed the hack into his email. "For your ears only. I assume the same person informed the media of my flight times and Heather's hospitalization. I can't blame reporters when they have a job to do. Face it, I look guilty. What's important is finding who developed and released the virus and if there's an antiviral. The FBI, CDC, and law enforcement are working to the same end, but I wish they'd speed up the process."

"I'm right there with you. I suppose the FBI suspect me, too."

"Count on it."

Andy stood and waved his empty mug. "I'm telling you this has Heather's signature stamped on it. She's getting even."

"You could be right."

"I need more coffee before we talk about how to make sense of what's happened." He filled his mug and added two packets of raw sugar.

"Are you interested in helping me clear my name?"

"Are you kidding?" Andy whirled around and grinned. "We work in a lab filled with crazy dangers. I'm fearless. Bring it on."

"I have a flight to New York tomorrow morning."

Andy startled. "Why?"

"To ID the man who punched me. His name's Simon Peale, and I want to ask him a few questions."

"Not real smart for a man in your physical condition. The confirmation of the flight is in your email."

"Right."

"I'd better come along as your bodyguard. You can't walk a straight line."

"I need you on the ground here." Chad shook his head. "I sound like the makings of a movie script."

Andy looked at Chad as though he swirled in a test tube. "What else have you uncovered 'cause you aren't the type to watch life happen?"

"I've outlined a plan." Chad pointed to his notebook. "We've got to be careful. We're not dealing with broken equipment or destroyed specimens. As much as I'm a fan of the FBI, they have eyes on us and so do the bad guys."

"No worries, Doc C. I'm a medical geek on research steroids. I've read every piece of information out there on the investigation and H9N15."

"The information written between the lines has my attention. Makes sense the FBI has surveillance teams assigned to Braden Taversty's parents and Decker Anslow's girlfriend."

"I'm a single guy. Want me to get close to her?"

Chad laughed. Andy's thick-rimmed glasses and his aversion to exercise didn't make him a candidate for the most-eligible bachelor in Houston. "I located the girlfriend, except contacting her raises the FBI's radar on us. Let's keep their role at the far end of the spectrum. If she's aware of the virus's origin, she wouldn't tell for fear of her life. Leave her interview to the professionals. I'm focused on something else."

"You're looking for the ones in Spain who hacked you?"

"Great thought, but the FBI techs are on that, too. I'd like for you to go through all my computer files." He pointed to a flash drive on the table between them. "Look for anyone we might have upset."

Andy pushed his glasses up his nose. "Lab reports? Billing? Scheduling?"

"All of it. Somewhere is the reason I've been singled out, and I intend to find the answers."

CHAPTER FORTY-NINE

CHAD WORE A BLACK HARLEY T-SHIRT that showcased the snake tattoo winding around his left bicep, the upshot of a drunken decision in his college days. He plopped on a worn ball cap, worn jeans he'd torn for the occasion, and the same tennis shoes from his last trip. He added sunglasses to cover his black eye and sat in the economy section. The sledgehammer to his head resisted every move. Agent McNally planned to meet him at the airport, and Chad had sent him a selfie in his new getup. A safe trip in and out. No reason for Chad to keep looking over his shoulder.

He'd asked to see the security video from the hospital with the time elements of thirty minutes before and after the assault, but he hadn't received an answer. He routed the second request through his attorney, who wasn't happy Chad's repeated actions occurred without legal representation.

Avoiding Heather ensured her safety and the cover of their possible reconciliation. Jordan told him the National Guard would fly her back to Adam's Island sometime today. Chad yanked his old phone from his jean pocket and pulled up a download of the Bible, easier to read than a clunky book. So out of his comfort zone, but if he were to have a conversation with Heather about God, then he had to read the handbook. Earlier, he'd googled where to begin reading for the first time, and most sites pointed to the book of John. Took him a few minutes to find it since the Bible had John and a 1, 2, and 3 John. Chad's parents had the faith thing in place before they died. While in high school, they joined a church. He had zero interest. To please Heather, he'd gone a few times. Back then he'd do anything to spend time with her, and the conversation stimulated his intellectual side. Soon, he returned to his former beliefs—science answered the questions rooted in the past, present, and future.

He navigated to John, the first chapter, verse one. He'd do his best to keep an open mind . . . Chad read until the plane touched down on the runway. Interesting story.

JFK airport flourished with activity. His senses were on alert. He'd made the flight reservations with his original phone to trap whoever had made the threat. At the time, his plan sounded smart. But now as he walked through the busy airport . . . fear rippled up his spine. He expected media or worse to be waiting for him outside where Agent McNally would pick him up in a black Ford SUV.

The moment Chad exited the airport, a small group of reporters watched the door. Hunger tracked across their faces to be the first to snap a pic or shove a mic into his bruised face . . . like prized prey. He stayed close to an older couple and hoped his disguise threw them long enough for McNally to appear.

The black SUV hugged the curb, but Chad had been in such pain when he rode in a similar FBI vehicle on his previous trip that he hadn't checked the license plates. A man stepped from the passenger side and opened the rear door. While the gesture looked promising, it could be a trap.

The driver's side opened and McNally waved. Chad hurried toward the SUV.

"That's Lawrence," a woman called.

"The FBI's picking him up," a man said.

He heard the cameras click.

Another flashed.

A mic planted in his face.

The nightmare from the hospital attack played in real time.

The passenger in the SUV grabbed his arm and assisted him into the rear of the vehicle. Once inside, he willed his heart to slow.

"Are you all right?" McNally pulled away from the curb.

"I think so. Guess the email hacker hasn't given up."

"Recognize anyone?" McNally said.

"No."

McNally wove in and out of New York's traffic to the FBI building. He spoke a few more words than their prior meeting but nothing substantial for Chad to lock on to. Once at the building, McNally showed Chad the security footage from the assault. Although Peale had avoided security cameras, a woman had identified him as the man who'd attacked him.

In a small FBI interview room, Chad and McNally faced Peale and his lawyer, Karen Hightower, a slender middle-aged woman who oozed with expensive tastes.

"Dr. Lawrence has identified Mr. Peale as the man who assaulted him, and he has a few questions," Agent McNally said.

"They're noninvasive," Chad said.

Hightower folded her hands on the table. "Your humor escapes me. My client doesn't have to answer anything."

Chad fixed his gaze on the charged man's face. "Mr. Peale, this past Saturday, you called me a 'murderer' and laid a fist into my face. I'll file charges unless you cooperate with the FBI by giving the name of who paid you $8,000 to attack me."

Not a muscle twitched. Mr. Peale must be accustomed to interrogation. "You're not making sense."

"Odd," Chad said. "Selective memory?" He turned to Hightower. "Who paid your retainer? I doubt if your services are pro bono. Your tailored suit didn't come from Amazon."

The woman lifted her lips in a smirk. "Where is your legal representation? No one agreed to take your case?"

Chad's attorney had an unmovable schedule and opposed Chad's decision to forge ahead alone. Hightower might not be far off. "I have an FBI agent with me."

"For the record—" Hightower leaned closer—"Mr. Peale made a mistake when he spoke to the FBI. Since then he has pleaded not guilty to the charges. Neither has there been any deposits to his bank account."

"Cash is an easy cover-up," Chad said. "There's a witness."

The woman aimed a cemented smile at him. "Strange, Dr. Lawrence, with all those people at the scene of the incident, why has only one person identified my client as the one who assaulted you? You're being investigated about a horrific crime that has killed over thirty innocent people and infected over a hundred suffering victims. Even if my client had pleaded guilty, his motive would appear to right your deplorable actions."

The name of the game was for the good of the people. Simon Peale had performed a justifiable act of retribution. Could Peale legally escape conviction? "I'm filing charges. I saw who hit me."

The woman's phone buzzed, and she read her screen. "Bad news, Dr. Lawrence. The woman who identified my client? She's withdrawn her statement, an error on her part. Guess it's your word against my client's."

CHAPTER FIFTY

HEATHER CRAWLED INTO HER BED on Adam's Island for a nap. The extra day in the hospital had built her energy, but her body still craved downtime to recuperate. Little Levi kicked more often, giving her sweet moments of joy. During those times, she touched his active body and whispered her love. Anticipation for who he might resemble spun like golden threads in her mind. Catherine read on her bed, no doubt to keep an eye on the pregnant woman who no longer had an appendix.

Before the helicopter transportation to quarantine, Heather had dragged her IV pole, which she'd referred to as another appendage, to meet Mr. Engels. The huge man with bulging biceps and stark carrot-colored hair sat upright in his bed. He expressed concern she'd tested positive for H9N15. "My appendix needed an escape plan." They chatted for a few minutes, and he relayed his appreciation for her paving the way for his wife and family to talk to him. Heather breathed a prayer of thanks for good news amid a difficult situation.

His memory of the time before boarding the plane and the

crisis afterward didn't further the investigation. He believed some-one planned the perfect crime.

"I understand Thomas Powell has pledged to assist us finan-cially," Mr. Engels said. "Very generous of him. My first impres-sion labeled him a rude idiot."

"You met him before the flight?"

"I stood behind him at Starbucks near our gate. The barista messed up his order, and he exploded. Shouted at her and turned the drink upside down on the counter. I told him his behavior looked like he needed a few lessons in manners. He ignored me and walked away. If not for getting tossed out of the airport, I'd have forced him to clean up his mess. On the plane, I saw him assist you in an arrest."

She left Engels's room and texted SAC Bischoff and ASAC Mitchell.

Now as a nap crept closer to Heather, she decided many rea-sons could have caused Thomas to overreact to a coffee order mis-take . . . or Bischoff could be on to substantial evidence. She filed the incident under "process later."

She'd drifted off when a call came in from Mitchell.

"Are you alone?" he said.

"I can be. Hold on while I walk outside."

"Are you cleared to be up?"

"Yes. Moving is good for me." She grabbed her sunglasses and inched her way to the door and hallway. "I'm a turtle. Slow but steady."

"Take your time. The turtle won the race."

"Right." She blinked back a little dizziness and grabbed the wall. Her secret.

They talked about unimportant things while she walked into a hot, sun-filled day, a reminder of home. Cotton-candy clouds as her mother called them. "Go ahead. I'm beyond ears and seated on a bench."

"Parker Karey has filed a ten-million-dollar suit against Lawrence Laboratories for damages incurred during loss of time from his job and the danger of contagion. Wanted you to have the information."

"Sounds like he jumped the gun without evidence of Chad's guilt. I'm sure the media is all over it."

"True. As if they needed more wood for the fire."

She'd check the latest after the call and before her nap. "Karey will make sure I find out about it. Do you have a few minutes for a series of what-ifs? I've had plenty of time to weigh what we've learned."

"Go ahead."

"Decker Anslow has reason to lie, and due to his Taliban loyalties, he won't offer info without special interrogation."

Mitchell chuckled. "There are those trained in persuasive tactics."

"Right. So why didn't the person who spread the virus pocket the pieces instead of flushing them into a business class toilet? That makes more sense. A plan of this nature required how to destroy evidence long before the flight."

"What happened?" Mitchell said. "Panic? The bad guy needed to use the bathroom? Risk of being caught with evidence on him? Fear of an arrest and prosecution? Or did the chain of events happen just as designed?"

"If the culprit is Karey, he might have gotten nervous," she said. "He leans toward the spontaneous side."

"I'm curious. How many people do you think are involved?"

"Minimum of three who carried out the development and distribution. Who is on your radar besides Chad, the Kareys, Taversty, Anslow, and Powell?"

"Dr. Andy Sheehan has the same skills as Chad," Mitchell said.

"If he is involved, I've really messed up reading people. Terrorists work to establish fear and ensue mass casualties—that's

Taversty and Anslow, and the virus accomplished both. In the meantime, we keep searching. Other than Andy working with Chad, the Kareys are after money, and Thomas Powell is a stretch." Heather spanned the area to ensure no one overheard her. "The virus supply is stored somewhere—a reality and our biggest problem. Where are the vials now, and what's their destination? I'm not alone in feeling like we're dealing with a ticking bomb."

"A judge declined our request to search every passenger and crew's luggage. Violated so many privacy laws, and he wasn't ready to sign off on a criminal search warrant to give us the legal authority to confiscate personal items, even if the virus release was termed terrorism. He cited just because a person was on the plane doesn't mean he or she had a criminal role."

She looked across the water to the shoreline. "Does the enemy term the virus release as successful?"

"Either way, we're afraid for the population until the guilty people are in cuffs and the virus remains are confiscated. The compromise of Chad's email and the phone threat don't add up. Agents Javier Rivera and Laura Tobias are working all angles. You know Chad best."

"I'll need to resign if I've made a huge mistake." She recalled his trip to New York. "My heart says he's being used. My training says he has the skills and knowledge. Do we ever know those who surprise us with bizarre crimes?"

"You understand the workings of the mind better than most."

"Doesn't mean I'm infallible. I saw on the FBI site Chad was scheduled to meet this morning with New York's FBI to identify the man who'd attacked him."

"It didn't go well." Mitchell relayed what happened.

"Who paid Peale's attorney?"

"An overseas account."

"Seems to be a pattern."

"A detailed one and a major concern. Lots of agents are on this,

Heather. Your role is vital. Contact me after your next encounter with any of our suspects." Mitchell concluded the call.

She logged onto a secure site and searched for updates on the investigation. Of the 267 passengers, occupations varied from retired to some aspect of business. Family vacations, music teachers, a pastor, two nurses but no one to raise additional concern to the FBI. None shared the same elementary school. A man and a woman attended a Houston middle and high school, and three were grads of A&M University. Zip codes past or present shared no commonality. Frequent medical clinics, restaurants, and entertainment spots hadn't been reported yet. Religious affiliations had no bearing. All appeared as dead ends, but Heather wasn't ready to discard everything that appeared irrelevant. The virus arrived on the flight with someone, and the person couldn't have done it alone.

Heather texted Thomas. **Back at Adam's Island. Want to chat later?**

CHAPTER FIFTY-ONE

HEATHER SAT WITH THOMAS on the bench she referred to as her remote office. The western sun was a huge fireball over New York City casting an amber glow over the water and tugging at the horizon. Breathtaking. The longer summer daylight offered more hours to enjoy the day. She valued light in the literal and metaphorical sense. The waves rolled in, a timeless reminder of stability when the world went awry.

"I hope I never lose sight of nature's beauty. It roots me in the good of our world."

"We take the blessings of our lives for granted." Thomas kept his distance on the other end of the bench. Gossip came with what she was doing, but his demonstration of respect for her as a married woman gave him extra points. For now anyway.

"Were you able to rest this afternoon?" Thomas said.

"Two-hour nap. I'm more tired than I care to admit. Between the surgery and my husband's visit, I'm exhausted." She yawned, and it wasn't for show.

"I'm surprised the FBI didn't stop him."

"An agent in Houston gave him permission. If the FBI had detained him, he'd have avoided the beating." Weariness tugged on her mind and body. "Arguing with me about our differences wasn't worth a concussion."

"I'm sorry for all you've been through." Thomas had a way of adding compassion into his words. Commendable if authentic.

"Everyone here has a story. If my husband is guilty of participating in the development of the virus, he needs to face a judge and jury." She shook her head. "Please accept my apologies for discussing a personal matter."

"No problem. One of the women from your room told several of us you're pregnant. Hope that's okay."

"You heard correctly." She hadn't asked to keep her pregnancy private.

"Mothers are special," he said. "They make sacrifices for their kids. Sleepless nights and long days. My mother always put me first."

"Mine raised me with lots of love and strong values."

"My mother passed twenty years ago. She's often in my thoughts. Is yours still living?"

"Very active and healthy." She drew in a long breath. "She's excited about being a grandmother. So's Dad."

"Never knew my father." His face hardened.

"Do you mind if I change the topic?"

"Go ahead."

She smiled. "Tell me about yourself. Did you always want to work with computers, develop software?"

"No, but I enjoyed math. Numbers make sense while other disciplines have variables. What interests you?"

"I enjoy behavioral science. Psychology fascinates me."

"What's your role at the FBI?"

"Behavior analyst."

"I should have known. I've seen you with the others. Kindness, control, and restraint."

She stared out over the water. "Thanks, but several here would disagree with you."

"Success means controversy. Did you always envision yourself an FBI agent?"

What she'd say wasn't hard to research. "I considered a career in psychology, but curiosity and an interest in law enforcement won out after college graduation. I received my master's in criminal justice from Sam Houston and applied to the FBI. And you?"

"Are you analyzing me?"

She forced a laugh while concentrating on his verbal and non-verbal communications. "You're far too intelligent for me to figure out."

"Agent Lawrence, you wouldn't have your current position if you weren't outstanding."

"I try."

"Grow up in Houston?" he said.

"Yes, and you?"

"Austin. I did my undergrad work at Baylor and my master's and doctorate at UT."

Mitchell had told her he was from Dallas. "And you learned how to bake in college."

"A skill I can always fall back on in the event the computer industry takes a nosedive."

"Very impressive. I saw your middle name on the manifest. Interesting."

He blew out his dislike. "Amadeus?"

"It's charming. Was your mother a classical music fan?"

"My grandfather." He waved his hand. "He died a long time ago." His tone deepened.

"Do you mind my questions?"

"Not at all. Keeps both our minds off our five-star resort. Were you on the flight to Germany in an FBI capacity?"

"Yes and no."

"Must be clandestine."

"Just personal. Any brothers or sisters?" she said.

"Just me and Mom. No one else."

Another lie. "I'm sorry. Every child needs a family . . ." She allowed the unspoken to persuade him that her thoughts were on herself.

His cell phone alerted him to a text. He read the screen. "Excuse me while I handle this."

He walked away and lifted the phone to his ear. "This can be taken care of without upsetting the team. Our purpose is to develop a solid relationship." He walked approximately thirty feet from her and turned his back. A problem at SDI? Personal?

A successful man leveraged his words, even used manipulation when necessary. Not a bad trait—she practiced the same. His lies about his family could be a protective measure for his dysfunctional childhood and just cause to wipe them from his life. Sometimes those wounds paved the way for the inconceivable. Did he have an unhealthy relationship with his mother? Or had Heather stumbled onto an honorable trait for a man who was innocent of any wrongdoing?

Her instincts told her something wasn't right about Thomas. He seemed too good to be true, a man who'd overcome a dysfunctional childhood to take a prestigious place in the business world. Shrewd tactics and mastery of critical situations were characteristics of brilliant people. Some were good and some were evil.

CHAPTER FIFTY-TWO

I'M PROUD OF MY ACHIEVEMENTS. I initiated the development of a virus strain that incorporates the life-threatening qualities of other diseases, capable of destroying millions of people all over the world. Distribution is easy—victims simply breathe.

Quarantine must be endured for a while longer, but I despise it. At times, I feel like I'm drowning in a whirlpool of anxiety with the bland food, deplorable housing, and planned community activities. I'm not accustomed to facing major obstacles. My methods are set in motion, and I detest complications. Instead I must cooperate with every person here. I struggle to remain complacent when I want to complain about normal creature comforts. In that regard, I've accomplished a milestone. This proves I can endure setbacks and move forward.

The CDC's attitude of congeniality fills me with contempt. Their hope for an antiviral will take months if not years to develop. Until then I have miles to travel.

My flawless design will be the architecture of twenty-first

century power. My calculations show wisdom and foresight to all those who crave the perfect crime. I've documented the testing and results, but no one will find my notes. The evidence has been destroyed.

Sonya's nudging and demands infuriate me while disrupting my thoughts. An alliance with an inquisitive woman disrupts the most stalwart of plans. She holds fast to her agenda, but she has no idea how I can shed cumbersome relationships.

She will be eliminated.

Heather will face the same end. She's using Thomas, and he's too stupid to see it.

CHAPTER FIFTY-THREE

DEPRESSION THREATENED to overwhelm Chad. Late evening, he sat at the JFK airport gate before his time to board for Houston. Déjà vu. Blinding pain seared his head, and the interview with Simon Peale soured his optimism. Most people were convinced Chad had developed H9N15, and a half-dozen motivations swirled out there. Although the FBI would eventually find the real criminal, many people had permanently stamped *murderer* on his forehead.

He pulled up his regular phone to check email. His unseen enemy used clever means this trip to blindside him—the airport media and Peale's attorney. Chad scrolled through the typical junk, delete, and read later until a message showed he hadn't escaped the people out to get him.

Your trip to New York failed again. Are you afraid? Start planning for your long jail sentence.

Chad mapped out a reply to the source, but his words were destined to return undeliverable. How could he be a threat to these people? The information they believed he possessed must be huge to monitor his actions. Why did the red laser light stay fixed on him? The implications scared him when the enemy had many resources and no boundaries.

His burner rang, and he longed to hear Heather's voice, but the number was from Andy's burner phone. Maybe he'd stumbled onto something in his scrutiny of the manifest. Chad answered.

"I've plopped on my investigator hat and looked into what we discussed," Andy said. "Nothing linked us to anyone on the flight except one person. What I discovered may be coincidental."

"I'm listening."

"Thomas Powell's charity paid my way through medical school. There was never a problem, and my grades were good. Remember the guy we interviewed last May for an assistant, Trey Alvinson?"

"Yes. You knew him in high school."

"The same. He was one of Thomas Powell's financial recipients, too. Trey applied to work at Lawrence Labs after he'd completed two years in a level 2 private lab."

"We hired him because of his interest in medical research, specifically viruses." Chad recalled the quiet young man, good communication skills and focused. "But he didn't show up for work."

"Right. I tried his cell phone all that day, but he never picked up or texted. Super annoying. The reason he didn't show was because he died in a swimming accident the previous day."

"How did you learn this?"

"Yesterday I spent time on a private Facebook page. It's a group made up of those who've been recipients of Powell's scholarships. Saw Trey's name, so I did some exploring. Checked other social media and saw he hadn't posted since right before he was scheduled to work for us. I learned he'd drowned in a terrible accident.

"I drove to his parents' home, and his mother talked to me.

Trey visited them on Saturday before his first day with us and asked to spend the night. While his parents went to breakfast on Sunday morning, he stayed to swim in the family pool. They returned and discovered he'd drowned. The police determined he'd slipped, bumped his head, and fell in. I confirmed cause of death online."

"Sad. I don't see a relationship to our problem."

"Maybe not," Andy said. "Guilt smacked me hard after talking to the Alvinsons. Trey and I were friends. I apologized for not checking on them and expressed my condolences. While talking to Mrs. Alvinson, Powell's name came up. Here is the peculiar part—Thomas Powell had a controlling interest in the level 2 lab where Trey worked."

Chad zeroed in on Andy's words. "What else?"

"Trey was researching a cure for dengue fever. Powell backed him. He and Trey spent a lot of time together, even two days before the drowning."

A chill swept over Chad. "This could be nothing. Can you arrange for me to talk to the Alvinsons?"

"Figured you'd say that. I'll arrange a visit for tomorrow morning."

"Both parents' contributions will give us an idea if this is worth pursuing. Or if we're two desperate men."

★ ★ ★

Javier met Chad at the Houston airport. "Thought I'd give you a ride home, and we could talk."

Chad studied the agent. "McNally met me in New York, and now you're giving me preferential treatment. Is this to talk about my latest threatening email, pick my brain, or something else?"

Javier stuffed his hands into his pants pocket. "All three, and a hard talk about your foolish detective work."

"What have you found?"

"Have you eaten?"

Chad's patience would fit in the bottom of a test tube. "I should keep track of how many times you refuse to answer a question or offer food." He lifted a finger. "But I figure no answer means a negative. And I'm not hungry."

Outside the airport, Javier swung toward the medical center and Chad's apartment. Having Javier transport him home yanked at his need to control every aspect of his life. Traffic relaxed, giving him a moment for his blood pressure to lower.

"I had time on the plane to concentrate on this mess," Chad said. "Where is Agent Tobias?"

"I assume where she's supposed to be."

"I'm reminded agents work in pairs."

"Usually."

"So I'm the focus of an undercover sting operation." Chad closed his eyes for a moment to clear the debilitating stab to his head. "Is that even the terminology today? Anyway, I started this private investigation to clear my name. Since the beginning of us working together, my email's been hacked, and the FBI traced the IP address to Spain. My life's been threatened. Let me add Simon Peale earned his $8,000 payment to level me. Today's episode with Peale's lawyer and the witness withdrawing her statement says someone is convinced I have incriminating evidence. Another email before I boarded the flight rounds out a miserable and unproductive day. If you don't have a positive swing on this, I suggest saving your pep talk."

"Whine much?"

If Chad had the energy, he'd punch him. "Where do Braden Taversty, Decker Anslow, and Parker and Sonya Karey fit? Do I have information the bad guy needs? If so, what?"

"I don't have your answers, just looking for evidence. By now you realize you've waded in shark-infested waters."

"My life and reputation are on the line." Heather's face walked across his mind. Was she in danger? "Please ensure the FBI continues to monitor my phone. Then you have reference to my outgoing and incoming calls."

"Do you expect the guilty person to call and confess?"

"I wish. Why haven't you inquired about Thomas Powell?"

"Why? Do you know him?"

"Never met him. He's a wealthy businessman. Lives here in Houston. Millionaire a few times over."

"What's your point?" Javier said. "Has he reached out to you?"

"No." Chad dipped his chin. "His company paid for my assistant's medical school—Dr. Andy Sheehan, a link worth investigation considering he's on Adam's Island."

"Flimsy connection. But I'll see what I can find out."

Chad huffed. "You mean you'll find out what you can tell me." He wasn't prepared to discuss Trey Alvinson until he talked to the young man's parents.

At Chad's apartment complex, Javier parked in front of the building and cut the engine. "I want to check your apartment." He pointed to a car. "Agent Tobias is here."

Chad opened the car door and waved at her. He laughed despite the circumstances. "You should have called for more backup. Somebody has my itinerary."

Agent Tobias greeted them, and the three rode the elevator up to his fourth-floor apartment. The door stood ajar.

Javier pulled his weapon. "Stay here." He and Agent Tobias entered the apartment.

Chad counted to five and walked inside. Sofa cushions lay on the floor, slashed. Cabinet doors flung open.

"Told you to stay outside," Javier called from the kitchen. "Do you ever listen to authority?"

"Sometimes." He did a 180 at the destruction and walked into his bedroom. Drawers lay on the carpet with the contents tossed aside. Bed linens were crumpled in a heap. His mattress and box spring leaned against the window wall. Clothes strewn from one side of the room to the other. He searched through his bathroom linen closet. "My laptop's gone."

"Anything someone could use?"

"I downloaded important files onto a flash drive before I left. Had notes, H9N15 observations, and what little I'd learned."

"Where is the flash drive?"

"In the Whole Foods coffee bean jar."

Javier and Tobias joined him in his bedroom. "Anything on it to use against you or aid the bad guy?"

"Everything we've discussed, including the IP address traced to Spain." Chad checked the glass container in the kitchen holding the coffee beans. It lay in pieces on the floor minus the flash drive.

"Looks like they found what they were looking for," Javier said.

How much worse could things get?

CHAPTER FIFTY-FOUR

CHAD AND ANDY APPROACHED the Alvinson home, a two-story brick traditional. Heather favored this style. Thoughts of her never left him no matter how hard he attempted to shove them away. He rang the doorbell. An FBI team had swept his ransacked apartment last night, and he'd spent the remainder of the hours in a hotel. The thieves had taken his laptop and flash drive—nothing else. They left the coffee beans amid the broken glass. The apartment management estimated three to four days before the renovation and repairs were completed.

He turned to Andy. "I'm prepared to do whatever it takes to find out if Trey is linked to the virus and what he and Powell researched together. While it's probably nothing, I'm tired of taking a backseat to whatever is going on."

"I'm angry his death might not have been an accident. Trey swam on the swim team in high school and college. You saw him, slim, buff."

"Whoa. Hadn't expected that. Do you want me to handle this?"

Andy shook his head. "I was friends with Trey for too many years to let this go. We have different reasons for probing this."

A white-haired woman answered, and Andy introduced Chad. Sadness hung over Mrs. Alvinson like a water-soaked umbrella. She invited them inside to a living area, where a tall, balding man introduced himself as Trey's father.

"Please, have a seat. Andy, Dr. Lawrence." Mr. Alvinson pointed to two chairs. "We know who you are and the accusations against you. Because of Andy's friendship with Trey, we've agreed to this meeting. But we have no idea why you want to talk to us." The Alvinsons squeezed together on the sofa. He wrapped his arms around his wife's shoulders.

"I'm sorry about your son's unfortunate accident," Chad said. "Did he have health issues?"

"No, sir. Since our son's death, my wife and I have asked ourselves why his untimely passing. It's impossible to move on with our lives with only memories to comfort us."

Chad allowed a moment of reverent silence. "Trey impressed us with his dedication to medical research." He stared into the man's clouded eyes. "We'd looked forward to his input at Lawrence Labs."

Mrs. Alvinson covered her mouth, then spoke. "He had dreams to help the world."

"Andy tells me he was conducting work at a private lab with a goal of developing a vaccine for dengue fever."

She nodded. "He'd visited a poor area in Ethiopia and witnessed those stricken with diseases, mainly dengue fever. From then on, his heart was bent on a cure. Thomas Powell had funded his medical school and learned of his interest. He contacted someone to invest in a private lab so Trey could continue. I'm sure he said a woman who lived overseas, but I never heard her name. Why the need for an investor when Powell had plenty of money?" She drew in a sharp breath. "Trey told us he'd discovered something important. And he'd tell us after he ran more tests."

"Did he keep notes or a computer file?"

Mr. Alvinson gripped his fist. "Powell has possession of those. He wanted to find another medical researcher to continue the work." His features set up like concrete. "He'd funded Trey's lab and claimed everything there belonged to him."

"But you wanted them as a reminder of your son's hard work." Chad voiced the anguish written on the couple's faces.

"My wife and I expressed a desire for Baylor College of Medicine to have his documentation. Didn't do any good. Powell was insistent, a hard man to deal with. Dr. Lawrence, how would our son's information help you?"

"Andy and I are searching for answers to help those stricken by a virus called H9N15, the one I'm accused of developing."

"No proof or you'd be behind bars," Mr. Alvinson said. "From the looks of your bruises, the trip to New York wasn't the best idea."

"True." Chad offered a grim smile. "Are you aware one of the people quarantined in New York is Thomas Powell?"

"Yes. Despise the man, but I don't want him dead."

"He hasn't been infected."

"I'm confused. Is Trey linked to this?" He straightened. "Did Powell mention our son?"

"No, sir. If your son has made medical discoveries, his notes may expedite the progress of a vaccine for other viruses. Since Powell and your son spent time together, did Trey tell you what they discovered?"

"Why? What am I missing? The FBI hasn't contacted us."

"Sir," Andy said, "they'd be here if they believed Trey's research could help this case. I'm the one responsible for our visit today. There's a Facebook group page for those who've been recipients of Mr. Powell's generosity, and I reached out to see what everyone was doing. When I learned Trey's death occurred the day before he was scheduled to start work at Lawrence Labs, I came by to talk to your wife. I regret I've not kept in contact."

Mr. Alvinson glanced out a window to the street. No doubt his thoughts reflected what Andy hadn't said. "Sorry, but I can't help you. Mr. Powell has Trey's information."

"Sir, are you certain Mr. Powell received all of Trey's research notes? Is there any place he could have put them?"

"Powell had them before Trey died. My wife and I requested a copy at the funeral, but he declined. We planned to read them together as a legacy before presenting them to Baylor."

Chad jumped in. "Did you consult an attorney?"

"We were told Mr. Powell had legal access. The cost to pursue legal action is expensive."

Chad despised what life and circumstances had done to these people. "Where is the lab located?"

"In an office building in the Memorial area. My wife and I checked for Trey's belongings and learned the lab had been closed. All the equipment, furniture, and personal items had been removed. We requested more info but got nowhere."

"Did you ask Powell why he closed the lab when he wanted someone to continue Trey's work?"

"He said the loss of our son hurt him so badly he'd decided to give up the project. Powell still claimed ownership." Mr. Alvinson's lips quivered. "It's an emotional whirlwind. One minute, I'm grateful for Trey's education, and the next I'm angry Powell confiscated the notes."

"Did you check Trey's apartment?"

"Someone had broken in and destroyed most of what he owned."

"What did the police say?"

"Open case."

Sounded familiar. "You have experienced a tragic loss." Chad meant every word. "We appreciate all you've told us."

Chad and Andy rose to leave, but the Alvinsons stayed seated.

"If Trey's research helped to develop a vaccine for a virus," Mr. Alvinson said, "would you give him recognition?"

Chad shifted. Was the couple aware of what Trey had discovered? "Yes, sir. We want to help those infected and to be blunt, clear my name. Your son's legacy would be intact."

Mr. Alvinson and his wife exchanged gazes. "We may be able to help you. We found a handwritten journal inside his duffel bag. We assume he left it that Saturday night as though he wanted us to find it. It contains some of his notes but little else, a mix of personal and professional reflections. There may be something you can use. His handwriting can be difficult to decipher. Neither of us have been able to read it all the way through without breaking down. Maybe when the pain softens."

Chad poured compassion into his words. "Can I look at the journal?"

Mr. Alvinson disappeared and returned with a thick leather binder and handed it to Chad. "Take all the pics you want, but it stays right here."

"I'd do the same in your position." Chad opened to the first page of handwritten entries.

"Three-quarters of the way through is an unusual statement," Mr. Alvinson said. "The pages aren't numbered but dated as in a journal, and the one I'm referring to begins July 20."

In my efforts to mutate the dengue virus to find a cure, I stumbled upon scary data results, a new virus.

November 23: I've decided my research is more important than I could ever imagine. If what I've found is already out there and has killed people, further testing will prove it. I will not stop until I discover an antiviral.

February 22: The results are conclusive. Mr. P. said he . . .

"What are those last two words," Chad said to Andy and passed the journal to the Alvinsons. No one could decipher them. Two or maybe three words scribbled together. "Andy and I will review this later."

Andy snapped pics over Chad's shoulder. Some days Trey doodled, and some days he didn't complete his thoughts. Chad chose not to comment on the entries where Trey mentioned concern for Mr. P.'s behavior but failed to record an explanation.

February 23: Mr. P. insists I keep the test results to myself. He says this will set my career in place.

April 5: Mr. P. and I will look at the final test results for the new virus and potential antiviral.

April 10: I've decided to apply to Lawrence Labs for a position. Medical research is my goal. Not what I fear is happening.

April 28: I'm confident in the testing. Nervous, too. To uncover a new virus is frightening, especially in the wrong hands. But the antiviral is there somewhere. How do I handle the issue of Mr. P.'s orders to keep the virus and the cure from the rest of the world? Tomorrow I will take a stand.

May 17: I refuse to argue with Mr. P. I'll begin at Lawrence Labs next week. I no longer want to work for Mr. P. My work is now in his possession, and my notes have disappeared from the lab's computer. He's changed the lock on the lab. I can't get inside without the security code, and he refuses to give it to me. Unless he's with me, I'm unable to work.

Mr. Alvinson tried twice to talk before the words finally came. "My wife and I aren't the least bit worried Thomas Powell's so-called best interests are threatened. He treated us like scum after Trey's death."

"Have you told anyone about the journal or the conversations with Trey?" Chad said.

"No. The lawyer knew of our son's death and our desire for his notes. No reason to share what we couldn't back up."

"I urge you not to talk to anyone about this but the FBI."

CHAPTER FIFTY-FIVE

THE REST OF THE MORNING and into the afternoon, Chad and Andy deliberated what they'd learned at the Alvinsons'. Andy refused to eat or drink his normal consumption of coffee. He claimed deadly viruses looked safer than what Thomas Powell might have done. Chad assured him the right people investigated the case. He downloaded the photos of notes from Trey's journal and copied them onto two flash drives, one for himself and one for Javier.

The unreadable post in the journal remained a mystery. From Trey's handwriting, an *e* was a straight line, and Chad and Andy found three of those. Chad deciphered two *l*'s and possibly a *y*.

Before Andy left him at the hotel, Chad scheduled an hour with Javier at the FBI building for late afternoon. Now the agent sat across from him in an interview room.

"Did you spend the night at your and Heather's condo?" Javier said.

"Not wise when we're in the middle of a divorce. The break-in is none of her concern."

"Or are you protecting her?"

Chad searched for a clever response. Javier continued. "Never mind. There's more going on beneath the surface with you two. For a man who wants to be free of his wife, you sure are sticking your neck out."

"Eight years of habit."

"Right. Could be love or guilt for the years she supported you. What do you have? Or should I ask what have you been up to?"

Chad summoned a smile. The agent had figured him out when it came to Heather. "First I want to confirm our conversation is videoed and recorded."

"It is."

"Did you trace the email I received in New York?"

"Yes. It led to an IP address in Norway, which means the source is an intelligent hacker with an agenda."

"I'm convinced Thomas Powell is behind the email hacks, and he paid Peale off as well as his fancy lawyer." Without the FBI or another well-equipped law enforcement agency to locate evidence, his discoveries were mere speculation.

"You're climbing a ladder. And the rungs are weak."

"You bet, and all the way to the top of truth. Were you aware Powell was connected to a medical research lab for one of his scholarship recipients?"

Javier studied him. "You have my attention."

"I've introduced new info or you're playing along." Chad relayed what he and Andy had learned from the Alvinsons. "Although Trey used the journal for personal reflections, Andy snapped pics of every page of his entries, and I have them. I understand why Powell claimed the research belonged to him and denied the Alvinsons a copy. Here's why I'm suspicious. Trey tells his parents he's working on something important. His journal states he's found a new virus and developed an antivirus. Powell takes control of the lab, and Trey drowns the day before he's to begin work for me. In some areas, Trey's handwriting is difficult to read."

He handed Javier the flash drive. "Even a medical geek like me saw the issues between him and Powell. Here's another tidbit to chew on—I met with Trey at Lawrence Labs three times before I hired him. I bet Powell found out."

Javier inserted the flash drive into his computer. "You've uncovered a few details the FBI can use."

"Wish I had the lab owner's name, and I assume it's a woman overseas." Chad reached for pen and paper between them and jotted the address where Trey had once worked. "It's closed but you might need this."

"The woman could be fictitious." Javier nodded his thanks and scooted the pad back to him. "I'll send the flash drive's content to our tech people to decipher Trey's handwriting. What else?"

"Trey had a girlfriend, but Powell insisted he break it off with her last November because she distracted him. I have her name, Leigh Masterson. This February he told Trey to move out of his parents' home because they interfered with his life pursuits, and he again complied. According to the journal, Powell demanded Trey abandon his social life until he finished the project. I do see how Powell's financial investment could dictate how Trey spent his off hours."

Javier looked beyond Chad at the wall. "You're saying the journal indicates Trey discovered a new virus and then developed an antiviral. If he and Powell are responsible for H9N15, we need to examine the research notes." He toyed with the pen. "What have you left out?"

"If I had all the answers, I'd no longer be a person of interest. Trey had confidence in Powell's financial support until the relationship took a possessive and maybe dangerous turn. Powell, a man with a deadly virus and in possession of an antiviral, stands to be one of the most powerful and wealthy men in the world. Wouldn't be the first time someone killed for either one. From his actions on Adam's Island, he's already achieved leadership status, and bringing an antiviral to the table raises him to sainthood."

"Paper thin."

Chad frowned. "Why?"

"If your conclusions are right, he's tossed a lot of money to cover criminal activities. No one goes to that much effort unless there's significant motivation."

"I gave you two, and over thirty people are dead!" Chad fought to calm his temper.

"None of those on the flight are linked to Powell."

"We both know a psychopath often chooses random victims," Chad said. "The truth is if I were an agent and presented this to you, we'd be mapping out an investigative strategy. And you'd have called in the big guns."

Javier dragged his hand over his face. "The FBI will want to talk to the Alvinsons and Leigh Masterson. Trust me, we are investigating this case in ways you can't imagine."

"So am I. Someone infected those people on the plane, and I will find who is behind it. One positive for my side is I'm convinced Powell is worried Trey gave me his findings, so I'm a significant target. Explains why I've been framed." He fought for composure. "That means my wife is in a precarious situation. I'm not ready to accept Trey's drowning was an accident and just anyone could have wrecked my apartment."

Javier made notes. He lifted his gaze to meet Chad's scrutiny. "What else?"

"I assume the FBI will look into Peale's lawyer and the origin of who paid for Trey Alvinson's lab and equipment. Where's the equipment now? Where was it purchased?"

"We'll find out. You claim Powell funded the lab to have Alvinson spend hours researching the dengue virus. He's successful with his results, but he doesn't want to work for Powell and takes a job at Lawrence Labs. Powell arranges an accidental death. Then you propose the virus was released at a calculated time on flight 3879. Huge risk and doesn't seem probable. What if the pilots were infected?"

"I looked into the plane's air ventilation system. The airflow in the cockpit would be the last affected by the virus," Chad said.

"So did Powell plan to parachute out?"

"Haven't put together his whole strategy yet. Which is why I came to you."

"The journal wouldn't hold up in a court of law."

"Admit it, Javier, every word I've said has nailed its mark. I've spent hours deliberating this. Parker Karey and his wife are suspects, but I have no idea why. He's not my favorite person with his lawsuit, but he could see an opportunity to make some money. Who knows? The Kareys could be working with Powell. But I'm going to find the evidence to show Powell masterminded H9N15."

"What if you're wrong?"

"I'd rather be wrong than do nothing, and here's my plan . . ."

CHAPTER FIFTY-SIX

HEATHER PICKED HER WAY along the shore to a favorite spot where she liked to sit, think, and pray. She smiled at the thought of the smooth rounded boulders resembling baby bottoms. Nature's beauty soothed her while she longed to be on the case from a different location than Adam's Island. Renewed strength energized her. Dr. Francisca and the surgeon had given her instructions to rest. She'd obey for Levi's sake. He was a strong little guy to weather the attacks against him.

Chad hadn't contacted her, which said her contingency to put their relationship back together had met with resistance. She shouldn't be disappointed, although a seed for a better future had taken root. Had her request to seek God exceeded his limit? Or had he viewed it as nagging?

The sandbox of her mind sifted through old memories allowing good times to build castles of hope.

A good outcome of the quarantine came with Catherine's and Tatum's friendship. Once they were all home again, they planned to meet regularly. She held her breath. Tatum's health dwindled. Not fair. Not right.

Her phone rang out its familiar summons. ASAC Mitchell.

"Free to talk?" he said.

"Yes. I'm at the shore."

He explained Chad's second email threat, the current state of his apartment, the situation surrounding Trey Alvinson, and Chad's conversation with Javier Rivera.

"Was an autopsy done on Trey Alvinson?" she said.

"No. The ME ruled drowning. Testimony from the parents point to unusual circumstances. If need be, we can request the body be exhumed."

"Is Chad no longer on your radar?"

"We're not ready to make the announcement and won't be until the lab's cleared. Rivera says he and Chad agreed on a plan. Have you given him a course in Investigation Tactics 101?"

Curiosity jogged across her mind. "I'm concerned for his safety. Is he in protective custody?"

"Refused."

"I'll talk to him." A twinge of alarm rang through her. "What's this plan?"

"To contact Powell and claim he has Trey's notes. Plans to offer him a deal."

"Blackmail? Chad's not trained. He'll get himself killed. We've been to the firing range, and he's a terrible shot. He doesn't own a gun. And the FBI approved his so-called crazy scheme?" Her voice rose. "Why didn't Rivera talk him out of it?"

"He tried, which is why I'm talking to you. We don't approve of his Captain America approach. The issue in asking you to call him isn't a good idea when his phone's been hacked."

"We have burner phones."

Mitchell snorted. "Why do two people who are separated use burner phones?"

"I suggested it after his attack. If we talked, I didn't want to risk the bad guys finding out."

"I don't understand. Why wasn't I informed?"

"Chad asked for a second chance. I said we'd discuss it after the investigation." She hesitated, sensing Mitchell's disapproval. "There are a few requirements on my end. But if he wanted to talk, a burner was the best option." She calculated the days left in quarantine. "I'll persuade Chad to forget his ludicrous plan, and I'll move closer to Powell."

"You're a great agent, Heather, but be careful. If Powell, the Kareys, or someone else is the killer, they'll have no problem eliminating those who get in their way."

"My point. I may want to kill Chad myself. So I don't need someone else doing the honors." She sighed.

"What if Chad has no wife or baby?"

His words jolted her. Her baby had survived insurmountable obstacles and beat the odds. "Just send me everything Chad's given you."

"Okay, will send now." Mitchell requested she check in after her next meeting with the Kareys or Powell. "Has your opinion changed about Chad's involvement?"

She prayed for divine guidance. "Yes. A guilty man doesn't put his life in jeopardy to prove himself innocent."

Minutes later, Heather still looked out over the water, listening to waves rush and crash against the shore. The rhythm that relaxed her body and soul. She'd focused so many weeks and months on Chad's faults. But had she dealt with her own? What blame did she share in their failed marriage? If she'd been gentler in her demands for him to talk about the last trip to Africa and Paul's death, could the heartache now have been avoided?

She'd watched their relationship spiral and tried to glue the broken pieces together . . . cooked his favorite foods, adhered to his schedule, searched for ways to make him happy. She catered to his every whim and ignored her own needs. No arguments. Keep the peace.

Codependency.

Heather swiped at a tear. She'd enabled Chad's drift to work obsession. She'd fed it, and her efforts for approval had driven him away. His respect for her vanished. Her own self-respect suffered, and her need for him grew in an unhealthy way.

Oh, God, what have I done?

Did she have the courage to accept the truth and move forward?

Own the problem.

Ask forgiveness from God and Chad.

Choose to change.

Determine not to fall into the codependency trap ever again.

Was she to stay married to Chad despite their differences?

Chad needed a wife who balanced him and whom he balanced. Little Levi needed a mother who loved, guided, and allowed him to make mistakes and learn from them.

So much easier said than done. That's where God came in.

With the fiery sun in a slow afternoon descent, Heather left the imaginary peaceful world along the rocky island shore and walked to the quarantine facility. The dinner hour approached, but first she needed to talk to Chad.

Heather grabbed a bottle of water from the recreation room. The words she needed to say to Chad rolled and rearranged in her mind. A handful of people were in the area, and one of them was Sonya Karey—the first time she'd seen the woman alone.

Heather unscrewed the bottle and took a long drink. Sonya wore her pink hair in a ponytail and no makeup, giving her a youthful appearance . . . or naive. "Hi, Sonya."

The young woman turned to the hallway.

"I'm not the enemy," Heather said. "I want the guilty person or persons arrested just like you."

She whipped around. "We have a difference in opinion."

"We, as in you and Parker? What do you think?" Heather studied her. Did she not have an identity outside of Parker? She pointed to two chairs. "Want to talk a little?"

"It's nearing dinnertime, and Parker will be expecting me."

"We have a good thirty minutes."

"I have nothing to say to you."

"Really? Your husband is looking for answers about the virus, and he believes I have them." Heather noted Sonya's fisted hands at her side. "But I don't. You could tell him that for me."

"Tell him yourself. Not my job to be your errand girl. You, on the other hand, have no idea what my husband is capable of doing."

Sonya made her way toward the cafeteria. It would take more than one encounter for Heather to make a friend.

CHAPTER FIFTY-SEVEN

CHAD LEFT A MESSAGE and his regular phone number with Thomas Powell's answering service. Betting hadn't made Chad's résumé, unless he deferred to calculating test tube data and projecting the results. He assumed Powell's response in two hours or less depended on the man's curiosity. Or a hit man had Chad in his sights waiting until he left his apartment. Andy planned to meet with Leigh Masterson—Trey Alvinson's ex-girlfriend—this evening, but Javier was left out of the loop on this one. If anything of value resulted, Chad would fill him in.

Fifty-five minutes later Chad's phone buzzed with a call, a number with no name. He touched Speaker and pressed Record. Just in case the FBI didn't record this call. "Dr. Chad Lawrence here."

"Dr. Lawrence, I feel like we're old friends."

"Your voice isn't familiar."

"Excuse me. Thomas Powell here. You wanted to talk?"

"I do. Let me get right to the point. I met with Trey Alvinson several times before his unfortunate accident, and he gave me incredible research notes."

"Trey talked to you three times, not several, and his notes are in my possession. Nothing there pertains to you. The owner closed the lab and shipped the equipment overseas. If you're interested in acquiring items for your laboratory, I'm not your man."

"I'm not interested in buying anything, Mr. Powell. I'm selling a valuable commodity. Trey made a copy of his findings, and he gave them to me. They're in a safe place."

"Why would I care? I'm not a medical researcher."

"You don't mind if I take them to the FBI? I'm sure they can sort them out."

"I'm confused. What are you referring to?"

"Let's toss out your story and get to the truth. My guess is the overseas investor is a sham, and you funded Trey Alvinson's research. He stumbled onto a potential virus, and you encouraged him to develop it and create an antiviral. You demanded he break off all social and family ties to concentrate on his work. Your attempt to rule his life caused him to leave your employment and work for me. You arranged an accident and disposed of the lab's equipment. Obviously you injected the antiviral to protect yourself. What I don't understand is why did you infect all those people on flight 3879?"

Powell laughed. "You, Dr. Lawrence, are suspected of releasing one of the deadliest viruses in the history of known medicine. According to the media, your reputation is destroyed, and I heard from a person here in quarantine that you're being sued for $10 million. Trey died in an unfortunate accident. Your attempt to coerce money from me is a plea from a desperate man who's destined to spend the rest of his life behind bars . . . or die by lethal injection."

"Those means are for the guilty. I'm innocent, and Trey provided the truth. But I commend you on covering your tracks. Clever. Well done."

"Why contact me now?" Powell said. "You've had plenty of time to give your alleged proof to the FBI and exonerate yourself."

"I'd like to work out a deal."

"For what? Do you and your beautiful pregnant wife need a little extra cash?"

Chad hadn't expected that response. "We're not speaking except through our lawyers. This conversation and potential business arrangement are between you and me."

"The media want ways to keep the story alive, and reporters will state and print whatever it takes. Dr. Sheehan lives alone, right?"

Chad cringed. "I have the evidence to put you away permanently."

"You're delusional, Dr. Lawrence. I am a victim in this tragedy. Your wife, on the other hand, could be involved."

"Heather is an FBI agent, and if the bureau had any reservations, she'd be wearing cuffs. The issue is my evidence proves you're responsible for funding the development of H9N15 and an antiviral. The transfer of notes will cost $10 million, same as Parker Karey's lawsuit. The question is, how important is Trey's research to you?" Chad hung up and ended the recording.

He transferred the conversation to a new laptop and placed the file in Dropbox. What had he accomplished? What if Chad had made a terrible mistake by contacting Powell without solid evidence of his involvement?

Heather brushed her teeth and slipped into pajamas. She slid her toothbrush and toothpaste into a plastic bag and sealed it. Weariness rolled through her like slow-moving clouds, but she would not close her eyes before calling Chad. The other women finished in the bathroom. She turned on the water to mask her voice and pressed in his burner number.

"This is Heather."

"Good to hear your voice. Are you healthy?"

"Yes. ASAC Mitchell told me your apartment had been broken into. I'd have offered the condo, but it would derail our separated status."

"My place will be suitable for habitation soon. No reason to jeopardize our story."

"I have four things to say if you can spare the time." Her voice trembled.

"Should I take notes?" His light laughter met her ears.

"I'm serious." Why did confessions have painful attributes? "First, I'm sorry for trying to fix things between us. My choices led me straight into codependency. Never again. No matter where our relationship leads, we are accountable for our own behavior."

"I used your codependent tendencies against you to stretch the boundaries of my own agenda. I'm sorry."

Heather closed her eyes. *Don't stop now.* "Second thing, I'm convinced you aren't responsible for H9N15. No doubts. If I'm wrong, I'll resign from the FBI."

"What?"

"You heard correctly. Third, I apologize for shoving faith down your throat. I preached at you, and my self-righteousness alienated you from any thought of a relationship with God. That decision is between you and Him."

"I've read the book of John and started Luke. By using archeological proof to confirm the Bible's validity, my mind's open. Non-biblical sources show Jesus Christ existed. It's the whole God knows all and is in control that I'm struggling with. If questions come to mind, I'll call you. Remember when we were first married and discussed the reality of God?"

Heather shivered. "Sure. If I don't have the answers, I'll find someone who does."

"Would you rather I talk to Jordan?"

"It's your choice." She'd think through his reading the Bible later.

"Okay, you said four things?"

"Mitchell gave me a little scary update."

He chuckled—been a long time since she'd heard any signs of humor from him, and this was the second instance in the same conversation.

"I'm worried you're in too deep. If Powell is behind the virus, he's not an amateur. He'll find a way to eliminate you or pay an assassin."

"He's already done that in New York. I accepted more of his repercussions when I gave him my deal."

Her heart thumped as hard as their baby's kick. "Tell me you're teasing. ASAC Mitchell claimed you planned to threaten blackmail."

"Right. May not have been my most intellectual move."

"No kidding. You've chosen to anger a big dog, and his bite could be for keeps. You botched an FBI investigation. In view of your crazy plan, I'm surprised Javier hasn't arrested you."

"I told him his objections made sense."

"He thought you'd changed your mind. For the record, jail is safer than your apartment. Let me hear the recording." And he did. She bit her tongue to stop the bubble of anger. Chad hadn't uncovered a thing that could be proven in court. "If his threats are legit, his next target is Andy."

"If I'd taken the time to think about the conversation beforehand, I would have seen the best way to get to me is through someone else. At least it wasn't you."

"He's too smart to come after me. I'm a trained agent—think through my actions."

"I'm sorry. I had no idea he'd turn the tables on me. Watch your back. His threats against Andy may be real or he could blind-side us.

"I understand your position as an agent, and other than the National Guard, you're the only law enforcement inside quarantine. Another reason for me to push on with what I've discovered."

"Stay out of this, Chad. I mean it. Let the FBI handle what they do best."

CHAPTER FIFTY-EIGHT

CHAD'S MIND SPUN in a vortex of what-if scenarios. He slammed his fist into his palm and paced the hotel room. He needed no more persuasion—Powell was knee-deep in the virus scandal. Why didn't the FBI see through the obvious?

Glancing at the late hour, he texted Andy to find out about his conversation with Leigh Masterson.

Andy returned the text. **Thought it might be too late to call. I'm awake.**

Andy's number lit up on Chad's burner phone. "How was your evening?"

"Hard. I approached Leigh at her workplace, a high-end women's shop near The Woodlands Mall. I told her I was a friend of Trey's and wanted to talk. We met for coffee when she got off work, and the moment I mentioned his research, she shut me down. I went the route of our longtime friendship and the shock of his death. She kept me at a distance until I asked if Trey had given a reason for ending their relationship. She said no. She cried for a long time. I didn't know whether to wait it out or comfort her. I gave her napkins to blow her nose. Once she got past that, she said Trey had called her the Sunday morning of the accident. He told her he loved her and wanted to get back together. He'd taken steps to get away from Thomas Powell dictating his life. The power and control had gotten scary. She refused him. The next day she learned he drowned."

"A lot of regret there. I'll relay the conversation to Agent Rivera. Although he's not happy with my investigation." Chad paused. "A lawyer would discount her testimony by stating Trey didn't give her proof of Powell threatening harm."

"You analyze too much, Doc. Let the legal types sort out the evidence. I asked Leigh if she'd give a statement to the FBI. She wasn't sure."

Chad agreed with an inner voice that sounded like Heather's. "I want you to stop the amateur sleuthing. The danger keeps mounting, and I apologize for dragging you into this."

"What am I supposed to do with my idle time?"

"Take a vacation, read, study, work out, find a nice girl, schedule watching a Marvel marathon. Just keep your distance from me until Powell is arrested. If you need to contact me, use this burner."

"Why? What's the change?"

"He threatened you."

"So do many of the invisible particles we test at the lab."

"This isn't the same."

"Can still kill. Nope, Doc C. I'm all in. You can't do this alone."

"I'll chance it, Andy. You're an intelligent, great guy, and I want my assistant to stay in one piece. G'night." He ended the call.

A text sounded from Andy. **Picking up Leigh tomorrow night after her work. I have Javier Rivera's card.**

I wish you'd back off.

Ain't happening.

Be careful. What time are you to meet her?
9:30.
Call when you're on your way home. Chad continued to stress. No way around it. His career, his wife and child, and those whose friendship mattered were swinging from a thin rope over shark-infested waters.

Andy was right. Chad analyzed every cell of life, and the God thing played into it. Chad had learned 95 to 99 percent of a person's belief system was prompted by the subconscious. If he were to find out if God was real, then he had to ignore the inner doubts. Trust in faith. Believe in an invisible deity. The concept slammed against his scientific, prove-me mode of operation. But helplessness snapped at him.

From what Chad had read in the Bible, God was perfect, but an infallible character also meant every word of the Bible was accurate. Back to his foundation for not giving in to an all-knowing God—the Bible's message was written by real men who made mistakes, were selfish, greedy, and exhibited every flaw imaginable. Chad admitted his skepticism. He needed concrete data, but right now, he longed for someone or something to rectify the virus situation.

Was the threat against Andy worthless dribble and nothing more? Were the Alvinsons in danger? Jordan? The other nagging reality was the FBI, CDC, and law enforcement agencies didn't share their progress with him. Their reasoning made sense, but the secrecy didn't mend his safety net.

Chad rested his face in his hands. Andy was clueless about investigative work. For that matter, Chad knew little. He didn't own a gun or have self-defense skills. But he could follow Andy tomorrow night and keep an eye out for one of Powell's hired thugs.

He reached for his legal pad and pen. If he accomplished anything tonight, he'd work on an idea brewing about the virus.

CHAPTER FIFTY-NINE

HEATHER HAD SLEPT FITFULLY. Her conversation with Chad, the virus, the baby, all rolled through her mind. The roast beef dinner wasn't to her liking, and now her stomach growled. Stupid hormones.

The cafeteria had fruit in the fridge, but Heather had her sights on ice cream, a chocolate, peanut butter ice cream sandwich. With extra peanut butter. She knew the spot where the little packages of the creamy delicacy were stored. The more the tan, gooey treat assaulted her, the more her mouth watered. She tossed back the blanket, slid into flip-flops, and grabbed her robe. Had she lost her mind? People were dying. A virus had the potential to kill people around the world. And she was hungry?

Embarrassing.

Shameful.

And true.

In the cafeteria Heather greeted Doris, the unofficial dorm mom, and the man called Tex who cooked breakfast and sometimes lunch. Both drank coffee in the stillness of the early morning. Heather headed straight for the freezer area. The kids might have depleted the supply of ice cream treats. She searched and wrapped her cold fingers around what she wanted.

"Want to sit with us?" Doris said.

"Love to." Heather grabbed a paper plate, knife, and an individual packet of peanut butter before swinging a leg over the bench beside Doris.

"Do I see cravings?" Doris said.

"Pitiful, I know. Never have I done this." She peeled back the ice cream and smothered it in peanut butter. Taking a bite, Heather allowed the treat to bathe her mouth in creamy goodness.

"If you want an omelet, I can whip it up."

With her mouth full, she shook her head at Tex.

Thomas entered the area. "Looks like a party on Adam's Island."

Tex gestured to the bench. "Join us."

"Let me get some coffee first." Thomas filled his cup and sat opposite Heather. "Peanut butter, huh?"

"Keep it to yourself. Once the kids figure it out, my concoction will be gone."

"Have you ever listed the many ways to enjoy peanut butter?" Thomas said.

"Is this a trick question?"

"The winner gets kicked off the island."

Tex chimed in. "With a year's supply of Jif."

She smiled. "Let me count the ways I can whip up a peanut butter craze."

"With peanut butter, I can always top you."

She groaned at his pun. "These are my favs, other than ice cream—pickles, pickles and mayo, bananas, bologna, donuts, chocolate, chip dip with jelly, latte, bacon, cookies, French toast . . . and waffles."

Thomas sipped on his coffee as though contemplating his

answer. "You forgot a wrap, cupcakes, ice cream, taco, meatballs, grilled with fried onions, and sushi."

Heather grimaced. "A few of those are disgusting. Have you eaten all of them?"

"Yes. And they're good." He leaned back on the cafeteria bench. "When I was a kid, Mom and I explored the many facets of peanut butter. Great memories."

Doris smiled. "I grew up on a farm along the Mississippi River. Twelve of us, and our best breakfast was pancakes with sorghum molasses and peanut butter."

"Those keep your mom forever in your heart," Thomas said. "My best days were with my mom."

"The older I get, the more I find I'm just like her." Doris glanced at her watch. "Time to make my runs." She rose from the bench with an empty cup. "See you later."

Tex followed suit with a declaration breakfast arrived in three hours and the biscuits were calling his name.

Heather sat alone with Thomas. She'd use every minute. "What do you envision for your future? You're already super successful."

"Family for starters."

Perfect answer if he intended to impress an FBI agent. "Mine, too. Do you have business goals? Are there areas to explore besides software?"

He propped his elbow on the table and rested his chin. "I've been researching ventures beyond SDI. I've funded college and university students in various studies. Now I want to invest in at-risk kids."

"Community centers?"

He nodded. "And summer camps. I want to encourage varied interests for boys and girls. Offer free tutoring, sports instruction, libraries, cooking, and crafts. Show the many career opportunities out there. Equip them with basic living skills. The community centers would need to be where the kids live so they can be encouraged when faced with opposition. I've checked out an area for a summer camp in Colorado where the kids can get away from their hardships. They could fish, hike, learn survival techniques, the value of teamwork, and enjoy nature."

"Commendable." And she meant it. "How do you fight resistance to your projects?"

"Let me try one of those ice cream bars before answering." He retrieved one from the freezer. With his back to her, he paused. His shoulders tightened. He returned and tossed the ice cream on the table. His face resembled granite. His nostrils flared, and his features twisted. "I have people on my payroll who take care of problems." His voice dropped and flattened to a menacing timbre. "I keep my hands in all endeavors and hire those who know how to perform tasks my way." The curtain had fallen on Thomas's virtuous facade.

"I see how that would work to your advantage," she said.

Whitened knuckles gripped the edges of the table. "Accomplishing my purpose is a life choice."

"Which is?"

"Protect those who can't protect themselves."

If she interviewed him within FBI capacity, she'd ask him to explain. Later she'd deliberate the change in voice, tone, and demeanor. "So many people owe you for their education and a better life. Has anyone ever disappointed you?"

He sneered, ugly, threatening. "Students who didn't value exceptional grades lost their funding. Business associates who displayed dishonesty or unethical practices were fired. Employees who attempted to cheat me don't receive a second chance. No one who ever betrayed me has escaped." He frowned. "Except two, and they will receive their reward."

"I trust the judicial system."

He buried his face in his hands and clutched his temples.

"Are you okay?"

Seconds ticked by. He lifted his face, grinned, and unwrapped the ice cream bar. "This looks really good."

A transition occurred before her, night to day . . . Dr. Jekyll and Mr. Hyde. If she hadn't seen the switch, she'd swear it didn't happen.

He bit into the ice cream bar. "Moving forward on assisting at-risk kids invigorates me. And you? What are your long-term goals?"

"Possibly instructing new recruits at Quantico. The idea of training the next generation of special agents inspires me."

"You're a strong woman and a good role model for others. We have no choice but to endure each day in quarantine until we're released."

She thanked him. "My commitment to the FBI drives me to reach out to those who are hurting."

"It shows."

"If you'll excuse me, I'm heading back to bed." Heather said her goodbye and walked back to her room.

Was this the man whom the FBI believed exposed people to a killer virus? Had he caused Trey Alvinson's death? Did he work with Parker and Sonya Karey? What if his friendship was calculated to endear her to him and not the other way around? A game of wits for two people with opposite agendas.

She'd witnessed a glimpse of insanity that might have morphed into evil.

CHAPTER SIXTY

CHAD NEEDED TO APOLOGIZE to Jordan for his past lousy attitude and thank him for his friendship. Last night's research on the virus provided a conversation opener—not that he needed an excuse to talk to his old friend. He'd spent most of the night contemplating the virus and his conversation with Heather. Lots of soul-searching with no results but misery. He pressed in Jordan's number using his burner and expected to leave a message. But Jordan surprised him and answered.

"Hey, Chad. What's up?"

"Needed to thank you for putting up with me since the virus scare. I've been a jerk."

"At times, yes. You've also been stupid and almost got yourself killed. If the tables were turned, you'd be there for me."

"Yes, I would. I've examined and reexamined Heather's medical history to figure out why she's immune to H9N15, other than the r-naught factor. Have we missed a vital aspect that's shared by many of the unaffected people and those who are recovering?"

Jordan sighed. "I'm afraid this thing will take months, years to resolve."

He'd not mention a possible antiviral . . . yet. "I stumbled onto a random theory. Would you mind looking at Heather's records?"

"My computer is in front of me. Give me a sec. While I'm doing this, I'll say 43 percent haven't been infected. The r-naught factor seems to be the biggest player here. Heather's one unique characteristic is she's pregnant." Jordan's fingers clicked on the keyboard. "Okay, I have her test results and medical history. What do you want me to see?"

"Five months ago, she received the quadrivalent flu vaccine. Her dad contracted type A and B flu strains at the end of December and a third undetermined in February. We chose the vaccinations in February as a precaution. The vaccines may have built her immunity."

"Give me a little time while I compare patient records. Can I get back to you?"

"Sure."

Three hours later, Jordan returned the call. "Sorry. Been busy with a situation here in quarantine."

"New outbreak?"

"No. A person here has complained of migraines, and I wanted to take a look at the blood tests. The person needs a neurologist, and I recommended admitting him to Jamaica Hospital for additional testing."

"Do you have other cases that relate the migraines to the virus?"

"No, but I'm not discounting any potential symptom. Aside from why I'm late getting back to you, I have interesting data to report on our earlier conversation. None of the deceased victims' medical records reflect vaccinations for strains A or B in the last two years. Also, of the patients in serious and critical condition, none were vaccinated for A or B flu strains in the last year. I checked how many who'd received the quadrivalent vaccine contracted the virus. I discovered three, and they are recovering."

"When did they take the vaccine?"

"During the previous flu season, which was seven to nine months ago. Heather received the vaccination under five months. The quadrivalent flu vaccine being a factor is a stretch, but in our context, it may be the breakthrough we needed. We need tests and confirmation, but I can't discount the data. We may be on our way to either a cure or treatment for H9N15. Some patients have recovered better than others, and not all those who have improved were vaccinated. They are lucky to have strong bodies."

"I hate to sound optimistic," Chad said. "But I am."

"Hold on to your thoughts," Jordan said. "I'm requesting further testing now. Researchers are busy seven days a week. If this supports our theory, every person subjected to the virus should receive the quadrivalent vaccine as soon as possible. It may not affect all those who are in serious condition. However, it may lessen the symptoms. These people and their families need hope. Chad, thanks. This is progress."

"I just made a suggestion. Heather terms hope as the God factor. Maybe she's right."

"Good to hear you haven't discounted God's hand. I don't want to announce our theory until I discuss it with the team. I'll keep you updated. Wish I had time to talk, but I have a meeting in five."

"And my attorney is scheduled to call."

"Be careful. From what happened to you in New York, you've upset the wrong people."

"If I fail, I'll leave a positive legacy for my son."

"He'd rather have his dad."

"Good point. When this is over, I may need you to give me a few pointers on fatherhood."

"Deal. Talk to you later, buddy."

★ ★ ★

Jordan had summoned Heather to his office. He said the matter was urgent. Each step brought a different question, and none of them had answers.

Seated in his office behind a closed door, she scrutinized the ever-deepening worry line in his face. "What's happened?"

"Bad news. Tatum passed."

A sharp inhale meant to stop the tears failed.

"I'm sorry. I know you two had become friends in the short time here. Her parents have been notified."

She nodded. A hint of speaking would plummet her emotions. "Can I have their contact information?"

"I knew you'd ask." He handed her a folded piece of paper. "I'm meeting Catherine in the cafeteria. Stay here for as long as you like."

She unfolded the contact information with shaking fingers and stared at her phone. Tatum, the young woman with dreams of serving God. Dead. Would this misery ever end?

CHAPTER SIXTY-ONE

CHAD HAD BECOME the master of disguise since being accused of an atrocious crime. Finding alternate ways to change his looks had become a game. Andy brought him wigs, weird hats, and a variety of sunglasses, and they laughed with each wild look. If only Chad could snap his fingers and disguise his BMW with a new paint job. Taxis and Ubers worked when Andy wasn't available. But tonight he trekked out on his own. He exited the rear of his apartment building dressed in faded jeans, a T-shirt, Walmart readers, a braid that scratched his neck, and an Astros cap. No one approached as he hurried to covered parking. Maybe the media had moved on to something else. Who was he kidding?

He drove to Andy's apartment and kept his distance until the kid left. Andy needed to replace his twelve-year-old Chevy if he expected to impress a woman. Except Chad had the geek mind-set, too. The tail was a little tricky in his BMW, but Chad managed. The kid parked in front of a high-end specialty store while Chad circled the area and parked about a hundred feet away.

His burner phone rang—Andy.

"Didn't trust me, huh?" the kid said.

Chad chuckled. "I'd make a lousy PI. But I'm here, and I'm staying. Want me to come inside?"

"Nope. I got this."

"Okay. Have a good time." Chad clicked off and turned on the latest news.

Five minutes before the store closed, a white van pulled up. The passenger and side doors opened, and two men exited wearing black masks. Each carried what looked like high-powered rifles. *No, this can't be happening.*

The driver reversed and whipped the van around so the passenger side faced the entrance of the store. Chad memorized the license plate number. He grabbed his phone, dropped it on the floorboard, and snatched it again. The men rushed the front door. Two shots cracked from inside the store.

With trembling fingers, he pressed in 911. "A robbery in progress." He gave the store's address and van's license plate number. "I saw two masked men enter the store carrying guns. Shots were fired."

"Sir, avoid the crime scene."

He hung up and opened his car door. He refused to sit by and do nothing while Andy faced the wrong end of a gun. For the first time in his life, he longed for a weapon.

Sirens whined and flashing blue lights signaled oncoming police cars.

Chad closed the distance on the store's entrance, fifty feet, forty feet—

The two black-masked men emerged from the store and jumped into the van's open side door while the vehicle sped away. Two police cars raced in pursuit of the van. Two additional police vehicles screeched to a halt in front of the store.

An officer shouted at him, "Get out of the way, sir. A crime is in progress."

Chad stopped and three officers raced past him. The fourth maintained a position outside the door.

Chad pressed in Andy's number and approached the officer. The cell rang five times. Andy didn't pick up. "My friend's in the store. I'm a doctor."

The officer whipped his attention through the glass front and spoke into his radio. He slipped it back onto his belt and opened the store's door. "Go ahead. A customer was shot twice. An ambulance is en route."

He rushed to the far south corner, where three women huddled together and officers worked the area. A dark-haired young woman knelt on the floor over a man bleeding from the left side of his neck and abdomen.

Andy.

"I'm a doctor." Chad dropped to the floor to check for vitals and make an initial assessment. His fingers found a faint pulse. "I need something to apply pressure to these wounds! Andy, this is Doc C. Can you speak to me?"

Andy's eyelids didn't flutter.

One woman handed him a box of tissues, and the young woman beside him shrugged off a lightweight jacket. He pressed it into Andy's abdomen wound.

"The ambulance is here," an officer said.

A bullet had gone through his neck, but the stomach wound was another matter. Blood pooled the floor, the signs of draining life.

A paramedic joined him. "You're a doctor?"

"Yes. Victim has two gunshot wounds. I'll insert an IV while you bandage him. He needs to be on the road to the hospital ASAP. His name is Dr. Andy Sheehan. He's allergic to penicillin, and he's diabetic. Pass that on if you get to the hospital before I do."

The paramedics spun into action while Chad administered the

Lactated Ringer's solution. Within minutes, Andy stabilized and the paramedics lifted him onto a stretcher.

"Take him to Memorial Hermann," Chad said. "I'll follow you."

"Sir," said the young woman who'd been at Andy's side. "Will he be all right?"

"I hope so. Are you Leigh Masterson?"

"Yes." Her pale face and quivering lips told him of the trauma she'd witnessed. "This . . . is horrible. Bizarre."

Chad watched the paramedics heading to the front of the store. "What happened?"

"The men didn't take anything. It seemed they were looking for Andy and one shot him twice."

An icy chill spread through Chad—confirmation of an earlier suspicion. He blamed Powell and his network of henchmen for every hitch since the virus unleashed. Chad vowed that the killer would pay for his crimes.

At the hospital, Chad phoned Andy's parents in Missouri and explained their son had been shot in a store robbery and required surgery. They planned to leave for Houston within the hour. Driving was faster than arranging a flight.

He called Javier and passed on the bleak news. "Tonight was not a coincidence but a planned shooting."

"I'm heading to my car," Javier said. "Should take me about forty or so minutes. For the record, the FBI doesn't believe in coincidences."

"Good to know. Look, I don't need a sitter. You have things to do."

"Too late. I'm on my way. How bad is Andy?"

"In my opinion, he'll recover from the neck wound. A GSW to the abdomen can be fatal. I'm hoping the bullet missed vital organs."

"How long until you have word?"

"Depends on what the surgeon finds and how long it takes to repair the damage."

"All right. If anything changes before I get there, call me. I'll see what I can find out."

★ ★ ★

Chad drank Diet Coke, coffee, and repeated to stay alert while the doctors repaired Andy's battle-torn body. If he believed in God, he'd be praying. Javier found Chad in the surgery waiting room. No news from the surgeon.

"The shooters disappeared, and the police weren't able to track them," Javier said. "I learned the van was found in a residential area. Stolen. Police are sweeping for fingerprints."

"Want to bet it's clean?" Overwhelming guilt coursed through him. "This is my fault. If something happens to Andy, I'll take the blame to my grave."

"You might take it to jail. I told you to leave the investigation alone."

"Are you here to arrest me?"

"Haven't decided."

"I asked Andy to help prove my innocence."

"His decision. Just when I think you're an asset, you pull something stupid."

Chad neither agreed nor refused.

"Powell used a burner phone to call you."

"Is it admissible in court?"

"We'd have to prove it." Javier rose to his feet. "I'm tired of the FBI looking like a rookie team of recruits." He paused. "The words in Trey Alvinson's journal that stumped you? They were referring to Powell claiming he'd destroy him."

"And he did." Chad's burner phone rang, and the number showed the devil himself. "Powell's got guts."

"Answer it," Javier said.

"This is Dr. Lawrence."

"Do we really need the formals?" Powell said. "After all, you recognized my number."

"What do you want?"

"I'm stuck here in quarantine and saw the news. Dr. Sheehan had a nasty run-in with a couple of thugs. Heard he received two gunshots. How sad. May not live. Looks like those associated with Trey are cursed. They all run into bad luck."

"Or it's a pattern against the innocent." Chad longed to trap him, shake up his saintly image. His anger burned calm, an unusual response for him. "The police will find the shooters."

"Don't count on it. Other regretful information has come to my attention. How unfortunate your computer is missing. I fear your enemies know everything you've learned about the virus. The CDC is desperate to find an antiviral. May never happen."

"I believe in medical advances and the investigative work of the FBI," Chad said.

"I have big plans. First, to make sure you pay for your part in H9N15."

Chad's blood pressure soared.

"I have a solution," Powell said. "I can ensure all charges against you are removed. Parker and Sonya Karey have been busy casting the blame on you. All you need do is give up your work in the US and take an overseas position. I'll call you on Monday at noon Houston time for your decision. If you choose my way, I'll clear your record when you arrive at your new destination."

"And if I refuse?"

"As I said to you before, danger haunts Adam's Island."

CHAPTER SIXTY-TWO

CHAD LOOKED OUT AT A NEW DAY through the window in Andy's hospital room. While a sun-bathed Saturday morning and cloudless sky looked promising, the weather masked the turmoil. Powell had given him an ultimatum, and Chad wrestled with giving in to an overseas position to keep Heather safe. Not one more person would pay for Chad's fumbling of a criminal case.

"Hey, Doc," Andy whispered. "I'm gonna live."

Chad smiled and faced him. "You're a lucky man."

He stared at the beeping and humming equipment monitoring him. "I hurt but it does feel good to be alive. What's the surgery prognosis?"

"You'll be good as new—just need time to heal. One bullet went through your neck but clean. The one to your abdomen did a little more damage, but surgery repaired the problem." Andy attempted to sit, but Chad eased his shoulders down. "I'll help you move about after the doctor makes his rounds."

"Okay. Doc C., the shooters came in looking for me."

"I figured that. Leigh was here for a long time. Poor girl was afraid to leave you. I sent her home to rest, but she texted me a few minutes ago and will be here in an hour."

"I saw her face when I was shot." His face tightened with an obvious stab of pain.

"We can talk later."

"Gotta say this. Powell is behind this."

"Right, and the FBI is on it."

"Were the shooters caught?"

"No."

"Not surprised?" Andy closed his eyes. "I'm going to take a quick nap before Leigh arrives. Besides, you need some sleep and a shower."

Chad chuckled. "Thanks for the analysis."

"Go on home. Call me later."

"An officer is posted outside your door 24-7."

Near the shoreline, on her favorite round stone, Heather typed Tatum's parents an email about their daughter . . . the bravery on the plane . . . the kindness, encouragement, love for others, delightful humor, and her heart for God. The phone call to them hadn't been enough. Heather swiped at tears beneath her eyes and pushed Send from her iPad. The best way to honor Tatum and all the victims of H9N15 focused on finding the guilty ones.

She recorded her observations about Thomas into a secure FBI site. Their early morning conversation stayed fresh in her mind allowing her to type word for word the dialogue and body language. A force within him displayed strange behavior, and another force shoved aside the angry man and brought back Thomas. A sign of a dissociative identity disorder.

The sea groaned, and she turned her attention to the lapping waves. Nothing. Must be her own thoughts keeping pace with the chaotic march inside her.

She concentrated on Thomas. The disorder normally occurred because the victim had experienced severe mental or physical abuse as a child. She'd been told of a childhood bullying problem and abandonment by his father. The combination of the two traumas could have caused him to dissociate himself from the pain in the way of memories, emotions, actions, or sense of identity. If Thomas suffered from a type of DID, one personality might not be aware of the other.

Mr. Engels said Thomas dumped coffee on a Starbucks counter when a barista made a mistake with his drink.

ASAC Mitchell's number showed up on her phone's screen, and she answered.

"I need to tell you about an incident," he said.

Her pulse sounded in her ears. "Go ahead."

Mitchell told her about Andy receiving two gunshot wounds in an apparent robbery, the surgery, and the circumstances surrounding the shooting.

"How is he?"

"Surgeons repaired the damage. He'll recover. Javier states Chad is in bad shape, blames himself. Believed he should have followed Andy inside the store and prevented the outcome."

"He hasn't contacted me. His habit is to process info before reaching out, and he's shouldering responsibility."

"You know him well."

"At least the man he used to be. Doesn't it sound like the robbery was staged to keep Andy from talking to Leigh Masterson?"

"Looks that way. When we make an arrest, the guy and whoever's working with him are looking at a long time in jail."

The dubious statement shouldn't have bothered her . . . Did he still think Chad was involved? "Keep me posted on Andy, and I'll reach out to Chad." She prayed for Andy, an innocent young man who'd been the target of a killer. "I have an update about Thomas Powell."

"All right."

She explained her experience with Thomas. "I'm requesting we probe deeper into the bullying scenario, and I'm interested in his twin brother's and parents' medical history."

"On it."

"If a mental issue lines up with this case, Thomas Powell may not have any recollection of his crimes."

"How is dissociative identity disorder treated?" Mitchell said.

"Unfortunately medical testing can't diagnose DID. And I doubt he'd agree to a psychiatrist or psychologist evaluation when we have no basis for it. For now, I request a consultation with an FBI psychiatrist to examine his medical history."

"Without a diagnosis, we have little to go on but hard facts."

"And the high probability of an unstable man," she said. "Can the FBI move ahead on an interview with Oliver or Jackson Powell? Either man may have witnessed mental instability or have a recollection of Thomas's behavior prior to the boys' separation. If you can arrange an interview, I'd like to be on the call."

"I'll see what I can arrange."

"Thomas said he helped pay for his grad school expenses by working at a bakery in Austin. The name is Flour Power. I've looked online and confirmed its existence. If the same people still own the bakery, they might have seen mood swings. Meanwhile I'll work my way into conversations that could trigger a personality switch."

"Good job, Heather."

"Two more things. Have any of Thomas's girlfriends viewed an emotional or mental issue? Is it possible to ask them if he demonstrated questionable moods?"

"I'll keep you in the loop."

She closed her iPad case and breathed in the salty air. Today had sent the investigation in unexpected directions. She trembled and attempted to process the dreadful news of the day.

What else could go wrong?

Heather walked along the grounds to the back entrance of the compound. An osprey, a gray-and-white dancer, dove into the water and emerged with a fish. She could pitch a tent here.

Staring out over the water, a strange object jutted up from the shoreline. At first Heather believed it was sea-washed rock. She crept closer, out of curiosity, and the object now resembled driftwood.

Twenty feet from the object, a leg appeared.

Another leg and torso.

Heather raced toward the body.

Sonya Karey.

CHAPTER SIXTY-THREE

BACK AT HIS APARTMENT after leaving Andy to rest, Chad opened the Bible he'd purchased at the JFK airport. What he'd read couldn't be real. To believe the Bible, he must believe God inspired the book. But he didn't believe in God, so how could he trust the Bible as the Word of God?

If God existed and He had all this power thing, why didn't He speak to Chad and end the uncertainty?

Why didn't He rectify the situation with whoever was responsible for the virus and ease Chad and Heather's angst?

Why had He allowed Andy to face a shooter?

The morning wore on. Chad read blog posts and articles in a mix of the virus investigation and medical research. His eyes blurred from the repeated information. How grand if the CDC confirmed the quadrivalent flu virus vaccine helped protect the immune systems of those who'd been exposed to H9N15.

Javier called after the noon hour and invited Chad to join him that evening for a lecture by a respected scientist hosted by a lawyer friend. "It will divert your attention for a couple of hours."

"Depends on how Andy is doing."

"How is he? Vitals still good?"

"He's improving. We talked a little. He's skeptical the shooting was a robbery."

"We'll ensure security is in place while he's hospitalized."

"A safe house after he's released?"

"That's the plan. The lecture would get your mind off the situation."

Chad sighed. "Tell me about it."

"Professor Alister McGrath from Oxford. Doctorates in theology and molecular biophysics."

"Why would he appeal to me?"

"Your bio says you're an atheist, but there's a Bible on your table. Tells me you're wrestling with God. You're cerebral, and the lecture topic examines the thoughts of Richard Dawkins and C. S. Lewis, a discussion on life from both the atheist and the Christian worldviews. I figured it would appeal to your intellect. I'd need to pick you up at six to get there in time."

"Even if I'm at home, I—"

"Chad, pacing the floor of your apartment doesn't close the case or heal Andy any faster."

"All right. Won't be the first time a lecture bored me."

Javier snickered before a see-you-later comment.

Chad settled in with his laptop and searched online for Alister McGrath. Definitely a highbrow intellectual and internationally respected for his work in science and theology. At one time McGrath had been against any notion of God. How had a brilliant mind accepted the gibberish?

Later that night, Chad walked away from the lecture intrigued by what he'd heard. The connection between science and religion grasped his attention, and McGrath's words challenged him to study the Bible.

"Are you deep into your reflections and if you find credibility in God?" Javier said.

"Both. I remember a statement made by Thomas Aquinas where he points out the universe's tendency toward order. Like him, I don't believe chaos produces order."

"Did you ever attend church?"

"No. My folks wanted me to join them when I was a teen, except my atheism beliefs were intact. I went a few times with Heather. Never found a theory or belief that clicked."

"I'd be afraid to step out my door without my convictions. Faith, family, and keeping others safe. Those are what matter to me."

"You aren't the first man I've met who's prioritized life in a similar way."

Once home, Chad watched an online video interview of McGrath's faith journey. Afterward Chad added two of the man's many books and two of C. S. Lewis's books to his Kindle. Every biblical reference found him checking his Bible for verification. He read the first of McGrath's books until 6:30 a.m. and finished it after downing coffee and a banana. At 9ish, he ended the book and slept on the sofa for three hours, then started a C. S. Lewis book.

He walked to the window of the living room and peered out over the city. *God, I've always said I had to see You to believe. Have I seen You all along and worn blinders?*

Chad finished the second C. S. Lewis book and began the second McGrath title. An invisible force drove him to continue reading throughout the day with a break to eat or drink. Sunday night became more thirst for knowledge and kept him glued to the page. At 3 a.m., he set aside the books and the Bible. Chad had suffered for what he couldn't accomplish in his life—finding a cure for Ebola and other life-threatening viruses, saving Paul, trying to prove his innocence, protect Heather and his unborn son, and too many other problems to list. If God were real, Chad wanted Him on a call list. The idea of one more day in this misery shattered his beliefs in himself.

Science. Math. Theology. God had created these to help humans understand themselves.

God. Chad didn't need to understand why He did things. If Chad comprehended it all, then God wouldn't be God.

Order. God created order organization. Only perfection could accomplish such a feat.

Redemption. Chad couldn't save himself when the world around him crumbled.

Jesus Christ. He had to be the true Son of God. Who else could take the world's sins upon Himself?

Forgiveness. Chad had given up on forgiving himself for all the wrongs he'd done.

Reality. Life as he'd lived it never satisfied him. It pushed him to be more, do more, be responsible for everything.

Chad balled his hand into a fist. The thought of one more breath on his own made him want to die now. But Chad wanted to live . . . with purpose. He made his decision for Christ, one birthed in desperation, humility, and a need for a Savior.

Chad was a new man, reborn into the family of God. Strange how the decision for Christ filled him with a rare and satisfying peace . . . and on a Monday morning before coffee. He'd written a ton of God questions in his notebook. Yet neither Jordan, Heather, nor Javier had time for a fledgling Christian who had stubborn as his middle name. Their skills were needed to end the virus madness.

Heather and their son needed protection, and not the kind Chad could provide. If he refused Powell's demands, Heather faced a perilous future or death. Removing himself from her life kept her and their son alive. Conceding to Powell also made him look like a liar and even guilty of the accusations.

The answer lay within his love for her and his new faith.

He'd call Powell before noon and agree to his terms.

He flipped open the lid on his laptop and contacted Doctors Without Borders for a list of permanent positions overseas. Within an hour, Chad had a job offer in Uganda. He thanked the director and accepted the position. He'd leave for Kampala, Uganda, in one week.

Javier brought lunch to Chad's apartment at 11:15, his usual manner of opening a discussion. The two sat at the kitchen counter, drank coffee, and ate deli sandwiches while Chad contemplated what he'd say.

"Have you processed the lecture?" Javier said.

"That might take a while." Chad stated his and God's newfound relationship.

"Congratulations." Javier grinned. "The wife and I have prayed for you. How can I help? Comments?"

Chad was clueless about how God answered prayer. Lightning bolts? Supernatural texts? But Javier had stepped into his life unexpectedly, and the two had developed an unusual friendship. Trembling, he buried his face in his hands.

"I assume this is about Powell's demand for you to leave the country. It's the reason for my visit." He pointed at the clock on the microwave. "You have twenty minutes before his call. Tell me where you stand."

"I have no choice." Chad explained his and Heather's discussion about a possible reconciliation. "Now I've broken her trust by telling you."

Javier waved away the comment. "You've come a long way since we first met."

"So have you."

"I deserve that."

"I take the real jerk award. Anyway, I accepted a job offer in Uganda. I plan to book a flight after I talk to Powell, and I want to leave in a week. I'm thinking it will satisfy him." Chad studied Javier. "Since you and other agents are aware of Powell's demands, is there a plan?"

Javier wadded the paper remains of his lunch and stuffed them into the deli bag. "Tell Powell what you've done. Book your flight. Give him the info about the job and request he keep his end of the bargain."

"Catch him off guard in hopes he makes a mistake?"

"Right. We anticipate he'll make arrangements to have you killed wherever you land. He's gone to a lot of trouble to destroy you."

"I'd considered the possibility of walking into a death trap."

"We're working our end of the case in ways I can't share."

"From what I've experienced and learned, Thomas Powell has spun cycles with this. The why baffles me. Online sources list his IQ at a genius level, making him capable of putting an intricate plan into place."

"True." Javier stared out the small kitchen window. "Powell's personality and motives are unraveling. Sit tight. The FBI will handle protection."

"Wish we could move Heather out of danger." Helpless best described him.

"She has to know the latest development."

"I wanted to keep her out of it."

"If you don't tell her, she'll learn the truth and feel betrayed."

"You're right. I'll call her, tell her about my faith, and Powell's ultimatum."

"This will work out."

God had paved the way for him to talk to Javier. Trusting God . . . was foreign, and Chad had fought it all the way. His relationship with God surfaced to another thought—they were unified in the same struggle.

His phone rang. He snatched it. "You're right on time, Powell. I've accepted a job in Uganda . . ."

CHAPTER SIXTY-FOUR

THE FLOUR POWER where Thomas worked his way through college still thrived. Heather sat outside Adam's Island in the afternoon sunshine and read through an agent's interview. The daughter of the bakery's original owners now owned and managed the small business. She remembered Thomas and described him as charismatic and a hard worker. She'd been much younger then and suggested talking to her parents. At the older couple's home, the agents found the two baking cupcakes for a neighbor child's birthday. The man confirmed Thomas had worked over three years for them.

"Can you describe him?" an agent had said.

"Brilliant and talented boy until he lost his temper with a customer. I had to let him go."

"What happened?"

"Thomas had an argument with a man who insisted he'd been shorted on a donut order. Instead of agreeing with the customer,

Thomas went nuts. The wife and I didn't recognize him. He grabbed two jelly donuts and smashed them into the man's face, then chased him outside. Knocked him down and choked him. We pulled Thomas off the man and dismissed him. The man filed assault charges but later dropped them."

"Ever see Thomas again?" the agent said.

"Why are you interested in him? He's successful and rich."

"This is only an inquiry."

"I have nothing else to tell you. It was a long time ago."

"Do you remember the date?" the agent said.

"I do." The older man provided the month, day, and year.

Odd he remembered when the incident occurred . . . Heather closed her laptop screen. One agent had posed questions, and the partner recorded what transpired. Curiosity sent her back online. She used the date Thomas assaulted the man and searched Austin newspaper archives until she found a possible explanation for the older couple's reluctance to relay info. Two days after Thomas lost his job, a fire broke out at night in the bakery. Investigators determined faulty wiring caused the blaze and not the bakery owners' negligence. Heather saw the couple had three children in middle grade and high school at the time. Reason for them to protect those they loved. She sent ASAC Mitchell an email.

Her burner phone buzzed, and she responded to Chad.

"Hey, how are you feeling?" he said.

She still treasured the sound of his voice. Hard to get past it. "Getting stronger. How is Andy?"

"Much better. Going to a safe house today. His parents will stay with him, and his mom's a nurse. Leigh Masterson has been at the hospital since he was shot."

"Oh, something happening there?"

"Maybe so. Tell me, how's the little guy?"

"Kicking."

Chad laughed. "An indication of things to come?"

"I'm sure of it."

"Have you thought of a name?"

"Yes."

"The one you wanted before we were married? Levi McCoy?"
Thank goodness, he couldn't see the tears. "The same."

"Solid, Heather. Biblical, too."

What had he said?

"I have news." He paused. "God and I are on the same page."
She couldn't stop the flow of emotion. "Chad, I'm thrilled.
How did this happen?"

He relayed the lecture, the books and Scripture he'd read—the
whole experience. "Fought God until He won."

She digested his new faith and the chances he was taking to
clear his name. Blessings in the middle of uncertainty. *Thank You.*
So many issues to work through. Jumping back into married life
without the benefit of talking through the dysfunction was a detri-
ment to both of them. But faith held their hands.

"I'm sorry for all those times I've hurt you. Remember when
I said you hadn't made me happy for months? It was never your
job to make me happy. I'm sorry, Heather. The faith thing has me
excited and a little afraid."

"We never learn it all. I'd like to shout this around the world."
She sighed. "But we can't, not yet anyway."

"Right. It's dangerous for you and risks your part of the investigation. Do you mind if I tell Jordan?"

"He'll be overjoyed." She watched gray clouds move closer.
"You're in too deep with your personal investigation, and I'm concerned it's too late for you to simply stop. The consequences of
attempting to solve a crime solo can have serious repercussions.
You. Andy. And a woman was murdered here. Reality is her death
has to be connected. No one's been arrested. No apparent motive."

"What kind of man sits by while others are suffering?"

"Selfishness was never an attribute I admired, but it might keep you safe. File this away—I never wanted to be protected. I wanted my husband. When we said, 'I do,' we promised to walk through the good and bad together."

"And we will work out our differences and honor our vows. I can tell you what I've been up to, but are you sure you want to hear it?"

"All of it. ASAC Mitchell told me you'd attempted a blackmail call to Thomas Powell."

He told her the things he'd done. She held her angst, but fear for him tore through her.

"There you have it," he said. "Javier has my findings. I told Powell I'd be leaving for Uganda in a week to take a position for Doctors Without Borders."

"Chad, this isn't a problem you can split like a cell. Go to a safe house until the FBI makes an arrest. There's no reason to take an overseas job."

"I'll do anything to help bring justice to all those who've been affected by the virus and keep you safe. My eyes are in the rearview mirror."

"Promise me you'll be careful."

"I have to do this."

"Is Andy aware of our discussions?"

"Nope. He's convinced you and Powell are in this together."

"Loyal Andy. And your decision to follow Jesus?"

"We haven't discussed it. I've asked him to use my burner phone when we talk. Powell and his cohorts must have followed him to find out he'd met with Trey's ex-girlfriend." He hesitated. "I want the new man in me to be real, not a phase that wears off. Strange, but the time alone during the virus scare has given me hours to evaluate myself as though God was preparing me to meet Him . . . as though the accusations against me were for a reason. Does that make sense?"

"Definitely. I'd hoped the FBI's announcement of your lab's

initial clearance and the fake photo of you and Taversty would make your life easier."

"Not yet. I'll breathe easier soon. In the meantime, I keep digging."

God, help him. Help us find an end to all the tragedies.

Huge raindrops pelted her. "Hey, Chad. A storm's rolling in, and it's starting to rain."

"Get inside and be safe. Call me when you can."

She echoed the same for him. While he'd embraced God, he hadn't discarded his risk-taking streak. Neither of them had.

CHAPTER SIXTY-FIVE

THROUGH EAR-PIERCING CRACKS of thunder and blinding lightning, Heather jogged from her shore respite to the quarantine unit. Huge raindrops drenched her while her phone buzzed. Once inside the building, she returned a call to ASAC Mitchell.

"Why are you out of breath?" he said.

"It's pouring, and I was outside." Thunder shook the building.

"I hear it."

The darkened sky pulled her attitude into an even grayer mood. The quarantine and all the heartache it tossed at the victims had to end soon. "Tell me you have good news."

"I do. One of Thomas Powell's ex-girlfriends gave us a statement."

Heather scanned the hallway to ensure privacy. A cluster of people talked about fifteen feet from her. "Hold on. I'm on the move."

"From the storm?"

"For privacy." She found a secluded small room used as a library.

About fifty *National Geographic* magazines and a few worn copies of books were scattered on every conceivable surface. Closing the door, she gave him the all clear. "Is this the woman who had a yearlong relationship with him?"

"Right. The woman's scared. Dated Powell for six months before he lost his temper. She didn't agree with something he'd said. He beat her. Broke her nose and jaw. He claimed it was the first time he'd ever lost control. He paid her medical expenses and deposited a hefty amount into her bank account in exchange for her to keep her mouth shut."

"And she still stayed with him for a year. How did you persuade her to talk?"

"The agent told her Powell may have exhibited violent tendencies with others. The agent assured her the interview was confidential, and she'd not be called to testify unless charges were brought against him."

"The facts mysteriously appear, don't they? All we need do is fit them together." She picked up an issue of *National Geographic* and focused on the title of an article: "To build the cities of the future, we must get out of our cars." The words reminded her of how she must continue to gain Thomas's trust no matter how uncomfortable.

"Heather, once quarantine is over, where will Powell go? Will he return to Houston and continue building his financial empire? Take off to a place where we can't touch him?" Sarcasm laced Mitchell's words. "Law enforcement and medical researchers haven't had a breakthrough with the virus. And there's nothing in Powell's records to show he has a personality disorder. You saw a glimpse of DID, but not to an extent we can link him to any crimes."

"Sir, I respectfully disagree with your conclusion. I'll make sure I have plenty of opportunities to view the real man once he's back to his normal routine. I'll encourage our friendship and encourage him to keep in touch."

"Face it, Powell could be leading you along since you're FBI. If what we suspect is true, he has a far-reaching network."

"Every investigation has high stakes. He's been in his dorm since yesterday, missed dinner last night and breakfast. If he's absent tonight, I'll ask Jordan to check on him. For the record, just you and Jordan Radcom know Chad and I are talking."

"I talked to Javier earlier and learned about the relocation to Uganda. I assume you have more info than I do."

"Thomas implied I could be hurt if Chad refused to leave the country." Weariness settled on her. "I understand from your standpoint, Powell could be innocent and Chad the culprit."

"I'm persuaded otherwise. But I need proof."

"I believe in Chad. He's not a killer. No doubts. He'll do anything to help end the case."

The call ended and she opened the library door. Thomas towered above her.

Heather touched her mouth. "Thomas, you scared me. Are you all right?"

His gray eyes softened. "A migraine hit me hard. I have my own meds. Knocked me out cold. But I've risen from the dead and am hungry enough to eat the whole dinner buffet."

If the migraine was a new development since exposure to the virus, why did he have his own meds? Suspicions nipped at her mind. Thomas wouldn't be the first person to ensure his medical records deleted information.

"How's the pain now?" she said.

"Only a little dull headache. The reason I was looking for you is one of the teen girls is looking for a table tennis partner tonight. Thought of you, and I misplaced your cell number. I went looking and asked everyone I met. A woman told me you'd headed into the library."

"Glad you found me. Tell the teen I'd be glad to play."

"She's waiting for you in the recreation area."

Heather fished into her shoulder bag and pulled out a business card. "Don't lose this one."

"I'll make sure it's in my contacts." He pocketed the card, and Heather stepped into the hall. Something about the conversation sent acid up her throat. How much had Thomas heard between her and ASAC Mitchell?

CHAPTER SIXTY-SIX

THE FOLLOWING MORNING at breakfast with Catherine, Jordan strode to the podium, his shoulders erect and his gait relaxed.

"Good morning, everyone. We are less than a week from the end of our quarantine. We've bonded, made new friends, and grieved an experience we never want to repeat. You are a courageous group of people, and I'm honored to have spent these days with you. With any contagion, a percentage of people exposed will not show any symptoms. Scientists are always baffled by this phenomenon and refer to it as the r-naught factor. Until yesterday, the CDC concluded you fell within this explanation. With renewed enthusiasm, I give you new and exciting information. Those working with the CDC have developed a vaccine to help with the symptoms and may even prevent others from contracting the H9N15 virus. We've studied the health records of all the people infected and discovered those who received the quadrivalent flu vaccine within the last six months have not been affected by the virus. Those who received the vaccine within the last ten months are recovering at a much faster rate. Much testing is ahead, but it is a breakthrough."

Heather recalled the date she received the quadrivalent vaccine. She rose to her feet with the group and applauded.

Thank You.

"Good news," Catherine said between claps. "A blessing for all of us."

"Hopeful. I received the vaccine in February." She couldn't stop the giggle. "That's why I've escaped the virus."

"I've seldom heard you laugh," Catherine said. "It's good for the soul."

"We all need more of it."

"I wish your personal life held more promise."

"My little son has made me exceedingly happy." Heather patted her stomach. "I hope you're a part of his life, too."

Jordan gestured for them to sit. "We released the announcement to the media about ten minutes ago. We need a cure for H9N15, and I repeat this is not a cure." He pointed to the back of the room. "The vaccine is available, and three of us are ready to administer the injections. We can't compel you to receive it, but we are encouraging it as a precaution. If you've received the vaccine in the last six months, there isn't a need to repeat it. Once you are home, consult your physician and adhere to his recommendations."

Jordan instructed the crowd to form lines in the rear of the room according to their last name. There, medical workers recorded vital information and gave injections. Heather walked outside to thank God for helping so many desperate people.

"Heather, were you vaccinated?" Thomas walked her way.

"I had mine five months ago. And you?"

"I'm going to wait until my doctor in Houston evaluates my records. I'm healthy. Could be among the r-naught group, but I was a sickly child."

She filed Thomas's new tidbit of information, one more fact about the complex man. "The doctors strengthened your immune system."

"Whatever they did helped me over the past weeks. What about you?"

She explained her dad had been infected with three flu viruses, and she took precaution in February. "Chad took the vaccine, too. Adds a unique spin to his FBI status."

"My regrets."

Carpe diem. "I'm thinking aloud here, but if he knew the vaccine would protect me from H9N15, then using it against me isn't valid."

"Makes sense the accusations aren't substantial." Thomas winced and rubbed his temples. "Migraine's back. I need to stretch out."

"Sure. Hope you feel better."

He moved toward the compound. Stiffened. And stopped near a rock cropping.

"Do you need to sit for a few minutes?" she said.

He whirled around and faced her. His nostrils flared. She'd seen the transformation before, and the alternate side of Thomas glared at her.

"The quadrivalent flu vaccine is an illusion." The words fell from his lips like poison. "Nothing stops or cures the virus." He pushed on to the compound.

Heather detected a slight limp, a trait not visible before. The migraine had either caused pain throughout his body or the announcement of the quadrivalent flu vaccine had triggered a possible dissociative identify disorder episode. Or both.

Heather informed Jordan of Thomas's headache and let him handle approaching the man. She texted Thomas to check on him, but he neglected to respond.

How surprising the daily routine in quarantine had become a

new normal. Even the time seemed to pass faster. She continued her walks outside and spent hours with Catherine, Jackie, and Ada. Still no progress on the investigation.

On Tuesday morning, the quarantine was officially over. Heather handed a soldier her luggage and stepped onto the ferry transporting the passengers and crew to New York and home. They'd been told to prepare themselves for an awaiting press, a few moments of flashing cameras, and questions. She planned to avoid them. New York's FBI had an escort ready to drive her to their office before a flight home. A few from Jamaica Hospital would be released today, Mia included. Although Heather's schedule negated saying goodbye to Mia in person and meeting her family, the two had talked earlier and promised to keep in touch.

Laughter resounded among the quarantined. Hope swirled in a euphoric state of a better tomorrow. Catherine shed tears. Life without Roy meant a time of grief and planning a memorial service. Many of those on the flight faced the same unsteady future.

Tomorrow morning, she'd attend an informal gathering at Mercy Community Church, where Tatum's father pastored. There she'd talk with Tatum's family, Kirk Durgin's widow, Catherine's family, and Maria's family about her relationship with the deceased. Other family members and friends might be attending, too.

A helicopter whirled above and landed near the building. Thomas emerged from the compound rolling a suitcase and climbed inside. Her opportunity to establish more of a relationship took flight.

She texted him. **Have a safe trip home.**

Within moments, he returned a message. **Didn't want the media attention. Can I call in the morning? I'd like to talk about something.**

Yes. I'll be leaving the house at 9 a.m.

Thomas sounded like his old self or more like his other self. What did he want to discuss?

Heather met SAC Fielder in his New York office, a formality, but he did thank her for the investigative work conducted on Adam's Island.

"We're investigating Sonya Karey's murder," he said. "We've taken Parker Karey into federal custody. He doesn't have an alibi during the time of his wife's death, and we're also investigating if he had a role in the virus."

"I intend to file charges against him for threatening a federal officer."

He nodded. "This morning we received an update on Decker Anslow," he said.

"And?"

"An assassin got to him in a German cell."

"Taliban?"

"They're taking credit. He kept his mouth shut, so whatever he and Taversty knew went to their graves. We are working with the Germans to find answers. We'll get to the bottom of who mastermined the virus."

She explained Thomas Powell's apparent migraine the last few days and his helicopter departure. "I'll continue my role until arrests are made."

"ASAC Mitchell tells me Jackson Powell, Thomas's twin, will be at the Houston office tomorrow afternoon. You'll be part of that meeting."

"Is this a result of the FBI's interview in Salzburg?"

"Yes. Oliver, the father, and Jackson Powell initially refused to discuss Thomas. Oliver hung up on the agent, but Jackson later offered a few words. The brothers haven't seen each other since they were boys, and Oliver preferred to keep it that way, even to the point of denying Thomas as his son. Two days later Jackson contacted the agent with a willingness to travel to Houston's FBI, but under the condition Thomas wouldn't be notified. He assured the agent he'd cooperate once he was here. ASAC Mitchell made the arrangements."

"Any idea why he wanted an FBI face-to-face?"

Fielder shook his head. "They've lived in London all these years. If the boys' mother had wanted her maternal rights, she could have legally obtained them. We have no record of any communication between the parents. Unusual situation."

"I'm thinking Jackson Powell has information we can use."

"Hold on to that thought. For a case against Thomas to hold up in court, we must find evidence pointing to him. In the meantime, we have other viable suspects."

CHAPTER SIXTY-SEVEN

ARRIVING HOME SEEMED ODD and yet familiar. The comforts relaxed and soothed her while the tragedies slammed unbidden memories. What good would ever come from the virus's release? Granted, Chad had found a relationship with God, and a vaccine relieved the virus symptoms for many, but what about those who'd suffered, died? How long before arrests led the way for justice?

She'd been on EDT in New York, and the transition to CDT meant she wakened at 5:30. She showered and started her day, digging into the latest updates about Decker Anslow. Curiosity surrounding Jackson Powell's arrival to Houston's FBI kept her monitoring time. She wanted to be early at Mercy Community Church to greet those who'd attend. Mom and Dad wanted to be there to support her, but both had doctor appointments. She'd have dinner with them tonight.

She contacted Chad to remind him to keep his distance.

"I need to help in some capacity," he said. "I have nothing to lose and everything to gain."

"Only your life and the father of our son? Leave the problem solving to investigators. Soon this will be over."

Thomas called at 8 a.m. "Are you acclimated to the new time?"

"Not yet. You?"

"Same. Does work start on Monday?"

"Have meetings at ten and two."

Thomas groaned. "I'd like to ask you something, but I don't want to be presumptuous or offend you."

"Go ahead."

"We have the beginnings of a friendship from our ordeal. The days, weeks, and months ahead for you will be difficult, and I'd like to be your friend."

"We both have busy lives."

"True. I'm proposing friendship."

She tapped her chin. "Chad used to be my best friend."

"I'd like to fill the vacancy with slow steps. Nothing else. My dealings with women in the past have been . . . arm candy. That's not how I think of you."

She hesitated—purposely. "I like the idea of a friend. I may need a sounding board, other than my parents, through the ongoing virus investigation and the days ahead."

"I'd like the role of your brother-friend."

"Okay." She forged ahead. "The situation with Chad is complicated. Sometimes I feel sorry for him."

"Why? He abandoned you and he's suspected of developing a virus with global implications."

She appeared to put her words together while she hoped her concocted story showed similarities between the two men. "He had a rough childhood. Parents didn't understand his interest in science. Bullied because of extreme shyness. He knew loneliness, ridicule—a lot of anxiety. He didn't have friends until medical school, where he met Jordan Radcom. Jordan is troubled about Chad's possible involvement." She shoved believability into her words. "As a behavior analyst, I despise how bullies victimize their prey."

"Regretful, Heather. I admit the pity gene for him escaped my chemical makeup. If he's guilty, he must be punished for his actions."

"And I'd be the first to cuff him. My comment wasn't a justification for any crime but a reason."

"The foundation for a psychopath. That remark wasn't necessary. I'm sorry if I've upset you."

"You haven't. I need a brother-friend."

"Are you up to a call later on tonight? Not too late."

"I'm having dinner with my parents. How about I call you?"

"Great. Think about a nap before your afternoon meeting."

"First, this morning, I'm talking to a few of the victims' family and friends."

"Take it easy on your first day back."

"I will. And thanks."

If Thomas were the killer and viewed her as the enemy, how long would he keep up the charade? Her instincts told her he'd make a mistake, and it was up to her to lay slippery ground.

CHAPTER SIXTY-EIGHT

HEATHER PARKED in the front parking area of Mercy Community Church, a magnificent brick and stone building that spread over a huge campus. The cross seemed to touch heaven. Catherine had commented on the church's size, and now Heather saw for herself.

She'd meet Tatum's parents in the foyer so they could chat before the others arrived. She dreaded and looked forward to talking with the grieving people. The important thing was to help people find closure, and her experiences with their loved ones could help.

She walked to the designated area, her steps slow while she prayed for guidance. A tall man opened the door . . . Tatum had his eyes. But hers had sparkled and his were dim.

"My wife is waiting in my office," he said. "We want to hear everything you can tell us about our daughter . . ."

Forty-five minutes later in the church's chapel, Heather ended her experiences with the victims represented. She shared happy moments and courageous ones. Catherine tried to talk about Roy, but her emotions stopped the flow of words. Heather embraced her and told of Catherine's role in comforting her and others during quarantine. Tatum's father prayed, concluding with an invitation for them to share coffee, lunch, and conversation in the fellowship hall.

Heather felt the exhaustion in every inch of her body. Thomas's urging for her to rest made sense if she had the time. She eased onto a folding chair and breathed in. People were making friends. They shared a bond, one that would never be forgotten.

A short woman approached her. "I'm Lynda Durgin. You look very tired, dear. Pregnant women need to take extra time to care for themselves."

"I will soon." Heather added a smile.

"Do you mind if I sit and chat?"

"Please do. You're Kirk's wife, right?"

"Yes. Thank you for befriending him." She closed her eyes. "I'm remembering how thrilled he was to be invited to play in Salzburg. He spent hours rehearsing. Kirk used to say a violin was like a child. It could sing the sweetest love song, cry, or fill others with laughter."

"I'm sorry I never heard him play."

Lynda reached into her purse and handed Heather a CD. "I was hoping you'd say that. Here is his last recording."

"Thank you." Drat hormones were making her a weeping mess.

Lynda patted her arm. "This is a small token of my appreciation. If not for you, I wouldn't have Kirk's violin. God bless you."

At the FBI office, Heather and Mitchell peered through the one-way glass at Jackson Powell, the twin who shared a resemblance to Thomas.

Mitchell's drawn features showed he bore pressure on every

level. "Take the lead on the interview. You know Thomas better than I do."

No need to state they were getting nowhere in finding evidence. She opened the door and entered the room. After shaking Jackson's hand and introductions made, the two agents sat across a table from him. The twin had the same gray eyes minus the sharp intensity. His facial structure was relaxed, a trait she'd rarely noted in Thomas.

"Thank you for coming to Houston," she said. "After a few formalities, we can discuss your brother."

"Yes, ma'am." His British accent reflected the many years in London.

"Your full name is Jackson Wolfgang Powell."

"Yes. My twin brother is Thomas Amadeus Powell."

Jackson confirmed Thomas's middle name. "A parent must have been a classical music enthusiast."

"Our father."

Thomas had said his grandfather had given him the middle name. "Our agent in London said you refused an interview concerning your brother. Then you volunteered to fly here. What changed your mind?"

He drew in a ragged breath. "I'm not sure where to begin. I made the decision after I read Thomas had been on a flight that had experienced the release of an unknown virus. Although he hadn't been infected, he was in quarantine. Further online reading stated the flight was en route to Frankfurt, Germany, at the same time as the Salzburg music festival. Our father played his final violin concert there, and I played in the orchestra accompanying him. I doubt the trip to Frankfurt was a coincidence. Thomas had threatened us in January of this year. I don't suspect anything concerning the source of the virus, but I'm worried my brother's purpose for taking the overseas trip is bound to his hatred for us."

He tapped his right fingers on the table, a gesture she'd viewed in Thomas. "My brother was calculating as a boy, vindictive, too. I imagine those traits worsened with the abuse he received from our father and the bullying at school."

"Sir, can you back up a little?" Heather said. "I'm not following."

"Would you like to hear the whole story?"

"Yes, please."

He moistened his lips. "Our father believes music is life. From the moment we were born, Thomas and I were subjected to listening only to classical music. As soon as we could talk, instruction began with hours of practice. I inherited our father's music ability. Thomas did not. He failed at learning to play an instrument and at vocal attempts, while I excelled in violin, piano, and cello. Thomas chose reading and science above any interest in music. Father ridiculed him, and I became the favorite. As long as I made Father happy and performed to his musical preference, I was given everything I wanted.

"I'm sorry. This story is difficult. Our mother tried to protect Thomas. She encouraged his interests and became his champion when Father verbally and physically attacked him. Father turned his contempt on her, too, always throwing a wobbly about something. We were a family at war. Thomas wasn't healthy and stuttered, more reasons for our father to shame him.

"I mimicked my father regarding Thomas but not our mother. At one point, Thomas contracted rheumatic fever and missed six weeks of school. Father said the disease should have killed him. I never forgot Thomas telling me he hoped one day a horrible sickness killed our father. Although I sided with our father on many occasions, his actions were harsh, cruel. I was afraid if I stepped in for Thomas or Mother, I'd become the next victim.

"The stuttering problem grew worse. At our eighth birthday party, our father asked me to play the cello. One of the boys asked what instrument Thomas played, and Father said all he knew how to do was talk like an idiot and imitated Thomas's speech. The news spread around school. The bullying against Thomas increased. Our father said and did unspeakable things to him." He rubbed his palms together. "We'd go out to eat or to a movie, and Father would demand Thomas stay in the car because he was an embarrassment. On our eleventh birthday, Father left with me to England. To the best of my knowledge, he never contacted my mother or Thomas again."

Pity rolled through Heather for Thomas's miserable childhood. The abuse by no means justified murderous actions, but his background showed how mental degradation could have developed. "You said Thomas had threatened you and your father. Tell us more."

"Last January he phoned our father in London. His words were 'You and Jackson will pay for abandoning Mom and me. Both of you.' I urged Father to talk to someone at the MPS—London Metropolitan Police Services—or a barrister. Father ignored me. He still thinks of Thomas as the little boy who disappointed him, and as he told your agent, he has but one son."

"And you?"

"From what I've learned, Thomas is highly intellectual and successful."

"If your brother had your contact information, why didn't he follow through with his threat in London? Why even call?"

"I don't know. If he did envision our demise, I assume the crowd at the music festival and the numerous countries represented offered Thomas a means to blend in while carrying out his actions."

Jackson made sense. But many questions lingered. "Are you afraid of your brother?"

He hesitated. "As boys, he displayed peculiar behavior." He stared at the wall before him. "Cruelty to animals. He'd draw pictures of killing people, rather gruesome. He bullied children younger than us."

"Were any of his actions aimed at you?"

"I'd rather not say. Happened a long time ago, and when I think back on how he was treated, I feel nothing but remorse." Anguish etched his features. "During my stay, I plan a drive to Dallas to see where our mother is buried, one of the reasons for my trip. She never showed partiality or said a condemning word about our father."

Heather forged ahead. "You never checked on your mother?"

"I saw no reason." He buried his face in his hands. "I was busy, selfish, and time passed. I must make amends with Thomas. I'll stop by his office once we're finished here."

ASAC Mitchell, who'd been quiet to this point, cleared his throat. "Mr. Powell, we appreciate your cooperation. We are investigating your brother on a matter of extreme importance. It's in our best interests and yours to discourage a face-to-face at this point. We prefer noncommunication with Thomas until our case is concluded."

Jackson gripped his hands. "What is his suspected crime?"

"That's confidential."

"He hasn't been charged or he'd be in custody. Sir, I'm no fool, and my guess he's a suspect in a serious incident. In any event, I need to settle the past and petition my brother for forgiveness." He peered into Mitchell's face. "I am committed to restoring my relationship with Thomas."

"How long are you in the States?"

"Ten days but I'm willing to stay longer." Jackson's gaze swung from Mitchell to Heather. "Ma'am, you were in quarantine with Thomas. I gather you know him? Do you feel he's dangerous?"

"We became friends. I can't confirm his threats, but I don't think you should ignore them. How did he respond to your father's bullying? I'd like specifics."

"Withdrew to his room. We didn't share a room. Our father believed separation fueled my music ability."

"Tears?"

"At first, but after a few instances, he appeared resigned to Father's demands. Emotion escaped him. Frightening, and I often wished I could read his thoughts."

"Did he ever fight back?" Heather said. Jackson shook his head. "What other instances could help us connect with your brother?"

He ran his hands through his hair, another mannerism she'd seen in Thomas. "He said one day he'd build a bomb to kill our father, but he was afraid our mom might be hurt. I wanted to tell Father, but we left the States a couple of days later."

"Were there happy times with your brother?"

"When Father was gone, we'd play together like boys. The moment Father returned, Thomas changed, as though forced to be a different person. A defense mechanism." Jackson studied the table as though it held more interest than anything in the room.

"Mr. Powell, are you okay?" Heather said.

He lifted his head. "I've had considerable time to think about my brother. I'm fearful Thomas suffered a personality disorder resulting from our father's treatment, that he's mad. If I'm right, then the disorder may still be prevalent."

Jackson's words reinforced what she'd witnessed. "You were eleven years old at the time. You needed a method to survive the dysfunction, a means of self-preservation. If your conclusions about Thomas are right, he's a threat to others and himself."

"While neither of you will tell me the reason Thomas is under investigation, I'll speculate. A virus breaks out on the flight, a deliberate action according to the media, and Thomas escapes contracting it. Something has prompted the FBI's suspicion."

Heather allowed Jackson's words to settle. "What is the real reason you're here?"

"We want the same thing—the truth. Seeing me would serve as

a reminder of our childhood, trigger an episode or prove my fears are false. There are no legal ramifications for me to ask him if he planned to kill our father and me. And if the situation arises, I'll ask him if he is involved with the virus."

"Why now after all these years?"

"If I hadn't been such a coward, I'd have reported our father's abuse to a teacher or a neighbor. My intentions are to put a dent in my past mistakes with my brother. To ease my conscience, I will support Thomas whether he's at fault in a crime or innocent."

CHAPTER SIXTY-NINE

JACKSON POWELL LEFT THE FBI BUILDING after promising not to contact Thomas until Saturday. Heather and ASAC Mitchell tossed ideas about how to force Thomas to confess his crimes, and now they had a plan, a shaky one, but Heather believed in it.

"Jackson gave us incredible information," she said. "Now we have time to implement my idea. Chad wants to help."

Mitchell frowned. "Aren't you concerned about his safety? SWAT is all we need."

"Chad has already taken way too many chances. I'll request he wear a vest, and I'll be wired. He said he has nothing to lose and everything to gain."

"Sounds biblical."

"Sort of. I don't want him hurt or worse, but I accept his reasoning."

"This has risky all over it, Heather—a huge hole. Who in their right mind wants to visit the zoo in August? Heat index has been well over a hundred degrees for the past five days. My wife ran hot and hotter when she was in your condition."

"I understand what you're saying, but your reasons against staging an operation there are the same as why it will work. I'll tell Thomas I'm taking Friday off, and I'd like for us to spend the morning at the zoo. It opens at nine. Not crowded yet or miserable." She navigated her phone to the zoo's website. "There's a new avian conservation center."

"A what?"

"Birds."

Mitchell worried his lip. "Your theory is Chad's confrontation and your questions will push Thomas into his other personality?"

"Exactly."

"And then what?"

"Confession. Action on his part. My dad says the purpose of light is to illuminate, and the new information on the Powell brothers explains even more why Thomas has to be stopped." Mitchell continued to hesitate, and she braved forward. "We're confronting Thomas. How he responds will be heard and witnessed by agents."

"What if the ploy fails? He's sure to see your hand in it. The FBI would look like idiots after he's been nominated for sainthood. Don't get me started on the media's take."

"It's a gamble." She held up her palm. "Do you have a better idea? If so, let's hear it."

"No." He rubbed his face. "At 10 p.m. tonight, the FBI will declare Lawrence Labs is cleared, and Chad will be exonerated."

"Thomas will be in a bad mood before he arrives at the zoo, which helps the confrontation."

Mitchell huffed. "I'll just call you Agent Optimism."

"Perfect. Shall we run this by SAC Bischoff before we confirm with Chad?"

"Are you prepared to offer more reasons why this ludicrous idea will work?"

"Don't argue with a pregnant woman. You should have learned that after three kids."

CHAPTER SEVENTY

HEATHER NEARLY FELL ASLEEP during dinner at her parents. They laughed and cried. Dad claimed she must have gained two pounds. No mention of Chad, and she valued their discretion. All was in place for tomorrow. Now for God to bless their efforts.

Crawling into bed at 8:10 p.m., her thoughts drifted to Lynda Durgin. Kirk didn't have the opportunity to play his violin at the music festival . . . A thought twisted. Kirk played violin like Oliver Powell. What were the chances Kirk was a part of the same concert?

Heather startled awake. She opened the CD from Lynda and searched for contact information. A phone number was listed for bookings. Grabbing her phone, she pressed in the numbers. A woman answered.

"Lynda?"

"Yes."

"This is Heather Lawrence. Are you free to talk?"

"Sure. How can I help you?"

"Was your husband scheduled to play in the same concert as Oliver Powell?"

"How did you guess? Did Kirk tell you?"

"No. It occurred to me it was Oliver Powell's last concert."

"You must follow him, too. When Kirk received the invitation, he thought he'd have to turn it down. We've been supporting his mother in a nursing home, and we simply didn't have the money for the trip. Then a miracle happened. An anonymous person offered to fully fund his trip including expenses."

Heather gasped. Kirk's seat on the plane was directly behind Thomas. "Did your husband meet this person?"

"No. The money was directly deposited into our bank. We have no idea who the benefactor was."

Heather thanked the woman. This was a vital link, and yet it wasn't proof. Ten seconds later, she phoned ASAC Mitchell.

CHAPTER SEVENTY-ONE

HEATHER SPOTTED THOMAS walking across the zoo's parking lot to the entrance and waved. He'd maneuvered his red Fiat to take up an additional parking place. If she had a fancy sports car, she might do the same. Agents were in place—a woman pushed a stroller minus a child, a man posed as a photo enthusiast, and two other men would follow Heather and Thomas inside. She wore an ear-wire recording device concealed in her earring.

Thomas approached her dressed in tan cargo shorts, a knit pullover shirt, and hosting the confidence from quarantine days. He grasped her hand and squeezed it. An unholy eeriness about him sent chills up her arms despite the rising temps.

"I have our tickets." She faked enthusiasm in her voice. "This will be so fun."

"Of all the things I imagined us to do, a zoo isn't one of them. Did you catch the heat index for this afternoon?"

"We'll be finished long before then, unless we're having way too much fun."

"Or die of heatstroke."

Once inside, they walked toward the northwest side of the zoo, where the avian display sounded of birds. She kept her eyes and ears open to the surroundings and the colorful birds and habitat. They moved toward the children's petting zoo. The ripe odor of animals sent an uneasy sensation to her stomach.

"The kids' area is my specialty," he said.

She willed her body to cooperate with the mission. They paid for pellets and laughed at the sheep and goats racing toward them. If she wasn't convinced Thomas had planned several murders, she'd enjoy herself.

Heather pointed to an adorable Shetland pony. "I'll be over there."

At that moment, a goat butted Thomas's behind. He plopped knees-first onto the ground. "I've been humbled." He brushed off the dirt and whatever else covered him.

Laughter bubbled up from her toes. "Wish I'd been fast enough to video that."

"No thanks. The idea of seeing my knees in *Forbes* would ruin my image."

They followed a trail to the African forest. An elephant trumpeted. A lion roared his kingship. And the temps soared right along with the humidity.

Thomas stopped at the white rhino exhibit and snapped a pic. "These are one of my favorite animals."

"Why?"

"Ready for a few facts?"

"Go for it."

"Rhinos are the second largest land mammal. The elephant holds the number one spot. They live to be around fifty years old. But what I like is they are semi-social and territorial. Complex. Like me. White rhinos have lousy vision but a keen sense of smell

348

and hearing. I have a couple of blind spots, but I pay smarter people to be my eyes."

She observed the huge animal. "How fast does a rhino run?"

"White ones have the edge with twenty to twenty-four miles per hour."

"Don't think I'd want to make a rhino mad, especially the bulls."

"I've been chased in a jeep. All the excitement I needed."

Heather pointed to the Twiga Café. "How about a heat break? I could use something cold to drink."

"I'm already there."

The air-conditioning bathed their faces, and she chose a corner table, a habit to see who entered the front door. Thomas bought iced teas and scooted his chair across from her. "I've cooled off just holding the cold paper cups." He glanced around at the few people in the café. "You know, Heather, the stock market rises and falls. The weather gets hotter. The media wants to announce an arrest so people will relax about the virus." He stretched his neck. "As much as I'm thrilled to be off Adam's Island, I'm worried another virus breakout will take innocent lives."

"I have the same fear."

"Taversty is dead. Chad's name has been cleared. Parker Karey is locked up—"

"Do you suspect him?"

"He's one strange man. Remember when you saw him and Sonya in the hallway with me?" She nodded and he continued. "He wanted an astronomical amount deposited into his bank account. His reasoning was the quarantine had destroyed his chances to secure the job he wanted in Frankfurt."

"Not true. The company in Frankfurt stated they'd not fill the position until they talked to him."

Thomas took a drink of the iced tea. "He's a parasite."

"He's also a widower."

"Between us, I wouldn't be surprised if he killed Sonya."

From the corner of her eye, she saw Chad walk in. "Oh no," she whispered. "We have company."

Thomas stared. His face reddened.

Chad walked their way wearing a plastered-on smile that didn't really look like him. "Mr. Powell, we finally meet face-to-face."

"Heather and I were just discussing parasites. How did you find us?"

Chad pulled a chair to the table. "I still have access to her online calendar." He tossed a glare at her. "You have lousy taste, Heather. Can't you do any better than this?"

"My personal life is not your concern. You walked out on me, remember? Now, please go."

"I won't be long," Chad said. "Need to pack for an extended trip to Uganda."

"We have nothing to discuss," Thomas said.

"Neither of us do." Heather pointed to the door.

"First, I need a moment with Mr. Powell. I'd like to celebrate my new status. Does Heather know about our deal?"

"What deal?" She reached inside her shoulder bag and trailed her fingers along the barrel of her Glock.

"If I take a permanent trip overseas, you'd be safe."

Heather turned to Thomas. "Safe from what?"

"Don't pay any attention to him," Thomas said. "He's a murderer, and it's only a matter of time before evidence surfaces to keep him permanently behind bars."

Chad leaned onto the table and folded his hands. "I've made a few discoveries. Then I'll leave you two alone."

Thomas held an unruffled pose. "I wouldn't want to interfere with your vacation."

"Five minutes is all I need." Chad turned to Heather. "I think it's fair for you to know he has a few skeletons in his closet."

"And why would I believe you?"

Chad focused on Thomas. "I'll start with a young man, Trey Alvinson, a recipient of one of Powell's scholarships. In this case, medical school. After graduation, Powell set him up in a class 2 lab so Trey could study viruses. According to Alvinson's parents, Trey researched a cure for dengue fever and stumbled onto a new virus. Powell requested he hold back on the discovery and develop an antiviral. While employed for Powell, he applied to Lawrence Labs for a position."

"Trey's parents gave you unreliable information." Thomas settled back in his chair.

"In his journal he wrote you insisted he have his own apartment. True?"

"Yes. As his mentor, I encouraged him to seek complete independence. Grow up. Mature."

"You also asked him to break off with his girlfriend because he needed to concentrate on his research."

"True again. She was a leech, and Trey had a promising career ahead of him."

"Did you change the locks on the lab doors, ensuring Trey could only be there with you?"

"His strange behavior walked a thin line between endangering others or himself. Viruses can be fatal as Heather and I witnessed. I changed the locks as well as confiscated his lab notes. They are worthless scribbles."

"I hired him after three interviews," Chad said. "He was a good fit for Lawrence Labs. Odd thing is he drowned the day before reporting to work."

Sadness passed over Thomas's features. "I remember. A terrible loss. His parents requested his notes, but those are mine. Grief from losing Trey caused me to close down the lab."

"Where is the equipment?"

"I think you've asked enough questions, Dr. Lawrence. I'll answer this last one before you leave, but remember I already told you the equipment belonged to an investor in Europe. The person has taken possession. The end. Done." Thomas lowered his voice. "You can leave now."

"Don't you think it's remarkable Trey researches for a cure to a life-threatening virus? He chooses to leave your employment and ends up dead. An unknown virus is unleashed on board a flight of innocent people, and you're unaffected?"

Thomas snorted. "Leave or I'll contact security."

"I have one more question. Have you told Heather about your twin brother, Jackson?"

She startled. "A brother? Thomas, you said you were an only child."

"He's a liar."

"Don't think so," Chad said. "I talked to Jackson last night. He's in Houston. Told me an interesting story, tragic, too. Your childhood must have left you emotionally crippled, especially with the abuse from your father."

Heather poured shock into her words and face. "Thomas, what is he talking about?"

Thomas sneered. "Heather, let's go."

"Let's put this to rest," she said. "Do you have a brother?"

"No."

Chad scrolled through his phone and displayed a photo of Jackson Powell. "Take a look at the twin."

Heather gingerly picked up Chad's phone. "I don't under-stand." She tilted her head to Thomas. "Can you explain this to me?"

Thomas's face distorted. He pulled a Beretta Pico from his pocket, covered it with a napkin, and aimed it at Chad. "Heather, keep both your hands on the table."

She met his demands, regretting she hadn't retrieved her weapon sooner. "Is this true? Did you know Trey had stumbled upon an unknown virus before you booked the flight to Germany?"

"My dear, the world is filled with brilliant, smiling monsters. I'm one who likes to show his teeth. But that's not my name. I'm Shield, the one destined to take retribution for Thomas." A feral look met her more menacing than any of the predatory animals.

"Where is Thomas?"

"I got rid of him." He turned the napkin-covered Beretta toward her. "I'm the one in charge."

CHAPTER SEVENTY-TWO

THE CONVICTION IN THOMAS'S VOICE put Heather on alert mode. "What's going on?"

Thomas bent closer to the table as though the three shared an intimate conversation. His hand stayed fixed on the napkin and the weapon. "Yes, I knew all about Trey's plan to abandon me. The kid was an ungrateful recipient of my generosity. How dare he leave me for Lawrence Labs. He deserved to drown."

"Was it an accident?" Heather whispered the words so not to attract attention from the many people filling the café.

"Hardly not."

"Did Thomas or Shield kill him?"

"Who do you think?" Thomas's eyes flashed anger, yet she had to dig deeper for the evidence. The female agent with the stroller entered the café and sat across the room.

"What happened on board the flight?"

"I see no reason to hide my ingenuity. I dispensed the virus through a breath freshener, but clumsy Thomas dropped it and a flight attendant stepped on the container. Thomas panicked and flushed it down the toilet to cover his tracks. I saw his blunder and acted. I already had every person's background in business class. Heather, you were always my ace. FBI. Husband a medical researcher." He pointed to Chad with his free hand. "Luck smiled on me. Learned about your marital status, and it all fell into my lap. So very easy to implicate you, which I did as soon as the plane landed at JFK."

"You exposed my wife and every person on the flight to a deadly virus?" Chad said.

Thomas smirked. "My design was for Kirk Durgin to infect Oliver and Jackson. Half of the people on the flight intended to vacation in Salzburg for the music festival. Imagine the international crowds. But instead of the virus taking two to three days, the symptoms occurred in two to three hours." He wagged his finger. "Can't figure out what accelerated the incubation period. None of the testing pointed to a rapid progression. It's an issue to address when opportunity presents itself. I'll have the formula revised and make sure it performs according to my expectations for future applications."

"Future applications?" Heather whispered. "Thomas, you can't be serious."

His eyes flared. "My name is Shield. By the way, thanks for letting Thomas play hero on the plane. He's always had a weak spot for the underdog, and his financial contributions on the island played well into my strategy. Throwing money away on a useless cause to help the needy is like starting a bomb fire with hundred-dollar bills."

"Thomas is a good man," she said.

"He's a sniveling coward. He tried to talk me out of eliminating Oliver and Jackson, but I'd worked on this since I was ten years old."

"How did Kirk Durgin become a part of your plan?"

Thomas laughed. "What have you figured out?"

She moistened her lips. "I'm sure you can fill in the blanks. He was invited to play at your father's last concert. Kirk's son posted on Facebook that Kirk would need to decline because of lack of funds. Your computer is set to display all instances of your father, brother, and the Salzburg music festival. You became a generous benefactor. I'm thinking you manipulated your seat on the plane to ensure he received a dose of the virus."

"Smart woman. Everything worked out. All I needed was patience. If Trey hadn't stumbled onto the new virus, I intended to use another contagion."

She calculated how to take Thomas down, but a couple and two small children sat beside their table. "Who are Oliver and Jackson?"

"Thomas's dad and brother. Not sure I'd call them family."

"Are there more vials of the virus?"

"I carry one with me all the time." He sighed. "On the plane, I started reading a thriller novel on my iPad. It had been on the bestseller list for six weeks in a row, but the plot failed to keep my attention when the nauseous smells of those showing signs of the virus penetrated my nostrils. My sound-canceling headphones weren't adequate to muffle the wretched cries of agony. The vomiting, the blood, the respiratory issues resulting in the deaths were all characteristic of the virus's symptoms, just much sooner than expected."

"But we became friends." She tried to make a connection to the Thomas she knew.

"That wasn't me. Thomas never listens, which is why he won't be back."

"Shield," Heather said, "I'm sorry Thomas disappointed you."

"Repeatedly. Quarantine disgusted me. The idea of one bathroom for four men and the hard beds not even three feet apart made me feel like I was in a closet. Voicing the unacceptable conditions was dangerous, and I'd rather Thomas be viewed as a model resident. So I endured the miserable conditions like a lab rat."

"Did you pay Simon Peale to attack Chad?"

"Not a difficult task. I have connections with the right people. His attorney is a smart attorney, follows orders."

She wanted to ask him more about Trey's death, but how far could she push him when his hand beneath the napkin was wrapped around a gun? "Is Parker on your payroll?"

"He and Sonya gave new meaning to greed."

"What do you mean?"

"Your FBI people will discover it soon enough."

"You killed her?" she said.

He snorted. "Despised that whining woman."

What hadn't he schemed? "What's next for the virus?"

"The setback is nothing but a challenge for me to strengthen the virus's ability to kill so the latest quadrivalent flu vaccine is useless. I'll reveal the antiviral at the right time. I'll make millions more and be one of the most powerful men in the world." He smiled at her, then Chad. "Ready? We have places to go."

"Where?" Chad said.

"My choice. I can see the media headlines now—poor deranged Dr. Lawrence saw me and Heather together and lost it. He shot her and himself. My gun doesn't have serial numbers. Heather, leave your purse right where it is. Stand slowly, both of you. I'll have my gun aimed at Chad while we emerge arm in arm. We'll exit through the zoo and on to my car. Anyone approaches us or we're followed, I'll kill you two and release the virus." He reached into his pocket and produced a breath freshener.

"Take me and leave Heather alone." Chad's voice held a calmness she remembered from years ago.

"Not the plan. Stand. Both of you."

Heather and Chad obliged. She kept her gaze leveled on the

deranged man. "Will Thomas show up at your car? I can talk to him if you like."

"He doesn't have the guts to show his face."

"You're a smart man, Shield. I like you much better than him."

"Forget the flattery." He hooked his right arm under her left, the napkin over the Beretta and resting against his side. The woman agent acted as though her baby needed attention, but the café continued to fill with people. Thomas held the vial disguised as a breath freshener in his left hand. Both weapons were positioned precariously close to his fingertips. If he released either one, innocent people would be sacrificed. She'd signed up for taking risks, but not endangering the crowd, her baby, or her husband.

Chad, don't do anything stupid.

Outside the café, the trio walked toward the zoo entrance. FBI SWAT and other agents waited for the right moment to stop Thomas. They'd heard he had a vial of H9N15, and she had no reason to doubt he'd use it.

Thomas jerked her hard. "Those two men were here when we arrived. If it's FBI, you two are dead."

"I have no idea who they are."

They walked twenty feet with the entrance in sight. Many women and children lined up outside the ticket booth. Young and old wore yellow T-shirts bearing the name of a day care. She'd assumed the heat would deter visitors.

Please, get inside the zoo.

"To the parking lot," Thomas said. "My car's there."

At the sight of his two-seater Fiat Spider, her idea to take him down dwindled.

CHAPTER SEVENTY-THREE

THE HEAT HELD NO MERCY, much like Thomas's demands. The agents would keep their distance, and SWAT had them in their scopes. The problem . . . the vial of H9N15 in Thomas's hand. Any unexpected movement, and he'd trigger it. Heather had no reservations that he'd use it.

A day care bus pulled into the parking lot.

Thomas lifted his left hand containing the vial and spoke into his Apple Watch. Within seconds, he arranged for a helicopter to pick him up at an address not his home or office.

But SWAT and agents heard.

Reaching his sports car, Heather did a mental check for where snipers hid. "How do you plan to do this, Shield? Which one of us will you eliminate first?"

"You, of course."

"I'd rather take the first bullet," Chad said.

"Noble, but not wise." Thomas clutched Heather around the

throat, jammed the barrel of the gun into her temple, and scanned the area. "Who else knows about our zoo excursion?"

"No one," Heather whispered through the viselike pain. "I scheduled it on my calendar. That's all. Believe me, Shield, I had no idea Chad would check up on me."

"Looks like you both lost. Here's what's going to happen." Thomas squeezed her against the front of him. "Chad, get into the passenger seat."

He hesitated, his face pale and rigid. The sound of excited children broke through the air.

"Now, or I'll shoot her. Heather, you're going with me to the driver's side."

She saw the foresight in his plan. SWAT wouldn't have a clear shot. Chad opened the car door. He stared into her face. "I'm sorry."

Thomas seethed. "Shut up."

Chad slid inside, but Heather didn't hear the door click shut. She dragged her feet while Thomas moved around the front of the car to the driver's side. She seized his left hand with the vial and aimed for a punch to his face. Thomas stopped her maneuver.

"Open the door," he said. When she did, he stepped back and aimed at Chad's face.

Heather screamed and slammed her head back against his.

The Beretta sent a bullet into Chad's thigh.

She lifted her right leg and slammed her heel into Thomas's groin. He doubled over. She grabbed the barrel of his gun and twisted his wrist back. It snapped. The pain sent him to his knees.

The gun dropped onto the concrete, but he still held fast to the weaponized freshener. She kicked the gun and reached for the vial.

Thomas managed to shove her aside still gripping the virus in his left hand. He pointed it toward the children pouring from the day care bus.

Someone shouted for the crowd to get back.

Heather lunged at him, peeling back the fingers wrapped around the deadly virus. Rage exploded from him with incredible strength. Agents rushed Thomas and held him down.

Heather struggled with the vial until it was in her hands. Agents took over and one helped her stand. She hurried to Chad, who'd stumbled out of the car and onto the pavement. Blood puddled onto the cement. She pressed on the wound, a sickening reminder of all the case had cost them.

Sirens grew louder. "Help's coming," she whispered. The ambulance pulled into the parking lot amid screams of children and adults.

"I love—"

"I love you. Now hush. You need your strength."

"Is . . . it over?"

"Done. Thomas is in custody. The FBI has evidence. Honey, the nightmare has ended."

Hours later, Thomas sat in an FBI interview room with ASAC Mitchell and Heather. He tugged at his handcuffs and faced her. Since the arrest he'd fought agents and shouted with language she'd not repeat.

Thomas seethed. "Where's my attorney?"

"We've called him. So calm down." Deep lines dug into his forehead, and with his anger and red face, she questioned a complete mental or physical collapse.

"You have nothing. No evidence. Do your sweep of my home and office. Agents won't find a thing." He laughed, a deep-throated sound that came from Shield's persona.

"Our conversation at the zoo was recorded. Every agent heard your confession."

"I'll be out on bail in an hour. This is entrapment."

"Read the definition of entrapment before you put all your money there," she said. "You confessed to murdering Trey Alvinson. You claimed to have released the deadly virus to a man en route to Salzburg."

"Watch the legal process play into my hands." He cringed as though he hurt.

"Headache?" Pain lines on his face wove with evident hatred.

"None of your business."

Thomas needed immediate professional psychiatric care, hospitalization, and medication. He wasn't competent from one moment to the next. She formed her words carefully. "I have someone who wants to see you."

"Who? I'm not answering any more questions until I have my attorney."

"Your brother, Jackson. He found out you were in quarantine and flew to Houston."

"Is Oliver with him?"

"Jackson's alone."

"He always had the good luck. While I'm in cuffs, I can't kill him."

"He wants to talk," Heather said. "Your choice. You told me you didn't have a brother."

"That was Thomas, and between the two of us, I told you the majority of lies."

"Who committed the most crimes?"

"Ask him. I'm waiting until I have legal counsel."

Heather looked at a man who'd slipped into a personality disorder as a child to protect himself. "Do you want to talk to Jackson?"

"Sure. He can breathe easily until I'm out of here. Nothing in our conversation will implicate me."

Mitchell nodded into the one-way window for Jackson to be

escorted in. The brother joined them, and Mitchell pointed to a chair across from Thomas. How hard this must be for Jackson.

"Thomas, I'd recognize you anywhere." Jackson folded his hands on the table. His quivering voice indicated his nervousness.

"It's Shield. And my face has been all over the Internet."

"True. I'm not sure where to begin or how long you're willing to listen. But I'll make this fast since your attorney is on his way. I apologize for the years we were together as boys. I should have stood up for you countless times instead of siding with Father or ignoring his inexcusable actions toward you and our mother."

"She's dead."

Jackson choked back a sob and swiped at his nose. "I'm sorry."

Thomas exploded with the similar curses he'd tossed at her. "A little late, Jackson."

"We could start over, commit to a relationship as it should have been."

"I grew up fine without you, made millions, and I don't need you now."

"What if I need my brother?" Jackson said.

"You're as weak as Thomas. You deserve each other."

Jackson slowly rose. "I've read the charges and what you're up against. Regardless of the outcome, I'm staying in Houston for as long as it takes."

CHAPTER SEVENTY-FOUR

CHAD LOWERED THE BAG of Tex-Mex food outside the door of his and Heather's condo. His gut fluttered with the anticipation of a kid on a first date. He leaned on a cane and pressed the bell. The roses in his other hand tickled his nose.

"You can do this," Javier said from the end of the hallway. He'd driven Chad there and waited to see if Heather would let him inside with a surprise visit.

Tonight Chad planned for them to start over in their relationship by dating her as she deserved. He'd been a lousy husband, and no number of heroic attempts to save his wife's life made up for the hurt he'd caused. His plan wavered from how to give her room to choose him to outright falling to his knees and begging forgiveness. She said she loved him, but was that enough? She might laugh all the way through the drama.

Heather opened the door, her eyes wide. "Chad, you should be at home. Did your doctor release you? Did you drive here?"

He presented the roses and she inhaled the rich fragrance.

"This is not how I planned our evening," he said. "The doctor released me. Javier drove me here after we stopped at Gringo's." He glanced at the bag beside him. "I have southwest egg rolls, diablo chicken, fajitas, and queso loco."

Tears welled her eyes. "This is what we ordered on our first date. You shouldn't have gone to all this trouble."

"It's a start for being a jerk. You saved my life today."

"You took a bullet for me."

"Are you two okay?" Javier called from down the hall.

Heather laughed and waved at him. "I'm letting him in. You're relieved of taxi duty."

"What time should I pick him up?"

"I'll be his chauffeur. Thanks."

Chad peered into his wife's green eyes. Her beauty stole his breath.

"Are you okay?" She reached out to steady him.

"I'm good. Just thinking I'd like to kiss every freckle on your cheeks."

She shook her head. "I think you're hungry. Come inside, and let's have dinner before you get delirious. You brought a ton of food."

"For you, Levi, and me."

"You've made me incredibly happy."

"We have a long way to go, but I'm going to be the man God purposed for me."

"I called Andy this afternoon," she said. "He apologized for thinking I'd framed you."

"He's a good man."

"I also talked to Jordan, and he and his family are planning a Houston visit."

After a feast, they held hands on the sofa and listened to Andrea Bocelli croon an Italian love song. Chad had no clue what the words meant, didn't matter. "How is Thomas Powell?"

"In a psychiatric hospital undergoing an evaluation by a team of doctors. He's been given a sedative until proper medication is determined. May never leave."

"He'll get help, and he won't harm himself or others. Can't imagine a father abusing his son like Jackson described."

"I've seen and read about horrible cases in my career, but this one is at the top of the list."

"Is he willing to turn over Trey's notes to the CDC?"

Heather shook her head. "Shield claims they are in a safe place, and he'll go to his grave with the information. Five containers with vials of H9N15 were found in the lining of his computer case. Terrifies me at what he intended to do."

"Maybe with the right prescriptions, he'll choose to help the authorities." Chad closed his eyes and bit back a stab of pain. His right thigh hurt from where the doctors had removed a bullet. His head pounded, too. To take a pain pill when he wanted to be alert with Heather contradicted his new-man determination.

"Nurse Heather to Dr. Chad. I assume the doctor prescribed pain pills, but in order for them to work, you have to take them."

He forced a grin. "I wanted to see you and not fall asleep."

"Take the bed, and I'll sleep right here." She patted the sofa cushion.

He opened his eyes. "Over my dead body."

"Close. I'm not taking you back to the apartment tonight. Neither will I let you call Javier or a taxi."

"You're a hard woman, Agent Lawrence." He frowned but he loved the bantering. He loved her.

"Better get used to it. The last several weeks have toughened me up."

He laughed, couldn't help it. "Okay, I'll stay, but I'm taking the sofa. My beautiful pregnant wife will sleep in her bed. And I'll make breakfast."

"Since when do you cook?"

"Forced into it in my single weeks—the worst mistake of my life." He paused. "But God used tragedies to draw me to Him and back to you."

She kissed his cheek. "We'll make it, Chad. God's on our side."

"I love you, Heather. Please forgive me."

"I do."

He looked at her with a tilt of his head. "I do?"

"As in the promise I made eight years ago." She laid her head on his shoulder. "I want to take this slow and steady and sure."

"Whatever it takes. I'm committed to us. Ready for Christian counseling and do the hard work."

"Want to seal it with a kiss?"

And they did.

CHAPTER SEVENTY-FIVE

Heather slid her oversize self onto the passenger seat of Chad's BMW. She waved at Catherine in the parking lot of Mercy Community Church. She and Chad had attended for the sixth week in a row after visiting several other churches. This one felt right, as though they were at home.

Chad switched on the engine and adjusted the heat. Although the pregnancy left her hot most of the time, the steady rains of Houston in January chilled them to the bone. "Great service," he said. "I keep learning more about God and realizing how far I have yet to go."

She reached across the seat and wrapped her hand around his. Warm wetness soaked her and the seat. "Hey, honey."

He flashed his blue eyes at her. "Yes."

"Is my overnight bag in the trunk?"

"Yes." He blinked. "He's coming?"

"Are you ready?"

"No. I mean yes. Are you all right?" He placed the car in reverse and backed out.

"I'm good. Excited. No rush. You can relax and drive."

"As in practice my breathing?" He pulled in behind a line of cars exiting the parking lot.

"From the look on your face, I'll take any kind of breathing." He gripped her hand. "We're going to be parents."

"Yes, Chad." She released his hand and steadied herself for the second contraction, ten minutes apart. "We have plenty of time."

He stopped for a red light and picked up his phone. "I'm calling your parents. . . . This is Chad. I'm taking Heather to the hospital. Ah, that's the one. See you soon. Thanks. I will." The light changed, and he placed his phone between them.

"They'll meet us there. They're praying, and they love you."

She closed the heat vent.

"Hold on when the pain comes. You're not doing this alone."

She whispered thanks. Sweet man. They'd come a long way in the past five months. He'd withdrawn his application from the CDC and reopened his lab with the stipulation of an eight-hour workday, five days a week. The time spent together was better than in the early years of their marriage. The rough spots were talked through, and they learned healthy arguing methods from the counselor. She no longer retreated to their bedroom in tears, and he no longer left the condo in a rage.

The contraction squeezed harder, then slowly let up.

The tragedy that had threatened their lives had drawn them together. Love was more important than prestige, power, and position. Chad called those the three p's destined to destroy a man—or a woman. Laughter, long walks, deep discussions, and prayer time were priorities. He studied the concept of merging faith and science and found the two connected—the more he dug, the deeper his faith grew.

The aftermath of the case was like seeing how a puzzle fit

together. Decker Anslow and Braden Taversty had planned an attack on the US by helping to smuggle in weapons to cell groups. Parker Karey was exonerated of federal charges, and she dropped hers. Thomas Powell remained in a secure hospital, and Jackson visited him regularly. The twin had accepted a position with the Houston Symphony, much to their father's anger. He disowned Jackson, too.

Thomas as Shield destroyed all of Trey's notes. Chad had told her a deadly pathogen had means of resurfacing. If a cure existed before, another researcher would find the antiviral.

Chad sped through a yellow light.

"Honey, an accident or a speeding ticket will slow us down."

He let off the gas. "Sorry."

"You are a doctor."

"I was thinking the same thing. I prefer a hospital setting and watching your doctor deliver Levi instead of me."

Heather touched her stomach and squeezed Chad's hand. They'd prayed daily for little Levi—to embrace life, love, and one day reach up to an amazing relationship with God. The beginnings of a third contraction hinted Levi wasn't wasting time. She held her breath and calculated ten more minutes to the hospital.

This wouldn't be the first time a Lawrence had their own time-table.

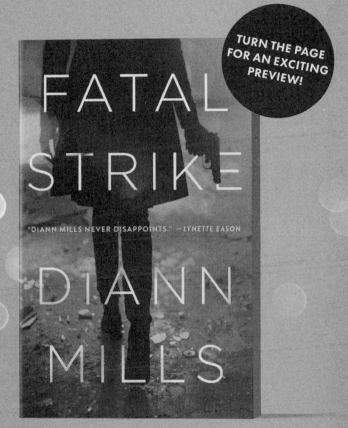

5

IN THEIR BRIEF SEARCH of Judge Mendez's office, Jon Colbert and Leah Riesel didn't turn up anything of note. Jon contacted Houston FBI for a team to image the computer, sweep the room, and request a search warrant for the judge's courthouse office. He hoped the FBI team had better luck.

In his truck with Leah beside him, Jon drove down Thirty-Second Street toward the home of Edgar Whitson, the witness to this morning's crime. Leah had called him as a courtesy to make sure he was home.

Galveston police officers surrounded St. Peter's on the corner. Jon parked half a block away from the church near the Whitson home, a freshly painted white bungalow facing seaward and backing up to the church. With residences lining only one side of the street, the chances of neighbors having cameras that might have picked up those who'd dumped the judge's body decreased.

An elderly man with a full head of snow-white hair stepped out of the house onto a porch bordered with yellow roses as thick as dandelions in spring. An American flag waved from one porch post, and a Texas flag saluted them on the other. As Jon and Leah approached the porch, the man introduced himself. Jon reached out and shook his hand. "I'm Agent Colbert, and this is my partner, Agent Riesel."

She grasped his hand. "We appreciate your willingness to talk to us."

"I fought in the Punchbowl in 1951, the Korean War." He nodded. "The families here on the island who've been hurt need to see justice served." Mr. Whitson returned her smile. "Miss, the FBI's doing a great job of recruiting pretty gals."

"Thank you."

"The wife's lying down. Feeling a bit puny today. The older we get, sleeping comes full circle like we're babies again."

"I'm sorry," she said. "We won't be long."

"Whatever y'all need. Come on inside, where it's cooler." He opened the door to a living room bright with sunlight. Usually older people lived in the dark, at least in Jon's experience. The scent of freshly brewed coffee met his nostrils.

Mr. Whitson led the way into the kitchen. "Made a new pot a few minutes ago. Want a cup?"

"A jolt of caffeine sounds wonderful," Leah said.

"You, sir?"

"Never met a cup of coffee I didn't like." The three filled their cups, rich and dark like Jon preferred. He picked up a framed wedding photograph near the coffeemaker. A much younger Edgar, dressed in his Marines uniform, stood erect beside a lovely petite woman.

"That's me and the missus some sixty-five years ago. The war was over, and we were ready to put it behind us."

Jon handed it to Leah. "What a beautiful couple." She glanced up. "Mr. Whitson, you're still the same size as you were then."

He laughed. "I'll be sure to tell the missus. She complains about my middle. Our granddaughter's an interior decorator, and she says pictures don't go in the kitchen. But I don't care."

"Me, either." Leah peered at the vintage photo. "Looks perfect here."

"Mr. Whitson, we'd like to record your testimony." Jon held up his cell phone. "Are you okay with that?"

The older man hesitated. "But can you keep my name out of it for the missus's sake? The Venenos won't take kindly to me talking to you folks."

"We'll keep your name from the media," Jon said. "In fact, we'll be knocking on your neighbors' doors too. If your information leads to an arrest and the case goes to court, we'll make sure you and your wife are protected."

"Good." Mr. Whitson nodded. "Let's take our coffee out back. Been thinking about the view from there, and you might want to take a few pictures."

"Mr. Whitson, you're a smart man," Jon said. "Might need to recruit you."

Leah held up her phone to Jon. "I'll take the pics if you'll record."

Outside, humidity dripped from plants and flowers. Jon complimented him on his vegetable garden. Huge red tomatoes, green and red bell peppers, and two varieties of lettuce. Jon gazed about sixty feet over the five-foot-tall bush line to the rear door of St. Peter's. "What happened this morning?"

"I woke early, before 6 a.m., and thought I'd pick a fresh tomato from the garden. Me and the wife like 'em for breakfast. I went outside and heard a commotion at the back of the church, like a thump. I peered over there and saw two men at the rear door. They walked down the steps to a car parked real close. One of them slammed the trunk. Drove off. Didn't think much about it until I saw the police show up around 8:30. I went over and learned a body had been found at the church. I told an officer I needed to talk to whoever was in charge. They connected me to Chief of Police Everson. He told me the FBI had been called in to work the case. Before you two got here, I heard on the news about Judge Mendez's body left at St. Peter's back door."

"Are you sure of what you saw?" Leah said. "It's still dark then."

"There's a light pole in the church's parking lot, and I have one mounted back here on my garage." Mr. Whitson pointed to both. "The lights showed me the man's face who shut the trunk. He looked familiar, but I didn't place him until Agent Riesel called me about your visit." He yanked a weed shooting up from a bottlebrush. "Thought I got all them boogers."

Jon wanted to be that spry one day. "Can you give us a name?"

"Hate to accuse a man of a vicious crime. But why were those men back there unless they were up to no good? The man was Dylan Ortega. He and his mother belong to St. Peter's, like me and my wife. Well, his mom attends regular, and he's there at Christmas, Easter, and Mother's Day. You know, a holiday Christian."

"And you're sure his name is Dylan Ortega?"

"Yes, sir. When he was younger, he'd help me pull weeds in

my flower beds and keep the yard looking good. Great kid then. I speak to him when he comes to church. He's changed in his looks—longer hair and an earring. Not judging those things, only noticing a difference. Sorry to say he did time for burglary a while back."

Jon jotted down the need for a background on Ortega. "Can you describe the second person?"

"Similar build. Wore a baseball cap over his eyes."

"Make of car?"

"When it backed out under the pole light, I caught sight of the hood. Looked like a Mustang. Dark color."

"Dylan Ortega might have a legitimate reason for being at the church."

"There isn't Mass then, and even in my day young people didn't go to confession at 6 a.m." The older man was blunt and spot-on.

"Anything else?"

"Don't think so."

"We appreciate your coming forward. If you think of anything you've missed, please contact us." Jon gave him his business card.

"If what I saw brings justice in the judge's death or either of those other victims, I'm glad I spoke up." He arched his shoulders. "Oorah."

DISCUSSION QUESTIONS

1. Heather is taking off on a vacation without her husband. What decisions is she wrestling with? What advice would you give her as she faces life-changing choices?

2. As Heather's fellow passengers fall ill on the plane, she wonders why God would allow so many to succumb. What does she tell her seatmate Mia about faith? What answers do you have for these types of questions?

3. Why does Chad say he's seeking to divorce Heather? Are these marital problems things they could overcome? Why or why not? What does the Bible say about divorce? What qualities are needed for successful marriages?

4. Why is Chad so resistant to the "God thing" Heather has going? How would you approach sharing the gospel with someone like him?

5. Heather is quick to offer compassion and assistance to others but reluctant to accept it for herself. Why is it sometimes hard to be on the receiving end of such acts of kindness? What can you do to show someone kindness today?

6. Even after Chad learns that he and Heather are expecting a child together, he's resistant to the idea of reaching out to his wife. What excuses does he give? What eventually changes his mind?

7. When Chad's name surfaces as a person of interest in the deadly virus infection, what makes Heather think he might be guilty?

8. In this story, the media is quick to spread unsupported allegations, and this misinformation is believed as the truth. How does the author's portrayal of the media compare to real-life agencies? What techniques can you use to discern the truth and avoid falling for "fake news"?

9. Chad tends to want to squash his emotions, favoring logic and scientific reasoning over feelings. When might his approach to life be appropriate or even necessary? When should emotions be allowed to control a person's actions or reactions?

10. Heather recognizes that her relationship with Chad has reached an unhealthy place. What steps does she take to try to change her interactions with him? What other things might you suggest Heather do to establish healthier boundaries?

11. Chad's revelations about God bring him to a surprising conclusion about his relationship with Heather and the importance of his work. What does he begin to understand as he reads and learns more about God? In what ways does his thinking line up with the truth of Romans 8:28?

12. How do you feel about the way mental illness is portrayed in this story? How are people afflicted with mental illness perceived, both in the story and in real life? What can be done to avoid negative stereotypes?

ABOUT THE AUTHOR

DIANN MILLS is a bestselling author who believes her readers should expect an adventure. She combines unforgettable characters with unpredictable plots to create action-packed romantic suspense novels.

Her titles have appeared on the CBA and ECPA bestseller lists; won two Christy Awards; and been finalists for the RITA, Daphne du Maurier, Inspirational Reader's Choice, and Carol Award contests. *Firewall*, the first book in her Houston: FBI series, was listed by *Library Journal* as one of the best Christian fiction books of 2014.

DiAnn is a founding board member of the American Christian Fiction Writers and a member of Advanced Writers and Speakers Association, Sisters in Crime, and International Thriller Writers. She is codirector of the Blue Ridge Mountains Christian Writers Conference, where she continues her passion of helping other writers be successful. She speaks to various groups and teaches writing workshops around the country.

DiAnn has been termed a coffee snob and roasts her own coffee beans. She's an avid reader, loves to cook, and believes her grandchildren are the smartest kids in the universe. She and her husband live in sunny Houston, Texas.

DiAnn is very active online and would love to connect with readers through her website at diannmills.com or on Facebook (facebook.com/DiAnnMills), Twitter (@DiAnnMills), Pinterest (pinterest.com/DiAnnMills), and Goodreads (goodreads.com/DiAnnMills).

TYNDALE HOUSE PUBLISHERS IS CRAZY4FICTION!

Fiction that entertains and inspires

Get to know us! Become a member of the Crazy4Fiction community. Whether you read our blog, like us on Facebook, follow us on Twitter, or receive our e-newsletter, you're sure to get the latest news on the best in Christian fiction. You might even win something along the way!

JOIN IN THE FUN TODAY.

 crazy4fiction.com

 Crazy4Fiction

 @Crazy4Fiction

CP0021